Praise for
The Wrong Man

"Katzenbach knows his characters so well and takes us so deep into their lives. . . . A lot of scary novels work intellectually—you admire the nasty characters, the shrewd plotting—but this is one that works emotionally. . . . [Katzenbach] persuades us that we might be all too vulnerable to a relentless psychopath who could attack with both a knife and a computer. . . . The ultimate stalker novel."

—*The Washington Post*

"Crisp prose and solid characterizations."
—*Entertainment Weekly*

"My heart was pounding during the last one hundred pages of *The Wrong Man*. The suspense is nearly intolerable, and the notion that one determined man can wreak such havoc on ordinary people is harrowing. This is an astonishingly patient and thrilling novel."

—ANITA SHREVE

"Bestselling Katzenbach keeps the pages turning in this unsettling tale of obsessive love."
—*Booklist*

"A powerful and complex story . . . The author deftly shifts perspective among his central characters, raising this page-turner above the run-of-the-mill by making all of them emotionally credible."

—*Publishers Weekly* (starred review)

"Reading Katzenbach's new thriller *The Wrong Man* is like riding the bullet train through hell—a chilling, exhilarating reminder of how precious is our 'ordinary' life and how devious are the ways of evil. Pilgrim, get on board."

—LES STANDIFORD

Also by John Katzenbach

FICTION
The Madman's Tale
The Analyst
Hart's War
State of Mind
The Shadow Man
Just Cause
Day of Reckoning
The Traveler
In the Heat of the Summer

NONFICTION
First Born: The Death of Arnold Zeleznik, Age Nine:
Murder, Madness and What Came After

THE
WRONG
MAN

A NOVEL

JOHN KATZENBACH

BALLANTINE BOOKS • NEW YORK

2007 Ballantine Books Mass Market Edition

Copyright © 2006 by John Katzenbach

Published in the United States by Ballantine Books, an imprint of The Random House Publishing Group, a division of Random House, Inc., New York.

BALLANTINE and colophon are registered trademarks of Random House, Inc.

Originally published in hardcover in the United States by Ballantine Books, an imprint of The Random House Publishing Group, a division of Random House, Inc., in 2006.

ISBN 978-0-345-46484-2

Cover design: Carl D. Galian
Cover photographs: buildings © Alamy; figure © Jupiter Stock

Printed in the United States of America

www.ballantinebooks.com

OPM   9   8   7   6   5   4   3   2   1

For the usual suspects:
wife, children, and dog.

THE
WRONG
MAN

"Would you like to hear a story? An unusual story."

"Of course."

"Okay. But first you must promise something: that you will never let on where you heard it. And if you ever tell it again, under any circumstances, in any location, in any format whatsoever, you will conceal enough of the story so that it can never be traced back either to me, or to the people I'm going to tell you about. No one will ever know if it is true, or not. No one will ever be able to uncover its precise source. And that everyone will always immediately assume it's exactly like all the other stories you tell: made-up. Fiction."

"That seems overly dramatic. What sort of story is it?"

"It's a story about killing. It happened a few years ago. But then again, perhaps it didn't happen. Do you want to hear the story?"

"Yes."

"Then give me your word."

"All right. You have my word."

She had an odd look of concern, something a little deeper than trouble, in her eyes. Her voice had an undercurrent of profound misgiving. She leaned forward and took a deep breath and said, "I suppose you could say it started with the moment he found the love letter."

1

The History Professor and the Two Women

When Scott Freeman first read the letter that he found in his daughter's top bureau drawer, crumpled up and stuffed behind some old white athletic socks, he knew immediately that someone was going to die.

It was not the sort of sensation that he could instantly have defined, but it overcame him in much the same way that any feeling of impending dread might, finding a distinct cold place deep within his chest. He remained rooted in his place, while his eyes repeatedly traveled the words on the sheet of paper: *No one could ever love you like I do. No one ever will. We were meant for each other and nothing will prevent that. Nothing. We will be together forever. One way or another.*

The letter was not signed.

It had been typed on common computer paper. The type font had been italicized, to give it an almost antique sensitivity. He could not find the envelope that it had been delivered in, so there was no handy return address, not even a postmark that he could check. He put the letter down on the bureau and tried to smooth out the creases that gave it an angry, urgent appearance. He looked again at the words and tried to imagine them to be benign. A puppylike protest of love, nothing more than a temporary infatuation on the part of some college classmate of Ashley's, a crush, and that she had kept it concealed for no real reason, other than some misplaced romantic foolishness. *Really,* he told himself, *you are overreacting.*

But nothing he imagined in that moment could overcome the sensation icing him inside.

Scott Freeman did not think of himself as a rash man, nor

was he quick to anger, or prone to swift decisions. He liked to consider every facet of any choice, peering at each aspect of his life as if it were the edge of a diamond, examined under a microscope. He was an academic both in trade and nature; he wore his hair shaggy-long, to remind himself of his youth in the late sixties, liked to wear jeans and sneakers and a well-worn corduroy sports coat that had leather patches on the elbows. He wore one set of glasses for reading, another for driving, and he was always careful to have both pairs with him at all times. He kept fit by a daily dedication to exercise, often running outdoors when the weather was suitable, moving inside to a treadmill for the long New England winters. He did this, in part, to compensate for the occasions when he would drink heavily alone, sometimes mixing a marijuana cigarette with Scotch on the rocks. Scott took pride in his teaching, which allowed him a certain daily flamboyant showmanship when he looked out across a packed auditorium. He loved his field of study and looked forward to each September with enthusiasm, and little of the cynicism that afflicted many of his colleagues at the college. He thought he had the most steady of lives and feared that he put too much excitement in the details of the past, so occasionally he indulged in some contradictory behavior: a ten-year-old Porsche 911 that he drove every day unless it snowed, rock and roll blaring from the stereo. He kept a battered, old pickup truck for the winters. He had an occasional affair, but only with women near his own age, who were more realistic in their expectations, saving his passions for the Red Sox, the Patriots, the Celtics, and the Bruins, and all the college's sports teams.

He believed that he was a man of routine, and sometimes he thought that he'd had but three real adventures in his adult life: Once, while kayaking with some friends along the rocky Maine coast, he'd been separated from his companions by a strong current and sudden fog and found himself floating for hours in a gray soup of quiet; the only noise surrounding him had been the lapping of the wavelets against the plastic kayak sides, and the occasional sucking sound of a seal or porpoise surfacing close by. The cold and damp had enveloped him, creeping closer, dimming his vision. He had understood that he was in danger, and that the extent of his trouble might be far greater than he could imagine, but he'd kept calm and waited until a coast guard boat had emerged from the vaporous mist that had enclosed him. The captain had pointed out that he'd only been yards away from a powerful offshore current that in all likelihood would have swept him seaward, and so he became significantly more frightened after his rescue than he'd been when he'd actually been at risk.

That had been one adventure. The other two were of greater duration. When Scott was eighteen and a freshman in college in 1968, he had refused to obtain a student deferment from the draft, because he felt it morally unacceptable to allow others to be exposed to dangers that he was unwilling to share. This heady romanticism had sounded highminded at the time, but had been eviscerated by the arrival of a letter from the draft board. In short order he'd found himself drafted, trained, and on his way to a combat support unit in Vietnam. For eleven months he'd served in an artillery unit. His job had been to relay coordinates received over the radio to the fire mission commander, who would adjust the height and distance on the battery of guns, then order the rounds released with a great whooshing sound that always seemed much deeper and more profound than any thunderclap. Later, he had nightmares about being a part of killing beyond his sight, beyond his reach, almost out of his hearing, wondering, when he'd awakened in the deep of night, if he had killed dozens, maybe hundreds, or perhaps no one. He'd rotated home after almost a year, never once having actually fired a weapon at anyone he could see.

After his service, he'd avoided the politics that gripped the nation and delved into his studies with a singlemindedness that surprised even himself. After seeing war, or, at least, an aspect of it, history comforted him, its decisions already made, its passions reverberating in time passed. He did not speak of his time in the military and now,

middle-aged and carrying a degree of tenured respect,
doubted that any of his colleagues knew he'd been a part of
the war. In truth, it often seemed to him as if it had been a
dream, perhaps a nightmare, and he'd come to think that his
year of conflict and death only barely existed.

His third adventure, he knew, had been Ashley.

Scott Freeman took the letter in his hand and went over
and sat down on the edge of Ashley's bed. It had three pil-
lows on it, one of which, inscribed with a needlepoint heart,
he'd given her on Valentine's Day more than ten years earlier. There were also two stuffed bears, which she'd named
Alphonse and Gaston, and a frayed quilt, which had been
given to her when she was born. Scott looked at the quilt and
remembered that it had been a small joke, in the weeks before Ashley's birth, when both her prospective grandmothers had given the child-to-be quilts. The other one, he knew,
was on a similar bed, in a similar room, at her mother's
house.

His eyes traveled over the rest of the room. Photographs
of Ashley and friends taped to one wall; knickknacks; handwritten notes in the flowing, precise script of teenage girls.
There were posters of athletes and poets, a framed poem by
William Butler Yeats that ended with the words *I sigh that
kiss you, for I must own, that I shall miss you when you have
grown,* which he'd given her on her fifth birthday, and which
he'd often whispered to her as she fell into sleep. There
were photographs of her various soccer and softball teams,
and a framed prom picture, taken in that precise moment of
teenage perfection, when her dress clung to her every new-
found curve, her hair dropped perfectly to her bare shoulders, and her skin glowed. Scott Freeman realized that what
he was looking out upon was the collected stuff of memories, childhood documented in typical fashion, probably no
different from any other young person's room, but unique in
its own way. An archaeology of growing up.

There was one picture of the three of them, taken when
Ashley was six, perhaps a month before her mother left him.
It had been on a family vacation to the shore, and he thought

the smiles they all wore had a helpless undercurrent to them, for they only barely masked the tension that had dominated their lives. Ashley had built a sand castle with her mother that day. The rising tide and waves poured over their every effort, washing every structure aside despite their frantic digging of moats and pushing together of sand walls.

He searched the walls and desk and bureau top, and he could see no sign of anything even the slightest bit out of place. This worried him more.

Scott looked down at the letter. *No one could ever love you like I do.*

He shook his head. That was untrue, he thought. Everyone loved Ashley.

What frightened him was the notion that someone could believe the sentiment expressed in the letter. For a moment, he tried again to tell himself that he was being foolish and overprotective. Ashley was no longer a teenager, no longer even a college student. She was on the verge of joining a graduate program in art history in Boston and had her own life.

It was unsigned. That meant she knew who sent her the letter. Anonymity was as strong a signature as any written name.

By the side of Ashley's bed was a pink telephone. He picked it up and dialed her cell phone number.

She answered on the second ring.

"Hi, Dad! What's up?"

Her voice was filled with youth, enthusiasm, and trust. He breathed out slowly, instantly reassured.

"What's up with you?" he asked. "I just wanted to hear your voice."

A momentary hesitation.

He didn't like that.

"Not too much. School is fine. Work is, well, work. But you know all that. In fact, nothing seems to have changed since I was home the other week."

He took a deep breath. "I hardly saw you. And we didn't get much chance to talk. I just wanted to make sure that everything is okay. No troubles with the new boss or any of your professors? Have you heard anything from that program you've applied to?"

Again, she paused. "No. Nothing really."

He coughed once. "How about boys? Men, I guess. Anything I should know about?"

She did not immediately answer.

"Ashley?"

"No," she said quickly. "Nothing, really. Nothing special. Nothing I can't handle."

He waited, but she didn't say anything else.

"Is there something you want to tell me about?" he asked.

"No. Not really. So, Dad, what's with the third degree?"

She asked this question with a lightheartedness that didn't match his own sense of worry.

"Just trying to keep up. Your life zooms along," he said. "And sometimes I just need to chase you down."

She laughed, but with a slightly hollow tone. "Well, that old car of yours is fast enough."

"Anything we need to talk about?" he repeated, then scowled, because he knew she would notice the redundancy.

She answered quickly, "No. For the second time. Why do you ask? Is everything okay with you?"

"Yes, yes, I'm fine."

"What about Mom? And Hope? She's okay, isn't she?"

He caught his breath. The familiar way she used the name of her mother's partner always took him aback, though he knew he shouldn't be surprised after so many years.

"She's fine. They're both fine, I guess."

"So what's with the call? Something else bugging you?"

He looked at the letter in front of him.

"No, not at all. No particular reason. Just catching up. And anyway, that's what dads do: We're always bugged. We worry. All we can imagine are worst-case scenarios. Doom, despair, and difficulty, lurking at every turn. It's what makes us the uniquely boring and deadly dull people we are."

He listened to her laugh, which made him feel a little bit better.

"Look, I'm heading into the museum and we're going to lose service. Let's talk again soon, okay?"

"Sure. Love you."

"I love you, Dad. Bye."

He placed the phone back on the cradle and thought that sometimes what you don't hear is much more important than what you do. And, on this occasion, he had heard nothing but trouble.

Hope Frazier watched the opposing team's outside midfielder closely. The young woman tended to overplay her side of the field, leaving the defender behind her exposed. Hope's own player, marking back closely, didn't yet see the way she could use the risks taken by her opposite number to create a counterattack of her own. Hope paced a small ways down the sideline, thought for a moment about making a substitution, then decided against it. She removed a small pad of paper from her back pocket, seized a stub of pencil from her jacket, and made a quick notation. Something to mention in training, she thought. Behind her, she heard a murmur from the girls on the bench; they were accustomed to seeing the notebook come whipping out. Sometimes this meant praise, other times it turned into laps after the next day's practice. Hope turned to the girls.

"Does anyone see what I see?"

There was a momentary hesitation. High school girls, she thought. One second, all bravado. The next, all timidity. One girl raised her hand.

"Okay, Molly. What?"

Molly stood up and pointed at the outside midfielder. "She's causing us all sorts of problems on the right, but we can take advantage of her recklessness . . ."

Hope clapped her hands. "Absolutely!" She saw the other girls smile. No laps tomorrow. "Okay, Molly, warm up and go into the game. Go in for Sarah in the center, get the ball under control, and start something in that space." Hope went over and sat in Molly's spot on the bench.

"See the field, ladies," she said quietly. "See the big picture. The game isn't always about the ball at your feet, it's about space, time, patience, and passion. It's like chess. Turn a disadvantage into a strength."

She looked up when she heard the crowd raise their voices. There had been a collision on the far sideline, and she could see a number of people gesturing for the referee to issue a yellow caution card. She could see one particularly irate father storming up and down the sideline, arms waving wildly. Hope stood up and took a few strides toward the touch line, trying to see what had taken place.

"Coach . . ."

She looked up and saw the nearside ref waving at her.

"I think they need you . . ."

She saw that the opposing team's coach was already half-jogging across the field, and so she rapidly set forth, after grabbing a bottle of Gatorade and an emergency kit from her bag. As she made her way across, she angled herself close to Molly.

"Molls . . . I missed it. What happened?"

"They clashed heads, Coach. I think Vicki got the wind knocked out of her, but the other girl seems to have gotten the worst of it."

By the time she arrived at the spot, her player was already sitting up, but the opposing team's player lay on the ground, and Hope could hear muffled sobbing. She went to her own player first. "Vicki, you okay?"

The girl was nodding, but she had a look of fear across her face. She was still gasping for breath.

"Does anything hurt?"

Vicki shook her head. Some of the players had gathered around, and Hope dismissed them back to their positions. "Do you think you can stand up?"

Vicki nodded again, and Hope took her by the arm and steadied her as she rose. "Let's sit on the bench for a bit," she said calmly. Vicki started to shake her head, but Hope gripped her arm more tightly.

On the nearby sideline, the one parent had raised his voice

further and was now verbally assaulting the other coach. No obscenities had spilled as yet, but Hope knew they couldn't be far behind. She turned to the sideline.

"Let's stay calm," she told him. "You know the rules about taunting."

The father shifted his glance to her. She saw his mouth open, as if to say something, then stop. For a second, he seemed about to release his anger. Then the barest restraint showed on his face, and he glared at Hope, before turning away. The other coach shrugged, and Hope heard him mutter, "Idiot" under his breath. She steered Vicki away and slowly began to escort her across the field. Vicki was still a little wobbly, but she managed to say, "My dad gets crazy." The words were spoken with such simplicity and so much hurt that Hope understood, in that second, there was far more to that moment than a collision on the field.

"Maybe you should come talk to me about it after practice this week. Or come into the guidance office when you have a free period."

Vicki shook her head. "Sorry, Coach. Can't. He won't let me."

And there it was.

Hope squeezed the teenager's arm. "We'll figure it out some other time."

This, she hoped was true. As she seated Vicki on the bench and substituted a new player into the game, she thought to herself that nothing was fair, nothing was equal, nothing was right. She glanced across the field, to where Vicki's father stood, a little ways apart from the other parents, his arms crossed, glaring, as if counting the seconds that his daughter remained out of the game. Hope understood, in that moment, that she was stronger, faster, probably better educated, certainly far more experienced at the game. She had acquired every coaching license, attended advanced training seminars, and with a ball at her own feet, she could have embarrassed the lumbering father, dizzying him with sleight of foot and change of pace. She could have displayed her own skills, alongside championship trophies and her NCAA All-American certificate, but absolutely none of it would have made an iota of difference. Hope felt a streak of frustrated anger, which she bottled, alongside all the other, similar moments, in her heart. As she thought these things, one of her players broke free down the right and in a fast, almost imperceptible bit of skill, thundered the ball past the keeper. Hope understood, as the team jumped up and cheered at the goal, all smiles, laughter, and high fives, that winning was the one thing, and perhaps the only thing, that kept her safe.

Sally Freeman-Richards remained in her office, waiting in the October half-light, after her secretary and both her law partners had waved their good-byes and set off in the evening traffic for their homes. At certain times of the year, especially in the fall, the setting sun aggressively dropped behind the white spires of the Episcopal church on the close edge of the college campus and would flood through the windows of the adjacent offices with a blinding glare. It was an unsettled time of the year. The glare had an unwitting, dangerous quality to it; on several occasions students hurrying back from late-day classes had been hit crossing the streets by drivers whose vision had been eradicated by windshield-filling light. Over the years, she had observed this phenomenon from both sides, once defending an unlucky driver, in another instance suing an insurance company on behalf of a student with two broken legs.

Sally watched the sunlight stream through the office, carving out shadows, sending odd, unidentifiable figures across the walls. She appreciated the moment. Odd, she thought, that the light that seemed so benign could harbor such danger. It was all in where you were located, at just the wrong moment.

She sighed and thought that her observation, at least in a small way, defined much of the law. She glanced over toward her desktop and grimaced at the stack of manila envelopes and legal files that weighed down one corner. At least a half dozen were piled up, none of which were much more than legal busywork. A house closing. A workplace compensation case. A small lawsuit between neighbors over a disputed piece of land. In another corner, in a separate file cabinet, she kept the cases that intrigued her more, and which really were the underpinnings of her practice. These involved other gay women throughout the valley. There were all sorts of pleadings, ranging from adoptions to marriage dissolutions. There was even a negligent-homicide defense that she was taking second chair on. She handled her caseload with expertise, charging reasonable rates, holding many hands, and thought of herself at her best as the lawyer of wayward, misplaced emotions. That some sense of payback, or debt, was involved, she knew, but she didn't like to be nearly as introspective about her own life as she was frequently forced to be about others'.

She seized a pencil and opened one of the boring files, then just as quickly pushed it aside. She dropped the pencil back into a jar labeled WORLD'S BEST MOM. She doubted the accuracy of this sentiment.

Sally rose, thought that there was nothing really pressing that required her to work late, and was wondering idly whether Hope was home yet, and what Hope might concoct for dinner, when the phone rang.

"Sally Freeman-Richards."

"Hello, Sally, it's Scott."

She was mildly surprised to hear her ex-husband's voice.

"Hello, Scott. I was just on my way out the door . . ."

He pictured her office. It was probably organized and neat, he thought, unlike the chaotic clutter of his own. He licked his lips for an instant, thinking how much he hated that she had kept his last name—her argument had been that it would be easier on Ashley as she grew up—but hyphenated in her own maiden name.

"Do you have a moment?"

"You sound concerned."

"I don't know. Perhaps I should be. Perhaps not."

"What is the problem?"

"Ashley."

Sally Freeman-Richards caught her breath. When she did converse with her ex-husband, it was generally terse, to-the-point conversations, over some minor point left over from the detritus of their divorce. As the years had passed since their breakup, Ashley had been the only thing that truly kept them linked, and so their connections had been mostly the stuff of transportation between houses, of paying for school bills and car insurance. They had managed a kind of détente, over the years, where these matters were dealt with in a per-functory, efficient manner. Little was ever shared about whom they had each become or why; it was, she thought, as if in the memories and perceptions of each, their lives had been frozen at the moment of divorce.

"What's the matter?"

Scott Freeman hesitated. He wasn't precisely sure how to put what was troubling him into words.

"I found a disturbing letter among her things," he said.

Sally also hesitated. "Why were you going through her things?"

"That's really irrelevant. The point is, I found it."

"I'm not sure it is irrelevant. You should respect her privacy."

Scott was instantly angered, but decided not to show it. "She left some socks and underwear behind. I was putting them in her drawer. I saw the letter. I read it. It troubled me. I shouldn't have read the letter, I guess, but I did. What does that make me, Sally?"

Sally didn't answer this question, although several replies jumped to her mind. Instead, she asked, "What sort of letter was it?"

Scott cleared his throat, a classroom maneuver to gain himself a little time, then simply said, "Listen." He read the letter to her.

When he stopped, they both let silence surround them.

"It doesn't sound all that bad," Sally finally said. "It sounds like she has a secret admirer."

"A secret admirer. That has a quaint, Victorian sound to it."

She ignored his sarcasm and remained quiet.

Scott waited for a moment, then asked, "In your experience, all the cases you handle, wouldn't you think this letter had overtones of obsession? Maybe compulsion? What sort of person writes a letter like that?"

Sally took a deep breath and silently wondered the same thing.

"Has she mentioned anything to you? About anything like this?" Scott persisted.

"No."

"You're her mother. Wouldn't she come to you if she was having some sort of man trouble?"

The phrase *man trouble* hung in the space in front of her, glowing with electric anger between them. She didn't want to respond.

"Yes. I presume so. But she hasn't."

"Well, when she was here visiting, did she say anything? Did you notice anything in her behavior?"

"No and no. What about you? She spent a couple of days at your place . . ."

"No. I hardly saw her. She was off visiting friends from high school. You know, off at dinner, back at two a.m., sleep to noon, and then paddle around the house until she started all over again."

Sally Freeman-Richards took a deep breath. "Well, Scott," she said slowly, "I'm not sure that it's something to get all that bent out of shape about. If she's having some sort of a problem, sooner or later she's going to bring it up with one of us. Maybe we should give Ashley her space until then. And I don't know that it makes much sense to assume there's a problem before we hear that there is one directly from her. I think you're reading too much into it."

What a reasonable response, Scott thought. Very enlightened. Very liberal. Very much in keeping with who they were and where they lived. And, he thought, utterly wrong.

•

She stood up and wandered over to an antique cabinet in a corner of the living room, taking a second to adjust a Chinese plate displayed on a stand. A frown crossed her face as she stepped away and examined it. In the distance, I could hear some children playing loudly. But in the room where our conversation continued, there was nothing other than a ticktock of tension.

"How, precisely, did Scott know something was wrong?" she asked, repeating my question back to me.

"Correct. The letter, as you quote it, could have been almost anything. His ex-wife was wise not to jump to conclusions."

"A very lawyerly approach?" she demanded.

"If you mean cautious, yes."

"And wise, you think?" she questioned. She waved her hand in the air, as if dismissing my concerns. "He knew because he knew because he knew. I suppose you might call it instinct, but that seems simplistic. It's a little bit of that leftover animal sense that lurks somewhere within all of us, you know, when you get the feeling that something is not right."

"That seems a little far-fetched."

"Really? Have you ever seen one of those documentaries about animals on the Serengeti Plain in Africa? How often the camera catches a gazelle lifting its head, suddenly apprehensive? It can't see the predator lurking close by, but . . ."

"All right. I'll go along with you for a moment. I still don't see how—"

"Well," she interrupted, "perhaps if you knew the man in question."

"Yes. I suppose that might help. After all, wasn't that the same problem facing Scott?"

"It was. He, of course, at first truly knew nothing. He had no name, no address, no age, description, driver's license, Social Security card, job information. Nothing. All he had was a sentiment on a page and a deep-seated sensation of worry."

"Fear."

"Yes. Fear. And not a completely reasonable one, as you point out. He was alone with his fear. Isn't that the hardest sort of anxiety? Danger undefined, and unknown. He was in a difficult situation, wasn't he?"

"Yes. Most people would do nothing."

"Scott, it would seem, wasn't like most people."

I remained quiet, and she took a deep breath before continuing.

"But, had he known, right then, right at the beginning, who he was up against, he might have been . . ." She paused.

"What?"

"Lost."

2

A Man of Unusual Anger

The tattoo artist's needle buzzed with an urgency that reminded him of a hornet flying around his head. The man with the needle hovering over him was a thickset, heavily muscled man, with multihued, entwined decorations creeping like vines up both arms, past his shoulders, and swirling around his neck, ending in a serpent's bared fangs beneath his left ear. He bent down, like a man considering a prayer, the needle in hand. He stooped to the task, then hesitated, looking up and asking, "You sure about this, man?"

"I'm sure," Michael O'Connell replied.

"I never put a tat like this on anybody."

"Time for a first, then," O'Connell said stiffly.

"Man, I hope you know what you're doing. Gonna hurt for a couple of days."

"I always know what I'm doing," O'Connell answered. He gritted his teeth a little against the pain and leaned back in the tattoo parlor chair. He stared down and watched as the burly man began to work over the design. Michael O'Connell had chosen a scarlet heart with a black arrow driven through it, dripping blood tears. In the center of the pierced heart, the tattoo would have the initials AF. What was un-usual about the tattoo was the location. He watched the artist struggle a little. It was more awkward for him to put the heart and initials on the ball of the sole of O'Connell's right foot than it was for O'Connell to keep his leg lifted and steady. As the needle pierced the skin, O'Connell waited. It is a sensitive location. Where one might tickle a child or ca-ress a lover. Or step on a bug. It was the location best suited for the multiplicity of his feelings, he thought.

Michael O'Connell was a man with few outward connec-tions, but thick ropes, razor wires, and dead-bolt locks con-stricted him within. He was a half inch under six feet in height and had a thick, curly head of dark hair. He was broad through the shoulders, the result of many hours lifting weights as a high school wrestler, and trim through the waist. He knew that he was good-looking, had a magnetism in the lift of his eyebrows and the way he sauntered into any situation. He affected a kind of carelessness about his cloth-ing that made him seem familiar and friendly; he favored fleece over leather so that he would fit in with the student population better and avoided wearing anything reminiscent of where he had grown up, such as too tight jeans or T-shirts with tightly rolled sleeves. He walked down Boylston Street toward Fenway, letting the midmorning breeze wrap itself around him. It had a suggestion of November in its breath, swirling some fallen leaves and debris off the street into a small whirlwind of trash. He could taste a little of New Hampshire in the air, a crispness that reminded him of his youth.

His foot hurt him, but it was a pleasant pain.

The tattoo artist had given him a couple of Tylenol and placed a sterile pad over the design, but he had warned O'-Connell that the pressure of walking on the tattoo might be hard. That was all right, regardless how crippled he might be for a few days.

He wasn't far from the Boston University campus, and

he knew a bar that opened early. He limped along, making his way down a side street, hunched over a little, trying with each step to measure the shafts of electric hurt that radiated upward from his foot. It was a little like playing a game, he thought to himself. This step, I'll feel pain all the way to my ankle. This step, all the way to my calf. Will I feel it all the way to my knee, or beyond? He pushed open the door to the bar and stood for a moment, letting his eyes adjust to the dark, smoky interior.

A couple of older men were at the bar, seated with bent shoulders as they nursed their liquor. Regulars, he thought. Men with needs defined by a dollar and a shot glass.

O'Connell moved to the bar, slapped a couple of bucks down on the counter, and motioned to the bartender.

"Beer and a shot," O'Connell said.

The bartender grunted, expertly drew a small glass of beer with a quarter inch of foam at the top, and poured off a shot glass with amber Scotch. O'Connell tossed back the shot, which burned his throat harshly, and followed it with a gulp from the beer. He gestured at the glass.

"Again," he said.

"Let's see the money," the bartender replied.

O'Connell pointed. "Again."

The bartender didn't reply. He'd already made his statement.

O'Connell considered a half dozen things he might say, all of which might lead to a fight. He could feel adrenaline starting to pump in his ears. It was one of those moments where it didn't really matter if he won or if he lost, it was just the relief he would feel in throwing punches. Something in the sensation of his fist and another man's flesh was far more intoxicating than even the liquor; he knew it would erase the throbbing in his foot and energize him for hours to come. He stared at the bartender. He was significantly older than O'Connell, pale, with a pronounced gut around his waist. It wouldn't be much of a fight, O'Connell thought, feeling his own taut muscles contracting with energy, begging to be released. The bartender watched him warily; years

spent on that side of the bar had given him an understanding
of the way a man's face suggested what he was about to do.

"You don't think I've got the money?" O'Connell asked.

"Need to see it," the bartender replied. He had stepped
back, and O'Connell noticed that the other men at the bar
had shrunk away, their eyes lifted up to the dark ceiling.
They, too, were veterans of this particular conflict.

He looked at the bartender again. The man was too old
and too experienced in the world defined by the gloomy corners of the decrepit bar to be taken unawares. And, in that
second, O'Connell realized that the bartender would have
some ready source of man-made equality. An aluminum
baseball bat, or maybe a short-handled wooden fish billy.
Maybe something more substantial, like a chrome-plated
nine-millimeter or a twelve gauge. No, he thought, not the
nine-millimeter. Too hard to chamber a round. Something
older, more antique, like a .38 police special, safety disen-
gaged, loaded with wadcutters, so to maximize the damage
to flesh, minimize the damage to the property. It would be
located out of sight, in easy reach. He did not think he could
jackknife across the bar fast enough to reach the bartender
before the man grabbed the weapon.

So, he shrugged. He spun and stared at the man at the bar
a few feet away.

"What're you looking at, you old fuck?" he asked angrily.

The man refused to make eye contact.

"You want another drink?" the bartender demanded.

O'Connell could no longer see the man's hands.

He laughed. "Not in a shit hole like this." He rose and exited the bar, leaving the men behind in silence as he passed
through the door. He made a mental note to come back
sometime, and felt a surge of satisfaction. There was nothing, he thought, nearly as pleasurable in life as moving to an
edge of something, and teetering back and forth. Rage was
like a drug; in moderation, it made him high. But every so
often it was necessary to truly indulge; to get wasted with it.
He looked down at his watch. A little after lunchtime.
Sometimes Ashley liked to take a sandwich out onto the

Common and eat beneath a tree with some of her art class friends. It was an easy place to keep an eye on her without being seen. He thought he might just wander over and check.

Michael O'Connell first met Ashley Freeman by happenstance, some six months earlier. He was working as a part-time auto mechanic at a gas station just off the Massachusetts Turnpike extension, taking computer technology courses in his free hours, making ends meet by tending bar on weekends in a student hangout near BU. She had been coming back from a weekend ski trip with her roommates when the right rear tire had shredded after hitting one of Boston's ubiquitous potholes, a common enough winter-season occurrence. The roommate had nursed the car into the station, and O'Connell had replaced the flat. When the roommate's Visa card, maxed out by the weekend's excesses, had been rejected, O'Connell had used his own credit card to pay for the tire, an act of generosity and seemingly Good Samaritanism that hadn't been lost on the four girls in the vehicle. They were unaware that the card he used was stolen and had readily handed over their addresses and phone numbers, promising to collect the cash for him by midweek if he would just swing by and pick it up. The new tire, and the labor to install it, had come to $221. None of the girls in the car had understood for an instant how ironically small a sum that truly was, to allow Michael O'-Connell into their lives.

In addition to his good looks, O'Connell had been born with exceptionally sharp eyesight. It wasn't hard for him to pick out Ashley's outline from beyond a block's distance, and he sidled up against an oak tree, maintaining a loose surveillance. He knew that no one would notice him; he was too far away, there were too many people walking by, too many cars passing, too much bright October sunlight. And he knew as well that he had been lucky to develop a chameleon-like ability to blend into his surroundings. He thought that he should really have become a movie star, because of his capacity to always seem to be someone else.

In a run-down dive of a bar, catering to alcoholics and fringe criminals, he could be a tough guy. Then, just as easily, in Boston's massive student population, he could appear to be just another college kid. The backpack, filled to bursting with computer texts, helped form that impression. Michael O'Connell thought he maneuvered expertly from world to world, relying at all times on the inability of people to take more than a second to size him up.

Had they, he thought, they would have been scared.

He watched, easily picking out Ashley's reddish blond hair from the group. A half dozen young people were sitting in a loose circle, eating lunch, laughing, telling stories. Had he been the seventh member of that group, he would have turned quiet. He was good at lying and making up believable fictions about who he was, where he'd come from, and what he'd done, but in a group, he always worried that he would go too far, say something loose and unlikely, and lose the credibility that was important to him. One-on-one, with someone like Ashley, he had no trouble being seductive, creating a need for sympathy.

Michael O'Connell watched, letting rage grow within him.

It was a familiar sensation, one that he both welcomed and hated. It was different from the anger he felt when he was readying for a fight, or when he got into an argument with a boss at any number of the occasional jobs he held, or with his landlord, or the old lady who lived next door to his tiny apartment and who bothered him with her cats and leery-eyed stares. He could have words with any number of people, even come to blows, and it was to him next to nothing. But his feelings about Ashley were far different.

He knew he loved her.

Watching her from a safe distance, unrecognized and unobserved, he stewed. He tried to relax, but could not. He turned away because watching was too painful, but then, just as quickly, he twisted back, because the pain of not looking was far worse. Every laugh she emitted, tossing her head back, her hair shaking seductively around her shoulders, every time she leaned forward, listening to someone else, was agony. Every time she reached out and, even in the most inadvertent of motions, let her hand brush up against another's—all of these things were like ice picks driven deep into his chest.

Michael O'Connell watched and for nearly a minute believed he could not breathe.

She constricted his every thought.

He reached down into his pants pocket, where he kept a knife. It wasn't the Swiss Army multiuse-type knife that could be found in hundreds of backpacks throughout Boston's student universe. This was a four-inch folding knife, stolen from a camping goods store in Somerset. It had heft. He wrapped his hand around the knife and squeezed it tightly so that, although the blade was concealed within the handle, it still bit into his hand. A little bit of extra pain, he thought, helps to clear the head.

Michael O'Connell liked carrying the blade because it made him feel dangerous.

Sometimes he believed that he traveled in a world of about-to-bes. The students, like Ashley, were all in the process of turning themselves into something other than what they were. Law school for the soon-to-be-minted lawyers. Medical school for the ones who wanted to be doctors. Art school. Philosophy courses. Language studies. Film classes. Everyone was part of becoming something. On the verge of joining.

He wished, sometimes, that he'd enlisted in the army. He liked to think that his talents would have translated well into the military, if they could have seen past his difficulty taking orders. Perhaps he should have tried the CIA. He would have made an excellent spy. Or contract killer. He would have liked that. A James Bond type. He would have been a natural.

Instead, he realized, he was destined to be a criminal. What he liked to study was danger.

From a block away, he saw the group begin to stir. Almost in unison, they rose, brushing themselves off, unaware of anything other than their immediate halo of laughter and happy talk.

He moved forward, following slowly, not closing the distance, mingling with other people on the sidewalk, watching until Ashley and the others walked up some steps and into a building.

Her last class ended at four thirty, he knew. Then it would be over to the museum for two hours of part-time work. He wondered if she had plans for that night.

He did. He always did.

•

"But there's something I don't exactly get."

"What's that?" Her reply was patient, like that of a teacher with a slow child.

"If this fellow . . ."

"Michael. Michael O'Connell. Nice Irish name. Boston name. Must be a thousand of them from Brockton to Somerville and beyond. Makes one think of altar boys carrying incense, and choir practice, and firemen in kilts playing bagpipes on a brisk and cold Saint Paddy's Day."

"That's not really his name, is it? This is a part of the puzzle, correct? If I were to follow up, I wouldn't find a Michael O'Connell, would I?"

"You might. You might not."

"You're making this a little more difficult than it has to be."

"Am I? Isn't that for me to judge? I might be presuming that there will come a point when you're going to stop asking me questions and head out on your own, because you're going to want to know the truth. Already you know enough, at least to get started. You'll start comparing what I've said against what you can find out. That's the point of telling this. And making it a little difficult. You called it a puzzle. That would be apt."

Her voice was direct. If she meant to be coy, it didn't register in her words.

"All right," I said, "let's move forward. If this fellow Michael was really heading toward some sort of fringe life, working his way up the petty-crime ladder, where did Ashley fit in? I mean, she would have had a pretty good read on this guy in two seconds, right? She'd been well educated. She must have attended classes or gone to lectures about stalkers and that sort of man. Hell, there's even a segment on them in the state's high school health textbook. It's alphabetical, so it comes right before STDs. So she would have picked him out rapidly. And then done whatever she could to extricate herself. You're suggesting a sort of obsessive love. But this guy O'Connell, he sounds like a psychopath, and—"

"A psychopath in training. A nascent psychopath. A psychopath wannabe."

"Yes, well, I can see that, but where did the obsession come from?"

"Good question," she answered. "And one that should be answered. But you would be unwise to think that Ashley, despite her many strong qualities, was properly equipped to deal with the sorts of problems that Michael O'Connell presented."

"True enough. But what did she think she was involved in?"

"Theater," she replied. "But she just did not know what sort of production it might be."

3

A Young Woman of Ordinary Ignorance

Two tables away from where Ashley Freeman sat with a trio of friends, a half dozen members of the Northeastern University varsity baseball team were hotly arguing the relative virtues of either the Yankees or the Red Sox, engaged in a loud, frequently foulmouthed assessment of each team. Ashley might have been perturbed by the over-the-top noise, except that having spent many hours in student-oriented bars over her four academic years in Boston, she had heard the debate a multitude of times. Occasionally it ended in some pushing or maybe a quick exchange of blows, but more often just gave way to cascading torrents of obsceni-

ties. Often there were fairly creative suppositions about the
bizarre off-hours sexual practices of the players on either
the Yankees or the Red Sox. Barnyard animals figured fairly
prominently in these sexual inventions.

Across from her, her friends were in a passionate discussion of their own. The issue was a show over at Harvard of
Goya's famous sketches of the horrors of war. A group of
them had taken the T across town to the exhibit, and then
wandered, unsettled, through the black-and-white drawings
of dismemberment, torture, assassination, and agony. It had
struck Ashley that while one can always tell the citizens
from the soldiers in the drawings, there was no anonymity in
either role. And no safety, either. Death, she thought, has a
way of evening things out. It crushes spirit without regard to
politics. It is unrelenting.

She shifted about in her seat, a little uncomfortable. Images, especially violent images, creased her deeply and had
done so since she was a child. They lingered unwelcome in
her memory, whether they were Salome admiring the head of
John the Baptist in a gruesome Renaissance rendition, or
Bambi's mother trying to flee the hunters who pursued her.
Even the campy killings of Tarantino's *Kill Bill* unsettled her.

Her de facto date for the evening was a lanky, long-haired
BC psychology graduate student named Will, who was leaning across the table, making a point, while trying to narrow
the distance between his shoulder and her arm. Small
touches were important in courting, she thought. The slightest of shared sensations might lead to something more intense. She was unsure what she thought of him. He was
clearly bright and seemed thoughtful. He'd shown up at her
apartment earlier with a half dozen roses, which, he said,
was the psychological equivalent of a get-out-of-jail-free
card; it meant he could say or do something offensive or stupid and she would likely forgive him at least once. A dozen
roses, he said, would have been too many; she would likely
see through the artifice of it all, whereas half that number at
least held out some promise as well as some mystery. She
had thought this was funny, and probably accurate as well,

and so she was inclined to like him initially, though it wasn't long before she started to sense that he was perhaps just a meager bit too full of himself, and less likely to listen than he was to pronounce, which put her off.

Ashley pushed her hair back from her face and tried to listen.

"Goya meant to shock. He meant to thrust all the reality of war into the faces of the politicians and aristocrats who romanticize it. Make it undeniable—"

The last words of this statement were lost, overcome by a burst from the nearby table: "I'll tell you what Derek Jeter's good at. He's good at bending over and . . ."

She had to smile to herself. It was a little like being trapped in a uniquely Bostonian version of the twilight zone, caught between the pretentious and the plebeian.

She continued to shift about in her seat, maintaining a neutral distance that neither discouraged nor encouraged Will, and thought about how she had always been wildly unlucky in love. She wondered whether this was merely something that would pass, like so many moments growing up, or was, instead, a predictable vision of her future. She sensed that she was on the edge of something, but of what, she was unsure.

"Yes, but the dilemma with shocking and showing the true nature of war through art is that it never stops the war, but gets celebrated as art. We flock to see *Guernica* and we revel in the depth of its vision, but do we really feel anything for the peasants who were bombed? They were real one day. Their deaths were real. But their truth is subordinated by art."

This was Will-the-date speaking. Ashley thought it a wise observation, but, at the same time, one that a million politically correct college kids would have made. Ashley glanced over at the loud baseball players. Even alcohol-fueled, their argument was exuberant. She felt a twinge of doubt. She liked sitting at Fenway with a beer. She loved wandering through the Museum of Fine Art. For one long second she wondered which of the two arguments she really belonged in.

Ashley stole a sideways glance at Will, who she guessed was thinking that the fastest way to seduce her was with all sorts of pompous intellectualisms. This was standard graduate-student thinking. She decided to confuse matters for him.

Ashley shoved her seat back abruptly and stood up. "Hey!" she shouted. "You guys, where you from? BC? BU? Northeastern?"

The table of baseball players quieted immediately. Young men being shouted at by a beautiful girl, Ashley thought, always gets their attention.

"Northeastern," one replied, half-standing, making a small bow in her direction, with a Far Eastern sense of courtesy, a decorum mostly lost in the rowdy bar.

"Well, rooting for the Yankees is just like rooting for General Motors or IBM or the Republican Party. Being a Red Sox fan is all about poetry. At some crucial point, everybody makes their choice in life. Enough said."

The boys at the table exploded with laughter and mock outrage.

Will leaned back, grinning. "That," he said, "was succinct."

Ashley smiled and wondered if he wasn't all that bad after all.

When she was young, she thought it would be better to be plain. Plain girls, she knew, can hide.

Right at the start of her teenage years, she had gone through a dramatic phase of opposition to just about everything: loud, stamped-foot disagreeing with her mother, her father, her teachers, her friends, wearing baggy, sacklike, earth-colored clothing, putting a streak of vibrant red next to a streak of ink black in her hair, listening to grunge rock, drinking harsh black coffee, trying cigarettes, and longing for tattoos and body piercings. This phase had lasted for only a couple of months, just long enough for it to come into conflict with just about everything she did in school, both in

the classroom and on the athletic field. It cost her some
friends, as well, and it made those who did remain with her
a little wary.

To Ashley's surprise, the only adult who she'd been able
to speak with in any modestly civil fashion during this portion of her life had been her mother's partner, Hope. This
had surprised her, because a large portion of her inwardly
blamed Hope for the breakup of her parents, and she had often told friends that she hated Hope because of it. This un-
truth had bothered her, in part because she believed it was
more what her friends wanted to hear from her, and she was
unsettled by the idea that she might comply with their perceptions for that flimsiest of reasons. After grunge and
Goth, she had gone through a khaki-and-plaid preppy stage,
followed by a jock stage, then a couple of weeks as a vegan
eating tofu and veggie burgers. She had dabbled in acting,
delivering a passable Marian the Librarian in *The Music
Man,* written reams of heartfelt diary entries, fashioned herself at various times into Emily Dickinson, Eleanor Roosevelt, and Carry Nation, with a touch of Gloria Steinem and
Mia Hamm. She had worked building a house for Habitat
for Humanity and had once gone along with the biggest drug
dealer in her high school on a frightening visit to a nearby
city to pick up a quantity of rock cocaine, an event that had
turned up on a police surveillance camera and prompted a
call from some detectives to her mother. Sally Freeman-
Richards had been furious, grounded her for weeks, shouted
at her that she'd been extraordinarily lucky not to be arrested, and that it would be hard to regain her mother's trust.
Separately, Hope and her father had reached more benign
conclusions, talking more about adolescent rebellion, with
him remembering some pretty stupid things that he had done
while growing up, which had created some laughter, but had
mostly reassured her. She didn't think she was consciously
setting out to do dangerous things in her life, but Ashley
knew that on occasion she engaged in a risk or two, and that
she was fairly charmed to have avoided true consequences
up to that point. Ashley often thought she was like clay on a

potter's wheel, constantly turning, being shaped, waiting for the heat blast from some furnace to finish her.

She felt adrift. She did not particularly enjoy her part-time job at the museum, helping to catalog exhibits. It was a stuck-in-a-back-room, stare-at-a-computer-screen sort of job. She was unsure about the art history graduate program she was waiting to hear from and thought sometimes that she had fallen into these fields only because she was adept with pen, ink, and paintbrush. This troubled her deeply because, like so many young people, she believed that she should only do what she loved, and, as yet, she was unsure what that might be.

They had left the bar, and Ashley pulled her coat a little tighter against the evening chill. She realized that she should probably have been paying attention to Will. He was good-looking, attentive, and might just have a sense of humor. He had an odd, loping stride at her side that was disarming and, probably, on balance, was someone she might consider more carefully. But, she recognized, as well, that they'd been walking for nearly two blocks and only had fifty yards to go before they reached the door to her apartment, and he had yet to actually ask her a question.

She decided to play a small game. If he asked her something she thought interesting, then she'd give him a second date. If he only asked whether he could come upstairs with her, then he was going to get dropped.

"So you think," he said suddenly, "that when guys in a bar argue about baseball, they do so because they love the game, or because they love the argument? I mean, ultimately, there are no right answers, there is only team-based loyalty. And blind loyalty doesn't really lend itself to debate, does it?"

Ashley smiled. There was his second date.

"Of course," he added, "Red Sox love probably belongs in my advanced abnormal-psychology seminar."

She laughed. Definitely another date.

"This is my place," she said. "I've had fun tonight."

Will looked at her. "Maybe we could try a slightly quieter evening? It might be easier to get to know each other when we're not competing with raised voices and wild-eyed spec-

ulation about Derek Jeter's predilections for leather whips
and outsized sex toys and the orifices where they might be
imaginatively employed. Or deployed."

"I'd like that," Ashley said. "Will you call me?"

"I will indeed."

She took a single stride up onto the first step to her apartment, realized that she was still holding his hand, and turned
back and gave him a long kiss. A partially chaste kiss, with
only the smallest sensation of her tongue passing over his
lips. A kiss of promise, but one that implied more for days
to come, although not an invitation for that night. He
seemed to get this, which heartened her, for he stepped a
half pace back, bowed elaborately, and, like an eighteenth-
century courtier, kissed the back of her hand.

"Good night," she said. "I really did have a nice time."

Ashley turned and headed into the apartment building. Between the two glass doors, she turned and glanced back. A
small cone of light stretched from a bulb above the outer
door, and Will stood just on the back side of the wan yellow
circle, which faded quickly in the encroaching rich black of
the New England night. A shadow creased his face, like an
arrow of darkness that sought him out. But she thought nothing of this, gave him a small wave, and headed up to her place
feeling the natural high of possibility, pleased with herself
for not even considering a one-night stand, the hookup that
was so popular in the college circles that she was just on the
verge of emerging from. She shook her head. The last time
she had given in to that particular temptation had been truly
awful. She had been reminded of it earlier when her father
had called out of the blue. But, just as quickly, as she hunted
for the key to her apartment, she dismissed all thoughts of
bad nights past and let the modest glow of this night fill her.

She wondered how long it might take for Will-the-first-
date to call her and become Will-the-second-date.

Will Goodwin lingered in the darkness for a moment after
Ashley had vanished inside the second door. He felt a rush

of enthusiasm, a devil-may-care kind of excitement about the evening past and the evening to come.

He was a bit overwhelmed. The girlfriend of a friend, who had passed on Ashley's number, had informed him that she was beautiful and bright, if a bit mysterious, but she had exceeded even his fantasies in each regard. He thought he'd just managed to avoid the "boring" tag by the narrowest of margins.

Hunched over against a quickening breeze, Will stuck his hands deep into his parka and started walking. The air had an antique quality to it, as if each shiver it delivered were no different, passed down exactly the same with the same October chill that had sliced through generations who had traveled the Boston streets. He could feel his cheeks starting to redden from the night's determination, and he hustled toward the subway stop. He covered ground quickly, long legs now eating up the city sidewalk. She was tall, too, he thought. Almost five ten, he guessed, with a model's lithe look that even jeans and a baggy cotton sweater hadn't been able to conceal. He was a little astonished, as he dashed between traffic, crossing the street midblock, that she wasn't inundated with guys, which, he supposed, probably had something to do with an unhappy relationship or some other bad experience. He decided not to speculate, but to simply thank whatever lucky star had put him in contact with Ashley. In his studies, he thought, everything was about probability and prediction. He wasn't sure that the statistics he assigned to clinical work with lab rats could necessarily apply to meeting someone like Ashley.

Will grinned to himself and went bounding down the steps to the T.

The Boston subway, like that of most cities, has an otherworldly feel to it, when one passes through the turnstiles and descends into the underground world of transit. Lights glisten off white-tiled walls; shadows find space between steel pillars. There is a constancy of noise, as trains come, go, and rumble through the distance. The outside world is shut away, replaced with a kind of disjointed universe where wind, rain, snow, or even bright warm sunshine all seem a part of some other place and time.

His train arrived, making a high-pitched, screeching sound, and Will boarded quickly, along with a dozen others. The lights in the train gave everyone a pasty, sickly look. For a moment, he speculated about the other passengers, all either wrapped up in a newspaper, buried in some book, or staring out blankly. He leaned his head back and closed his eyes for an instant, letting the speed and sway of the train rock him a little like a child in his mother's arms. He would call tomorrow, he told himself. Ask her out and try to engage her on the phone a bit. He sorted through subjects and tried to imagine one that would be unexpected. He wondered where to take her. Dinner and a movie? Predictable. He had the sensation that Ashley was the sort of woman who wanted to see something special. A play perhaps? A comedy club? Followed by a late-night dinner at some place better than the usual burgers-and-beer hangout. But not too snobbish, he imagined. And quiet. So, laughter and then something romantic. Maybe not the greatest plan, he thought, but reasonable.

His stop arrived, and he bounded up and out, moving quickly, but a little haphazardly, as he rose through the station, out to the street. The Porter Square lights sliced through the darkness, creating a sense of activity where there was little. He hunched over against a blast of cold wind and worked his way out of the square, down a side street. His own place was four blocks distant, and he worked his memory, trying to decide on the right restaurant to take her to.

He slowed when he heard a dog bark, suddenly alarmed. In the distance, an ambulance siren broke through the night. A few of the duplexes and apartments on the block had the glow of television screens lighting up windows, but most were dark.

To his right, in an alleyway between two apartment buildings, Will thought he heard a scraping sound, and he turned in that direction. Suddenly he saw a black shape rushing toward him. He took a step back in surprise and held up his arm to try to protect himself and thought that he should cry out for help, but things were moving far too quickly, and he had only a single moment filled with shock and fear, and the vaguest of terrors because he knew something was coming at him fast. It was a lead pipe, and it swung through the air with a swordlike hiss, bearing inexorably down on his forehead.

•

It took me nearly seven hours over one long, eye-straining day, to find Will Goodwin's name in *The Boston Globe*. Except that it was a different name, under the headline POLICE SEEK MUGGER OF GRAD STUDENT, and ran in the local section, near the bottom of the page. The story was only four paragraphs and had precious little information, beyond that the injuries suffered by the twenty-four-year-old student were serious and he was in critical condition at Mass. General Hospital after being discovered by a passing early-morning pedestrian who spotted his bloody figure abandoned behind some aluminum garbage cans in an alleyway. Police were requesting assistance from anyone in the Somerville neighborhood who might have seen or heard anything suspicious.

That was all.

No follow-up either the next day or in the subsequent weeks. Just a small moment of urban violence, duly noted, registered and then, just as quickly, forgotten, swallowed up by the steady buildup of news.

It took me two more days working the telephones to get an address for Will. The Boston College Alumni Office said that he had never finished the program he was enrolled in and came up with a home address out in the Boston suburb of Concord. The phone number was unlisted.

Concord is a lovely place, filled with stately homes that breathe of the past. It has a green swath of town common with an impressive public library, a prep school, and a quaint downtown filled with trendy shops. When I was younger, I took my own children to walk the nearby battle sites and recite Longfellow's famous poem. The town has, like so many in Massachusetts, unfortunately let history take a backseat to development. But the house where the young man that I had come to know as Will Goodwin was an older place, early-colonial farmhouse in nature, less ostentatious than the newer homes, set back from a side road, some fifty yards down a gravel drive. In the front, someone had clearly spent time planting flowers in the garden. I saw a small plaque, with the date 1789, on the glistening white exterior wall. There was a side door that had a wooden wheelchair ramp built up to it. I went to the front, where I could smell the nearby hibiscus blossoms, and knocked gingerly.

A slender woman, gray-haired, but not yet grandmotherly, opened the door.

"Yes, may I help you?" she asked.

I introduced myself, apologized for showing up unannounced, but said that I was unable to call ahead because of the unlisted number. I told her I was a writer and was inquiring about some crimes that had taken place a few years back in the Cambridge, Newton, and Somerville areas and wondered if I might ask a few questions about Will or, better yet, speak with him directly.

She was taken aback, but did not immediately close the door in my face.

"I don't know that we can help you," she said politely.

"I'm sorry if I've taken you by surprise," I replied. "I just have a few questions."

She shook her head. "He doesn't . . . ," she started, then stopped, looking out at me. I could see her lower lip start to quiver, and just the touch of tears glistening in her eyes. "It has been . . . ," she tried, but then she was interrupted by a voice from behind.

"Mother? Who is it?"

She hesitated, as if uncertain precisely what to say. I looked behind her and saw a young man in a wheelchair emerging from a side room. His skin had a bleached, pale look, and his brown hair was a tangled, unkempt mass, stringy, long, and falling toward his shoulders. A Z-shaped, dull red scar on the upper right side of his forehead reached almost to the eyebrow. His arms seemed wiry, muscled, but his chest was sunken, almost emaciated. He had large hands, with elegant, long fingers, and I thought, as I looked at him, that I could see hints and whispers of whom he once was. He rolled himself forward.

The mother looked at me. "It has been very hard," she said softly, with surprising intimacy.

The rubber wheels on the chair squealed when he stopped. "Hello," he said, not unpleasantly.

I gave him my name and quickly explained that I was interested in the crime that had crippled him.

"My crime?" he asked, but clearly didn't really expect an answer, because he rapidly gave one himself. "I don't think it was all that special. A routine mugging. Anyway, I can't tell you all that much about it. Two months in a coma. Then this . . ." He waved at the chair.

"Did the police ever make an arrest?"

"No. By the time I woke up, I'm afraid I wasn't too much help. I can't remember anything from that night. Not a damn thing. It's a little like hitting the backspace key on your keyboard and watching all the letters of some piece of work disappear. You know it's probably somewhere in the computer, but you can't find it. It's just been deleted."

"You were coming home after a date?"

"Yes. We never connected again after that. Not that surprising. I was a mess. Still am." He laughed a little and smiled wryly.

I nodded. "The cops never came up with much, huh?"

He shook his head. "Well, a couple of curious things."

"What?" I asked.

"They found some kids in Roxbury trying to use my Visa credit card. They thought for a couple of days that they might have been the ones that mugged me, but it turned out they weren't. The kids apparently just found the card near a Dumpster."

"Okay, but why . . ."

"Because someone else found my wallet with all my ID— you know, driver's license, BC meal card, Social Security, health care, all that stuff, intact in Dorchester. Miles away from the Dumpster where the kids found the credit card. It was as if whatever was taken from me was scattered all over Boston." He smiled. "A little like my brains."

"What are you doing now?" I asked.

"Now?" Will looked over at his mother. "Now, I'm just waiting."

"Waiting? For what?"

"I don't know. Rehab sessions at the Head Trauma Center. The day I can get out of this chair. Not much else I can do."

I stepped back and his mother started to close the door.

"Hey!" Will said. "You think they'll ever find the guy that did this to me?"

"I don't know," I replied. "But if I find out anything, I'll let you know."

"I wouldn't mind having a name and an address," he said quietly. "I think I would like to take care of some matters myself."

4

A Conversation That Meant More Than Words

Crime, Michael O'Connell thought, is about connections.

If one doesn't want to be caught, he reasoned to himself, one must eradicate all the obvious links. Or at least obscure them so that they are not readily apparent to some plodding detective. He smiled to himself and closed his eyes for a moment to let the rocking of the subway train soothe him. He still felt an electric surge of energy throughout his body. Beating a man gave him a curiously peaceful sensation, even while he felt his muscles contract and tighten. He wondered if physical violence was always going to be this seductive.

At his feet was a cheap blue canvas duffel bag, the strap

loosely wrapped around his arm. In it were a pair of leather gloves, a second pair of rubber latex surgeon's gloves, a twenty-inch piece of common plumber's pipe, and the wallet belonging to Will Goodwin, although he hadn't yet had time to learn the man's name.

Five items, O'Connell thought, meant five different stops on the T.

He knew he was being overly cautious, but told himself that a devotion to precision would benefit him. The pipe was undoubtedly marred with blood from the man he'd beaten. So were the leather gloves. He guessed that his clothes also contained traces of material, and maybe his running shoes, as well, but by midmorning he would have run everything through several hot-water cycles at the local Laundromat. So much for microscopic links between the man and himself. The duffel bag was destined for a Dumpster in Brockton, the lead pipe for a construction site downtown. The wallet, after he'd removed the cash, would be abandoned in a trash barrel outside a T stop in Dorchester, and the credit cards would be scattered around some streets in Roxbury, where he hoped some black kids would pick them up and start using them. Boston was still divided by race, and he guessed that those kids would get blamed for what he'd done.

The surgeon's gloves, which he'd used beneath his leather gloves, could safely be discarded on the way home. Especially if he tossed them into a waste basket not far from Mass. General Hospital, or Brigham and Women's, where even if they were spotted, they wouldn't attract any special attention.

He wondered whether he had killed the man who had kissed Ashley.

There was a good chance. His first blow had caught him up around the temple, and he'd heard the bone crack. The man had dropped fast, slamming back against a tree, which was lucky, because it muffled the sound as he had tumbled over. Even if someone had overheard something, curiosity pricked, and looked out the window, both he and the man who'd kissed Ashley were obscured by the trunk of the tree and several parked cars. It had been an easy matter to drag him back into the shadows of the alleyway. The kicking and punching had taken only a few seconds. A burst of savagery almost like a sexual climax, unrelenting, explosive and then finished. As he shoved the unconscious body behind some metal canisters, he'd removed the man's wallet, rapidly packed his homemade weapon into the duffel, and, moving quickly, cut through the darkness back to the Porter Square subway station.

It had been incredibly easy. Sudden. Anonymous. Vicious.

He wondered for an idle second or two who the man was. He shrugged. He didn't really care. He didn't even need to know his name. Within an hour or two, the only possible thing that conceivably connected him to the man he'd left in the alleyway was asleep in her own apartment, unaware of anything that had taken place that night. And when she did become aware, she might go to the police. He doubted it, but the chance, even if slight, existed. But what could she say? In his pocket was a ticket stub for a movie theater. It wasn't much of an alibi, but it covered the time when the kiss had taken place and would be enough for any policeman who wouldn't believe her in the first place, especially after the wallet or the credit cards showed up all the way across town.

He leaned his head back, listening to the sound of the subway train, a curious kind of music hidden in the unrelenting noise of metal against metal.

It was a little before five in the morning when Michael O'-Connell made his next-to-last stop. He picked a station more or less at random and rose up out into the last darkness of the night into the area around Chinatown, near the downtown financial district. Most of the stores were shuttered and closed, and the sidewalk was empty. It did not take him long to find a pay phone that was operating, and he shivered against the chill. He pulled the hood of his sweatshirt over his head, giving him an anonymous, monklike appearance. He worked fast. He didn't want a lazy patrol car making a last sweep through the narrow streets to spot him, stop, and ask questions.

O'Connell deposited fifty cents and dialed Ashley's number.

The telephone rang five times before he heard her sleep-groggy voice.

"Hello?"

He paused, just to give her a second or two to fully awaken.

"Hello?" she asked a second time. "Who is it?"

He remembered a cheap, white portable phone by the side of her bed. No caller ID, not that it would make a difference.

"You know who it is," he said softly.

She did not reply.

"I told you. I love you, Ashley. We are meant for each other. No one can come between us."

"Michael, stop calling me. I want you to leave me alone."

"I don't need to call you. I'm always with you."

Then he hung up the phone, before she had a chance to. The best sort of threat, he thought, wasn't stated, but imagined.

It was almost dawn when he finally made it back to his apartment.

Perhaps a half dozen of his neighbor's cats were milling about in the hallway, mewling and making other annoying sounds. One of them hissed when he approached. The old lady who lived across from him owned somewhere more than twelve cats, perhaps as many as twenty, called them all by a variety of names, and set out food dishes for the occasional stray that happened by. *Owned,* he thought, was a relative term. They seemed to come and go pretty much as they pleased. She'd even put an extra litter box in a corner of the hallway to accommodate their needs, which gave the corridor a thick, unpleasant smell. The cats knew Michael O'-Connell and he knew the cats, and he didn't get along with any of them any better than he did with their owner. He considered them strays, a step above vermin. They made him sneeze, and his eyes water, and were forever watching him with feline wariness whenever he entered the building. He didn't like it when anyone or anything paid any attention to his comings and goings.

O'Connell aimed a kick at a calico who strayed within his reach, but missed. Getting sluggish, he told himself. The result of a long but exciting night. The calico and companions skittered away as he unlocked his apartment door. He looked down and saw that one, a black-and-white with an orange streak, lingered momentarily near the food dish. It must be new or else stupid not to take its cue from the others, who kept their distance from him. The old woman wouldn't be up for an hour, maybe longer, and he knew her hearing was getting pretty shaky. He glanced down the hallway for a moment. None of the other tenants seemed to be stirring. He could never understand why no one else complained about the cats, and he hated them for it. There was an old couple, from Costa Rica, who spoke poor English. A Puerto Rican man who, O'Connell guessed, supplemented his machinist's job with an occasional B and E occupied one of the other apartments. Upstairs were a pair of graduate students, who occasionally filled the hallway with the pungent smell of marijuana, and a gray-haired, sallow-faced salesman who preferred to spend his extra hours weepy and immersed in a bottle. Other than complaining about the cats to the superintendent—an older man with fingernails encrusted with years of dirt, who spoke in an accent that was indecipherable, and who clearly hated to be bothered with repairs—O'Connell had little to do with any of them. He wondered if any of the other tenants even knew his name. It was all just a quiet, dingy, unimpressive, cold place, either an end for some or a transition for others, and it had an impermanence that he liked. He looked down, as he opened his door, and wondered whether the old woman actually kept track of her cats. He doubted that she had an accurate count.

Or that she would miss one.

He rapidly bent down and seized the black-and-white roughly around the midsection. The cat squealed once, clawing at him in surprise.

He looked down at the sudden red scratch on the back of his hand. The thin line of blood was going to make what he had in mind much easier.

Ashley Freeman lay back in her bed.

"I am in trouble," she whispered out loud.

She remained that way, barely moving until the sunlight moved steadily through her window, past the frilly, opaque shades that gave the room a little-girl feel. She watched as a shaft of daylight moved slowly along the wall across from her bed. Some of her own works were hung there, some charcoal drawings done in a life-figure class, one of a man's torso that she liked, another of a woman's back that curved sensuously across the white page. There was also a self-portrait that she'd done, which was unusual in that she had only drawn half of her face in detail and left the remainder in obscurity, as if it were shadowed.

"This can't be happening," she said, again out loud, but this time a little louder.

Of course, she noted inwardly, she didn't know what *this* was. Not yet.

•

I called her later that day. I didn't bother with pleasantries or small talk, but just launched into my first question: "Exactly where did Michael O'Connell's obsession come from?"

She sighed. "That's something you need to discover for yourself. But don't you remember the electricity of being young and coming unexpectedly across that singular moment of passion? The one-night stand, the chance encounter. Have you gotten so old that you can't remember when things were all possibility?"

"All right. Yes," I said, perhaps a little too hastily.

"There was only one problem. All those moments are more or less benign, or, at the very most, simply embarrassing. Red-faced mistakes, or moments you keep to yourself and never mention to another soul. But that wasn't the case this time. Ashley, in a moment of weakness, slipped once, and then, abruptly, found herself enmeshed in a briar patch. Except a briar patch isn't necessarily lethal, and Michael O'Connell was."

I paused, then said, "I found Will Goodwin. Except his name wasn't Goodwin."

She hesitated, a small catch in the words that slowly came over the phone line. "Good. You probably learned something important. At the very least, your understanding of Michael O'Connell's, ah, *potential* should have grown through your meeting. But that's not where it all began, and it's probably not where it all ends, either. I don't know. That's for you to figure out."

"Okay, but—"

"I have to go. But you understand, in a way, you're at the same point Scott Freeman was, before things started to get . . . well, I'm not sure what the right word is. Tense? Difficult? He knew some things, but not very much. Mostly what he had was an absence of information. He believed that Ashley might be at risk, but he didn't know how, or exactly where or when, or any of the things that we first ask ourselves when we perceive a threat. All Scott Freeman had were several disturbing items to wonder about. He knew it wasn't the start and he knew it wasn't the finish. He was like a scientist, thrown into the middle of an equation, trying to guess which way to go in order to find an answer."

She paused, and for the first time I felt a bit of the same chill.

"I have to go," she said. "We'll speak again."

"But—"

"Indecision. It's a simple word. But it leads to evil things, does it not? Of course, so can being foolishly decisive. That's more or less the dilemma, isn't it? To act. Or not to act. Always an intriguing question, don't you think?"

5

Nameless

When Hope came through the front door of her house, she instinctively clapped her hands twice. She could already hear the sound of her dog's paws as he rushed from the living room, where he spent much of his time staring out the front picture window, waiting for her to return home. The sounds were utterly familiar to her: first the thud, as he leapt down from the sofa that he wasn't allowed on when there was an actual human around to tell him *no,* then the scrabbling noise that his toenails made against the hardwood floor, as he slipped and pushed the Oriental rug out of position, and finally the urgent bounding, as he headed to the vestibule. She knew enough to put down any papers or groceries in anticipation of the greeting.

There is nothing, she thought, in the entire world that is as emotionally unencumbered as a dog's greeting. She knelt down and let him cover her face with his tongue, his tail beating a steady tattoo against the wall. It is a truism for dog owners, Hope thought, that regardless of what else is going wrong, the dog always wags its tail when you come through the door. Her dog was of oddly mixed parentage. A vet had suggested to her that he was the clearly illegitimate offspring of a golden retriever and a pit bull, which gave him a shortish, blond coat, a snubby nose, a fierce and unmitigated loyalty minus the nasty aggressiveness, and a degree of intelligence that sometimes astonished even her. She had acquired him from a shelter where he'd been shunted as a puppy, and when she asked the shelter operator what the pup's name was, she'd been told that he hadn't been christened, so to speak. So, in a fit of slightly devilish creativity, she'd called him Nameless.

When he was young, she'd taught him to retrieve wayward soccer balls at the end of practice, a sight that never failed to amuse the girls on whatever team she happened to be coaching. Nameless would patiently wait by the bench, silly grin on his face, until she gave him a hand signal, then would bolt across the pitch, rounding up each ball and pushing it with his nose and forelegs, racing back to where she waited with a mesh bag. She would tell the girls on the team that if they could learn to control the ball at speed the way Nameless did, then they would all be all-Americans.

He was far too old now, couldn't see or hear as well, and had a touch of arthritis, and collecting a dozen balls was probably more than he could handle, so he went to practice less often. She did not like to think about his ending; he'd been with her as long as she'd been with Sally Freeman.

She often thought that if it had not been for Nameless the puppy, she might not have succeeded in her partnership with Sally. It had been the dog who had forced Ashley and her to find a common ground. Dogs, she thought, managed that sort of thing pretty effortlessly. In the days after the divorce, when Sally and Ashley had come to live with her, Hope had been greeted with all the impassiveness that a sullen seven-year-old could muster. All the anger and hurt Ashley felt had pretty much been ignored by Nameless, who had been overjoyed at the arrival of a child, especially one with Ashley's energy. So Hope had enlisted Ashley in exercising the puppy with her, and training him, which they did with mixed results—he was adept at retrieving, clueless when it came to the furniture. And so, by talking about the dog's successes and failures, they had reached first a détente, then an understanding, and finally a sense of sharing, which had broken through many of the other barriers that they'd faced.

Hope rubbed Nameless behind the ears. She owed him far more than he owed her, she thought. "Hungry?" she asked. "Want some dog food?"

Nameless barked once. A stupid question to ask a dog, she thought, but one they certainly liked to hear. She walked into the kitchen and grabbed the dog bowl off the floor, as she began to think about what she might prepare for Sally and herself for dinner. Something interesting, she decided. A piece of wild salmon with a fennel cream sauce and risotto. She was an excellent cook and took pride in what she made. Nameless sat, tail sweeping the floor, anticipating. "We're the same, you and I," she said to the dog. "We're both waiting for something. The difference is, you know it's dinner, and I'm not sure what is in store for me."

Scott Freeman looked around and thought about the moments in life when loneliness appears completely unexpectedly.

He had slumped into an aging Queen Anne armchair and stared out the window toward the darkness creeping through the last October leaves on the trees. He had some papers to correct, a class lecture to prepare, some reading he needed to do—a colleague's manuscript had arrived in the day's mail from the University Press and he was on the peer-review panel, and there were at least a half dozen requests from history majors for advice on course selections.

He was also stymied in the midst of a piece of his own writing, an essay on the curious nature of fighting in the Revolutionary War, where one moment was endowed with utter savagery, and another, with a kind of medieval chivalry, as when Washington had returned a British general's lost dog to him in the midst of the battle of Princeton.

Much to do, he thought. Out loud, to no one except himself, he said, "You've got a full plate."

And in that moment, it all meant nothing.

He considered this thought and realized instead, it *might* all mean nothing.

It depended upon what he did next.

He looked away from the fading afternoon light and let his eyes scour across the letter that he'd found in Ashley's bureau. He read each word for the hundredth time and felt as trapped as when he'd first discovered it. Then, he mentally reviewed every word, every inflection, every tone, in everything she had said to him when he'd called her.

Scott leaned back and closed his eyes. What he had to do was try to imagine himself in Ashley's position. You know your own daughter, he told himself. What is going on?

This question echoed in his imagination.

The first thing, he insisted to himself, was to discover who'd written the letter. Then he could independently assess the person, without intruding on his daughter's life. If he was skillful he could reach a conclusion about the individual without involving anyone—or, at least, not involving anyone who would tell Ashley that he was poking around in her private life. When, as he hoped was true, he discovered that the letter was merely unsettling and inappropriate and nothing more, he could relax and allow Ashley the freedom to extricate herself from the unwanted attention and get on with her life. In fact, he could probably manage all this without even involving Ashley's mother or her partner, which was his preferred course of events.

The question was how to get started.

One of the great advantages of studying history, he reminded himself, was in the models of action that great men had taken through the centuries. Scott knew that at his core he had a quiet, romantic streak, one that loved the notion of fighting against all hope, rising to desperate occasions. His tastes in movies and novels ran in that direction, and he realized there was a certain childish grace in these tales, which trumped the utter savagery of the actual moments in history. Historians are pragmatists. Cold-eyed and calculating, he thought. Saying "Nuts" at Bastogne was remembered better by novelists and filmmakers. Historians paid more attention to frostbite, blood that froze in puddles on the ground, and helpless mind- and soul-numbing despair.

He believed that he'd passed on much of this heady romanticism to Ashley, who had embraced his storytelling verve and spent many hours reading *Little House on the Prairie* and Jane Austen novels. In part, he wondered, if this might be at least a little bit of the basis for her trusting nature.

He felt a small acid taste on his tongue, as if he'd swallowed some bitter drink. He hated the idea that he'd helped to teach her to be confident, trusting, and independent, and now, because she was all those things, he was deeply troubled.

Scott shook his head and said out loud, "You're jumping way ahead here. You don't know anything for certain, and in fact you don't even know anything at all."

Start simply, he insisted. Get a name.

But doing this, without his daughter finding out, was the problem. He needed to intrude without being caught.

Feeling a little like a criminal, he turned around and went up the stairs of his small, wood-framed house, toward Ashley's old bedroom. He had in mind a more thorough search, hoping for some telltale bit of information that would take him beyond the letter. He felt a twinge of guilt as he went through her door and wondered a little bit why he had to violate his own daughter's room in order to know her a little better.

Sally Freeman-Richards looked up from her plate at dinner and idly said, "You know, I got the most unusual call from Scott this afternoon."

Hope sort of grunted and reached for the loaf of sourdough bread. She was familiar with the roundabout way that Sally liked to start certain conversations. Sometimes Hope thought that Sally remained, even after so many years, something of an enigma to her; she could be so forceful and aggressive in a court of law, and then, in the quiet of the house they shared, almost bashful. Hope thought there were many contradictions in their lives. And contradictions created tension.

"He seems worried," Sally said.

"Worried about what?"

"Ashley."

This made Hope put her knife down on the plate. "Ashley? How so?"

Sally hesitated for a moment. "It seems he was going through some of her things and he came across a letter she received that disturbed him."

"What was he doing going through her things?"

Sally smiled. "My first question, too. Great minds think alike."

"And?"

"Well, he didn't really answer me. He wanted to talk about the letter."

Hope shrugged a little bit. "Okay, what about the letter?"

Sally thought for a minute, then asked, "Well, did you ever, I mean, like back in high school or college, ever get a love letter, you know the type, professing devotion, love, undying passion, total commitment, over-the-top I-can't-live-without-you sorts of statements?"

"Well, no, I never got one. But I suspect the reasons I didn't were different. That's what he found?"

"Yes. A protest of love."

"Well, that sounds pretty harmless. Why do you suppose he was bent out of shape about it?"

"Something in the tone, I'm thinking."

"And," Hope said, with a touch of exasperation, "what precisely would that be?"

Sally considered what she was going to say before saying it, a lawyer's cautiousness. "It seemed, I don't know, *possessive*. And perhaps a bit manic. You know, the *If I can't have you, no one can* sort of thing. I think he was reading too much into it."

Hope nodded. She chose her own words carefully. "You're probably right. Of course," she added slowly, "wouldn't it be a greater error in judgment to underestimate a letter like that?"

"You think Scott was right to be worried?"

"I didn't say that. I said that ignoring something is rarely an answer to a question."

Sally smiled. "Now you sound like a guidance counselor."

"I *am* a guidance counselor. So it probably isn't all that crazy that upon occasion I actually sound like one."

Sally paused. "I didn't mean for this to be an argument."

Hope nodded. "Of course." She wasn't sure that she agreed with this, but it was a much safer thing to say.

"It seems, sometimes, that every time Scott's name comes up, when we're talking, that we end up arguing about one thing or another," Sally said. "Even after all these years."

Hope shook her head. "Well, let's not talk about Scott. I mean, after all, he's not really much of a part of who we are, is he? But he's still a part of Ashley's life, so we should deal with him in that context. And anyway, even if Scott and I don't exactly get along, that doesn't mean I automatically think he's crazy."

"Okay, fair enough," Sally replied. "But the letter . . ."

"Has Ashley seemed out of touch, or distant, or anything out of the normal lately?"

"You know as well as I. *No* is the answer. Unless you've noticed something."

"I don't know that I'm all that great at spotting emotional undercurrents in young women," Hope said, although she knew this statement was the opposite of the truth.

"What makes you think I am?" Sally asked.

Hope shrugged. The entire conversation was going wrong, and she couldn't tell if it was her fault. She looked across the dining room table at Sally and thought that there was some tension between them that she couldn't quite put a name to. It was like seeing some hieroglyphics carved into a stone. It was speaking a language that should be clear, but was just beyond her grasp.

"When Ashley was last here, did you notice anything different?"

As Hope waited for Sally to reply, she went over all the dynamics of Ashley's last visit. Ashley had breezed in with all the usual bluster, confidence, and a million plans all going on at once. Sometimes standing next to her was a little like trying to grab the trunk of a palm tree at the height of a hurricane. She simply had a natural velocity to her.

Sally was shaking her head and smiling. "I don't know," she said. "She was doing this and that and meeting up with one person or another. High school friends she hadn't seen in years. It seemed like she hardly had a moment for her boring old mom. Or her boring old mom's partner. Or, I suppose, for her boring old dad either."

Hope nodded.

Sally pushed back from the table. "Ah, let's just see what happens. If Ashley has a problem, she's likely to call and ask for advice or help or whatever. Let's not read anything into anything, okay? Actually, I'm sorry I brought it up. If Scott hadn't been so upset . . . Actually, not upset. But concerned. I think he's just getting a little paranoid in his old age. Hell, we all are, aren't we? And Ashley, well, she's got all that energy. Best thing is to just step aside and let her find her own way."

Hope nodded. "Spoken like a wise mother." She began to clear the dishes, but when she reached for a long-stemmed wineglass, the glass broke in her hand, a piece of the base simply breaking off and shattering as it hit the floor. She looked down and saw that the tip of her index finger was bleeding. For a moment she watched the blood gather and then drip down across her palm, each droplet welling up through the slice, synchronized to her heartbeat.

They watched a little television, and then Sally announced that she was going to bed. This was an announcement, not an invitation, not even accompanied by the obligatory kiss on the cheek. Hope barely looked up from some college essays she was reviewing, but she did ask Sally if she thought it was possible for her to get to a game or two in the upcoming weeks. Sally was noncommittal as she headed up the stairwell to the bedroom they shared on the second floor.

Hope slumped back into a spot on the sofa, looked down as Nameless shuffled over to her, and then, hearing the water running in the upper bathroom, slapped her palm on the seat next to her, inviting her dog up to her side. She never did this in front of Sally, who disapproved of Nameless's cavalier attitude toward furniture. Sally liked everyone's roles carefully defined, Hope thought. Dogs on the floor. People in seats. As little messiness as possible. This was the lawyer in her. Her job was to sort out confusions and conflicts and impose reason upon situations. Create rules and parameters, set out courses of action and define things.

Hope was far less sure that organization meant freedom.

She enjoyed some clutter in her life and had what she thought was a slightly rebellious streak.

She idly rubbed Nameless's fur, and he thumped his tail once or twice while his eyes rolled back. She could hear Sally moving about, then saw the shadow thrown by the bedroom light disappear from the stairwell.

Hope put her head back and thought that perhaps their relationship was in far more trouble than she could imagine, although she was hard-pressed to say exactly why. It seemed to her that for much of their last year together Sally had lived in a world of distraction, her mind elsewhere, all the time. She wondered if someone could fall out of love as quickly as they fell into it in the first place. She exhaled slowly and shifted in her seat and exchanged her fears for her partner to fears for Ashley.

She did not know Scott well and had probably only spoken to him on a half dozen occasions in nearly fifteen years, which, she conceded to herself, was unusual. Her impressions were gathered mostly from Sally, and Ashley, but she thought that he wasn't the sort of person to go off half-cocked about something, especially something as trivial as an anonymous love letter. In her job, both as a coach and as a private-school counselor, Hope had seen so many bizarrely dangerous relationships, and she was inclined to be wary.

She rubbed Nameless again, but he barely budged.

It was trite, she thought, for someone of her sexual persuasion to mistrust *all* men. But on the other hand, she was aware of the damage that runaway emotions could do, especially to young people.

Raising her eyes, she looked up at the ceiling, as if she could see through the plaster and wallboard and determine what Sally was thinking as she lay in bed. Sally had trouble sleeping, Hope knew. And when she did manage to drift off, she tossed and turned and seemed troubled by her dreams.

Hope wondered whether Ashley was having the same trouble sleeping. That was a question she realized she should probably acquire the answer to. But exactly how to do this eluded her.

At that moment, Hope had no idea that more or less the same dilemma was also keeping Scott awake.

•

Boston has a chameleon-like quality that seems different from that of other cities. On a bright summer morning, it seems to burst with energy and ideas. It breathes learning and education, constancy, history. A headiness that speaks of possibility. But walk the same streets when the fog comes rolling in off the harbor, or when an edgy frost is in the air or the dirt-streaked residue of winter snow litters the streets, and Boston becomes a cold, gritty place, with a razor harshness that belongs to a far darker side.

I watched a late-afternoon shadow creep slowly across Dartmouth Street and felt hot air coming from the Charles. I couldn't see the river from where I stood, but I knew it was only a few blocks distant. Newbury Street, with its trendy shops and upscale galleries, was nearby. So was the Berklee College of Music, which filled the adjacent sidewalks with aspiring musicians of all varieties: budding punk rockers, folksingers, aspiring concert pianists. Long hair, spiked hair, streaked hair. I could also see a homeless man, mumbling to himself, rocking back and forth, back to the wall of an alleyway, hidden in part by shadows. He might have heard many voices, or one craving, it was hard to tell, as I turned away. On the street nearby, a BMW honked at some students jaywalking against the light, then accelerated with a squeal of tires.

For a moment, I paused, thinking that what made Boston unique was its ability to accommodate so many different currents, all at once. With so many different identities to choose from, it was no wonder that Michael O'Connell found a home here.

I did not know him well, yet. But I had the inkling of a feel for him.

Of course, that was the same mystery Ashley faced.

6

A Taste of What Was to Come

She waited until midday, unable to move from her bed, until sunlight came pouring through the windows and the city streets beyond her apartment walls hummed and buzzed reassuringly. She spent a few moments staring out through a streaked pane of glass, as if to tell herself that with all the normal ebb and flow of another typical day, nothing much could be out of order. She let her eyes follow first one person, then another, as people walked up the sidewalk into her field of vision. She did not recognize anyone, and yet, everyone was familiar. They all fit into easily identifiable types. The businessman. The student. The waitress. There seemed to be a world of purpose just beyond her reach. People moved about with determination and destination.

Ashley felt like an island in their midst. She wished for an instant that she had a roommate or a best friend. Someone to confide in, who would sit on the other side of the bed, sipping tea, ready to laugh or cry or voice concern at the most modest of prompts. She knew a million people in Boston, but none she would trust with a burden, and certainly not a Michael O'Connell burden. She had a hundred friends, but no Friend. She turned to her desk, littered with half-finished papers, art history texts, a laptop computer, and some CDs. She rummaged around until she came up with a small piece of scrap paper with some numbers on it.

Then, with a single deep breath, Ashley dialed Michael O'Connell's phone number.

It rang twice before he picked it up.

"Yes?"

"Michael, it's Ashley."

She let silence fill the line. She wished that she had mapped out what she was going to say in forceful phrases and unequivocal statements. But, instead, she let emotions overcome her.

"I don't want you to call me anymore," she blurted out.

He said nothing.

"When you called this morning, I was asleep. It scared the hell out of me."

She waited for an apology. An excuse, perhaps, or an explanation. None came.

"Please, Michael." It sounded a great deal as if she were asking him for a favor.

He did not reply.

She stammered on, "Look, it was just one night. That's all. We had some fun, and a few drinks, and it went a bit farther than it should have, although I don't regret it, that's not what I mean. I'm sorry if you misunderstood my feelings. Can't we just part as friends? Go our own ways."

She could hear his breathing on the other end of the line, but no words.

"So," she continued, aware that everything she said was sounding more and more lame, increasingly pathetic, "don't send me any more letters, especially like the one you sent the other week. That was you, wasn't it? It had to be. I know you have a busy life and a lot on your mind, and I'm wrapped up with my work and trying to get this graduate school thing going, and I just don't have time for a serious relationship now. I know you'll understand. I just need my space. I mean, we're both involved in so many different things, it's just not the right time for me, and I bet it's not really the right time for you. You can see that, can't you?"

She let this question hang in the air, surrounded by his silence. She grasped at the quiet as if it were an acquiescence on his part.

"I really appreciate your listening to me, Michael. And I wish you the best, really, I do. And maybe, sometime in the future, we can be better friends. But not right now, okay? I'm sorry if this disappoints you. But if you really love me like you say, then you'll understand I need to be on my own and can't be tied down right now. You never can tell what the future might hold, but now, in the present, I just can't handle it, okay? I'd like to end this as friends, okay?"

She could hear his breathing on the other end of the line. In and out. Regular, unhurried.

"Look," she said, exasperation and a little desperation creeping into her words, "we don't really know each other. It was just once and we were both a little drunk, right? How can you say you love me? How can you say these things? We're perfect for each other? That's crazy. You can't live without me? That makes no sense. None. I just want you to leave me alone, okay? Look, you'll find someone else, someone who's just right for you, I know. But it's not me. Please, Michael, just leave me alone. All right?"

Michael O'Connell didn't say a word. He simply laughed. It came across the phone line as something alien and distant when nothing she'd said was in the smallest way funny or even ironic. It chilled her completely.

And then he hung up the telephone.

For a few seconds she stood, staring down at the receiver in her hand, wondering whether the conversation had actually happened. For a moment she wasn't even sure that he *had* been on the other end of the line, but then, she remembered his one word, and that was unmistakable, even if he was almost a stranger. She carefully hung up the phone and looked around the apartment wildly, as if expecting someone to jump out at her. She could hear the muted sounds of traffic, but it did little to lessen the sensation of total and complete solitude that crept over her.

Ashley slumped down on the edge of her bed, suddenly

exhausted, tears welling up in the corners of her eyes. She felt incredibly small.

She had no real grasp of the situation, other than the feeling that something was just starting to pick up speed, moving dangerously forward—not yet out of control, but on the verge. She dabbed at her eyes and told herself to get a grip on her emotions. She tried to layer a sense of toughness and determination over the residue of helplessness.

Ashley shook her head hard. "You should have planned what you were going to say," she said out loud. Hearing her own voice bounce around the narrow space of her small apartment unsettled her. She had tried to come across as forceful—at least, that was what she had wanted—but instead had seemed weak, pleading, whining, all the things that she thought she wasn't. She forced herself up off the edge of the bed. "God damn it to hell," she muttered, adding, "What a goddamn fucking mess." She followed this with a wild torrent of obscenities, spewing every nasty, harsh, and inappropriate word she could recall into the still air around her, a waterfall of frustrated anger. Then she tried to reassure herself. "He's just a creep," she said loudly. "You've known creeps before."

This, Ashley knew inwardly, was untrue. Still, she felt better hearing her own voice speaking with determination and ferocity. She searched around, found a towel, and walked purposefully into her small bathroom. Within a few seconds, she had the shower running hot, and she'd stripped off her clothes. As she stepped under the steaming stream of water, she thought to herself that the conversation with Michael O'Connell made her feel dirty, and she scrubbed her skin red, as if trying to remove some unwanted smell, or deep stain, that lingered despite all her efforts.

When she stepped from the shower, she looked up into the mirror and dabbed away some of the steam from the glass, looking deep into her own eyes. Make a plan, she told herself. Ignore the creep and he'll just go away. She snorted and flexed the muscles in her arms. She let her eyes linger over her body, as if measuring the curve of her breasts, her flat stomach, her toned legs. She was fit, trim, and good-looking, she thought. She believed herself strong.

Ashley walked into her bedroom and got dressed. She had the urge to wear something new, something different, something that wasn't familiar. She shoved her computer into the backpack, then checked to see if she had cash in her wallet. Her plan for the day was more or less the same as always: some studying in the library wing of the museum amid the stacks of art history books, before heading over to her job. She had more than one paper that needed massaging, and she thought to herself that immersing herself in texts and prints and reproductions of great visions would help get her mind off Michael O'Connell.

Certain that she had everything she needed, she grabbed her keys and thrust open the door to the corridor.

Then she stopped.

She looked down and felt a sudden, awful coldness creep through her. Ice seemed to choke her throat.

Taped to the wall opposite her door were a dozen roses.

Dead roses. Wilted and decrepit.

As she stared, a bloodred petal almost blackened by age dropped off and fluttered to the floor, as if driven there not by a breath of wind, but by the mere force of Ashley's gaze. She fixed her eyes helplessly on the display.

Scott sat at his desk in his small office at the college, twiddling a pencil between the fingers of his right hand, pondering how one intrudes on the life of one's nearly grown-up child without being obvious. If Ashley were still a teenager, or younger, he could have used a natural blustery forcefulness, demanding her to tell him what he wanted, even if he caused tears and insults and all sorts of standard parent-child dynamics. Ashley was right in that half age between youth and adulthood, and he was at a loss precisely how to proceed. And every second that he delayed doing something, his sense of concern doubled.

He needed to be subtle, but efficient.

Surrounding him were history texts on shelves and a cheaply framed reproduction of the Declaration of Independence. At least three photographs of Ashley rode the corner of his desk and the wall across from where he sat. The most striking was of her in a high school basketball game, her face intense, her red-blond ponytail flying, as she leapt up and seized the ball from two opponents. He had one other photo, but he kept it in the top drawer of his desk. It was a picture taken of him when he was just twenty years old, just a little younger than his daughter was now. He was sitting on an ammunition box, next to a glistening stack of shells, right behind the 125-millimeter howitzer. His helmet was at his feet, and he was smoking a cigarette, which, given the proximity of so much explosive ordnance, was probably a poor idea. He had an exhausted, vacant look on his face. Scott sometimes thought the photo was probably his only real remembrance of the time he'd spent in the war. He had had it framed, then kept it secret. He did not even think that he'd ever shown the picture to Sally, even when Ashley was due and they thought they were still in love. For a moment, he wondered if he could remember a time when Sally had ever asked him about his time in the war. Scott shifted about in his seat. Thinking about his past made him nervous. He liked considering other people's history, not his own.

Scott rocked back and forth.

In his imagination, he began to replay the words of the letter. As he did so, he had an idea.

One of the both good and bad qualities that Scott possessed was an inability to throw away cards and slips of paper with names and phone numbers. A slight pack-rat-type obsession. It took him nearly a half hour of rummaging about in desk drawers and file cabinets, but he finally found what he was seeking. He hoped the cell phone number was still accurate.

On the third ring, he heard a slightly familiar voice. "Hello?"

"Is this Susan Fletcher?"

"Yes, who is this?"

"Susan, this is Scott Freeman, Ashley's father . . . you remember from freshman and sophomore year . . ."

There was a momentary hesitation, then a brightening on the other end. "Mr. Freeman, of course, it's been a couple of years."

"Time really passes fast, doesn't it?"

"Sure does. Gosh, how's Ashley? I haven't seen her in months and months."

"Actually, that's why I'm calling."

"Is there a problem?"

Scott hesitated. "There might be."

Susan Fletcher was a whirlwind sort of young woman, always balancing a half dozen ideas and plans between her head, her desktop, and her computer. She was small, dark-haired, intense almost to a fault, and endlessly energetic. She had been scooped up by First Boston as soon as she had graduated and worked in their financial planning division.

She stood in front of her cubicle window, staring out, watching as airplane after airplane descended into Logan Airport. She had been a little unsettled by her conversation with Scott Freeman and wasn't precisely sure how to proceed, although she had reassured him that she would take charge of the situation.

Susan liked Ashley, although it had been nearly two years since they'd actually spoken. They had been tossed together as roommates freshman year in college, a little astonished at how different they were, then even more astonished when they discovered they got along quite well. They'd stuck together for a second year, before each had moved off campus. This had resulted in significantly less contact, though when they had managed to get together, it had been marked by a singular sense of comfort and laughter. They now shared little in common; if she used the bridesmaid's test— would she choose Ashley to be in her wedding party?—the answer was no. But she felt a great deal of affection for her onetime roommate. At least, she thought she did.

She glanced over toward the telephone.

For some reason that she couldn't quite determine, she was uneasy about what Ashley's father had asked of her. On the simplest level, it was more than a little like spying. On the other hand, it could be nothing more than some misguided paternal concern. She could make a phone call, be reassured, call Scott Freeman back, and everyone could get on with whatever they were doing. And the added benefit would be getting in touch with a friend, which was rarely a bad idea.

If there was some irritated fallout, it would be between Ashley and her father. So, with only the smallest of misgivings, she seized her desk phone, glanced out one final time at the first streaks of darkness slicing across the harbor, and dialed Ashley's phone.

It rang five times before being picked up, right to the moment when Susan thought she was going to have to leave a message.

"Yes?"

Her friend's voice was curt, which surprised Susan. "Hey, free-girl, how's it going?" She used Ashley's freshman-year nickname with a soft familiarity. The only course they had ever taken together had been a first-year seminar on women in the twentieth century, and they had agreed, after a couple of beers one night, that free-*man* was sexist and inappropriate, free-*woman* sounded pretentious, while free-*girl* fit pretty well.

Ashley waited on the street outside the Hammer and Anvil, jacket collar pulled up against the wind, feeling cold seeping through the pavement into her shoes. She knew she was a couple of minutes early. Susan was never late. It simply wasn't in her nature to be delayed. Ashley glanced down at her watch, and as she did, she heard a car horn blare from the street just beyond where she was standing.

Susan Fletcher's beaming grin penetrated the early night as she rolled down the window. "Hey, free-girl!" she shouted with genuine enthusiasm. "You didn't think I'd keep you waiting, did you? Go in and get us a table. I'm gonna park up the street. Be two minutes, max."

Ashley gave a wave and watched as Susan peeled away from the curb. Pretty fancy new car, Ashley thought. Red. She saw Susan pull into a Park and Lock a block away and then went into the restaurant.

Susan drove up to the third level, where there were far fewer cars and she could pull the new Audi into a space where it was unlikely anyone else would park next to her and ding the door. The car was only two weeks old, half a present from her proud parents, half a present to herself, and she was damned if she was going to let the wear and tear of downtown Boston diminish its shiny newness.

She tapped the alarm system, then headed out to the restaurant. She moved quickly, took the stairs instead of waiting for the elevator, and within a couple of minutes she was inside the Hammer and Anvil, stripping off her over-coat and striding toward where Ashley waited, two tall glasses of beer waiting on the table in front of her.

The two embraced.

"Hey, roomie," Susan said. "It's been too long."

"I ordered you a beer, but thought maybe now that you're a hotshot businesswoman and Wall Street denizen, maybe a Scotch on the rocks or a dry martini would be more appropriate."

"This is a beer night. Ash, you look great."

This, Susan thought, wasn't exactly true. Her onetime friend had a pale, nervous look about her.

"Do I?" Ashley asked. "I don't think so."

"Something bugging you?"

Ashley hesitated, shrugged, and looked around the restaurant. Bright lights, mirrors. Toasts at a nearby table, intimacy between a couple at another. A happy buzz of voices. It all made her feel as if what had happened to her that morning were something that had taken place in some bizarre parallel universe. Nothing surrounded her in that moment except a carefree sense of anticipation.

She sighed. "Ah, Susie, I met a creep. That's all. He kinda freaked me out a little. But no big deal."

"Freaked out? What did he do?"

"Well, he hasn't exactly *done* anything, it's more what he implies. Says he loves me, I'm the girl for him. No one else will do. Can't live without me. If he can't have me, no one else can. All that sort of useless crap. Doesn't make sense. We only hooked up once and that was a big mistake. I tried to let him down gently, told him thanks but no thanks. Kinda hoped that was that, but when I headed out today, he left me some flowers outside my door."

"Well, flowers, that sounds almost gentlemanly."

"Dead flowers."

This made Susan pause. "That's not cool. How'd you know it was him?"

"Didn't figure it could be anyone else."

"So, what are you going to do?"

"Do? Just ignore the creep. He'll go away. They always do, sooner or later."

"Great plan, free-girl. Sounds like you've really thought that one through and through."

Ashley laughed, although it wasn't funny. "I'll figure something out. Sooner or later."

Susan grinned. "Sounds like that calculus course you took freshman year. If I recall correctly, that was your approach for both the midterm and then, when that lesson hadn't sunk in, the final."

"I should never have done well in math in high school. My mother pretty much steered me into that mistake. I guess she learned her lesson. That was the last time she ever asked me what courses I was taking."

Both young women leaned their heads together and shared a laugh. Few things in the world are as reassuring, Ashley thought, as seeing an old friend, one who was now in a new and separate world, but who still remembered the same old jokes, no matter how different the two of them had become. "Ah, enough about the creep. I met another guy, who seemed pretty cool. I'm hoping he'll call me back."

Susan smiled. "Ash. Living with you the first thing I learned was that the boys always called *you* back." She didn't ask another question, nor did she hear Michael O'-Connell's name. But in a way, she thought, she had already heard enough, or close to enough. Dead flowers.

On the street outside the Hammer and Anvil after a good deal of food and drink and more than a few old and familiar jokes, Ashley gave her friend a long embrace. "It has been great to see you, Susie. We should get together more often."

"When you get this grad school thing up and running, call me. Maybe a regular get-together, once a week, so that you can bring all your artistic sensibilities to my complaints about stupid bosses and dumb business models."

"I'd like that." Ashley stepped back, staring up into the New England night. The sky was clear, and beyond the diffuse streetlights and buildings, she could just make out the canopy of stars dotting the blue-black sky above.

"One thing, Ash," Susan said as she began to hunt in her pocketbook for her keys. "I'm a little concerned about the guy who's been bugging you."

"Michael? Michael O'Creep," Ashley said with a dismissive wave, and a voice that even she knew sounded like a lie. "I'll be rid of him in a couple of days, Susie. Guys like that just need the big, strong *no* and then they whine and complain for a few days, until they go out to some sports bar with their beer buddies, and all agree that one hundred percent of all women are bitches, and that's all there is to it."

"I hope you're right. But still, I'd be a lousy friend if I didn't tell you that you can call me anytime. Day or night. If this guy doesn't disappear."

"Thanks, Susie. I appreciate that. But not to worry."

"Ah, you remember, free-girl, worrying was always my strongest quality."

They both laughed, embraced again, and with a grin Ashley turned and headed down the street, ambling through each streak of light reflected from the neon signs above storefronts and restaurants. Susan Fletcher watched her for a moment, before turning away. She was never sure precisely what to make of Ashley. She mingled naïveté with sophistication in a mysterious fashion. It was no wonder that boys were attracted to her, yet, in truth, Susan thought, she remained isolated and elusive. Even the way she moved, slipping away into the shadows, seemed almost otherworldly. Susan took a deep breath of cool night air, tasting the frost on her lips. She felt a little uncomfortable that she hadn't told her friend that Scott was behind their whole meeting, that her call earlier that evening hadn't been by chance. She shifted her feet a bit, a little uncomfortable with not being completely honest either with her friend, nor having truly found out much for her friend's father. Michael O'Creep, she thought to herself. And dead flowers.

It was either nothing or something terrifying, and Susan didn't know which. Nor did she know which of those polar opposites she would report to Scott Freeman.

She snorted out loud, dissatisfied on both counts, and started walking fast toward the Park and Lock a block distant. She had her keys in her hand, and her finger on the Mace canister attached to the key chain. Susan didn't fear much in life, but knew also that a little bit of prevention went a long way. She wished that she had worn more sensible shoes. As she marched forward, she could hear the sound of her feet against the pavement, mingling with nearby noises from the street. And yet, in that second, she was overcome with a sense of loneliness, as if she were the last person left on the street, downtown, perhaps in the city itself. She hesitated, peering around her. She could see no one on the sidewalk. She paused and tried to stare into a nearby restaurant, but the window was curtained. She stopped and took a deep breath and pivoted about.

No one. The street behind her was empty.

Susan shook her head. She told herself that talking and

thinking about some creep guy had unsettled her. She inhaled slowly, letting her lungs fill with crisp air. *Dead flowers.* Something in that statement played some discordant
chord within her, making every stride she took seem indecisive. Again she paused. She was startled, felt cold, pulled
her overcoat closer to her, and leaned into her pace, moving
more rapidly through the shadows.

She swiveled right and left, saw no one, but had the sensation that she were being followed. She told herself she was
alone, but that wasn't reassuring, so she simply hurried.

Within a few paces, she felt an odd electricity, more now
as if she were being watched. Again she hesitated, letting her
eyes drift up and around, inspecting windows in office buildings, looking for the pair of eyes she was convinced were assessing her every step, and again coming up with nothing that
even suggested to her a reason for the cold, nervous, throat-
tightening sense of fear that was surely taking her over.

Be reasonable, she insisted to herself. And again, she
picked up her pace, so that now she was moving almost as
rapidly as her heels would allow her. She had the feeling
that she had done everything wrong, that she had violated all
her be-safe-in-the-city rules, that she had allowed herself to
be distracted and had put herself in a vulnerable position.
Only she couldn't see any source of a threat, which only
made her stumble forward more rapidly.

Susan lost her balance and slipped, catching herself, but
dropping her pocketbook. She grabbed at her lipstick, a pen,
a notebook, and her wallet, which had scattered about the
sidewalk. She stuffed these back into the satchel and threw it
over her shoulder.

The entrance to the Park and Lock was only a few feet
away, and she half-ran to the glass doors. She thrust herself
inside the narrow entranceway and breathed out hard. On the
other side of the thick cinder-block wall was the kiosk where
the attendant collected each driver's cash upon exiting. She
wondered, if she called out, whether he would hear her.

She doubted it. And she doubted whether he would do
anything anyway.

Susan lectured herself. Take charge. Find your car. Get going. Stop acting like a child.

For an instant, she stared over at the stairwell. It was dark and filled with shadows.

She turned away, punched the elevator button, and waited. She kept her eyes on the series of small lights that monitored the elevator's descent. Third floor. Second floor. First floor. Ground. The doors opened with a shudder and a rattle.

She stepped forward, then stopped.

A man, wearing a parka and a ski hat, and averting his face so that she could not see it, burst past her, nearly knocking her to the ground. Susan gasped and reeled sideways.

She raised her hand as if to ward off a blow, but the figure had already thrust himself through the doors to the stairwell, disappearing in a blur, so quickly she hardly had time to comprehend anything about him. He wore jeans. The ski hat was black and the parka, navy blue. But that was it. She couldn't tell whether he was short or tall, thickset or skinny, young or old, white or black.

"Jesus Christ," she wheezed out loud. "What the hell was that?"

For a moment, she listened, but could hear nothing. As quickly as the man was there, he was gone, and she felt her loneliness and solitude redouble. "Jesus," she repeated. She could feel her heart racing, pounding adrenaline in her temples. Fear seemed to have painted itself throughout her, covering reason, rationale, and her own sense of self. Susan Fletcher struggled, trying to regain control over herself. She willed each limb to respond. Legs. Arms. Hands. She insisted to her heart and throat that they recover, but she didn't trust her own voice again.

The elevator doors started to close, and Susan reached out abruptly, stopping them. She forced herself into the elevator and punched the 3 button. She felt a small sense of relief when the doors closed, leaving her alone.

The elevator creaked and rose past 1. Then, at level 2, it slowed and stopped. It shuddered slightly when the doors opened.

Susan looked up and wanted to scream, but no sound came out.

The man who had burst past her was standing in front of the doors. Same jeans. Same parka. But now the ski cap was pulled down into a mask, so that all she could see were his eyes, boring in on her. She thrust herself back against the rear wall of the elevator compartment. She could feel herself shrinking, almost falling, just from the pressure like a wave that came from the man. It was like an undertow of fear, pulling her off balance, threatening to sweep her away and drown her. She wanted to strike out, defend herself, but Susan suddenly felt nearly helpless. It was as if the man behind the mask were shining a light in her eyes, blinding her. She gasped words, with no idea what she was saying, wanting to cry for help, but unable to.

The man behind the mask did not move.

He did not step forward. He simply stared at her.

Susan pushed herself back into a corner, feebly holding a hand in front of her face. She thought she could no longer breathe.

Again, he did nothing. He just eyed her, as if memorizing her face, her clothes, the look of panic in her eyes. Then he whispered, *"Now I know you."*

And then, just as abruptly, the elevator doors slowly crept shut.

•

There was no urgency this time, when I called her. She seemed curiously blank, as if she had already played out my questions and her answers in her mind, and as if I was following a script.

"I'm not sure that I understand Michael O'Connell's behavior. I think I'm getting a feel for him, and then . . ."

"He does something you find unexpected?"

"Yes. The dead flowers, there's an obvious message, but . . ."

"Sometimes isn't what frightens us most deeply not something unknown, but something understood and anticipated?"

This was true. She paused, then picked up again.

"So, Michael didn't precisely behave as you might immediately imagine. You don't see the value in instilling fear?"

"Well, yes, but . . ."

"To be utterly, completely helpless and filled to overflow with terror one instant, and then, in a flash, to have it seemingly disappear."

"How can I be sure that it even *was* Michael O'Connell?" I demanded.

"You cannot. But if the man in the ski mask in the parking garage truly had rape or robbery on his mind, then wouldn't he have attempted one of those things? The circumstances were perfect for either of those crimes. But someone with a different agenda behaves unusually and unpredictably."

When I was slow to respond, she hesitated, as if considering her words.

"Perhaps you should look not only to *what* happened, but also to the impact of what happened."

"Okay. But steer me in the right direction."

"Susan Fletcher was a capable, determined young woman. She was savvy, cautious, expert in many things. But she was deeply wounded by her fear. Being scared that profoundly can do that. Terror is one thing. The residue of terror is just as crippling. That moment in the elevator made her feel vulnerable. Powerless. And in that way, any potential assistance she might have rendered Ashley in the days to follow was effectively removed."

"I think I see . . ."

"A person with the skills and determination that might have put her in the forefront of helping Ashley was instantly relegated to the periphery. Simple. Effective. Horrifying."

"Yes . . ."

"What was really happening, though?" she suddenly asked me. "What was far worse? What was far more terrifying than anything he'd done up to that point?"

I thought for an instant, before replying, "Michael O'Connell was learning."

She remained silent. I could picture her gripping the telephone with one hand, reaching out with the other to steady herself. Her knuckles would be white as she fought against something I didn't yet understand. When she finally did respond, it was almost whispered, as if the words took great effort on her part to speak. "Yes. That's right. He was learning. But you still don't know what happened to Susan next."

7

When Things Began to Become Clear

Scott didn't hear from Susan Fletcher for forty-eight hours, but when he did, he almost wished he hadn't.

He had busied himself the way all academics do, going over his upcoming spring-semester syllabus, designing the structure of several lectures, catching up on some correspondence from various historical societies and inquiry groups. And, in actuality, he hadn't expected a rapid response from Susan Fletcher. He knew he had put her in an awkward position, and a part of him half-expected a blistering phone call from Ashley, along the *Why are you butting into my private business?* line, and he didn't really have much of an answer for that question.

So he let the hours pass without allowing himself to feel overly anxious. There was no profit in being nervous, he told himself, when he caught his eyes wandering toward the black telephone waiting silently on the edge of his desk.

When it finally did ring, he was startled. At first, he did not recognize Susan Fletcher's voice.

"Professor Freeman?"

"Yes?"

"It's Susan . . . Susan Fletcher. You called me the other day . . . about Ashley."

"Of course, Susan, I'm sorry. I didn't expect you to call back so soon."

This was untrue, of course. He'd hoped she would be prompt.

She hesitated, and Scott heard a catch in her throat. "Is something wrong?" he asked, his own voice betraying him slightly.

"I don't know. Maybe. I can't be sure."

"What about Ashley?" Scott blurted out, then immediately regretted switching the focus away from the troubled tones he heard in Susan's voice.

"She's okay," Susan said slowly. "At least, she seems to be okay, but she does have a problem with some guy, like you suspected. At least, I think she does. She didn't really want to talk about it."

Each word came timorously, almost as if she thought someone was listening in.

"You sound uncertain," Scott said.

"I've had a difficult couple of days. Since I saw Ashley. In fact, that was the last good thing. Seeing her."

"But what happened?"

"I don't know. Nothing. Everything. I can't tell."

"I'm confused. What do you mean?"

"I had an accident."

"Oh my goodness," Scott said. "That's terrible. Are you okay?"

"Yes. Just shaken up. My car is pretty messed up. But no broken bones. Maybe a little concussion. I've got a great big welt across my chest and it feels like my ribs were bruised. But other than being sore and disoriented, I'm okay, I guess."

"But what . . ."

"The right front tire flew off. I was doing close to seventy . . . no, maybe a little more, close to eighty, and the front tire came detached. I was really lucky, though, because I felt the car start to swerve, and the front end started to shimmy, and so I pounded on the brakes. I was decelerating fast when it actually came off. Then I lost control."

"My God . . ."

"Everything was spinning around, and there was all this noise. It was like someone was screaming in my ear, and I could feel this hyperalertness because I knew I couldn't do anything about what was happening. But I was really lucky. I hit those collapsible barrier things, you know, the big, yellow barrel types that are filled with sand to cushion the impact."

"The wheel came off?"

"Yeah. That's what the trooper told me. They found it a quarter mile back down the road."

"I've never heard of that before."

"Yeah. Neither had the trooper. Nearly new car, too."

Scott paused, and there was a small silence.

"Do you think . . ." He stopped.

"I don't know what to think. One minute I was flying down the highway, the next . . ."

Again he was silent, and after a moment Susan spoke softly.

"I was going so fast because I was scared."

This word caused Scott to listen. He remained quiet throughout Susan Fletcher's recital of the evening with Ashley. He asked no questions, not even when he heard the name Michael O'Creep, which was the best that she could recall. Things were jumbled in Susan's memory, and more than once he could hear frustration in her voice, as she struggled to get details right. He guessed this was the result of her mild concussion. She was apologetic, but this, Scott thought, was unnecessary.

She did not know if anything that had happened to her related in any way to Ashley. All she knew was she went to see her and then things that terrified her had taken place just as soon as she'd hugged her friend good-bye. She was fortunate to be alive.

"Do you think that this guy that Ashley's involved with had anything to do with what took place?" Scott asked, unwilling to believe in a connection, just filled with a nervousness that he couldn't quite describe.

"I don't know. I don't know. Probably just coincidence. I

don't know. But, I think," Susan said, almost whispering, close to tears, "that if it's okay with you, I won't be calling Ashley for a little while. Not until I get my act back together again."

Scott hung up the phone thinking that he had a choice of possibilities: nothing. Or maybe the worst thing he could imagine.

We were meant for each other.

He tried to swallow, but his throat was completely dry.

Ashley moved down the street rapidly, as if her pace on the sidewalk could keep up with the thoughts crowding her head. The phrase *You're being followed* hadn't really fully formed in her consciousness, but a lingering sense of something being out of order dogged her. She carried a small bag of groceries in her arms, and her backpack was stuffed with art books, so she felt a little awkward every time she paused and let her eyes cruise around the street, trying to assess what was making her feel so unsettled.

Nothing that she could see was in the slightest out of the ordinary.

The city is like that, she thought to herself. Out in her home in western Massachusetts, things were a little less cluttered, and so, when something was out of place, it was a little more apparent. But Boston, with its constant flow and energy, defied her ability to see when something had changed. She felt a little hot, as if the temperature around her were rising, which confused her, because the opposite was true.

She swept the street with her eyes. Cars. Buses. Pedestrians. The same view that she was familiar with. She pricked up her ears. The same steady hum and beat of daily life. She did a small inventory of her senses and found that none were registering anything that would prompt the small electric currents of anxiety that she felt.

And so, she ignored the sensation.

She set out, at a quick march down the sidewalk, turning

off the main roadway onto the side street where her apartment was located midway down the block.

There is a pretty clear distinction in Boston between apartments for students and apartments for people with actual jobs. Ashley was still in the student world. The street had an acceptable shabbiness, a little extra grime that to young eyes seemed to add character, but to those who had left it behind only spoke of impermanence. The trees planted in small swaths of grass seemed a little stunted, as if they didn't get enough sun. It was an indecisive street, much like the people who lived there.

Ashley lurched up to her place, balanced the grocery bag on her knee, and undid the door. She felt a sudden exhaustion as she closed the door behind her and locked it.

Ashley looked around, pleased no more dead flowers were waiting for her.

It took her less than five minutes to put the granola, yogurt, spring water, and salad fixings away in the small refrigerator. She found a bottle of beer in the crisper and opened it, taking a long swig. Then she went into her small living room, relieved to see that no messages were on her answering machine. She took another drink, told herself that she was being a little foolish, because there were any number of people she did actually want to hear from. Certainly she hoped that Susan Fletcher would follow up on their dinner. And then there was the hope that Will Goodwin would call for that second date. In fact, as she went through a mental list, she thought that it was truly dumb to allow Michael O'Connell to isolate her. And, she told herself, she'd been pretty straightforward with him the other day, and maybe that would be the end of it.

The more she replayed the conversation in her mind, the more it took on a forcefulness that it probably didn't deserve.

She kicked off her shoes, slid into her desk chair, punched on her computer, and hummed to herself as it booted up.

To her surprise, more than fifty new e-mails were waiting for her. She looked at the addresses and saw that they came from virtually everyone that she had in her electronic address book. She moved the cursor over the first, from a coworker at the museum, a girl named Anne Armstrong, and opened the e-mail. Ashley leaned forward to see what her acquaintance had to say. Except the e-mail wasn't from Anne Armstrong.

Hello, Ashley. I've missed you more than you
can imagine. But soon we will be together forever,
and that will be great. As you can see, there are fifty-
six e-mail messages after this one. Do not delete them.
In them is important information that you will need.
I love you more today than yesterday. And tomorrow
I will love you even more.
Forever yours,
Michael

Ashley wanted to shriek but no sound could rise through her throat.

•

At first, the garage owner was not particularly eager to help.

"Let me get this straight," he said, wiping greasy, oil-stained hands on an equally filthy rag. "You want to know something about Michael O'Connell? Tell me why."

"I'm a writer," I said. "He figures in a book I'm working on."

"O'Connell? In a book?" The question was followed by a short burst of forced laughter. "Must be some sort of crime story."

"That's right. It's some sort. I'd appreciate any help."

"We get fifty bucks an hour here to fix your car. How much time do you think you're gonna need?"

"That depends on how much you can tell me."

He snorted. "Well, that depends then on what it is you want to know. I worked side by side with O'Connell the entire time he was employed here. Of course, that was a couple of years back, and I haven't seen him in a long time. That's a good thing. But, hell, I was the one that gave him his job, so I could tell you some stuff. But then, I could also be fixing the transmission on this Chevy, too, you get what I mean?"

We had circled around my question, and I thought we

would find ourselves nowhere in a couple of minutes. So I reached into my back pocket, grabbed my wallet, and rapidly counted out $100. I put this down on the counter in front of where I was standing. "Just the truth," I said. "And nothing that you don't know firsthand."

The man at the garage eyed the money. "About that son of a bitch, sure." He reached out his hand, and like some hard-bitten character in a million Hollywood potboiler movies, I placed my palm down on the money, holding it on the counter. The mechanic grinned, showing white teeth with gaps.

"One question first," the man said. "You know where O'-Connell is now?"

"No. Not yet. But I'm going to find him sooner or later. Why?"

"He's not the sort of guy I necessarily want to piss off. Come looking for me with questions of his own. Like why I talked with you in the first place. He's not someone you would want asking you those types of questions. And unhappy about it, too."

"I'll keep this conversation confidential."

"Those are big, fine words. But how do I know, Mr. Writer, that you'll do what you say?"

"I guess that's the chance you're going to take."

He shook his head, but at the same time eyed the money. "Bad odds. Especially where that guy is involved. Wouldn't want to be trading peace of mind for a lousy hundred bucks." He took a moment, muttered, "Screw it," under his breath, then shrugged. "Michael O'Connell. He worked here for about a year, and after about two minutes I made damn sure that he worked the same shift that I did. I didn't much want him stealing me blind. He was the smartest bastard that ever changed some spark plugs in here, that's for damn certain. And very cool, too, about how he stole money. Mean and charming as hell, all at the same time, if you can imagine it. Like you would hardly know it when you got taken. Most of the guys that I hire to pump gas in this place are either college kids trying to make a little extra money, or guys that couldn't pass one of the mechanics certification courses at the big dealerships, so they end up here, instead. Either they're too young to know how to steal or too dumb. You know what I mean?"

I didn't answer that question, but took a long look at the gas station owner. He was probably close to my own age, but too much time underneath a car in the summer heat and winter frost had given him creases around the eyes and at the corners of his face. Smoking, too, hadn't helped, and he took the moment to stick a cigarette between his lips, ignoring his own NO SMOKING sign prominently displayed on the back wall. He had a way of speaking directly toward me, but twisting his head slightly, so that it seemed as if whatever he said came out sideways.

"So, he started working here . . ."

"Yeah. He worked here, but he wasn't really working here, you get my drift?"

"No. I don't."

The gas station owner rolled his eyes. "O.C. put in the hours. But fixing old carbs and doing inspections wasn't really his thing. Not exactly where he figured his future lay."

"What was?"

"Well, replacing a perfectly good fuel pump with a rebuilt one was. Then selling the good one and pocketing the difference. Taking an extra twenty bucks in cash from whoever walked in to make sure some old clunker passed its Massachusetts State emission test was another. Whacking a front ball joint with a hammer and then telling some Boston College kid they needed a new set of brakes and an alignment was."

"A scam artist?"

The mechanic smiled. "That was it. But you're just scratching the surface with O'Connell."

"Okay, what else?"

"He took computer courses at night, and he was into every damn thing you could do with a laptop. The boy was a regular fountain of knowledge. Credit-card fraud. Identity theft.

Double billing. Telephone cons, you name it, he had a handle on it. And in his spare time, he used to scan every damn website, newspaper, magazine, whatever, looking for new ways of stealing. He used to keep folders filled with clippings, just to keep himself up-to-date. You know what he used to say?"

"What?"

"You don't have to kill someone to kill them. But if you really want to, you can. And, if you really know what you're doing, ain't nobody going to catch up with you. Not ever."

I wrote that down.

When the gas station owner saw my pencil scratching across the notepad, he smiled, and he reached out and took the money off the counter. I let him pocket the $100. "You know what the damn stupidest thing was?"

"Okay, what?"

"You'd think that a guy like this would be looking for some big score. Trying to find a way to get rich. But that wasn't exactly it, with O'Connell."

"What was it, then?"

"He wanted to be perfect. It was like he wanted to be great. But he wanted to be anonymous, too."

"Small-time?" I asked.

"No, you're wrong. He knew he was going to be big. Ambition. He was strung out on it, like it was some sort of drug. You know what it's like to be around some guy who's just like an addict, but it ain't cocaine up the nose or heroin filling up his veins? He was drunk all the time with all sorts of plans. Always getting ready for the big deal. Like it was just waiting for him out there somewhere and he was closing in on it. Working here, whatever he did, it was just a way of passing time, filling in the blanks, all along the path. But it wasn't exactly money or fame he was interested in. It was something else."

"You parted ways?"

"Yeah. I didn't want to end up getting used whenever the hell he figured out what he was going to do. But someday he was going to take down something. You know what they say,

'The end justifies the means.' Well, that was O'Connell. Like I say, the boy had big ideas."

"But you don't know——"

"Don't know nothing about what happened to him. Saw enough, though, to keep me pretty scared."

I looked at the mechanic. *Scared* didn't seem as if it would normally be a part of his vocabulary. "I don't get it," I said. "He scared you?"

The garage owner took a long drag of his cigarette and let smoke curl up around his head. "You ever meet somebody that's always doing something different from what he's doing? I don't know, maybe that don't make sense, but that was O'Connell. And when you called him on it, when you called him on anything, he would look at you with this way where he just stared right like you weren't there, and he was taking down something about you and putting it somewhere, because someday he was going to find a way to use it against you."

"Against you?"

"One way or the other. He was just the sort of man, you just didn't naturally want to get in his path. Stand to the side a bit, that would be okay. But get in his way, or get in the way of what he wanted . . . well, that would be something you'd want to avoid."

"He was violent?"

"He was whatever he needed to be. Maybe that was what was so scary about him."

The man took another deep, deadly inhale of the smoke. I didn't ask another question, but he added, "You know, Mr. Writer man, here's a story. Once about ten years ago, I was working here real late, you know, two, three in the morning, two kids come in, next thing I know, I've got a big, shiny steel nine-millimeter stuck up in my face, and one kid is yelling *'Motherfucker this'* and *'Cocksucker that'* and a whole lot of *'I'm gonna bust a cap in your face, old man'* type bullshit, and I thought, truly and honestly, that was going to be it, that he was going to do it, while his goddamn partner cleaned out

the register, and I ain't particularly religious, but I was muttering every Our Father and Hail Mary I could think of, 'cause
this was the end, no doubt about it. Then the two kids took
off, with hardly a word, left me laying on the floor behind the
counter needing a change of underwear. You get the picture?"

I nodded. "Not pleasant."

"No, sir. Not pleasant at all." He smiled and shook his head.

"But what did O'Connell have to do with that?"

The man shook his head slowly and exhaled.

"Nothing," he said carefully. "Not a single damn thing. Except this: Every time I ever talked to Michael O'Connell and
he didn't say nothing back, just listened and looked right at
me that way he had, it reminded me of looking into that
black hole of that kid's pistol. Same feeling exactly. There
weren't no time I talked with him that I didn't wonder if what
I was saying meant I was gonna die."

8

A Beginning of Panic

Ashley bent toward the computer screen, assessing each
word that flickered up in front of her. She had been locked
into position for more than an hour and her back was tightening up. She could feel the muscles in her calves quivering
a little, as if she'd run farther on that day than was her usual
jogger's norm.

The e-mail messages were a dizzying array of love notes,
electronically generated hearts and balloons, bad poetry that
O'Connell had written, much better poetry that he'd stolen
from Shakespeare or Andrew Marvell and even Rod McKuen.
It all seemed impossibly trite and childish and yet chilling.

She tried writing down different combinations of words
and phrases from the e-mails to deduce what the message

was. There was nothing so obvious as a word italicized or placed in boldface that would have made her task simpler. As she closed in on her second hour of inspection, she finally tossed down her pencil, frustrated with her efforts. She felt stupid, as if there were something she was missing that would have been apparent to any crossword or acrostics puzzle fan. She hated games.

"What is it?" she shouted loudly at the screen. "What are you trying to say? What are you trying to tell me?"

She could hear her voice rise, stretching into unfamiliar pitches.

She scrolled back, starting at the beginning, then blistering through each message, one after the other, so they flashed up on the computer screen and then disappeared.

"What? What? What?" she yelled as each went past her eyes.

And then, in that second, she saw it.

The message from Michael O'Connell wasn't contained in the e-mails that he'd sent.

It was that he'd been able to send them at all.

Each one had come from a different name on her address list. Each was from him. That they were grade-school-level testimonials of undying love was irrelevant. What was critical was that he had managed to insinuate himself into her own computer. And then, through a clever choice of words, managed to get her to read every message he'd sent. And, she understood, the likelihood was that by opening one, she had opened some sort of hidden electronic door. Michael O'Connell was like a virus, and now he was nearly as close to her as he would have been if he'd actually been seated next to her.

With a small gasp, Ashley leaned back hard in her chair, almost losing her balance, feeling a sense of dizziness as if the room were spinning around her head. She grabbed the arms of the chair with her hands and steadied herself quickly, took several long, deep breaths to regain control over an accelerating heart.

She turned slowly and began to let her vision creep over

the small world of her apartment. Michael O'Connell had spent precisely one night here, and it had been a truncated night, at that. She had thought they were both a little drunk, and she'd invited him up, and she tried to replay what had taken place in her current, scared-sober imagination. She berated herself for being unable to recall just exactly how much he'd had to drink. One drink? Five? Had he been holding back while she indulged? The answer to that question had been lost in her own nervous excesses. There had been a nasty looseness to the night, a mood of abandon that she was unfamiliar with and was out of character for her. They had clumsily fallen out of their clothes, then coupled frantically on her bed. It was rapid, edgy lovemaking, without much tenderness. It had been over in a few seconds. If there was any real affection in the act, she could not remember it. It had been an explosive, rebellious release for her, right at a time when she was vulnerable to poor choices. On the rebound from a noisy, unpleasant breakup with her junior-year boyfriend, who'd lingered into her final year despite some fights and general dissatisfaction. Graduation and career and school uncertainty dogging her every step. A sense of isolation from her parents, her friends. Everything in her life had seemed to her to be forced, to be a little misshapen, out of tune, and out of sync. And into that turmoil came a single bad night with O'Connell. He was handsome, seductive, different from all the students that she'd dated through college, and she had overlooked the singular way that he'd stared at her across the table, as if trying to memorize every inch of her skin and not in a romantic way.

She shook her head.

The two of them had slumped back on the bed in the aftermath. She had grabbed a pillow and, with the room swerving unsteadily and a sour taste in her mouth, plummeted into sleep. What had he done? she asked herself. He had lit a cigarette. In the morning, she had risen, not inviting him for a second tumble, making up some story about needing to be at an appointment, not offering any breakfast, or even a kiss, just disappearing into the shower and scrubbing herself under steaming water, sudsing every inch of her body, as if she'd been covered with some unusual smell. She had wanted him to leave, but he had not.

Ashley tried to recall the brief morning-after conversation. It had been filled with falsehoods, as she had distanced herself, been cold and preoccupied, until finally he had stared at her in an uncomfortably long silence, then smiled, nodded, and exited without much further talk.

And now, all he talks about is love, she thought. Where did that come from?

She pictured him going through the door, a cold look on his face.

That recollection made her shift about uncomfortably.

The other men she had known, even if only briefly, would have exited either angry or optimistic or even with a little bravado after the one-night stand. But O'Connell had been different. He'd merely chilled her with silence, then removed himself. It was, she thought, as if he were leaving, but he'd known it wasn't for long.

She thought to herself, sleep. Shower. Plenty of time with her back turned. Had she left the computer on and running? What was strewn about her desktop? Her bank accounts? What numbers? What passwords? What did he have time to find and steal?

What else had he taken?

It was the obvious question, but one she didn't really want to ask.

For an instant, the room spun again, and then Ashley rose and, as quickly as she could, raced to the small bathroom, where she pitched forward, head over the glistening toilet bowl, and was violently, utterly sick.

After she cleaned herself up, Ashley pulled a blanket around her shoulders and sat on the edge of her bed, considering what she should do. She felt like some shipwrecked refugee after rough days adrift at sea.

But the longer she sat there, the angrier she got.

As best as she could tell, Michael O'Connell had no claim on her. He had no right to be harassing her. His protests of undying love were more than a little silly.

In general, Ashley was an understanding sort, one who disliked confrontation and avoided a fight at almost all costs. But this foolishness—she could think of no other word—with a one-night stand had really gone too far.

She threw the blanket off and stood up.

"God damn it," she said. "This is ending. Today. Enough of this bullshit."

She walked over to her desk and picked up her cell phone. Without thinking about what she was going to say, Ashley dialed O'Connell's number.

He answered almost immediately.

"Hello, lover," he said almost gaily, certainly with a familiarity that infuriated her.

"I'm not your lover."

He didn't reply.

"Look, Michael. This has got to stop."

Again, he didn't answer.

"Okay?"

Again, silence.

After a second, she wasn't even sure he was still there. "Michael?"

"I'm here," he said coldly.

"It's over."

"I don't believe you."

"It's finished."

There was another hesitation, then he said, "I don't think so."

Ashley was about to try again, but then she realized he had hung up.

She cursed, "You goddamn son of a bitch!" then redialed his number.

"Want to try again?" he answered this time.

She took a deep breath.

"All right," Ashley said stiffly, "if you won't make this easy, I guess we can do it the tough way."

She heard him laugh, but he did not say anything.

"Okay, meet me for lunch."

"Where?" he asked abruptly.

For an instant she scrambled about, trying to think of the right place. It had to be someplace familiar, someplace public, someplace where she was known and he wasn't, somewhere she was likely to be surrounded by allies. All this would give her the necessary gumption to turn him off once and forever, she thought.

"The restaurant at the art museum," she said. "One this afternoon. Okay?"

She could sense him grinning on the other end of the line. It made her shiver, as if a cold breath of air had seeped through a crack in the window frame. The arrangements must have been acceptable, Ashley realized, because he had hung up.

•

"So I suppose," I said, "in a way this is all about recognition. Everyone needed to see what was happening."

"Yes," she replied. "Easy to say. Hard to do."

"Is it?"

"Yes. You know we like to presume that we can recognize danger when it appears on the horizon. Anyone can avoid the danger that has bells, whistles, red lights, and sirens attached to it. It's much harder when you don't exactly know what you're dealing with."

She thought for a moment, while I remained quiet. She was drinking iced tea and lifted the glass to her lips.

"Ashley knew."

Again she shook her head. "No. She was scared, true. But just as much as she was frightened, she was annoyed, which truly hid the desperate nature of her situation. And, in reality, what did she know about Michael O'Connell? Not much. Not nearly as much as he knew about her. Curiously, although at a distance, Scott was closer to understanding the real nature of what they were up against, because he was operating far more out of instinct, especially at the beginning."

"And Sally? And her partner, Hope?"

"They were still outside fear. Not for much longer, though."

"And O'Connell?"

She hesitated. "They couldn't see. Not yet, at least."

"See what?"

"That he was beginning to truly enjoy himself."

9

Two Different Meetings

When Scott was unable to reach Ashley either on her landline or on her cell phone, he felt a sweaty sort of anxiety, but he immediately told himself it amounted to nothing. It was midday, she was undoubtedly out, and he knew his daughter had on more than one occasion left the cell phone charging back at her place.

So, after he'd left brief "Just wondering how things are going" messages, he sat back and worried whether he should be worried. After a few moments feeling his pulse rate rise, he rose and paced back and forth across the small office. Then he sat down and maneuvered through some busywork, responding to student e-mails and printing out a couple of essays. He was trying to waste time at a moment when he wasn't sure that he had time to waste.

Before long he was rocking ever so slightly back and forth in his desk chair while his mind fastened on moments in Ashley's growing up. Bad moments. Once, when she had been little more than a year old, she'd come down with severe bronchitis, and her temperature had spiked and she'd been unable to stop coughing. He'd held her throughout the night, trying to comfort her, trying with soothing words to calm the hacking cough and listening to her breathing grow increasingly shallow and difficult. At eight in the morning, he'd dialed the pediatrician's office and been told to come straight in. The doctor had leaned over Ashley, listening to her chest, then swung about and coldly demanded to know why Scott and Sally had not taken her to the emergency room earlier. "What?" the doctor had questioned. "Did you think that by holding her all night she would get better?"

Scott had not answered, but, yes, he'd thought that by holding her she would get better.

Of course, antibiotics were a wiser choice.

When Ashley started to split her time between her two parents' homes, Scott would be up pacing in his bedroom, waiting for her to come home, unable to prevent himself from conjuring up all the worst cases: car accidents, assaults, drugs, alcohol, sex—all the nasty undercurrents to growing up. He knew that Sally was asleep in her bed those late nights that Ashley the teenager was out rebelling at Lord knows what. Sally always had trouble handling the exhaustion of worry. It was, Scott thought, as if by sleeping through the tension, it never actually happened.

He hated that. He'd always felt alone, even before they were divorced.

He grasped a pencil and twiddled it between his fingers, finally cracking it in half.

He took a deep breath. *"What? Did you think that by holding her all night she'd get better?"*

Scott told himself that worry was useless. He needed to do something, even if it was completely wrong.

Ashley arrived at her job perhaps ten minutes earlier than normal, her pace driven by anger, her usual leisurely walk replaced this day by a quick-time, jaw-set preoccupation with Michael O'Connell. For a couple of seconds, she looked up at the huge fortresslike Doric columns marking the museum entrance, then she turned and swept her eyes across the street. She was pleased with herself. Where she worked was filled with the colors of her world, not his. She was comfortable among the pieces of art; she understood each, she could feel the energy behind every brushstroke. The canvases, like the museum, were immense, taking up great patches of wall space with their insistence. They intimidated many of the visitors because the paintings dwarfed everyone who stepped in front of them.

She felt a touch of satisfaction within her. It was the perfect place to extract herself from Michael O'Connell's crazy claims of love. Everything here was *her* world. Nothing was *his*. The museum would make him seem small and inconsequential. She expected their meeting to be quick and relatively painless for both of them.

She played it out in her head. Firm, but uncompromising. Polite, but strong.

No high-pitched complaints. No more whiny *please*s and *leave me alone*s.

Just direct, to the point. End of story. Finished.

No debate about love. No discussion about possibility. Nothing about the one-night stand. Nothing about the computer messages. Nothing about the dead flowers. Nothing that would lead itself into a wider exchange. Nothing that he might take as criticism. A clean, unencumbered break. Just, Thanks. Sorry. It's over. Good-bye forever.

She even allowed herself to imagine that once she'd gotten through this meeting, perhaps Will Goodwin would call. It surprised her that he hadn't. Ashley wasn't really familiar with boys who didn't call back, and so she was a little unsure how to feel. She spent some time thinking about this, as opposed to Michael O'Connell, as she made her way through the museum offices, nodding to the people she knew, and allowing herself to fill up with the benign normalcy of the day.

At lunchtime, she made her way to the cafeteria, took a seat at a small table, and ordered a glass of overpriced fizzy water, but nothing to eat. She had positioned herself so that she could see Michael O'Connell when he came up the museum steps and through the wide glass doors to the entrance. She glanced at her watch, saw that it was 1:00 p.m. straight up, and leaned back, knowing he would be prompt.

She felt a small quiver in her hands, and a little sweat in her armpits. She reminded herself, No kiss on the cheek. No handshake. No physical contact whatsoever. Just point at the seat opposite her and keep it simple. Do not get sidetracked.

She took a $5 bill—which would more than cover the price of her single glass of water—and put it in her pocket, where she could extract it rapidly. If she had to stand up and exit, she wanted to be able to move freely. She congratulated herself for thinking of this precaution.

Anything else? she asked herself. No loose ends. She felt excited but blank inside after performing a mental rundown of her plan.

She looked through the plate-glass windows, expecting to see him. A few couples hove into view, then a family, two young parents dragging a bored six-year-old. There was an odd-looking elderly pair of men, who were slowly walking up the expanse of steps, pausing, as if on cue, to rest before continuing. Her eyes swept the sidewalk, and far down the street. There was no sign of Michael O'Connell.

At ten past the hour, she started to squirm in her seat.

At quarter past, the waiter came over and politely but firmly asked her if she wanted to order.

At one thirty, she knew he wasn't coming. Still, she waited.

At two, she put the $5 on the table and left the restaurant.

She took one last glance around, but Michael O'Connell was nowhere she could see. Feeling a black emptiness within her, she headed back to work. When she reached her desk, she put her hand on the telephone, thinking she should call him and demand to know where he was.

Her fingers hesitated.

For an instant, she allowed herself to think that perhaps he'd simply chickened out. He'd understood that she was going to dump him once and for all and decided not to hear the bad news in person. Maybe, she thought, he's out of my life already. In that case, the call was unnecessary and, in fact, would defeat the purpose.

She didn't think she could be that lucky, but it certainly was a possibility. She could be suddenly, abruptly, delightfully free.

A little unsure about precisely what had happened, she

went back to work, trying to fill her head with the humdrum of the job.

Ashley worked late, although she didn't need to.

It was spitting rain outdoors when she exited the museum. A cold, angry sort of rain that played a drumbeat of loneliness on the sidewalk. Ashley tugged on a knit cap and pulled her coat tight as she set out, head down. She gingerly walked down the museum's slick steps to the sidewalk and started to turn up the street, then her eyes caught a red neon reflection glistening from a storefront opposite her. The lights seemed to wash into the glare from automobile headlights that swept past. She was not sure why her eyes were pulled in that direction, but the figure she saw was ghostlike.

Standing just to the side, so that he was halfway in the light, halfway in a shadow, Michael O'Connell waited.

She stopped sharply.

Their eyes locked across the street.

He was wearing a dark stocking cap and an olive-drab, military-styled parka. He seemed both anonymous and hidden, but, at the same time, glowed with some intensity that she could not put a word to.

She felt a sudden heat within her and gasped for air, as if she'd suddenly turned short of breath.

He made no gesture. No sign other than his fixed stare that he even recognized her.

On the street in front of her, a car suddenly swerved to avoid a taxi, sending a sheet of light across her path. There was a sudden blaring of horns, and a momentary screech of tires against wet pavement. She was distracted for just an instant, and when she turned back, O'Connell was gone.

She recoiled again.

She looked up and down, but it was as if he had vanished. For a moment, she was unsure precisely *what* she had seen. He seemed more hallucination than reality.

Ashley's first step forward was unsteady, not in the same way that a drunken person at a party might take, or a bereaved widow at a funeral service might manage. It was a step filled with doubt. Again she pivoted, trying to spot O'-Connell, but she could not make him out. She was overcome with the sensation that he was right behind her, and she abruptly turned around, nearly colliding with a businessman hurrying down the street. As she lurched out of the man's path, she almost bumped into a couple of young people, who managed a quick "Hey! Watch out!" before sliding past her.

Ashley turned and followed them, her feet sloshing through puddles, moving as quickly as she could. She kept swiveling her head, searching right and left, but without success. She wanted to turn and check behind her, but she was too scared. Instead, she barreled on, almost running.

Within a few seconds she was at the T station, and she pushed her way through the turnstile, almost relieved by the crowds and the harsh, glaring lights of the platform.

She craned her head forward, trying to pick O'Connell out among the knots of people waiting for the train. Once again, he was nowhere. She turned and stared at the people coming through the turnstiles and up the stairs, but he wasn't among them. Still, she wasn't at all certain that he wasn't there. She couldn't see through every clutch of people, and posters and stanchions obscured her line of sight. She leaned out, wanting the train to come. At that moment, more than anything, she wanted to get away. She reassured herself that nothing could happen to her in a crowded train station, and as she told herself she was safe, she felt herself jostled from the back, and for a dizzying second, she thought she was going to lose her balance and fall onto the tracks. She gasped and jerked back.

Ashley swallowed hard and shook her head. She braced herself, tightening her muscles like an athlete anticipating the blow of contact, as if Michael O'Connell were directly behind her and ready to push her. She listened for the sound of his breathing in her ear, too crazed to turn and look. The approaching train filled the platform with harsh braking noises. She released a long breath of relief when the train slid to a stop in front of her and the doors opened with a whooshing sound.

She let herself be carried forward by the surge from the commuters and slid into a seat, immediately crammed between an older woman and a student, who slumped beside her smelling of cigarettes. In front of her a half dozen other riders clung to the metal hand straps and overhead bars.

Ashley looked up, right and left, inspecting every face.

With another whoosh, the doors closed. The train lurched once as it took off.

She was unsure why, but she swiveled in her seat and took a single glance back at the elevated train platform as the train started to pick up speed. What she saw almost made her choke, and it was all she could do to prevent herself from crying out in fear: O'Connell was standing right in the same spot where she'd been seconds earlier. He didn't move. He was statuelike, impassive. His eyes were once again locked on hers, as she was carried away by the accelerating train. As they pulled away from the station, O'Connell disappeared behind her.

She felt the rhythmic sway of the commuter train as it gathered speed, sweeping her away from the man who'd followed her. But no matter how fast it went, Ashley understood that the distance it placed between them was elusive and probably, ultimately, nonexistent.

•

The campus of the University of Massachusetts–Boston is located in Dorchester right next to the harbor. Its buildings are as graceless and stolid as a medieval fortification, and on a hot, early-summer day, the brown brick walls and gray concrete walkways seem to absorb the heat. It is a plain stepsister of a school. It caters to many seeking to take a second bite at education, with an infantryman's sensibility: not pretty, but critically important when you need it most.

I got lost once in the sea of cement, had to ask for directions, before finding the right stairwell that descended into a threadbare lounge outside a cafeteria. I hesitated for a moment, then spotted Professor Corcoran waving for me from one of the quieter corners.

Introductions were quick, a handshake and a little small talk about the unseasonably hot weather.

"So," the professor said as he sat down and took a swig of bottled water, "how *precisely* is it that I can help you?"

"Michael O'Connell," I replied. "He took two of your computer courses a few years back. I was hoping you might recall him."

Corcoran nodded. "I do, indeed. I mean, I shouldn't, really, but I do, which says something all in itself."

"How so?"

"Dozens, no, hundreds of students have passed through the same two courses he took from me, over the last few years. Lots of tests, lots of final papers, lots of faces. After a while, they all pretty much blend into one generic blue-jeans-wearing, baseball-cap-on-backwards, working-two-different-jobs-to-support-themselves-through-Second-Chance-U sort of student."

"O'Connell, though . . ."

"Well, let's say it doesn't surprise me to have someone show up asking questions about him."

The professor was a wiry, small man, with bifocals and thinning, sandy blond hair. He had a row of pens and pencils in his shirt pocket, and a battered, overstuffed, brown canvas briefcase.

"Okay," I said, "why doesn't it surprise you?"

"Actually, I always figured it for a detective who would show up with an inquiry or two about O'Connell. Or the FBI or maybe an assistant U.S. attorney. You know who comes to the classes I teach? Students who quite accurately believe that the skills they will learn will improve their financial outlook considerably. The problem is, the more adept the students become, the more clear it becomes how you can misuse the information."

"Misuse?"

"A nicer word than what the truth is," he said. "I have an entire lecture on law-breaking, but still . . ."

"O'Connell?"

"Most of the kids that choose, ah, the *dark side*," he said with a small laugh, "well, they're pretty much what you might expect. Overgrown nerds and losers to the *nth* degree. Mostly they just make trouble, hacking, downloading video games without paying licensing fees, or stealing music files or even pirating Hollywood movies before they're released to DVD, that sort of thing. But O'Connell was different."

"Explain *different*."

"What he was, was infinitely more dangerous and more scary."

"How so?"

"Because he saw the computer precisely for what it is: a tool. What are the sorts of tools a bad guy needs? A knife? A gun? A getaway car? Sort of depends on what crime you have in mind, doesn't it? A computer can be just as efficient as a nine-millimeter in the wrong hands, and his, trust me, were the wrong hands."

"How could you tell?"

"From the first moment. He didn't have that bedraggled, slightly-amazed-at-the-world look about him, like so many students. He had this, I don't know, a *looseness* to him. He was good-looking. Well put together. But he exuded a sort of dangerousness. As if he cared not one whit for anything other than some unspoken agenda. And when you stared closely at him, he had this truly unsettling look in his eyes. This don't-get-in-my-way look.

"You know, he handed in an assignment once a couple of days late, so I did what I always do, and which I tell every class about on the first day: I marked it down one full grade point for each day late. He came to see me and told me that I was being unfair. This was, as you would probably guess, not the very first time that a student had come to me complaining about a grade. But, with O'Connell, the conversation was somehow different. I'm not sure how he did it, but somehow I was in the position of justifying what I had done, not the other way around. And the more I explained that it wasn't unfair, the more his eyes narrowed. He could look at you the way some people might actually strike you. The impact was the same. You just knew you didn't want to be on the other end of that look. He never threatened, never suggested, never said or did anything overt. But every instant we spoke, I could feel that that was precisely *what* was happening. I was being warned."

"It made an impression."

"Kept me up at night. My wife kept asking me, 'What's the matter?' and I had to reply, 'Nothing,' when I *knew* that wasn't precisely true. I had the sensation that I managed to dodge something truly terrifying."

"He didn't ever do anything?"

"Well, he let me know, one day, in passing, that he'd just happened to find out where I lived."

"And?"

"That was it. And that was where it ended."

"How?"

"I violated every rule I have. Complete moral failure on my part. I called him in after a class, told him I'd been mistaken, he was absolutely one hundred percent right, and gave him an A on the assignment, and an A for the semester."

I didn't say anything.

"So," Professor Corcoran asked as he gathered his things together, "who did he kill?"

10

A Poor Start

Hope was in the kitchen, working on a recipe she had never tried before, waiting for Sally to get home. She tasted the sauce, which burned her tongue, and she cursed under her breath. It just did not taste right, and she feared that she was destined for a failed dinner. For an instant, she felt a helplessness that seemed far deeper than a kitchen disaster, and she could feel tears welling up in her eyes.

She did not know precisely why Sally and she were going through such a rocky period.

When she examined it all on the surface, she could see no reason for their extended silences and stony moments. There was no real anxiety at either Sally's legal practice or Hope's school. They were doing well financially and had the funds to take an exotic vacation or buy a new car, even redo the kitchen. But every time one of these indulgences had come up in conversation, it had been shunted aside. Rationales were given for why they shouldn't do one or the other. Hope thought that almost always whatever obstacle made whatever adventure impossible seemed to be raised by Sally, and this worried her deeply.

It seemed to her that it had been a long time since they'd shared something.

Even their lovemaking, which had once been both tender and filled with abandon, had been tempered of late. Its perfunctory quality unsettled her. And the occasions for sex had become far less frequent.

In a curious way the lack of passion suggested that Sally was seeking affection elsewhere. The notion that Sally was having an affair was totally ridiculous, and yet, completely reasonable. Hope gritted her teeth and told herself that to fantasize emotional disaster was to invite it, and to dwell on one suspicion or another only made her more anxious. She hated doubt. It wasn't really a part of her makeup, and to allow it in now, unbidden, was a mistake.

She looked up at the clock on the wall and was suddenly overcome with the urge to turn off the stove, grab her running shoes, and head out on a really hard, fast run. A little bit of daylight was left, and she thought that even if she was completely exhausted by the school day, and by soccer practice, still, a couple of miles at a near sprint was a good idea. When she had been a player, the one thing she could always count on near the end of a game was that she would have more energy than her opponents. She was never sure that this was really the result of extra conditioning, as her coaches always thought. She believed it had something to do with some inherent emotional capability, something that drove her, so at the end, when others were weakening, she had some extra strength that she could summon. A special reserve, perhaps, that became the ability to run hard when others were gasping, as if she could put off the pain of exhaustion until after the game.

She turned down the heat on the stove and quickly rose to the bedroom, taking the steps two at a time. It only took her a few seconds to strip off her clothes, throw on some shorts and an old red Manchester United sweatshirt, and grab her shoes. She wanted to get out the door before Sally came back, so that she wouldn't have to come up with an explanation why she felt driven to run at an hour when she was generally preparing dinner.

Nameless was at the bottom of the stairs wagging with mixed enthusiasm. He recognized the running outfit and knew that he was rarely included now. At one time he would instantly have been at her side, circling with enthusiasm, but now he was more than willing to escort her just as far as the door and then settle down and wait, which, she thought, seemed to be how Nameless interpreted his dog responsibilities.

Hope had paused to rub his head when the phone rang.

What she wanted, in that second, was to get away from all the troubles that were coursing within her, if only temporarily. She guessed the call would be Sally, maybe saying she was going to be late. She never seemed to call anymore to say she would be early. Hope didn't want to hear this, and her first instinct was to ignore the ringing.

The phone rang again.

She started toward the door, pulling it open, but stopped, turned, and took a dozen quick strides into the kitchen and seized the phone.

"Hello," she said briskly. No-nonsense.

"Hope?"

And in that second, Hope not only heard Ashley's voice, but a world of trouble behind it.

"Hello, *Killer*," she said, using a joke nickname that only the two of them knew about. "Something wrong?" She put a liveliness in her voice that belied not only her own situation, but the emptiness that she suddenly felt in her stomach.

"Oh, Hope," Ashley said, and Hope could hear the vacant echo of tears in her voice. "I think I have a problem."

Sally was listening to the local alternative-rock station on the car radio when the late Warren Zevon's "Poor, Poor Pitiful Me" came on, and for some reason she couldn't quite fathom, she felt compelled to pull to the curb, where she listened to the entirety of the song frozen in her seat, drumming her fingers on the steering wheel with the beat.

As the music flooded her small sedan, she held her hands up in front of her.

The veins on the backs were standing out, blue, like the interstates on a travel map. Her fingers were tight, maybe a little arthritic. She rubbed them together, trying to regain some of the suppleness they once held. Sally thought that when she was younger, much about her had been beautiful: her skin, her eyes, the curve of her body. But she had been proudest of her hands, which seemed to her to hold notes within them. She had played the cello growing up and had considered auditioning for Juilliard or Berklee, but at the last moment had decided to pursue a more general education, which had somehow evolved into a husband, a daughter, an affair with another woman, a divorce, a law degree, and her current practice and her current life.

She no longer played her instrument. She couldn't make the cello sound as pure and as subtle as she once could, and she preferred not to listen to her mistakes. Sally could not bear to be clumsy.

As she sat there in the car, the song began to wind down, and Sally caught a glimpse of her eyes in the edge of the rearview mirror and reached up and adjusted it so that she could look at herself. She was just shy of turning fifty, which some thought of as a milestone, but which she inwardly dreaded. She hated the changes in her body, from hot flashes to stiffness in her joints. She hated the wrinkles forming at the corners of her eyes. She hated the sag of skin beneath her chin and in her buttocks. Without telling Hope, she had taken a membership at a local health club and pounded away on the treadmills and the elliptical machines as often as she could get away.

She had taken to reading advertisements for cosmetic surgery and had even considered sneaking off to some fancy health spa, using an ostensible business trip as a cover. She was a little unsure of why she hid these things from her partner, but was smart enough to recognize that that in itself said all she needed to know.

Sally took a deep breath and turned off the radio.

For a moment, she thought that her entire youth had been stolen from her. She felt a bitterness on her tongue, as if everything in her life was predictable, established, and absolutely set in stone. Even her relationship, which in some parts of the country would have set people to whispered gossip across backyard fences and would seem exotic and dangerous, in western Massachusetts was about as boringly routine as the inevitable arrival of the seasons. She wasn't even much of a sexual outlaw.

Sally gripped the wheel of the car and let out a quick, angry shout. Not quite a scream, more a bellow, as if she were in pain. Then she glanced around rapidly, to make certain that no passing pedestrian had heard her.

Breathing hard, she put the car in gear.

What's next? she asked herself as she pulled back into traffic, aware that once again she was late for dinner. Some disease? She thought to herself that perhaps it would be breast cancer, or osteoporosis, or anemia. But whatever it was, it wouldn't be harsher than the uncontrolled anger, frustration, and madness that she felt ricocheting about within her and that she felt helpless to fight.

·

"So, the two women were having trouble?"

"Yes, I suppose you could say they were having *trouble*. But that wouldn't begin to capture the moment that Michael O'Connell arrived in their lives, and how his mere presence redefined so much that was happening."

"I get it," I said.

"Really? It doesn't exactly sound like you do."

We were seated in a small restaurant, near the front, where she could look through the plate-glass windows out onto the main street of the small college town we lived in. She smiled for an instant and turned back to me.

"We take a lot for granted, in our nice, safe middle-class lives, don't we?" she asked. She didn't wait for my answer, but continued, "Problems sometimes occur not only when we least anticipate them, but at moments when we are least equipped to deal with them." The edgy decisiveness in her voice seemed out of place on the fine, mostly lazy afternoon.

"Okay," I sighed, "so Scott's life wasn't exactly perfect, although, on balance, it wasn't that bad. He had a good job, some prestige, a more than adequate paycheck, which should have compensated at least some for middle-aged loneliness. And Sally and Hope were going through a difficult time, but still, they had resources. Significant resources. And Ashley, despite being well educated and attractive, was in something of a state of flux, as well. That's more or less the way life is, isn't it? How does it—"

She cut me off, lifting one hand like a traffic cop, while the other reached for a glass of iced tea. She drank before replying.

"You need perspective. Otherwise, the story won't make sense."

Again, I remained silent.

"Dying," she said finally, "is such a simple act. But you need to learn that all the moments leading up to it, and all the minutes afterwards, are terribly complicated."

11

The First Response

Sally was surprised that the front door was wide open. Nameless was plopped down by the entrance, not exactly sleeping, not exactly standing guard, but more or less accomplishing both. He picked his head up and thumped his tail at Sally's arrival, and she reached down and stroked him once behind the ears, which was pretty much the extent of her connection to the dog. She suspected that if Jack the Ripper had walked in, with a dog biscuit in one hand and a bloody knife in the other, Nameless would have locked in on the biscuit.

She could just hear the final words of a conversation as she set her briefcase down in the small foyer.

"Yes . . . yes. Okay, I've got it. We'll call you back later tonight. Don't worry, everything will be okay. . . . Yup. Later, then."

Sally heard the phone being returned to its cradle, then Hope exhale and add, "Jesus H. Christ."

"What was that about?" Sally asked.

Hope spun about. "I didn't hear you come in."

"You must have left the door open."

Sally eyed the running clothes and added, "Were you heading out? Or just coming back?"

Hope ignored the questions and Sally's tone and said, "That was Ashley. She's really upset. Turns out that she really has gotten sort of involved with some creep in Boston and she's starting to get a little scared."

Sally hesitated for an instant before asking, "What does *sort of involved* actually mean?"

"You should have her explain. But, as best as I understand it, she had a one-night stand with the guy, and now he won't leave her alone."

"Is this the guy who wrote the letter Scott found?"

"Seems to be. He's making all sorts of *We were made for each other* protests, when they don't make a damn bit of sense. The guy sounds a little out there, but again, you should have Ashley explain it to you. It will seem a lot more, I don't know, real, maybe, if you hear it from her."

"Well, my guess is this is really a mountain being made out of a molehill, but—"

Hope interrupted, "It didn't sound that way. I mean, we both know she can be overdramatic, but she sounded genuinely disturbed. I think you should call her back right away. It will probably do her some good to hear from her mother. Reassure her, you know."

"Well, has the guy hit her? Or threatened her?"

"Not exactly. Yes and no. It's a little hard to say."

"What do you mean *not exactly*?" Sally asked briskly.

Hope shook her head. "What I mean is that *I'm going to kill you* is a threat. But *We'll always be together* might be the same thing. It's just hard to tell until you hear the words for yourself."

Hope was a little taken aback. Sally was decidedly cool and irritatingly calm about what she was being told. This surprised her.

"Call Ashley," she repeated.

"You're probably right." Sally stepped to the telephone.

Scott tried Ashley on her regular phone, but the line was busy, and for the third time that evening he got the answering machine. He had already tried her cell phone, but that, too, had only produced the sound of her voice breezily requesting the caller to leave a message. He was more than a little bit put off. What, he wondered to himself, is precisely the point of all these modern forms of communication if one simply gets nowhere more efficiently? In the eighteenth century, he thought, when one received a letter carried over distance, it damn well meant something. By being closer, he thought, everyone had gotten much farther away.

Before his frustration built further, the phone rang. He seized the receiver.

"Ashley?" he asked rapidly.

"No, Scott, it's me, Sally."

"Sally. Is something wrong?"

She hesitated, creating just enough of a dark space in time for his stomach to clench and the world around him to darken.

"When we last spoke," Sally said, employing all her lawyer's sense of equanimity, "you expressed some concern about a letter you found. You may have been justified in your response."

Scott paused, wanting to scream at the professional reasonableness in her voice. "Why? What's happened? Where's Ashley?"

"She's okay. But she might indeed have a problem."

Michael O'Connell stopped at a small art-supply store before heading home. His stock of charcoal pencils was down, and he slipped a set into the pocket of his parka. He picked out a medium-sized sketch pad and took it to the counter. A bored young woman who sported an array of facial piercings, and hair streaked with black and red, was sitting behind the cash register, reading a copy of an Anne Rice novel about vampires. She wore a black T-shirt that said FREE THE WEST MEMPHIS THREE on it in large, Gothic-style print. For a brief moment, O'Connell was mad with himself. He should have filled his pockets with many more items, given the lax attention the girl was paying to the comings and goings in the store. He made a mental note to return in a few days as he forked over a couple of worn singles for the pad of paper.

He knew the clerk would never think to examine the pockets of someone willing to pay for something.

Misdirection, he thought to himself. He remembered playing football in high school. His favorite plays were always those designed with some element of deception. Make the other team believe one thing when another was actually happening. The screen pass. The double reverse. It was the key to much of his life, and he embraced it at every opportunity. Make people underestimate you. Make them believe one thing was happening when really, something far different was at stake.

It was, he thought, the game that made it all worthwhile.

The clerk handed him some change, and he asked, "Who are the West Memphis Three?"

She looked at him as if the simple act of communicating was somehow physically painful. She sighed, "They're three kids who were convicted of murder, of killing another kid, but they didn't do it. They kinda got convicted because of the way they looked, and all the Bible-thumpers down there who didn't like the way they dressed and talked about Goth stuff and Satan, and now they're on death row and it's unfair. HBO did a documentary about them."

"They got caught?"

"It wasn't right. Just because you're different doesn't make you guilty."

Michael O'Connell nodded. "Right. It just makes it easier for the cops to look for you. When you're different, you can't get away with anything. But if you're the same, you can do anything you want. Anything."

He headed back out into the evening. As he walked down the street, he took a modest inventory of information he'd acquired. There is a small fringe to society, he told himself, where one can travel with relative impunity. Stay away from the chain store with the security guard. Work at the service station where the owner is willing to cut corners and look the other way. Avoid robbing something from a Dairy Mart or 7-Eleven, because those places were robbed all the time and might have an off-duty cop moonlighting with a twelve-gauge hiding behind a two-way mirror. Always do what was unexpected, but only just so, which kept people off balance, but not alert.

Never rely on others.

It all came naturally to him, he thought.

Michael O'Connell trudged up the street to his apartment house, then up the stairs. As usual, the hallway outside his door was filled with the mewlings and meowings of his old neighbor's cats. As always, she had put bowls of food and water out for the animals. He looked down and several scurried out of his path. They were the smart ones because they recognized a threat, even if they couldn't quite determine what it was. The others milled about. He knelt down and held out his hand, until one of the least suspicious cats moved close enough for him to scratch it on the head. With a quick and practiced motion, he seized the cat by the scruff of the neck and carried it into his apartment.

The cat struggled for a moment, trying to twist and scratch, but O'Connell kept it firmly in his grip. He walked into the kitchen and pulled out a large ziplock bag. This one would join four others in his freezer. When he reached a half dozen, he would dispose of them in some distant Dumpster. Then start in again. He doubted the old woman's ability to keep an accurate count of her pets. And, after all, he'd asked her politely once or twice to limit their number. Failing to follow his suggestions, especially when so generously put, was in reality what was killing the cats. He was merely the agent of death.

Scott listened to his ex-wife and every second grew angrier.

It wasn't that his instincts had been ignored, nor that he'd been right all along. It was the orderly tone in her voice that infuriated him. But he decided that arguing with Sally wasn't going to do any good.

"So," she said, "I think, and Ashley does, too, that perhaps the best thing would be for you to go to Boston and maybe bring her home for the weekend, so she can really get a handle on what sort of problem this young man is likely to cause her."

"Okay," Scott said. "I'll go tomorrow."

"A little distance usually gives one some perspective," Sally said.

"You would know," Scott dug back. "How's your perspective?"

Sally wanted to respond with equal sarcasm, but decided against it.

"Scott, can you just go pick Ashley up? I'd go, but . . ."

"No, I'll go. You've probably got some court hearing or something that can't be postponed."

"As a matter of fact, I do."

"The drive back will give me a chance to really sound her out, anyway. Then we can come up with a plan or whatever. Or at least some sort of plan that's a little more comprehensive than merely bringing her home for the weekend. Maybe all that's called for is for me to go have a talk with this guy."

"I think, before we inject ourselves into the problem, we should give Ashley every chance to sort it out herself. Part of growing up, you know."

"That's the sort of totally reasonable and sensible point of view that I truly hate."

Sally did not answer. She did not want the conversation to disintegrate any further. And she recognized that Scott had some legitimate claim to being upset. It was the way her mind worked, seeing every word spoken as if it were light reflecting through a prism, with any particular shaft being important. This made her an excellent attorney and upon occasion a difficult person.

"Maybe I should go tonight," Scott said.

"No," Sally said quickly. "That would have an element of panic in it. Let's just proceed steadily."

They were both quiet for a moment. "Hey," Scott asked abruptly, "do you have any experience with this sort of thing?"

What he meant was legal experience, but Sally took it a different way. "No," she said suddenly. "The only man who ever said he would love me forever was you."

•

There had been a story in the local paper over the past few days that had captured much attention in the valley where I lived. A child, thirteen years old, had been placed in the tenth of a series of foster homes and had died under questionable circumstances. Police and the local district attorney's office were investigating, as was every ham-fisted news outlet for miles. But the facts of the case seemed murky, so dark and conflicted that the truth might never emerge. The child had died from a single gunshot wound, administered at close range. The foster parents said that the boy had found the father's handgun and been playing with it when it discharged. Or perhaps he wasn't playing with it but had committed suicide. Or perhaps the set of brand-new bruises on the child's arms and torso that the autopsy revealed meant that he'd been beaten or held down while something far more evil had taken place. Or perhaps the gun had been the source of a struggle between child and adult, discharging in an accident. Or, even darker, perhaps it was murder. Murder prompted by rage. Murder prompted by frustration. Murder prompted by desire. Murder prompted by nothing more than the lousy hand that life sometimes deals to those least equipped to bluff their way out of trouble.

It seemed to me that the truth is often impossibly elusive.

Each day for a week, the black-and-white photo of the dead child stared out at me from the pages of the newspaper. He wore a beautifully wry, almost shy smile, beneath eyes that seemed bright with promise. Maybe that was what drove the story, gave it the impetus that it had, before it was swallowed up and disappeared in the steady march of events; there was something dishonest in the death. Someone was cheated.

No one cared for the child. At least, no one cared enough.

I suppose I was no different from everyone else who read the story or heard it on the nightly news or discussed it over the proverbial watercooler. It hit anyone who had ever looked in on a sleeping child and imagined how fragile all life is, and how tenuous our grip on what passes for happiness can truly be. I guessed, in its own way, that this was what slowly became apparent for Scott and Sally and Hope.

12

The First Wayward Plan

Scott drove east the following morning, early enough so that the rising sun reflected off the reservoir outside the town of Gardner, momentarily filling the windshield with glare. Usually when he drove the Porsche up Route 2, with its long, empty stretches through some of the least scenic countryside in New England, he let the car fly. He'd been ticketed once by a humorless state trooper, who'd clocked him at over a hundred miles per hour, and who had started a series of quite predictable lectures, which Scott had ignored. When he drove alone and fast, which was as frequently as he could, he sometimes thought it was the only time that he truly failed to act his age. The rest of his life was dedicated to being responsible and adult. He knew inwardly that the recklessness he exhibited spoke of some larger issue within him, but he ignored it.

The car began to hum in the distinctive sound that the Porsche had, an *I can go faster, if you'll let me* reminder, and he settled into the drive, considering the brief conversation he'd had with Ashley the night before.

There had been no discussion of the reason for his trip to get her. He'd started to ask a question or two, but realized that she'd already spoken with both Hope and her mother, and so he was likely to simply be repeating questions already asked. So it had been all *I'll be there early* and *Don't bother parking, just beep, and I'll come running out.* He figured that once she got into the car, she would open up, at least enough for him to make some sort of assessment of the situation.

He wasn't sure what he thought, so far. The recognition that his first instincts upon reading the letter were correct didn't give him any satisfaction.

Nor did he know, now that he was heading toward Boston to pick up his daughter, just how worried he should be. In a slightly perverse way, he was looking forward to seeing her because he doubted that he would have many more opportunities to truly act like a father. She was growing up, and she didn't need him or her mother nearly as much as she did when she was a child.

Scott slid a pair of sunglasses down on his nose. He wondered, What does Ashley need now? A little extra cash. Maybe a wedding party sometime in the future. Advice? Not likely.

He punched the accelerator and the car jumped forward.

It was nice to be needed, but he doubted he would ever be again. At least, not needed in that small-child-and-parent way, where the smallest of problems can be magnified. Ashley was equipped to extricate herself from the problem. Indeed, he suspected she would demand this right. His role, he believed, was truly cheering from the sidelines, limited to making a modest suggestion or two.

When he had first seen the letter, he'd been filled with protective feelings that were reminiscent of her childhood. Now, as he drove to get her, more or less vindicated in his concerns, he glumly realized that his role was probably going to be small, and his feelings were best kept to himself. Still, as the stands of trees still carrying their fall colors swept past him, a part of him was overjoyed to be allowed into his daughter's life in something other than a peripheral way. Scott grinned *Can't catch me* as he headed down the highway.

Ashley heard the car horn beep twice, quickly peered out the window, and saw the familiar profile of her father in the black Porsche. He gave a small wave, which was both a greeting and a hurry-up gesture, because he was blocking the street and more than a few people who drive in Boston are willing to exchange words over the inconveniences of the narrow traffic lanes. Boston drivers take a sporting delight in honking and shouting. In Miami or Houston, that sort of conversation might produce handguns, but in Boston it is more or less considered protected speech.

She grabbed a small overnight bag and made sure that her apartment was locked. She had already unplugged the answering machine and turned off her cell phone and computer.

No messages. No e-mails. No contact, she thought, as she bounded down the stairwell and through the front door.

"Hi, beautiful," Scott said as she crossed the sidewalk.

"Hi, Dad." Ashley smiled. "Gonna let me drive?"

"Ah," Scott hesitated. "Maybe next time."

This was a joke between them. Scott never let anyone else drive the Porsche. He said it was for insurance reasons, but Ashley knew better.

"That all you're going to need?" Scott asked, eyeing the small bag.

"That's it. I've got enough stuff out there anyway, either at your place or Mom's."

Scott shook his head and smiled as he embraced her. "There was a time," he said with a fake, sonorous tone, "that I distinctly recall carrying trunks and suitcases and backpacks and huge, military-issue duffel bags, all crammed with completely unnecessary clothing, just to be sure that you would be able to change at least a half dozen times each day."

She smiled and headed toward the passenger door.

"Let's get out of here before some delivery truck comes along and decides to squash your midlife-crisis toy car," she said, laughing.

She put her head back on the leather headrest and momentarily closed her eyes, feeling, for the first time in some hours, safe. She breathed out slowly, feeling herself relax.

"Thanks for coming, Dad." A few words that said a great deal.

Their exchange distracted her as her father steered the small car out of her street. He, of course, wouldn't have recognized the figure sliding into the shadow of a tree as they went past, but she would have if her eyes had been open and she had been more alert.

Michael O'Connell stared after them, taking note of the car and the driver, and memorizing the license plate number.

•

"Do you ever listen to love songs?" she asked me. The question seemed to come out of the blue, and I hesitated for a moment before replying.

"Love songs?"

"Exactly. Love songs. You know, 'Yummy, yummy, yummy, I've got love in my tummy,' or maybe, 'Maria . . . I've just met a girl named Maria' . . . I could go on and on."

"Not really," I replied. "I mean, I suppose everyone does, to some degree. Isn't about ninety-nine percent of pop, rock, country, whatever, even punk, often about some sort of love? Lost love. Unrequited love. Good love. Bad love. I'm not sure what this has to do with what we're talking about."

I was a little exasperated. What I wanted to do was find out what the next step had been for Ashley. And I certainly wanted to get a better handle on Michael O'Connell.

"Most love songs aren't about love at all. They're about many things. But mostly about frustration. Lust, maybe. Desire. Need. Disappointment. Rarely are they about what love really is, which is, when you strip away all these other aspects, a . . . well, mutual dependency. The problem is, so often it is too difficult to see that, because we get obsessed with another one of these items on the love list, mistaking that for the be-all and end-all of the emotion."

"Okay," I said slowly. "And Michael O'Connell?"

"Love for him was anger. Rage."

I remained quiet.

"And it was as essential to him as the very breath of life."

13

The Most Modest of Goals

The throaty hum of the sports car lulled Ashley into sleep almost instantly, and she didn't stir for nearly an hour until she abruptly opened her eyes and sat up with a small gasp, disoriented. Scott saw her look about wildly and punch at the air in front of her for a second or two, before she slumped back again in the contoured seat of the car. She rubbed her hands across her face to clear the sleep from her eyes.

"Jesus," she said. "Did I pass out?"

Scott didn't answer the question. "Tired?"

"I guess. Maybe more like relaxed for the first time in hours. It just came over me. Feels kinda weird. Not bad weird, but not good weird, either. Just weird weird."

"Should we talk about it now?"

Ashley seemed a little hesitant, as if with each mile that slid beneath the Porsche's wheels, and Boston fading in the rearview mirror, whatever trouble she was in grew smaller and more distant. In that space of time, Scott asked a third question.

"Maybe you should just fill me in on what you told your mom and her partner," he said quietly, aware that he had given a stilted formality to Sally and Hope's relationship. "At least that way we'll all be up-to-date on the same stuff. It would make sense if we could all put our heads together and come to some sort of reasonable plan for you to follow." He wasn't sure that making a plan was exactly what Ashley was coming home to do, but it was the sort of thing she would expect him to say, and that in itself was likely to be reassuring.

Ashley paused, shuddered, and then said, "Dead flowers. Dead flowers taped outside my door. And then he followed me instead of meeting me at a restaurant like we'd agreed, where I was going to get rid of him, and it was just like I was some animal, and he was a hunter, closing in on me." She stared out the side window, as if organizing her thoughts in a way that would make some sense, then said with an immense sigh, "Let me start at the beginning, so you can understand it."

Scott slowed the car down to the speed limit and moved into the right-hand lane, where the Porsche almost never traveled, and without saying a thing, listened.

By the time they reached the small college town where Scott lived, Ashley had pretty much filled him in on her relationship, if it could be dignified with that word, with Michael O'Connell. She had glossed over the initial connection as much as possible, not exactly being comfortable discussing alcohol use and her sex life with her father, using seemingly benign euphemisms such as *hooked up* and *sloshed* instead of words that were dangerously more explicit.

For his part, Scott knew exactly what she was talking about, but restrained himself from probing too aggressively. There were some details, he guessed, that he'd rather not know.

He shifted the car once or twice when they left the highway and started beating their way through country roads. Ashley had grown quiet again and was staring out the window. The day had risen brightly, a high, pale blue sky overhead.

"It's nice," she said. "To see home again. You forget about how well you know a place when you're involved with so much other stuff. But there it is. Same old town common. Same old town hall. Restaurants. Coffee shops. Kids playing with a Frisbee on the lawn. Makes you think that hardly anything could be wrong anywhere." She breathed out with a snort. "So, Dad, there you have it. What do you think?"

Scott tried to force a smile that would mask some of the turmoil he felt.

"I think we ought to be able to find a way to discourage Mr. O'Connell without too much trouble," he replied, although he wasn't sure about what he was saying. Still, he made certain that his tones were filled with confidence. "Perhaps all that is really needed is a talk with him. Or maybe some distance—this could cost you some time before your graduate program gets going. But that's sort of the way life is. A little messy. But I'm sure that we can sort it out. He doesn't really sound like as much of a challenge as I initially feared."

Ashley seemed to breathe a little easier. "You think?"

"Yeah. I'll bet your mom has pretty much the same take on it as I do. In her practice she's seen some pretty tough guys, you know, in divorce cases or some of the low-rent crimes she handles. And she's seen her share of abusive relationships—although that's not exactly how I'd characterize this one—and so she's pretty competent when it comes to getting all this sort of stuff straightened out."

Ashley nodded.

"I mean, he hasn't hit you, has he?" Scott asked, although Ashley had already given him the answer.

"I said no. He just says we're made for each other."

"Yes, well, I may not know who made him, but I know who made you, and I doubt that you were made for him."

A small smile creased Ashley's face.

"And, trust me," Scott said, trying to make a small joke that might leaven the mood a little further, "it doesn't seem like such a substantial problem that any well-respected historian couldn't figure it all out. A little bit of research. Maybe some original documents, or eyewitness accounts. Primary sources. Some fieldwork. And we'll be right on track."

Ashley managed a small laugh. "Dad, we're not talking about a scholarly paper here."

"We aren't?"

This made her smile again. Scott turned in his seat, just

enough to catch all of the smile, which reminded him of a million moments and was more valuable than anything else in his entire life.

Saturday was game day at Hope's private school, so she was torn between getting over to the campus and waiting for Scott to arrive with Ashley. By experience, she knew that the morning sunshine would help dry the pitch, but not completely, so she expected something of a slogging, muddy game that afternoon. Probably a generation ago, the notion that girls would play in the mud was so alien that the game would have been canceled. Now, she was certain that the girls on the team were looking forward to the sloppy, messy conditions. Dirt-streaked and sweaty were positives now. Mud-defined progress.

She was hovering in the kitchen, half-watching the clock on the wall, half-peering out the window, her ears attuned to the unmistakable sound of Scott's car as he downshifted at the corner and came winding down their block. Nameless was waiting by the door. Too old to be impatient, but unwilling to be left behind. He knew the phrase *Want to go to a soccer game?* and when she spoke it, no matter how quietly, he would instantly go from near comatose to wildly overjoyed.

The window was cracked open and she could hear sounds from her neighbors' homes that were so routine for a Saturday morning that they were nearly clichéd: a lawn mower starting up with a cough and a roar; a leaf blower whining; high-pitched voices of children happily at play in a nearby yard. It was hard to imagine anything even vaguely approaching a threat to their orderly lives existed anywhere. She had no idea that nearly the same thought had struck Ashley only a few moments earlier.

When she looked away, she saw Sally standing behind her in the doorway.

"Will you be late?" Sally asked. "What time is the game?"

"I have some time."

"Today's game is important?"

"They're all important. Some are just a little more so. We'll be okay." Hope hesitated a bit, then added, "They should be along any second. Didn't Scott say he was leaving early?"

Sally, too, paused before replying, "I think we should ask Scott in, because he'll want to be a part of any decisions made."

"Good idea," Hope said, although she was less sure.

Anything that involved Scott put her in what would once have been termed an *awkward* position, but which went far deeper and was far more complicated. She believed Scott hated her, although he had never said anything so explicit.

At the very least, he hated the sight of her. Or maybe hated what she stood for. Or hated what she'd done to attract Sally or hated what had happened between them. Regardless, he carried within him a package of anger toward her, and she believed she was helpless to ever make him change.

"I wonder," Sally said, "whether it's a good thing for you to be here when he arrives and I tell him to come inside."

Hope was immediately angry with Sally, and disappointed at the same time. It seemed to her that it was completely unfair; enough years had gone by so that civil behavior was the norm between them, even if the undercurrents were always much stronger. She was pitched into fury by the idea that Sally would want to somehow accommodate Scott's feelings and trample over hers at the same time. She had put years into raising Ashley and, while she could not claim her as blood, felt that she had as much a stake in her happiness as anyone else.

She bit her lip before replying. Be judicious.

"Well, I don't think that's really fair. But if you think it is important, well, I'd bow to your superior knowledge in these matters."

This last bit might have sounded sincere or sarcastic. Sally was unsure which.

She took a step back, a little shocked at herself for even asking Hope to stand aside when Scott arrived. What am I doing?

"No—" she started to reply, but was interrupted by the sound of Scott's car coming up the slight rise to their house. "There they are."

"Well," Hope said stiffly, "I guess I'll be here, then."

Nameless bounced up, recognizing the sound of the car. They all went to the front door, and the dog shoved his way past their legs just as Scott slid the Porsche into the driveway. Ashley was out of the car almost as quickly as the dog exited, and she immediately bent down and stuck her face into his muzzle, then let him cover her with wet dog affection. Scott, too, stepped out of the car, a little unsure what the drill was going to be. He half-waved at Sally and nodded toward Hope.

"Safe and sound," he said.

Sally crossed the lawn to the drive, pausing only to embrace Ashley. "Don't you think you should come in, and we can figure out some sort of plan?" she said to Scott.

Ashley lifted her head toward her father and mother, waiting for a second. She was aware in that second how rarely they were ever within arm's length of each other. A well-defined distance always marked their meetings.

"It's up to Ashley," Scott said. "She might not want to just dive into the whole thing right now. Maybe she needs some lunch and a moment or two to decompress."

They both looked at Ashley, and she nodded, although she sensed that she was doing something cowardly.

"All right," Sally said with her take-charge lawyer's voice. "This afternoon, then. Say around four or four thirty?"

Scott nodded. Then he gestured toward the house. "Here?"

"Why not?" Sally said.

Scott could think of a dozen good reasons why not, but he managed to stifle them all. "Well, four thirty it is, then. We can have tea. That would be very civilized."

Sally did not respond to the sarcasm. She turned to Ashley. "Is that all you've brought with you?" she said, pointing at the overnight bag.

"That's it," Ashley said.

Hope, standing aside, watching and listening, thought that

Ashley had in truth brought much more. It just wasn't quite as obvious.

Ashley gingerly hip-hopped around the edge of the muddy field and took up a spot where she could see Hope coaching. Nameless was leashed to the end of the bench, but he thumped his tail when he spotted Ashley, then put his head back down. Lions, she thought as she looked over at him. They often sleep as much as twenty hours in an African day. Nameless looked to be closing in on that standard, although he wasn't very lionish in his attitude. Sometimes she wondered whether any of them would have survived if not for him. She was always disappointed that her mother didn't fully recognize Nameless's importance. Rescue dog, she thought. Seeing Eye dog. Guard dog. Nameless had metaphorically managed every role, and now he was old, nearly retired, but still almost a brother.

She let her eyes scan across the distant range of hills. The locals called the Holyoke Range a group of mountains, but she understood that that was exaggerating their significance more than a little. The Rockies are mountains, she thought. The local hills were given some undeserved grandeur, although on a fine fall afternoon they made up for their lack of elevation with generous streaks of red, brown, and russet.

She turned back to watch the game. It wasn't hard to imagine the time some five years earlier when she would have been out there in blue and white, running up and down the left side. She had always been a good player, although not like Hope. Hope always played with a kind of reckless freedom, but something had always made Ashley hold herself back.

She felt a curious thrill when the girl playing her old position scored the winning goal. She waited through the cheers and handshakes, then saw Hope unleash Nameless and roll a ball out toward the center of the field. Just one, Ashley realized, and not thrown nearly as far as he was once capable of retrieving. She watched as he gathered up the ball and gleefully pushed it back to Hope with his nose and forelegs, filled with dog joy. As Hope scooped up the ball and tossed it into a mesh bag, she saw Ashley standing to the side.

"Hey, Killer, you made it over. What did you think?"

Hearing the nickname that Hope had given her in her first varsity year made Ashley smile. Hope had come up with the name because Ashley had been too reticent on the field, too shy around the older players. So Hope had taken her aside and told her that when she was playing, she was to stop being the Ashley who worried about people's feelings and transform herself into Killer, who would always play hard, give no quarter and not expect any, and do whatever it took to walk off the field at the end knowing that she had left everything she had out on the pitch. The two of them had kept this secondary persona between themselves, not sharing it with either Sally or Scott or, indeed, any of the rest of the team. And Ashley had at first thought it silly, but had then come to appreciate it.

"They look good. Strong."

Hope looked past her. "Sally didn't come with you?"

Ashley shook her head.

"We're too young. Not enough experience," Hope replied, but she couldn't hide her disappointment behind her words. "But if we don't get intimidated, we might just do okay."

Ashley nodded. She wondered if the same could be said for her situation.

Scott sat a little uncomfortably in the center of the living room couch flanked by empty spaces on either side. Each of the three women was in a chair by herself, across from him. It had an odd formality to it, and he imagined that it was a little like sitting in a grand jury hearing room.

"Well," he said briskly, "I guess the first thing is, what do we really know about this fellow who seems to be bothering Ashley? I mean, what sort of guy is he? Where does he come from? The basics."

He looked over at Ashley, who looked as if she were sitting on a sharp edge.

"I've already told you what I know," she said. "Which isn't really that much."

She was coldly waiting for one of the other three to add something along the lines of *Well, you knew enough to let him into your place for a one-night stand,* but no one said this.

"I guess what I'm getting at, really," Scott said quickly, filling up a small silence, "is that we don't know if this guy O'Connell will just respond to a simple talking-to. He might. He might not. But a modest show of determination . . ."

"I tried to do that," Ashley said.

"Yes, I know. You did the right thing, really. But now I'm suggesting a little more forcefulness. Like me," Scott said. "Don't you think the first step here is not to assume the problem is greater than it is? Maybe all that's required is a bit of a showing. Dad muscle."

Sally nodded. "Maybe we can make it two-pronged. Scott, you go say to this guy, 'Leave her alone,' and at the same time we sweeten the approach by offering some cash. Something substantial, like five grand or so. That has to be a significant amount of money to someone working in gas stations and trying to get a degree in computer sciences on the side."

"A bribe to leave Ashley alone?" Scott asked. "Does that sort of thing work?"

"In many of the family disputes, divorces, child-custody cases, that sort of thing, my experience has been that a monetary settlement goes a long way."

"I'll take your word for that." Scott didn't believe her. He also had his doubts that talking to O'Connell would make any difference. But he knew the simplest path had to be tried first. "But suppose—"

Sally held up her hand, cutting off his question. "Let's not get ahead of ourselves here. The guy has behaved creepily. But as best as I can see, he hasn't really broken any laws yet. I mean, down the line we could talk about private eyes, calling the police, getting a restraining order—"

"Those sure work," Scott said sarcastically. Sally ignored him.

"—or examining other legal means. We could even have

Ashley move out of Boston. It would be a setback, sure, but it's always a possibility. But I think we should try the easiest first."

"Okay," Scott said, glad that Sally was thinking more or less along the same lines he was. "What's the drill?"

"Ashley calls the guy. Sets up another meeting. Take cash and your father. Do it in public. A little no-nonsense, forceful conversation. Hopefully, end of story."

Scott started to shake his head, but stopped. It made some sense to him. At least, enough sense to pursue it. He decided that he would follow Sally's plan, with a wrinkle or variation of his own.

Hope had remained silent throughout the conversation. Sally turned to her. "What do you think?"

"I think it's an appropriate approach," Hope said, although she did not believe any of it.

Scott was abruptly angry that Hope had been given any opportunity to speak. He wanted to say that she had no standing in the room, shouldn't even be here. Be reasonable, he told himself. Even if it's irritating. "Well, that's the plan, then. At least for starters, and until we know it won't work."

Sally nodded. "So, Scott, did you really want tea, or was that one of your jokes earlier?"

•

"I just have trouble believing . . . ," I started, then I stopped and decided to try a different tack. "I mean, they had to have some idea . . ."

"What they were up against?" she asked, but didn't wait for an answer. "They didn't know about the assault on the erstwhile boyfriend. They didn't know about the, ah, *accident* Ashley's friend had after their dinner. They didn't know anything about Michael O'Connell's reputation, nor the *impressions* he'd made on coworkers, teachers, you name it. The critical information that might have led them in a different direction. All they knew was—what was the word Ashley kept using? He was a *creep*. What an innocent word."

"Still, *talking to him*? Or *offering money*? Why would they think for a minute that this approach might work?"

"Why wouldn't it work? Isn't that what people do?"

"Yes, but—"

"You second-guess instantly. People always believe that they would have answers when the truth is, they wouldn't. What alternatives did they have, right then?"

"Well, they might have been more aggressive."

"They didn't know!" Her voice suddenly picked up in pitch and passion. She leaned toward me and I could see her eyes narrow and flash in frustration and anger. "Why is it so hard for people to understand how powerful the forces of denial are within each and every one of us? We don't *want* to believe the worst!"

She stopped, taking a deep breath. I started to speak, then she held up her hand.

"Don't you make an excuse," she said. "Don't you imagine that you wouldn't want to believe the safest thing, when in reality the most dangerous thing was lurking right there in front of you."

She took another deep breath. "Except for Hope. She saw it. Or, at least, she had some inkling . . . the vaguest of notions. But for one reason or another, and all of them goddamn wrong and foolish, she couldn't say anything. Not then."

14

Foolishness

Scott shifted about uncomfortably at the bar, nursing his bottle of beer, trying to keep one eye on the doorway to the restaurant and the other on Ashley sitting alone in a quiet booth. She kept looking up, playing with the silverware on the table, drumming her fingers nervously against the wood, while she waited.

He had coached her on what to say when she had called

Michael O'Connell and on what she was to do when he arrived. Scott had an envelope with $5,000 in hundred-dollar bills stuck in his jacket pocket. The envelope was stuffed to overflow, and it would make for an impressive wad of cash when tossed down on a tabletop; he was counting on it having an impact greater than the actual sum. As he thought about the money, he could feel sweat sticking unpleasantly beneath his arms. But he guessed that he was far better off than his daughter. She was all knotted up inside. Still, he believed her theatrical abilities would carry her through the meeting. Scott cleared his throat and took another long sip of beer. He flexed his muscles beneath his sports coat and reminded himself for the tenth time that day that a person willing to bully a woman was likely to cower when confronted with someone his own size and strength who was older and more resourceful. He'd spent much of his adult life dealing with students not much different from Michael O'Connell, and he'd intimidated more than a few of them. He signaled to the bartender to bring him another beer.

Ashley, for her part, felt nothing but cold ice and hot tension within.

When she had managed to reach O'Connell on his cell phone, she had been cautious, following a modest script that she and Scott had worked out on the drive back to Boston. Nonconfrontational, but not suggestive, either. The point, she had kept reminding herself, was to get him face-to-face, so that if it was necessary, her father could intervene.

"Michael, it's Ashley."

"Where have you been?"

"I had some out-of-town business."

"What kind of business?"

"The kind we should talk about. Why didn't you meet me at the museum the other day?"

"I didn't like the setup. And I didn't want to hear what you were going to say. Ashley, I really believe we've got a good thing going here."

"If you believe that, then meet me for dinner tonight. Same place we went for our first and only date. Okay?"

"Only," he had said. "But only if you promise it's not going to be the big kiss-off. I need you, Ashley. And you need me. I know it."

He had sounded small. Almost childlike. It had thrown her into some confusion.

She'd hesitated. "Okay, I promise. Eight tonight, okay?"

"That would be great. We've got lots to talk about. Like, the future."

"Great," she had breezily lied. She had hung up, and without saying a word about how scared she'd been when he'd followed her through the rain to the T. Not a word about dead flowers. Not a word about anything that truly chilled her.

Now, she made a conscious effort to keep her eyes off her father at the bar, watching the doorway, aware that it was nearly eight, and hoping that there wouldn't be a replay of the other day. The plan she had worked out with her father was simple: Get to the restaurant early, sit in a booth, so that when O'Connell came in, he would be trapped in his seat by Scott's sudden appearance, unable to walk out before they'd had a chance to speak to him. The two of them would be like a tag team, forcing him to agree to leave her alone. Strength in numbers. Strength in the public place. Psychologically, her father had insisted, they were more than a match for him, and they were going to control the situation from start to finish. *Just be strong. Be firm. Be explicit. Leave no room for doubt.* Scott had been decisive as he'd described what would happen. *Remember: There are two of us. We're smarter. We're better educated. We have greater financial resources. End of story.* She reached out and took a sip of water from the glass in front of her. Her lips were dry and parched. She suddenly felt as if she were adrift on a life raft.

As she placed the glass down, she saw O'Connell come through the door. She half-lifted herself up in her seat and waved to him. She saw him quickly sweep his eyes across the room, but she wasn't sure whether he'd seen Scott at the bar. She stole a quick look in her father's direction and saw that he had visibly stiffened.

She took a deep breath and whispered to herself, "Okay, Ashley. Up curtain. Cue music. Showtime."

O'Connell moved rapidly across the room and quickly slid into the seat across from her in the booth.

"Hey, Ashley," he said briskly. "Boy, it's great to see you."

She was unable to control herself. "Why didn't you come to lunch like we agreed? And then, when you tailed me . . ."

"Did it scare you?" he responded, as if he were listening to her tell a small joke.

"Yes. If you say you love me, why would you do something like that?"

He merely smiled, and it occurred to Ashley that she might not want to know the answer to that question. Michael O'Connell tossed his head back a little way, then bent forward. He tried to reach across the table and take her hand, but she swiftly put them both under the table on her lap. She didn't want him to touch her. He half-snorted, half-laughed, and leaned back.

"So, I guess this really isn't a nice romantic dinner for two, is it?"

"No."

"And I guess you were lying to me when you said this wasn't going to be the big kiss-off, weren't you?"

"Michael, I—"

"I don't like it when people I love don't tell me the truth. Makes me angry."

"I've been trying to—"

"I don't think you fully understand me, Ashley," he said calmly. No raised voice. No indication that they were speaking of anything more complex than the weather. "Don't you think I have feelings, too?"

He said this in a flat, almost matter-of-fact voice. *No, I don't,* flashed through her head, but instead, she said, "Look, Michael, why does this have to be harder than it already is?"

He smiled again. "I don't think it is hard at all. Because

it's not going to happen. I love you, Ashley. And you love me. You just don't know it yet. But you will, soon enough."

"No, I don't, Michael." As soon as she spoke, she knew it was the wrong thing to say. She was being concrete, and at the same time talking about the wrong thing, which was *love,* when she needed to be saying something far different.

"Don't you believe in love at first sight?" he asked almost playfully.

"Michael, please. Why can't you just leave me alone?"

He hesitated and she saw a small smile flit across his face, and she had the horrible thought, *He's enjoying this.*

"It seems to me that I'm going to have to prove my love to you," he said. Still smiling, almost grinning.

"You don't have to prove anything to me."

His voice sounded smug. "You're wrong. Completely wrong. I might even say *dead* wrong, but I wouldn't want to give you an inaccurate impression."

Ashley took a sharp, deep breath and realized nothing was going the way she'd hoped it would, then lifted her right hand to her hair, pushing it back from her face twice. This was the signal for her father to inject himself. Out of the corner of her eye, she saw him bolt from his seat at the bar and cross the small restaurant in three huge strides. As planned, he stood at the table, blocking O'Connell from rising from the booth.

"I don't think you are listening to her," Scott said. He spoke quietly, but with a cold forcefulness that he used on reluctant students.

O'Connell kept his eyes on Ashley.

"So, you thought you needed help?" he asked.

She nodded.

He slowly pivoted in his seat and looked up at Scott, as if measuring him.

"Hello, Professor," he said calmly. "Won't you have a seat?"

Hope quietly watched Sally as she worked on the *New York Times* crossword puzzle left over from the previous Sunday.

She never worked in pencil, tapping her pen against her front teeth, before finally committing letters to blocks and slowly, steadily filling in the blank spaces. The silences that she had become accustomed to, Hope thought, were growing even more frequent. She looked over at Sally and wondered what was making her so unhappy.

"Sally, don't you think we should talk about this guy that Ashley seems to have taken up with?"

Sally lifted her head when she heard Hope's question. She had been about to write down the answer to 7 ACROSS, four letters, the clue being *Murderous Clown* and the word being *Gacy*. She hesitated. "I don't know what there is to talk about. Scott should be able to handle this with Ashley. I'm hoping that he'll call sometime this evening and say it's all straightened out. *Finito.* Kaput. On with everything else. We're just out our share of the five grand."

"You're not afraid that this guy might be worse than we think?"

Sally shrugged. "He sounds to me like a nasty guy, sure. But Scott is pretty capable at dealing with college students, so my guess is, he's out of Ashley's life any minute now."

Hope framed her next question carefully. "In your experience, like in divorce cases and domestic disputes, are people bought off that easily?"

She knew that the answer was no and that on far more than a few occasions she had listened to Sally as she had vented at the dinner table, or even in bed later, over the pigheadedness of clients and their families.

"Well," Sally said with a lack of urgency that infuriated Hope, "I think we should just wait and see. No use in preparing for a problem that we don't know exists."

Hope shook her head. She couldn't help herself. "That's the damn stupidest thing I've heard in some time," she replied, her voice rising slightly. "We don't know if a storm is going to hit, so why buy candles, batteries, and extra food? We don't know that we're going to get the flu, so why get a shot?"

Sally put down the crossword puzzle. "Okay," she said, irritation creeping into her own words, "precisely what sort of batteries would you like to buy? What sort of inoculation is out there?"

Hope looked across at her partner of so many years and thought how little she really knew about Sally and about herself. They lived in a world where normal was defined differently, and Hope thought sometimes it was nothing but minefields.

"I can't answer you, you know that," she said slowly. "I just think we should be doing something, and instead, we're sitting around waiting for Scott to call and tell us everything is back to the way it was, and I don't imagine for an instant that we're going to get that call. Or, indeed, whether we deserve that call."

"Deserve?"

"Think about it while you finish your puzzle. I'm going to read for a bit." Hope took a deep breath, thinking that there were some far greater puzzles that Sally could be working on.

Sally nodded, dropping her eyes to the puzzle page in front of her. She wanted to say something to Hope, something reassuring, something affectionate, something that would defuse some of the tension around their house, but instead, she looked down and saw that 3 DOWN was *What the Muse Sang,* and she remembered that the opening of Homer's *Iliad* was "Sing, O muse, of the anger of Achilles." There were four blank boxes, with the last letter needing to be *E,* and so it was not hard for her to come up with *rage.*

Scott slid into the booth, pushing Michael O'Connell into the corner, as he'd planned. It was a tight fit. The waitress took that moment to arrive at the table, menus in hand.

"Give us a minute or two," Scott said to the waitress.

"Bring me a beer," O'Connell said. Then he turned to Scott. "I figure you've got this round."

There was a momentary silence, and then O'Connell

turned to Ashley. "You're filled with surprises today. Don't you really think that all this is between you and me?"

"I tried to tell you," she said, "but you wouldn't listen."

"So you thought bringing in your father . . ." He pivoted slightly and stared at Scott. "Well, I don't know. Just what exactly is he supposed to do?"

This question was directed at Ashley, but Scott answered, "I'm just here to help you understand that when she says it's all over, that means it's all over."

Again Michael O'Connell took a long time assessing Scott.

"Not exactly muscle. Not exactly persuasion. So, Professor, what's your deal? What have you got in mind?"

"I think it's time for you to leave Ashley alone. Get on with your life, so she can get on with hers. She's busy. Working. Going to grad school. Hasn't really got the time for a long-term relationship. Certainly not the one that you seem to suggest. I'm here to do what I can to help you see that."

O'Connell didn't seem fazed in the slightest by what Scott said. "Why do you think this is any of your business?"

"Your refusal to listen to what Ashley has said has made it my business."

O'Connell smiled. "Maybe. Maybe not."

The waitress brought O'Connell his beer, and he drank half of it in a large gulp. He grinned again. "What is it, Professor, that you got that's going to persuade me not to love Ashley? How do you know we're not perfect for each other? What do you know about me? I'll tell you: nothing. Maybe I don't look like what you expected for her, and maybe I'm not the sort of BMW-driving young executive with a Harvard MBA that you're counting on, but I'm a pretty capable guy at lots of things, and she could do a lot worse. Just because I don't fit your profile, I don't know that that means a damn thing."

Scott wasn't sure how to respond. O'Connell had thrust the conversation in a different direction than he'd expected.

"I don't want to know you," Scott said. "All I want is for

you to leave Ashley alone. I am willing to do whatever is necessary to help you understand that."

O'Connell paused, then said, "Somehow I doubt that. Whatever is necessary? I'm not thinking that that's really true."

"Name a price," Scott replied coldly.

"A price?"

"You know what I'm saying. Name a price."

"You want me to put a price tag on my feelings for Ashley?"

"Stop screwing around," Scott said. O'Connell's grin and the easygoing way he was handling the conversation were beyond irritating.

"I could never do that. And I don't want your money."

Scott reached into his jacket pocket and pulled out the $5,000 in the white envelope.

"What's that?" O'Connell asked.

"Five grand. Just for giving Ashley and me your word that you will stay out of her life."

"You want to pay me?"

"That's right."

"I never asked you for any money, did I?"

"No."

"So, this money isn't in response to anything I demanded, is it?"

"No. All I want is your word."

O'Connell turned to Ashley. "I never asked you for money, did I?"

She shook her head.

"I can't hear you," O'Connell said.

"No, you have never asked me for money."

O'Connell reached across and picked up the cash. "If I took it, it would be a gift, right?"

"In return for a promise."

He smiled. "All right. I don't want the money. But I'll give you the promise. I promise."

O'Connell kept the cash in his hand.

"You're going to leave her alone? Stay out of her life? Walk away and never bother her again?"

"That's what you want, right?"

"That's right."

O'Connell thought for a moment, then said, "Everyone gets what they want, huh?"

"Right."

"Except me." He looked over at Ashley, freezing her with a narrow look that she could not put a word to. The harshness of the look was compounded by a contradictory, devil-may-care smile that Ashley thought was one of the coldest things she had ever seen.

"That make this trip worthwhile, Professor?"

Scott did not answer. He was half-expecting O'Connell to throw the money down on the table or into his face, and he tensed his muscles, maintaining a rigid control over his emotions.

But instead of some dramatic gesture, O'Connell turned and once again stared at Ashley, letting his eyes burrow into her, so intensely that she squirmed in her seat. "Do you know what the Beatles sang, back in your father's time?"

She shook her head.

" 'I don't care too much for money, money can't buy me love . . . ' "

Keeping his eyes on Ashley, O'Connell slid the envelope into his jacket pocket, confusing the two of them. Then, still staring at her, he said, "Okay, Professor, time to let me up. I don't think I'll stay for dinner, after all. But thanks for the beer."

Scott moved aside, standing at the edge of the table while O'Connell, moving with surprising agility, slid out and stood. For a second he remained, his gaze still fixed on Ashley. Then, with a small grin, he turned about abruptly and rapidly walked across the restaurant toward the exit without once looking back.

They remained silent for almost a minute. "What just happened?" Ashley asked.

Scott did not reply. He was unsure. The waitress sidled back up, saying, "So, just two for dinner?" as she handed them menus.

Outside Ashley's apartment, the night seemed to have painted itself into shadows and shafts of stray distant light from streetlamps that barely argued against the growing autumn dark. There was no place to park, so Scott pulled the Porsche in front of a fire hydrant. He left the car running and turned to his daughter.

"Maybe you should come out west for a couple of days. Just until we're sure that this guy stands by what he said. Stay a couple of days at my place, then maybe a little bit of time with your mother. Let a little time and a little distance work for you."

"I shouldn't be the one who has to run and hide," Ashley said. "I have classes. I have a job."

"I know, but perhaps we should err on the side of caution."

"I hate that. I just hate it."

"I know. But, honey, I don't know what else to say."

Ashley sighed, then turned to her father and smiled. "He just freaked me out a little. It will be okay. Guys like him, Dad, they're really cowards when you get right down to it. Maybe he was strutting a bit when he took the money, but really he was pretty shut down. He'll go out, call me names when he's drinking with his buddies, and move on. I don't much like it, and you're out some cash . . ."

"Damnedest thing," Scott said. "He said he didn't want it, then he put it in his pocket. It was almost like he was tape-recording us. Saying one thing, doing another. Creepy."

"Well, let's hope it's all over."

"Yeah. Look, here's the drill. Any sign of him, and I mean anything, and you call home. Get your mom on the case, or Hope or me, right away. Anytime, day or night, got it? And I mean any sort of suspicion that he's been tailing you or calling you, or harassing you, or even just watching you, and you call. You get a bad *feeling* and you call, okay?"

"Yes. Look, Dad, Michael creeped me out, too. I'm not looking to be heroic here. I just want my life to go back to what it was, even if it wasn't all *that* perfect."

She sighed again, undid her seat belt, grabbed her purse, and took out her apartment keys.

"You want me to walk you up?"

"No. Just wait until I'm inside, though, if you don't mind."

"Look, honey, I don't mind anything. I just want you to be happy. And I'd like to forget about this whole incident, and Michael O'Connell, and watch you get your master's or doctorate in art history and have a wonderful life. That's what I want, and your mother, too. And that's what's going to happen. Trust me. And before too long you're going to meet someone special, and all this will just be like a little blip on the past. You'll never think about it again."

"A little nightmare blip." She leaned across and kissed him on the cheek. "Thanks, Dad. And thanks for driving and coming and helping and just, I don't know, for being who you are."

This made him feel quite wonderful, but he shook his head. "You're the special one."

Ashley got out of the car, and Scott gestured her toward the front of the apartment building. "Now get a good night's rest and call us tomorrow just to touch base."

She nodded. Scott had one other curious thought, which seemed to come out of some darkened place within him, and before he could stop himself, he asked, "Hey, Ashley, one thing bothered me."

She was about to shut the car door, but stopped and leaned in. "What's that?"

"Had you told O'Connell anything about me? Or your mother?"

"No . . . ," she said hesitantly.

"Like on that first and only bad date, did you talk about us at all?"

She shook her head. "Why?"

He smiled. "No reason. No reason at all. Get inside. Call tomorrow."

Ashley smiled, pushed the hair back from her eyes, and nodded. Scott gave her another smile, said, "It will only take me a couple of minutes to get home at this time of night. All the troopers have the night off."

"Don't ever grow up, Dad. It would disappoint me." Then Ashley closed the door and bounded up the steps to her building. It only took her a second or two to open the outside door, enter the sally port, then open the second door. She turned as she entered and waved to Scott, who still waited until he saw her heading up the stairs before he put the car in gear and pulled out of the hydrant slot, wondering, in that second, just precisely how it was that O'Connell had known to call him *professor*.

•

"So, they felt safe?"

"Yes. Safe enough. Not that exhilarating we-dodged-a-bullet sensation, but enough right for that moment. They still had some doubts and some concerns. Some residual anxiety. But, for the most part, they actually felt safe."

"But they shouldn't have?"

"Would I be telling you all this if that was the end of it all? Five thousand dollars and a so-long-see-you-later fare-thee-well?"

"Of course not."

"I told you. This is a story about dying."

When I failed to respond, she looked up and out a window. Sunlight seemed to catch her face, illuminating her profile. "Doesn't it make you wonder," she said slowly, "how things can be turned upside down in one's life so easily? I mean, what protects us? I suppose the religious fundamentalist would say faith. The academic would say knowledge. The physician might say skill and learning. The police officer might say a nine-millimeter semiautomatic pistol. The politician might say the law. But really, what is it?"

"You don't expect me to answer that question, do you?"

She tossed her head back and laughed out loud. "No. Not at all. At least, not yet. Of course, neither could Ashley."

15

Three Complaints

Each in his or her own way felt unease over the following days, almost as if a low-hanging cloud of deep gray fog had settled onto their lives. When Scott replayed the meeting with Michael O'Connell over again in his mind, it seemed curiously inconclusive one instant, then strangely decisive the next.

He told Ashley that he wanted to hear from her daily, just to make sure that things were okay, and so they set up a regular early-evening phone call. Ashley, even with her fiercely independent streak, had not objected. He was unaware that Sally had proposed precisely the same arrangement.

For her part, Sally suddenly found that nothing in her life seemed in order. It was a little as if she had become detached from all the anchors in her existence, with the single exception being Ashley, and even that was tenuous. The purpose for her daily phone calls to her daughter, she came to understand, had as much to do with regaining some sort of foothold on who she was herself as with being reassured that Ashley was okay. After all, she told herself, the incident with O'Connell was merely the sort of commonplace unpleasantness that all young people go through at some point.

But far more disturbing to her was the less-than-effective work she was doing in her law practice, and the growing tension between Hope and herself. Clearly, something was wrong, but she could not bring herself to focus on it. Instead, she threw herself into her various cases, but in a distracted, erratic way, where she would devote too much time to a small issue dogging one case, while ignoring large problems that shouted for attention in others.

Hope merely dragged herself through each day, wondering what was happening. Sally wouldn't really fill her in, she couldn't call Scott, and for the first time in all the years she and Sally had been together, she thought it was inappropriate for her to call Ashley. She threw herself into the team, as it pushed toward the play-offs, and into her counseling work with struggling underclassmen. She felt as if she were walking across shards of broken glass.

When Hope received an urgent message from the school's dean of faculty, it took her by surprise. The command was cryptic: Be in my office at 2 p.m. Sharp.

Some thin, wispy clouds were scudding across a slate-colored sky as Hope hurried across the campus to be on time for her meeting. She could feel a sullen pre-winter cold creeping through the air. The dean's office was in the main administration building, a remodeled, white Victorian home, with wide, brown wooden doors, and a fireplace in a reception area with a log burning. None of the students ever went there unless they were in deep trouble.

She pushed her way in, nodded to some of the office workers, and went up to the second floor, where the dean of faculty had his small office. He was a veteran of the school and still taught a section of Latin and a class in ancient Greek, clinging to classics that were increasingly unpopular.

"Dean Mitchell?" Hope said, peeking her head through his door. "You wanted to see me?"

In her time at the school, she had spoken with Stephen Mitchell perhaps a dozen times, maybe less. They had served on a committee or two together, in years past, and she knew he had happily attended a championship game she had coached, although his own preference was generally for the boys' football team. She had always thought him to be funny, in a grumpy prep school, Mr. Chips sort of way, and never thought of him as judgmental—which was her standard for most people. If they could accept who she was, then she was willing to go more than the extra mile to accept them. It went with the territory of living *an alternative lifestyle,* which was the odious phrase used where Sally and she lived, and which she despised, because it seemed utterly devoid of romance.

"Ah, Hope, yes, yes, yes, please do come in."

Dean Mitchell spoke with an antiquarian's wondrously precise sense of words. No slang words or verbal shortcuts for him. He was known to write comments like *I frequently despair for the intellectual future of the human race* on student papers. He gestured toward a large red overstuffed leather wing chair in front of his desk. It was the sort of chair that swallowed one up, making Hope feel ridiculously small.

"I got your message," Hope said. "How can I help you, Stephen?"

Dean Mitchell fumbled around for a moment, then spun and looked out the window, as if gathering himself to say something. She did not have long to wait.

"Hope, I believe we have a significant problem."

"A problem?"

"Yes. Someone has lodged an extremely serious complaint against you."

"A complaint? What sort of complaint?"

Dean Mitchell hesitated, as if already offended by what he had to say. He ran a hand through thin, gray hair, then adjusted his eyeglasses, before speaking in a heartbreaking tone, as if he were telling someone of a death in their family.

"It would fall under the unfortunate and common rubric of a sexual harassment complaint."

At nearly the same time that Hope was seated across from Dean Mitchell and hearing the words that she had dreaded almost all of her adult life, Scott was finishing up a session with an upperclassman from his Revolutionary War Readings seminar. The student was struggling. "Don't you see caution in Washington's words?" Scott asked. "But at the same time, isn't there a sense of determination?"

The student nodded. "It still seems too abstract. To deduce motive, opportunity. All the things that we believe Washington innately understood."

Scott smiled. "You know, the temperature tonight is supposed to really drop down. Frost expected, maybe even some flurries of snow. Why don't you take some of Washington's letters outside and read them by flashlight, or even better yet, by candlelight, around midnight right in the middle of the quad. See if they make some additional sense to you then."

The student smiled. "Seriously? Outside in the dark?"

"Absolutely. And, assuming you don't catch pneumonia, because you should only take a single woolen blanket out there to keep you warm and you should wear shoes that have holes in the soles, we can continue this discussion, say, middle of the week. Okay?"

The phone on his desk rang and he picked up the receiver as the student's back disappeared through the door. "Yes? Scott Freeman here."

"Scott, this is William Burris down at Yale."

"Hello, Professor. This is a surprise."

Scott stiffened in his seat. In the world of teaching American history, receiving a call from William Burris was similar to getting a call from the heavens. Pulitzer Prize winner, best-selling author, seated at an endowed professorship at one of the nation's leading institutions, and adviser, upon occasion, to presidents and other heads of state, Burris had impeccable credentials, with a taste for $2,000 Savile Row suits, which he had custom-made when he lectured at Oxford or Cambridge, or anywhere that could meet his six-figure fee.

"Yes, it has been some time, hasn't it? When did we last meet? At some society meeting or another?" Burris meant one of the many historical societies that Scott was a member of, and all of which would kill to have Burris list his name on their roster.

"A couple of years, I would imagine. How are you, Professor?"

"Fine, fine," Burris replied. Scott pictured him seated, gray-haired and imperious, in an office much like his own, except considerably bigger, with a secretary taking messages from agents, producers, editors, kings, and prime ministers, and shooing away students. "Yes, I am fine, even with the looming despair of a pair of losses by the football team to the evil empires of both Princeton and Harvard, an awful possibility this year."

"Perhaps Admissions can come up with an improved quarterback for next year?"

"One would hope. But, ah, Scott, that is not the purpose of this call."

"I did not think so. What can I do for you, Professor?"

"Do you recall a piece you wrote for us at the *Journal of American History* some three years ago? The subject was military movement in the days directly after the battles of Trenton and Princeton, when Washington made so many key and, dare I say it, prescient decisions?"

"Of course, Professor." Scott did not publish much, and this essay had been particularly helpful at influencing his own department not to cut back on the American history core courses.

"It was a fine piece, Scott," Burris said slowly. "Evocative and provocative."

"Thank you. But I fail to see what—"

"The work, ah, the writing, ah, did you have any, ah, outside assistance on formulating your themes and conclusions?"

"I'm not sure that I understand, Professor."

"The work, the writing, it was all your own? And the research, as well?"

"Yes. I had a student assistant or two, mostly seniors, help with some of the citations. But the writing and the conclusions were my own. I don't understand what you are driving at, Professor."

"There has been a most unfortunate allegation made in regard to that piece."

"An allegation?"

"Yes. A charge of academic dishonesty."

"What?"

"Plagiarism, Scott. I'm most sorry to say."

"But that's absurd!"

"The allegation in front of us cites some troubling similarities between your piece and a paper written in a graduate seminar at another institution."

Scott took a deep breath. Instantly dizziness circled around him, and he grasped the edge of his desk as if to steady himself.

"Who has made this complaint?"

"Therein lies a problem," Burris replied. "It came to me electronically, and it was anonymous."

"Anonymous!"

"But regardless of its authorship, it cannot be ignored. Not in the current academic climate. And certainly not in the public's eye. The newspapers are voracious when it comes to misdeeds or missteps in the academy. Likely, I hesitate to say, to jump to many erroneous conclusions, in a most embarrassing and ultimately incredibly damaging fashion. So, it would seem to me that the best approach here is to nip this allegation in the bud. Assuming, of course, that you can find your notes and go over every line, chapter, and verse, so that the *Journal* is satisfied that the allegations are incorrect."

"Of course, but . . . ," Scott sputtered. He was almost at a loss for words.

"We must, in this day of rampant second-guessing and dreadful microscopic analysis, seem purer than Lot's wife, alas."

"I know, but . . . ," Scott was stammering.

"I will send you by overnight courier the complaint and the actual verbiage. And then, I suspect, we should speak again."

"Yes, yes, of course."

"And, Scott"—the professor's voice was even, suddenly

cold and almost devoid of tone and energy—"I do hope that we can work all this out privately. But, please, do not underestimate the threat involved. I say this to you as a friend, and as a fellow historian. I've seen once promising careers destroyed for far less. Far, far less." The emphasis in the final words was unnecessary, but undeniably true.

Scott nodded. *Friend* was not a word he would have used, because when word inevitably got out in academic circles about this charge, he was likely to have none left.

Sally was staring out of the window at the dropping light of the late afternoon. She was in that odd state where a great deal was on her mind, and yet she wasn't specifically thinking about anything. There was a knock at her door and she spun about to see an office assistant standing sheepishly in the portal, a large white envelope in her hand.

"Sally," the assistant said, "this just came by courier for you. I wonder if it isn't something important . . ."

Sally could think of no pleading nor any other document that she was expecting to arrive in such urgent fashion, but she nodded. "Who is it from?"

"The state bar association."

Sally took the envelope and looked at it oddly, turning it over in her hand. She could not recall when she had received something from the association, other than dues requests and invitations to dinners, seminars, and speeches that she never attended. None of these ever came by overnight mail, return receipt required.

She tore open the package and removed a single letter. Addressed to her, it came from the head of the state bar, a man she knew only by reputation, a prominent member of a big-time Boston law firm, active in Democratic Party circles with frequent appearances on television talk shows and in newspaper society pages. He was, Sally knew, way out of her league.

She read the short letter carefully. Each second that passed seemed to darken the room around her.

Dear Ms. Freeman-Richards:

This is to inform you of a complaint received by the
state bar association regarding your handling of the
client accounts in the pending matter of *Johnson v.
Johnson,* currently before Judge V. Martinson in Superior Court, Family Division.

The complaint states that funds associated with this
matter have been diverted into a private account in your
name. This is a violation of M.G.L. 302, Section 43,
and is also a felony under U.S.S. 112, Section 11.

Please be advised that the bar association will need your
sworn affidavit explaining this matter within the week, or
it will be referred to the Hampshire County District Attorney's Office and to the United States Attorney for the
Western District of Massachusetts for prosecution.

Sally thought each word of the letter was caught in her
throat, choking her like some wayward piece of meat. "Impossible," she said out loud. "Absolutely fucking impossible."

The obscenity clattered around in the room. Sally took a
deep breath and spun to her computer. Typing rapidly, she
brought up the divorce action cited in the letter from the
bar association head. *Johnson v. Johnson* was not by any
description one of her more complicated cases, although it
was marred by real animosity between her client, the wife,
and her estranged husband. He was a local eye surgeon, father of their two preteen children, a serial cheater, whom
Sally had caught trying to move joint assets into an offshore, Bahamas bank account. He had done this particularly clumsily, taking out large cash amounts from their
jointly held brokerage account, then charging plane tickets
to the Bahamas on his Visa card, in order to get the extra
mileage. Sally had successfully moved the court to seize
assets and transfer them into her client account pending the
final dissolution of the marriage, which was scheduled for

sometime after Christmas. By her reckoning, the client account should have had somewhere in excess of $400,000 in it.

It did not.

She stared at the screen and saw that there was less than half that amount.

"That can't be," she said, again out loud.

As close to panic as she had ever been, Sally started to go over every transaction in that account. In the past few days more than a quarter million had been extracted through electronic means and transferred to nearly a dozen other accounts. She was unable to access these dozen through the computer, as they were in a series of different names, both of individuals whom she did not recognize and clearly questionable corporations. She also, to her growing anxiety, saw that the last transfer from her client account was made directly into her own checking account. It was for $15,000 and was dated barely twenty-four hours beforehand.

"That cannot be," she repeated. "How . . ."

She stopped, right at that second, because the answer to that question was likely to be complicated, and she had no ready answer. All she knew, right at that moment, was that she was likely to be in a great deal of trouble.

•

"There's something I just don't quite get."

"What's that?" she asked patiently.

"The *why* for Michael O'Connell's love. I mean, he kept saying he *loved* her, but what had he done in any way, shape, or form that came close to anything that anyone would understand as love?"

"Not too damn much, right?"

"Right. Makes me think that there was something far different on his mind."

"You may be correct about that," she replied, as distant, yet as seductive, as always.

She hesitated and, as she often did, seemed to pause to organize her thoughts cautiously. I sensed that she wanted to control the story, but in a way that I couldn't quite see. This made me shift about uncomfortably. I felt I was being used for something.

"I think," she said slowly, "that I should give you the name of a man who might help in this regard. A psychologist. He is an expert on obsessive love." She hesitated again. "Of course, that's what we call it, but in reality, it has little to do with love. We think of love as roses on Valentine's Day or maybe greeting-card sentiments. Chocolates in red, heart-shaped boxes, cherubic cupids with wings and tiny bows and arrows, Hollywood romance. But I think it has little to do with any of those things. Love is really much closer to all sorts of dark things within us."

"You sound cynical," I said. "And callous."

She smiled. "I suppose I sound that way. Coming to know someone like Michael O'Connell can, shall we say, give one a different perspective on what precisely constitutes happiness. As I've said, he redefined things for folks."

She shook her head. She reached down to a table and opened a small drawer, rummaging around for an instant or two, before coming out with a small piece of paper and a pencil. "Here." She wrote down a name. "Talk to this man. Tell him I sent you."

She put her head back and laughed, although nothing was funny. "And tell him that I waive any conflict-of-interest or physician-client privilege. No, better yet"—she wrote something down swiftly on the piece of paper—"I'll do that myself."

16

A Series of Gordian Knots

Ashley moved away from the window cautiously, just as she had every day for more than two weeks.

She was unaware of what was taking place with the three people who constituted her family, focused instead on the near constant sensation that she was being watched. The problem was, every time the feeling threatened to overcome her, she could find no concrete evidence to support it. A quick and sudden turn while walking to a class or to her job at the museum turned up nothing except some surprised and inconvenienced pedestrians behind her. She had taken to darting onto the T just as the train doors were closing, then intensely eyeing all the other passengers as if the old lady reading the *Herald* or the workman in the battered Red Sox cap could be O'Connell in some elaborate disguise. At home, she edged to the corner of the window in her apartment and peered up and down her street. She listened at her door for some telltale noise before exiting. She started varying her route when she went out, even if only heading to the grocery store or pharmacy. She purchased a telephone with caller ID. She spoke to her neighbors, asking them if any of them had noticed anything out of the ordinary or, in particular, if they had seen a man fitting Michael O'Connell's description hanging around the entranceway or by the street corner or maybe in back. None were able to help, in that none could recall seeing anyone like him acting suspiciously.

But the more she tried to force herself to imagine that Michael O'Connell wasn't anywhere near her, the closer he actually seemed to be.

She could not put her finger on something concrete and say out loud, "That's him," but dozens of small things, telltale signs, told her that he was neither out of her life nor really keeping much distance. She came home to her apartment one day and discovered that someone had scratched a large *X* in the paint on her door, probably using nothing more sophisticated than a penknife or even a spare key. On another occasion, her mailbox had been opened, and her paltry pile of bills, flyers, credit card offers, and catalogs had been strewn about the foyer.

At the museum where she worked, items on her desk kept being moved. One day the phone would be at her right hand, the next, shifted to her left. One day she came in and found the top drawer locked—something she never did, because she didn't keep anything remotely valuable inside.

Both at work and at her home, her phone would often ring once or twice, then stop. When she picked it up, it buzzed with a dial tone. And when she checked the caller identification, it came up with either a "private party" notation or a number she didn't recognize. She tried hitting *69 several times to redial the incoming call, but each time got a busy signal or electronic interference.

She was unsure what to do. In her daily phone calls with both Sally and Scott, she described some of these things, but not all, because some seemed simply too bizarre to mention. Others seemed to be the sort of ordinary mishaps that plague life—such as when the professor in one of her graduate courses was unable to access her undergraduate transcript electronically, and computer services at her college were unable to discover why a series of blocks were on her files. They removed these, but only after considerable effort.

When Ashley rocked in her chair alone in her apartment, watching the night close in outside, she thought that everything was O'Connell and nothing was O'Connell. With her uncertainty came frustration, followed by outright anger.

After all, she kept insisting to herself, he had given his word. She kept telling herself this, even if she didn't really believe one word of it. And the more she thought about it, the less reassuring it was.

Scott spent a restless night waiting for the package from Professor Burris at Yale to arrive by courier. Few things are more dangerous to an academic career than a charge of plagiarism, and Scott knew that he had to move swiftly and efficiently. His first step had been to find the box in his basement at home where he had stored all his notes for the piece for *The Journal of American History*. Then he had sent e-mail messages to the two students whom he'd enlisted three years earlier to help with the citations and research. He was lucky to have a contact address for both. He did not specify exactly what he had been accused of when he wrote them. He merely said that a fellow historian had asked some questions about the piece he'd authored, and he might need to rely upon their recollections of their work. It was just an effort to put them on alert, as he waited for the material in dispute to arrive on his doorstep.

It was all he could do.

He was at his desk at the college when the overnight deliveryman arrived, carrying a large envelope for Scott. He signed for it quickly and was just tearing into the envelope when the phone rang.

"Professor Freeman?"

"Yes. Who is this?"

"This is Ted Morris over at the college newspaper."

Scott hesitated. "Are you in one of my classes, Mr. Morris? If so . . ."

"No, sir, I'm not."

"I'm quite busy. But what is it I can help you with?"

He could sense some reluctance in the momentary pause before the student replied.

"We have received a tip, an allegation really, and I'm just following it up."

"A tip?"

"Yes."

"I'm not sure that I follow," Scott said, but this was a lie, because he knew exactly what was coming.

"There is an allegation, Professor, that you are engaged in a, well, for lack of a better phrase, an issue of academic integrity." Ted Morris was being careful about what he said.

"Who told you that?"

"Ah, is that relevant, sir?"

"Well, it might be."

"Apparently it came from a disgruntled graduate student at a Southern university. But that's about all I can tell you."

"I don't know that I know any graduate students at any schools down South," Scott said with a little false levity in his voice. "But 'disgruntled' is a description that unfortunately applies to just about every grad student at some point in their academic career. It pretty much goes with the territory, don't you think, Ted?" He dropped the formal *Mr.* from the student's name, just to underscore their respective roles. He had authority and power—or, at the very least, he wanted Ted Morris at the campus newspaper to think this.

Ted Morris paused and, to Scott's immediate dismay, wouldn't be distracted.

"But the question in front of us is simple. Have you been accused—"

"No one has accused me of anything. At least not that I know of," Scott scrambled quickly. "Nothing that isn't completely routine in academic circles—"

Scott took a long breath. He guessed that Ted Morris was writing down every word.

"I understand, Professor. *Routine.* But still, I think I should come speak with you in person."

"I'm pretty busy. But I have office hours on Friday. Come by then."

That would give him several days.

"We're under some deadline pressure here, Professor."

"I can't help you on that. I've always discovered that rushed things are inevitably confused or, worse, erroneous."

This was a bluff. But he needed to put off the student on the phone.

"Okay, Friday. And, Professor, one other thing."

"What's that, Ted?" he said with his most condescending voice.

"You should know that I string for the *Globe* and the *Times.*"

Scott swallowed hard. "Well," he said, affecting as much phony enthusiasm as he could, "that's excellent. There are many fine stories on this campus that those papers should be interested in. Well, see you on Friday, then," Scott said, hoping that he had deflected and obscured enough so that the student would simply wait until Friday before calling the city desk at either paper and with a few short words explode Scott's entire career.

He hung up the telephone thinking that he had never

thought he would be scared, no, terrified, of the sound of a student's voice. Then he quickly bent to the material from Professor Burris, anxiety filling him as he read every word.

Hope went into the ladies' room adjacent to the Admissions Office, knowing it was likely to be the one place on campus where she could be alone for a few moments. As the door shut behind her, she gave in to the turmoil within her and burst out in a deep, unbridled sob of despair.

The accusation against her had arrived at the dean's office via an anonymous e-mail, claiming that Hope had cornered a student in a steamy section of the women's locker room, just outside the showers, when the student was alone after a sports practice. The e-mail described how Hope had fondled the young woman's breasts and reached for her crotch, while all the time whispering to the fifteen-year-old about the many advantages of sex with a woman. When the teenager had resisted the advances, Hope had threatened to manipulate the student's grades if she ever complained to any authorities or to her parents. The e-mail ended by urging the school administration to "take whatever appropriate means necessary" to avoid a lawsuit, and perhaps criminal prosecution. It used such words as *predatory* and *statutory rape* along with *homosexual enlistment* to describe Hope's behavior.

Not one word of it was true. Not one moment described in such near pornographic detail had ever occurred.

Hope doubted the truth would help her in the slightest.

The ugly recitation of events played into all sorts of fears and wild, uninformed suppositions. It played to the worst in people, with coarse description and frightening images.

That it never happened, that she had no idea who the young woman was, that she made it a point *never* to enter the women's locker room at the gym without another faculty member present for precisely this reason, that she always carried herself with nunlike integrity whenever anything even vaguely sexual in nature came up at the school, and that she was careful never to flaunt her relationship with Sally—all suddenly meant nothing.

That the complaint was anonymous also meant nothing. Rumor and innuendo would fly around the school, and people would spend their time trying to guess who it had happened to, not whether it had ever happened. In a high school or private school setting, nothing is as explosive as allegations of illicit sexual behavior. A reasoned, cautious assessment of the charges would never take place, Hope knew. And her denials, forcefully delivered to the dean, probably wouldn't mean much. She worried, too, what the reaction would be in the community that she and Sally considered their home. Other women in partnerships like theirs would likely rally vocally and angrily to her cause. She could imagine rallies and speeches and newspaper articles and demonstrations outside the gates of her school, all ostensibly on her behalf. Many women like Hope hated being stigmatized and would want to stand up and refuse to be ignored. This was inevitable. And, she suspected, it would destroy any chance she had of quietly extricating herself from the situation.

She went over to the sink and splashed cold water on her face over and over, as if she could somehow wash away what might happen to her. She did not want to be anyone's cause, and she didn't want to lose the trust of the students that she had spent so many years building.

She had told the dean, "None of this happened. Nothing like this has ever taken place. How can I prove my innocence without names, dates, times, all that sort of information?"

He had agreed with her and had agreed, for the time being, to keep the allegation under wraps, although by necessity he was going to have to discuss it with the head of the school and maybe even inform the chairman of the board of trustees. Hope knew rumors were inevitable. She had started to say this, but then stopped, because she understood there was little she could do. The dean suggested she continue with ordinary school behavior until additional information became available. "Keep coaching, Hope," Dean Mitchell had said. "Win the league championship. Keep all your scheduled counseling appointments with students, but . . ." Then he'd hesitated.

"But what?" Hope had asked.

"Keep the door open at all times."

Staring at her red-rimmed eyes in the bathroom mirror, Hope had never in her life felt so vulnerable. She exited the bathroom, understanding that the world she had thought was safe had become incredibly dangerous.

Sally scrambled to make sense of the documents in front of her, all the time feeling as if the heat in the room had increased, sweat dripping from her, as if she were in the midst of an aggressive workout.

There was little doubt in her mind that someone had managed to acquire her electronic password and had subsequently wreaked havoc with her client account. She was furious with herself for not making the password more difficult to decipher. The case in question was a divorce, so she had come up with *DIVLAW*. By contacting security officers at the various banks that had received the deposits ripped from the supposedly sacrosanct client account, she was able to restore the greater part of the money, or at least put it in a freeze so that no one could access it. The banks had agreed to put electronic traps on some of the funds, so that anyone trying to withdraw any amount either through the computer or in person would be traced. But she was not completely successful at manipulating the money. Several transactions had been put through a dizzying series of deposits and withdrawals, ultimately disappearing into an offshore bank account that Sally could not penetrate, and when she called the banks, they were less sympathetic to her tale of identity theft than she would have hoped.

Her instinct was to hire her own lawyer, but she held off on this for the moment. Instead, she took the entirety of the home-equity line of credit that she had on the house she shared with Hope and deposited that amount back into the client account, zeroing it out, while at the same time putting herself, and her unwary partner, into significant debt. It would take some months, she thought, to earn the income to undo the financial damage that had taken place, but, she hoped, at least for the interim she was safe.

She drafted a letter to the state bar association carefully. It outlined some of the transactions and said that they were performed by an unknown party, but that she had restored the client account out of her own funds and, in concert with the bank, rendered it safe from another electronic assault. She hoped that this letter would forestall any action by a prosecutor, or state bar investigation, at least until she determined who had done this to her. She thought of requesting information about *who* had complained to the bar association, but, she knew, until they had decided to pursue the matter themselves, they weren't going to tell her how the complaint had arrived at their offices. So she was destined to be kept in the dark for some time to come.

Sally had never really thought of herself as a particularly tough-minded lawyer. Her strongest suit was mediation, getting opposing sides to agree. She hated those moments where compromise was no longer a possibility.

But when she wheeled around in her office chair, staring at the printed-out piles of paper transactions that littered her desktop, she felt nothing but despair. Whoever had done this, she thought, must truly hate me.

That posed a question that she was reluctant to ask, because no one manages to have a viable legal practice, especially handling the dissolutions of marriages, custody cases, and small-time criminal actions, without making some enemies. Most merely bluster and complain. Some take additional steps.

But who? she asked herself.

It had been many months since someone had angrily threatened her, at least in any sort of credible way. The thought that there might be someone out in the world with the patience and the ability to plan an attack against her made her bite down hard on her bottom lip.

Sally leaned back, swiveling about, and realized that she

was going to have to tell Hope about what had happened. She was unsure about doing this. There had been so much tension between them, and now, suddenly, they were in significant financial stress.

It did occur to her to call the police, because, after all, a robbery had taken place.

But this went against the grain for her, as it would many attorneys. And until she knew more or had a better picture of who had done this and why this had happened, she really didn't want a detective crawling all over a case file.

Sort it out, she told herself. Sort it out by yourself.

Sally grabbed her briefcase, stuffed as many papers into it as she could, and abruptly rose, moving rapidly out the door, grabbing her overcoat as she went. The offices had emptied out, and she locked up, then moved quickly through the stairwell and out to the street. For an instant, the cold air seemed to confuse her, and she lifted her hand to her forehead as if she were suddenly dizzy. In that second she could not even remember where she had parked her car. The world swirled around her, and she inhaled sharply once, almost as if she were having a panic attack. Her fists balled up and she felt a sudden jab of pain. Her heart was racing in her chest, her temples throbbing, and she seized a nearby wall to steady herself.

Sally told herself to be orderly, to be organized. Get control, she insisted.

Her car was where it always was, in the parking garage. She buttoned her coat and slowed her breathing to normal, feeling the pressure in her chest and in the pit of her stomach diminish. But as she regained control over all the sensations that had threatened to overcome her, she felt suddenly as if she were no longer alone. She spun about, but the sidewalk was empty, save for the few students crawling in and out of a nearby coffee shop. The traffic on the main street of town was moving along normally. A bus whooshed its air brakes as it settled into the stop across the street in front of an old theater. Everything she could see was as it should be. Everything was in place, settled and normal.

Only nothing was.

She took another deep breath and moved off steadily toward the garage. A part of her wanted to run, and it was all she could do to keep from breaking into a trot, as the evening darkness slid over her and wan light from streetlights and storefronts carved out small sanctuaries against the growing night.

•

"You know, even with this so-called release, and a signed one at that, I'm a little uncomfortable speaking of things told to me in confidence."

"That's your prerogative," I said, filled with false generosity. "I completely understand your position." In my words, I was trying to install the exact opposite suggestion.

"Do you?" he asked.

The psychologist was a small, impish sort, with curly hair streaked with gray that swirled haphazardly around his collar as if attached to odd and conflicted ideas hidden inside his scalp. He wore glasses that gave him a slightly buglike appearance, and he had a curious mannerism. He would finish speaking an idea, then wave his hand in the air to punctuate the words.

"After all," he continued, "I'm not sure that the impact that Michael O'Connell had on these people has yet been fully realized."

"How do you mean?" I asked.

He sighed. "I think one way you can consider this is to think of him entering their lives in much the same way as an auto accident, perhaps one caused by a drunk driver. A moment of loss, a moment of fear, a moment of conflict, however you want to see it. But the residue lasts for years, perhaps even forever. Lives changed. Ashes and agony for a very long time. That's what you're looking at, in this case."

"But—"

"I just don't know if I can speak about it," he said abruptly. "Some things said in this office need to be sacrosanct, even if I support your telling the story. Although I'm not sure that I do. Haven't really thought it through. And I sure as hell would hate to say one thing or another and then suddenly get a subpoena from some authorities, or have to open my door to a couple of Columbo-type detectives in ill-fitting suits, and playing a whole helluva lot dumber than they really are. Sorry."

I sighed, not really knowing whether to be frustrated or respectful. He gave a wide smile and shrugged.

"Well," I said, "so that my trip here isn't an entire waste, can you at least explain to me some of the ins and outs of O'Connell's obsessive love with Ashley?"

The psychologist snorted, suddenly angry. "Love. *Love!* My God, what had it to do with that word? There is one thing you need to know about the psychological makeup of a Michael O'Connell. It is about *possession.*"

"Yes," I said, "I suppose I can see that. But what did he get? It wasn't about money. It wasn't about desire. It wasn't passion. And yet, in a way, it seems, from what I know so far, that it was about all those things."

He leaned back in his chair, then rocked forward abruptly.

"You're being far too literal," he said. "A bank robbery says something concrete. Perhaps even the drug deal, or shooting the late-night clerk at the convenience store. Serial killing and repetitive rapes. Those sorts of crimes are far more easily defined. This was not. Michael O'Connell's proclaimed love was a crime about *identity*. And thus, became something far greater, far more profound. Far more devastating."

I nodded. I was about to say something else, but he waved his hand in that way that I'd already seen, quieting me.

"Actually, another thing you need to always keep in mind," he said hesitantly. "You must also understand that Michael O'Connell was..." he took a second to breathe in deeply ". . . *relentless.*"

17

A World of Confusion

For the first time in her relatively short life, Ashley felt as if her world were not only incredibly small, but now defined by so few things that it lacked anywhere that she could hide, anywhere she could escape to take a small breath of air and gather herself.

The minor irritations and small signs that she was being trailed and observed kept up steadily. Her telephone had become a weapon, filled with silences or heavy breathing. She no longer trusted her computer. She refused to check her e-mail because she could no longer tell who was sending it.

She told her landlord that she had lost her apartment keys, and he sent a locksmith around to replace the locks on the front door, although she doubted it did much good. The locksmith told her that the new locks would keep out most people, but not anyone who actually knew what he was doing. It wasn't hard for her to imagine that O'Connell would be in the category of people who knew what they were doing.

At her job at the museum some of her coworkers complained that they were getting odd anonymous phone calls and unsettling e-mails suggesting that Ashley was acting behind their backs on some project or bad-mouthing them to management. When Ashley tried to explain that this was all untrue, she thought she wasn't believed.

Completely out of the blue, one morning a gay coworker angrily accused her of being a closet homophobe. The charge was so ridiculous that Ashley was completely nonplussed. She was incapable of responding. Then a day or so later, a black coworker eyed her suspiciously and refused to have lunch with her that day. When Ashley followed her, trying to see what was wrong, she haughtily announced, "We have absolutely nothing to talk about. Leave me alone."

After her evening graduate course, Modern European Impressionist Artists, her professor called her into her office and told her that she was in danger of failing if she did not start attending classes.

Ashley was taken aback. Her mouth opened and she stared at the woman, who barely lifted her head from the stacks of papers, slides, and large, glossy art books that littered her desktop. Ashley tried to look around, find something to focus on, and stop the dizzy sensation that threatened to overtake her.

"But that's impossible," Ashley said. "I've been at every class. The sign-up sheets should have my signature right in the middle."

"Please don't lie to me," the professor said stiffly.

"But I'm not."

"One of the graduate assistants goes over these, then puts them into the department system," the professor said coldly. "Of the weekly lectures and additional slide presentations, which we've had more than twenty of so far, we can only find your name on two separate occasions. And one of those would be tonight."

"But I've been there every time," Ashley pleaded. "I don't understand. Let me show you my notes."

"Anyone can get someone to take notes for them. Or get someone to let them copy theirs."

"But I've been there. Really. I promise. Someone has made a mistake."

"Sure. Someone. A mistake. Right. It's all our fault," the professor spoke sarcastically.

"Professor, I think someone is deliberately sabotaging my attendance record."

The professor hesitated, then shook her head. "I've never heard of that. What purpose would anyone have . . ."

"An ex-boyfriend," Ashley said.

"I repeat, Miss Freeman, what purpose would that have?"

"He wants to control me."

The professor hesitated again. "Well," she said slowly, "can you prove this allegation?"

Ashley breathed in slowly. "I don't know how."

"You understand I simply can't take your word for this?"

Ashley started to respond, but the professor held up her hand, cutting Ashley off in midprotest. "I told everyone at the start, in the very first lecture, that attendance was required. I'm not heartless, Miss Freeman. If someone has to miss a single session, perhaps even two, I can see that. Conflicts arise. People get into trouble. But attending class and studying the material in the course is your responsibility. I do not think you will be able to pass this course. In fact, I'm not inclined—"

"Give me a test. A paper. Something that would let me demonstrate that I've grasped the elements of each lecture."

"I don't do special releases or give special treatment," the professor said briskly. "If I did, then I would have to do the same for every lazy or less than fully dedicated student who sat where you are sitting, Miss Freeman, quite willing to lie to my face and with one excuse or another, including my dog ate the homework and my grandmother died. Again. Grandmothers seem to die in my classes with depressing frequency and considerable regularity, and often many more times than once. So, no deal, Miss Freeman. Start coming to class. Get a perfect grade on the final—if you can, and I doubt it, because no one ever has—and perhaps I can eke out a passing grade for you. That remains to be seen. Have you considered some other field? I mean, perhaps art and graduate studies aren't what you should really be doing."

"Art has always been—"

The professor held up her hand again, shutting off Ashley's response.

"Really? Perhaps I am wrong. Regardless, good luck, Miss Freeman. You will need it."

Luck, Ashley thought, has nothing to do with anything.

She exited the professor's office into a corridor that

echoed with emptiness. Somewhere in a stairwell, or rising
from another floor, she could hear laughter, but it was dis-
embodied, almost ghostly. She stood, almost frozen in the
vacant space. He was there, watching her. She slowly pivoted, as if he were always just beyond her sight, like a
shadow trailing her. She listened for a sound, breathing, a
whisper, anything concrete that would inform her that he
was really there, but she could hear nothing.

Tears began to well up in Ashley's eyes. She had no
doubt that O'Connell had somehow managed to erase her
name from the class rolls. She slumped against a wall,
breathing in hard. All the hours she had spent in the
classes, all the attention she had paid, the notes taken, the
information, the knowledge, the appreciation of all the colors, shapes, styles and beauty of the artists studied in the
class were somehow, in that moment, rendered moot. It
was as if all those moments existed in some different universe where the Ashley that she thought she was went
about her life, well on her way to being the person that she
hoped to be.

He is making me disappear.

Anger filled her on a parallel course with despair. She
pushed herself off the wall. *This has got to stop.*

Scott remained at his desk, hamstrung by what he had read.
He felt as if something inside him had frayed. The words on
the pages in front of him wavered, like heat above a highway, and he could feel the earliest tightening of panic in his
chest.

Professor Burris had sent him a copy of his own article
published in the *Journal* and the computer printout of the
doctoral thesis written by a Louis Smith at the University of
South Carolina. The thesis had been submitted to that
school's history department some eight months prior to
Scott's article, and it had, at its core, an examination of much
of the same material. Their similarities were inevitable, and
both pieces had relied on some of the same source material.

But that wasn't the dangerous part. There was simply no denying that a half dozen key paragraphs were *word for word* the same in both. Professor Burris had helpfully highlighted the offending sections in yellow.

In a lengthy scholarly paper for an esteemed journal and in a 160-page double-spaced doctoral thesis, the offending paragraphs constituted only a tiny percent. And the observations they made were hardly of earth-shattering academic importance. But Scott knew that both those aspects were entirely beside the point. They were identical and that was that.

He had a sudden memory of the Red Queen in *Alice's Adventures in Wonderland.* Execution first, then we'll have the trial!

Scott had absolutely no doubt that he had written the sentences in front of him. Whatever hopes he'd had, that somehow one of his two student assistants had accidentally put the words in a note and that he'd used them without double-checking had disappeared. Their work was blameless.

His, on the other hand, apparently was not.

He reeled about in his seat, squirming in turmoil.

Professor Burris had not indicated what the source of the complaint was. Scott presumed it had come from the doctoral student, or from someone on the faculty at the University of South Carolina. Possibly some history buff—of which there were hundreds of thousands around the United States—had made the comparison, but he doubted he or she would have had the reach to enlist a historian as prominent as Burris.

It was almost midday before Scott, unshaven, bleary-eyed, and on his fourth cup of coffee, finally reached the acting chair of the USC History Department on the phone. To his surprise, the man was outgoing and helpful, and clearly unaware that any questions had been raised about Scott's work. Instead, the acting chair immediately assumed that the fault ran in the other direction.

"Why, certainly I recall that thesis," the acting chair said. "It received some very high marks from the entire panel. It was well researched and well written and, I believe, is in line for publication somewhere. And the young man, quite a fine student, and quite a fine fellow, I imagine has a terrific career ahead of him. But you say there is some question about the thesis? I find it hard to imagine—"

"I just want to examine some similarities. After all, we work in the same general area of expertise."

"Of course," the acting chair said. "Although I would hate to discover that a student here had engaged in any impropriety . . ."

Scott hesitated. He knew he had given the fellow historian the untrue impression that it was the onetime student who was potentially guilty of an academic felony. "You know, if I could speak with the young man, it might clear things up," Scott said.

"Why, of course. Let me just check . . ."

Scott was placed on hold for several nerve-racking minutes. He sat immobile waiting to resume the conversation that might cost him everything that he'd spent years constructing.

"Well, Professor Freeman, sorry to have kept you waiting. It's a little tricky for anyone to reach out and contact Louis. Young Mr. Smith took his newly minted doctorate and joined Teach For America. Sure as blazes isn't what most of our students do. Anyway, the number and address we have for him is in some place north of Lander, Wyoming, on an Indian reservation. I'll give you that now."

Scott called out to Wyoming, discovered that Louis Smith was stuck in a class of eighth-graders for several hours, left his name and number, and explained that it was urgent. When the phone finally rang, he grabbed at it.

"Professor Freeman? This is Louis Smith."

"Thanks for calling back," Scott said.

The young man seemed enthused. "I'm really honored that you would call, Professor Freeman. I've read everything you've ever published, especially on the early days of the Revolutionary War. That's my area, too, and I have to admit, I find it all fascinating, all the time. The military maneuvering, the political intrigues, the most improbable success. So many lessons for today. I mean, you can imagine on an Indian reservation how differently people view all those concepts of history that we take for granted." The young man spoke rapidly, nonstop. But before Scott could interject something, Smith paused and took a breath and apologized. "I'm sorry. I'm rambling. Please, Professor, to what do I owe the honor of this call?"

Scott hesitated. The boundless energy from the young teacher wasn't what he'd expected. "I've read your doctoral thesis . . ."

"You have! Oh, that's great, I mean, if you liked it? Did you think that I got it all right?"

"It's excellent," Scott said, a little taken aback. "And your insights are right on point."

"Thank you, Professor. I can't tell you how much that means. You know, you do all this work, and maybe it gets published by an academic press—I'm still hoping for that— but really hardly anyone except your board and maybe your girlfriend actually sees it. To find out that you've actually read it . . ."

"There is a question," Scott said stiffly. "There are some similarities between your thesis and a piece I did some months later."

"Yes. In *The Journal of American History*. I read it carefully, because we dealt with much the same material. But similarities? How do you mean?"

Scott took another deep breath. "I have been accused of plagiarizing some of the paragraphs you wrote. I did not, but I have been accused."

He stopped and waited. It took Louis Smith a couple of seconds to gather himself.

"But, that's crazy," he said. "Who accused you?"

"I don't know. I thought it might be you."

"Me?"

"Yes."

"No. Absolutely not. Impossible."

Scott felt dizzy. He had no idea what to think. "But I have in front of me a printout of your thesis, and I must say that there are paragraphs that are word for word the same. I don't know how this happened, but . . ."

"Impossible," Louis Smith repeated. "Your article came out months after my thesis was written, but you must have been doing your writing and research at more or less the same time. And there were delays in publishing my thesis. In fact, other than on the university website, which links to several historical sites, it's hard to get a copy. The idea that you managed to find it, and then adopt some of the language . . . well, this is a mystery. Can you read me the paragraphs that are the same?"

Scott looked down at the yellow-highlighted words. "Yes. In my article, on page thirty-three, I wrote . . ."

And Scott ran through both.

Louis Smith responded slowly. "Well, that's most curious, because the paragraph you read me that purports to be in both papers does not exist in mine. That is, I never wrote that. It's not in my thesis. I mean, the points are similar to conclusions I draw, but what you say is there, is not."

"But I'm reading from a printout of your thesis."

"I don't know for certain, Professor, but my immediate suspicion is that someone has tampered with the document you have in front of you. Do you know anyone who might do that?"

The wind had picked up, cutting razorlike across the pitch, and the daylight was fading in the west, making the world filmy gray and indistinct, as Hope gathered the team around her at the end of practice. The strands of hair that had escaped from ponytails were plastered to their foreheads with sweat. She had worked them hard, perhaps harder than she ordinarily would near the end of the season, but she had lost herself in running with them, feeling a release in breathlessness, as if the cold air was the only thing that could possibly distract her.

"Fine effort," she said. "As sharp as we've been all season. Two weeks before the play-offs. You will be tough to beat. Very tough. That's good. But there are seven other teams heading into the tournament who might be working just as hard. Now it becomes something more than physical. Now it's about desire. How do you want this year, this season, this team, to be remembered?"

She looked around at the glistening faces of young women who had come to understand that a prize can be attained by hard work and dedication. It finds a spot in their eyes first, Hope thought, then spreads right into their skin, so intense that it gives off a sort of heat.

She smiled at them all, but felt a deep hole inside.

"Look," Hope said carefully, "in order to win, we're all going to have to pull together. So is there anything anyone wants to say here in front of the team? Is there anything holding you back?"

The girls looked oddly at each other. Some heads shook back and forth.

Hope was unsure whether any rumors about her had begun to circulate. But she found it hard to imagine that there hadn't been some talk, yet. There are no secrets in some worlds, she thought.

The girls seemed to collectively shrug. She wanted to interpret this as support.

"Okay," she said. "But if there is anyone, and I mean anyone, who is bothered by something, anything, before we start the play-offs, they can come to me. Office door is always open. Or, if you don't want to talk to me, then see the athletic director."

She could not believe she was saying what she was. She had the sense to change the subject.

"This is, without doubt, the quietest you've ever been as a team. So quiet, in fact, that I'm going to assume you've all lost your voices because you've worked so hard. So, let's cancel the postpractice run. Give yourselves a cheer, a pat on the back, and then grab your bags and head on in."

This got a round of applause. No extra laps always worked.

Hope gave them a wave, sending them on their way. They are ready, she thought. She wondered whether she was.

Within seconds, the girls had started to make their way off the field, knotting into groups, and Hope could hear laughter. She watched them depart, then sat on the wooden sideline bench.

The wind had increased, and she hunched her shoulders against the cold. She thought to herself that being a part of something, such as the school and the team, was a large part of how she defined herself, and now that was in jeopardy. A shadow moved across the green grass of the field, making the earth seem black. Little in the world is as soul-deadening as being falsely accused, she thought. An empty fury filled her. She wanted to find the person who had done it and pummel him or her with her fists.

But whoever it was, at that moment, seemed to have no more substance than the darkness growing around her, and Hope, as angry as she was, instead put her head in her hands and sobbed uncontrollably.

•

"Ashley? Ashley Freeman? I haven't seen her in a while. Months. Maybe even more than a year. Does she still live in the city?"

I didn't answer that question, but asked, "You worked here at the museum at the same time as she did?"

"Yes. There were a bunch of us working toward various graduate degrees who filled part-time jobs here."

I was in the lobby of the museum, not far from the restaurant where Ashley had fruitlessly waited one afternoon for Michael O'Connell. The young woman working the reception desk wore her hair close-cropped on one side and spiked on the top, giving her a roosterlike appearance, and she sported at least a half dozen earrings in one ear and a single large, bright orange loop in the other, which made her seem curiously off balance. She looked up at me, with a small, youthful smile, and finally got around to asking the obvious question.

"Why are you interested in Ashley? Is something wrong?"

I shook my head. "I'm interested in a legal case that she was connected to. I'm just doing a little background work. Wanted to see where she worked. So, you knew her, when she was here?"

"Not very well . . ." The young woman hesitated.

"What is it?" I asked.

"I don't think too many people knew her. Or liked her."

"Really?"

"Well, I overheard one person once say that Ashley wasn't at all like who she pretended to be, or something like that. I think that was the general consensus. There was a lot of talk and speculation when she left."

"Why?"

"There was a rumor about some stuff found on her workstation computer that got her in trouble. At least that's what I heard."

"Stuff?"

"Like *way* different stuff. Is she in trouble again?"

"Not exactly," I replied. "But then, *trouble* might not be the right word."

18

When Things Got Worse

Michael O'Connell told himself that his best skill was waiting.

It was not simply a matter of biding his time or sitting around patiently. Real *waiting* required all sorts of preparations and planning, so that when the moment that he was anticipating arrived, he was already significantly ahead of everyone else. He conceived of himself as something like a director, the sort of person who can see an entire story, act by act, scene by scene, right to the end. He was a man who knew all the endings, because he alone constructed each and every one.

O'Connell was stripped to his boxer shorts, his body glistening. A couple of years back, while browsing in a used-book shop, he had come across an exercise-regimen book that had been popular in the mid-1960s. This particular book was drawn from the Royal Canadian Air Force manual on physical fitness and was filled with antique drawings of men in shorts doing squat thrusts, one-handed push-ups, and chin lifts. It also had curious exercises he performed, such as springing into the air and lifting his knees so that he could touch his toes. It was the opposite of all the Pilates, Billy Blanks, Body by Jake, and six-minute abdomen-exercise programs that dominated daytime television channels. He had become proficient in the RCAF exercises and beneath his loose-fitting, worn student garb sported a wrestler's physique. No vanity-driven health club membership or soul-ful, long runs alongside the Charles for him. He preferred to hone his muscles alone, in his room, occasionally wearing a headset blasting some pretentiously satanic rock group, such as Black Sabbath or AC/DC.

He dropped to the floor, raised his legs above his head, then lowered them slowly, pausing to hold his position three times before stopping with his heels just inches above the hardwood floor. He repeated this exercise twenty-five times. But on the final repetition, he remained in position, arms flat at his sides, holding himself immobile for one minute, then another. He knew that somewhere after three minutes he would start to feel discomfort, and two minutes later, dis-tress. After six minutes, he would feel significant pain.

O'Connell told himself that it really wasn't about devel-oping muscles any longer.

Now, it was about overcoming.

He shut his eyes and shunted away the burning in his stom-ach, replacing it with a portrait of Ashley. In his mind, he slowly drew each detail, with all the patience of an artist de-voted to duplicating every signature curve, every small, shad-owy recess. Start with her feet, the splay of her toes, the arch, the tautness of her Achilles'. Then move up the length of her leg, capturing the muscles in her calf, to her knee and thigh.

He gritted his teeth and smiled. Usually he could hold his position all the way past her breasts, after lingering a long time contemplating her crotch, finally to the long and willowy, sensuous curve of her neck, before he was forced to drop his heels to the floor. But as he grew stronger, he knew he would someday complete the mental painting, filling in the features of her face and hair. He looked forward to developing that strength.

With a gasp, he relaxed and his feet bounced hard against the floor. He lay for a moment or two, feeling sweat trickle down his chest.

She will call, he thought. Today. Perhaps tomorrow. This was inevitable. He had put forces into play that would ensnare her. She will be upset, he told himself. Angry. Filled with demands, none of which meant a thing to him. And, more critically, he reminded himself, this time she will be alone. Frantic and vulnerable.

He took a deep breath. For an instant he believed he could feel Ashley at his side, soft and warm. He closed his eyes and luxuriated in the sensation. When it faded, he smiled.

Michael O'Connell lay back on the floor, blankly staring up at the whitewashed ceiling and a single unshaded hundred-watt bulb. He had once read that certain monks in long-forgotten orders in the eleventh and twelfth centuries had remained in that position for hours on end, in utter silence, ignoring heat, cold, hunger, thirst, and pain, hallucinating, experiencing visions, and contemplating the immutable heavens and the inexorable word of God. It made absolute sense to him.

The thing that troubled Sally was a single offshore bank account that had received several modest deposits from her client's account. The sum in question was somewhere near $50,000.

When she had called the bank in Grand Bahama, they had been unhelpful, telling her that she would need an authorization from their own banking authority, implying that that was difficult to obtain, even for SEC or IRS investigators— and probably impossible for a single attorney operating alone, without subpoenas, or State Department threats.

What Sally could not fathom was why someone capable of raiding her client account had seemingly only stolen one-fifth of the amount. The other sums, arrayed through a near dizzying series of transfers back and forth through banks all over the nation, were still traceable, and, as best as she could tell, likely to be recovered. She had managed to have the sums frozen at nearly a dozen different institutions, where they rested untouched under different and transparently phony names. Why, she wondered, wouldn't someone have merely transferred all of the cash into the offshore accounts, where it was in all likelihood completely untouchable? The majority of the money was simply hanging out there, not stolen, but waiting for her to undergo the immense difficulty in recovery. It troubled her deeply. She could not say with any precision what sort of crime she was the victim of. The one thing she knew was that her professional reputation was likely to take a blow, at the least, and more likely be crippled significantly.

She was equally uncertain who had attacked her.

Her first suspicion, of course, fell on the other side in the divorce case. But she did not understand why the opponents would make such serious trouble for her—it would significantly postpone matters and make things more difficult, in addition to dragging out the action in court, which would only cost everyone more money. In a divorce, she was accustomed to people behaving irrationally, of course, but this stumped her. People were usually more blatantly petty and obnoxious when they tried to make trouble. And, so far, this assault had a subtlety that she had yet to fully understand.

Her second suspicion, then, became some other opponent in some other case. Someone she had bested in some year past.

This unsettled her even more, the idea that someone would harbor a need for revenge over some time, waiting months, perhaps even years, before acting. It was Sicilian in nature, and seemed to her to be something right out of *The Godfather*.

Sally had exited her office early and walked through the

center of town to a restaurant that sported a fake-Irish name and had a quiet and dark bar, where she nursed her second Scotch and water. In the background, she could hear the Grateful Dead singing "Friend of the Devil."

Who hates me? she asked herself.

Whoever it was, she knew that she needed to tell Hope. She dreaded this. With all the tension between them, this was the last thing they needed. Sally took a long pull of the bitter liquid. Someone out there hates me and I'm a coward, she thought to herself. A friend of the devil is a friend of mine. She looked at the glass, decided that there wasn't enough alcohol in the entire world to cover up how miserable she felt, pushed it away, and with what little remaining steadiness she had, started to make her way home.

Scott finished his letter to Professor Burris, then reread it carefully. The word that he'd chosen to describe what had taken place was *hoax*—he presented the allegation as if they had all been the subjects of some elaborate, yet mysterious, undergraduate prank.

Except, on this occasion, Scott wasn't laughing much.

The only part of the cautiously worded letter that he'd felt comfortable with was the portion where he'd recommended that Burris take a long look at the academic accomplishments of Louis Smith. Scott thought that perhaps he could give the fellow a boost in his career.

He signed the e-mail and sent it. Then he went back to his house and sat in his old, tattered wing chair and wondered what had just happened to him. He wasn't willing to believe that a single letter, even one as decisive as the one he'd just written, meant he was free from any problems. He still had the snooping campus reporter showing up at his office at the end of the week. The room grew dark around him as the day faded, and Scott knew that at some time in the future he would have to defend himself. That the charge had no substance, no credibility, was more or less irrelevant. Someone, somewhere, would believe it.

It all made Scott furious, and he sat clenching his fists, his head aching, wondering who had done this to him. He had no idea that many of the same questions were simultaneously plaguing Sally and Hope, and that if they all had known of one another's struggles, the source of their problems would be far more obvious to all of them. But they were all, by circumstances and bad luck, in their own orbits.

Ashley was putting her few things together and getting ready to leave the museum for the evening when she looked up from her desk and saw the assistant director hovering uncomfortably a few feet away.

"Ashley," he said, stilted, his eyes pivoting about the room, "I'd like a word with you."

She put down her small satchel and dutifully followed the assistant director into his office. The quiet museum seemed suddenly cryptlike, and their footsteps echoed. Shadows seemed to mar the art on the walls, defacing the shapes, deforming the colors.

The assistant director motioned to a chair, while he sat down behind his desk. He paused, adjusted his tie, sighed, then looked directly at her. He had the nervous mannerism of rubbing his hands together at odd moments. "Ashley, we've had some complaints about you."

"Complaints? What sort of complaints?"

He didn't exactly answer. "Have you been going through some difficulty of late?"

She knew the answer was yes but she didn't want to allow the assistant director into her private life any more than she had to. She thought him a wheedling, hollow man. She knew he had two young children at home in Somerville, a detail that rarely prevented him from hitting on every new, young female employee. "No. Nothing that unusual," she said, lying. "Why do you ask?"

"So," he said slowly, "you would say things were *normal* in your life? Nothing *new*?"

"I'm not sure what you're driving at."

"Your views, on the, ah, world at large, ah, haven't recently changed in some radical direction?"

"My views are my views," she said slowly.

He hesitated again. "I was afraid of that. I don't know you very well, Ashley. So I suppose nothing should really surprise me. But I have to say . . ." He stopped. "Well, let me put it this way: You know, at this museum we try to be pretty tolerant of other people's views and opinions and, well, lifestyles, I suppose you'd say. We don't like to be, ah, judgmental. But there are some lines that can't be crossed, wouldn't you agree?"

She had no idea what he was speaking about, but she nodded. "Of course. Some lines, yes."

The assistant director looked both sad and angry at the same time. He leaned forward.

"Do you really think that the Holocaust never happened?"

Ashley sat back in her chair. "What?"

"The murder of six million Jews was merely propaganda, and never really took place?"

"I don't follow . . ."

"Are blacks really an inferior race. Sub-Mongoloid? Little more than wild animals?"

She didn't reply, her voice disappearing in shock.

"Do Jews truly control the FBI and the CIA? And is purity of race truly the most important issue facing this nation today?"

"I don't know what you're—"

He held up his hand, red-faced. He gestured toward the computer on his desk. "Come over here and sign in with your ID and password," he said abruptly.

"I don't understand—"

"Just indulge me," he said coldly.

She rose from the chair, walked around to his side of the desk, and did as he asked. The computer jumped to life, played a familiar small fanfare, and a picture of the museum filled the screen, followed by a *Welcome Ashley* screen and the message *You have unread mail in your mailbox.*

"Okay," Ashley said. She stood up.

The assistant director abruptly pushed by her, seizing the keyboard.

"Here," he said furiously. "Recent searches."

Signed in on her name and password, he hit a rapid succession of keys. The image of the museum instantly disappeared, replaced by a large black-and-red screen. Martial music flooded the speakers, and a large swastika suddenly appeared, followed by a blast of music. Ashley did not recognize the "Horst Wessel Song," but she could immediately sense its nature. Her mouth opened in astonishment, and she tried to speak, but her eyes were riveted on the computer, which changed to an old black-and-white newsreel of a line of people raising their arms in a Nazi salute as *"Sieg Heil!"* was repeated a half dozen times. She recognized Leni Riefenstahl's *Triumph of the Will*. This faded and was replaced with a *Welcome to the Aryan Nation Web Site* page. A second screen followed instantly, which proclaimed, *Welcome Storm Trooper Ashley Freeman. Please type in your password to enter.*

"Do we need to go further?" the assistant director asked.

"This is crazy," Ashley said. "This isn't mine. I don't know how—"

"Not yours?"

"No. I don't know how, but—"

The assistant director pointed at the screen. "So, type in your museum password."

"But . . ."

"Indulge me," he said coldly.

She leaned over and typed it in. The screen immediately changed as the site opened up. It played another musical fanfare. Something from Wagner.

"I don't understand."

"Sure," he said. "Sure you don't."

"Someone did this to me. An ex-boyfriend. I don't know how, but he's very clever with computers and he must have—"

The assistant director held up his hand. "But you said nothing was unusual in your life. That was the very first thing I asked you, and you said *no. Nothing unusual.* An ex-boyfriend signing you up for membership in a hate group, at a modern-day Nazi website, well, I would consider that *unusual.*"

"It's, he's, I don't know . . ."

The assistant director shook his head. "Please don't offend me any further with any other lame excuses. This is your last day here, Ashley. Even if your excuse is the truth, well, we cannot have this, one way or the other. Nasty boyfriend, or true belief. Both are completely unacceptable in the atmosphere of tolerance we try to promote here. This is the pornography of hate. I won't allow it. And, to be frank, I'm not sure I believe you. We will mail you your final paycheck. Good night, Miss Freeman. Please do not come back here again. And please"—he added as he pointed to the door—"don't expect a recommendation."

Ashley alternated between tears of frustration and utter fury as she made her way back to her apartment through the fast-descending night. With each step, she grew angrier, so much so that she barely saw the shadows and darkness surrounding her. She quick-marched with military precision down the city streets, trying to decipher some plan of action, but unable to, her rage was so complete. She let it overcome her, so that her entire body quivered. No one in her right mind would allow someone to screw up her life so completely, and as she considered herself fully in her right mind, she decided that it was going to stop, that night.

She threw her jacket and backpack on the bed and went straight to the telephone. Within seconds, she had dialed Michael O'Connell's number.

His voice sounded sleepy, disconnected, when he answered the phone.

"Yes? Who is it?"

"You know goddamn well who it is," Ashley said in a voice that was on the edge of a shout, filled with bitterness.

"Ashley! I knew you'd call."

"You bastard! You've screwed up my work at school. Now you've cost me my job. What sort of creep are you?"

He was silent.

"Leave me alone! Why can't you leave me alone?"

He remained silent.

She picked up momentum. "I hate you! God damn you, Michael! I told you it was over, and it is! I never want to see you again. I can't believe you would do this to me. And you say you love me? You're a sick and evil person, Michael, and I want you out of my life. Forever! Do you understand that?"

He still didn't reply.

"Do you hear me, Michael? It's over! Ended. Finished. Completed. However you want to understand it, but it's all over. No more. Got it?"

She waited for a response and got none. Silence slithered around her, enveloping her like a vine.

"Michael?" She suddenly thought he wasn't there, that he'd disconnected and her words were simply disappearing into some immense electronic void. "Do you get it? It's over."

Again, all she heard at first was silence.

She thought she could hear his breathing.

"Please, Michael. It's got to be over."

When he did finally speak, it took her by surprise.

"Ashley," he replied almost brightly, a little laughter in his tone, as if he were speaking a different language, one that was utterly foreign to her. "It's just wonderful to hear your voice. I'm counting the days until we can get back together again."

He paused, then added, "Forever."

And then he hung up.

•

"But something happened?" I asked.

"Yes," she replied. "Something, actually many things, happened."

I watched her face and saw that she was struggling with

the details of what she wanted to say. She wore reluctance in much the same way that someone puts on a warm sweater in the winter, in anticipation of some wind and cold and a shift in the weather for the worse.

"Well," I said, a little exasperated by her oblique manner, "what's the context here? You got me into this story by saying that I was supposed to make sense of it all. So far, I'm not sure what I've really gathered. I can see the games that Michael O'Connell was working. But to what end? I can see the crime taking shape—but what crime are we thinking about?"

She held up her hand. "You want things to be simple, don't you? But crime isn't so simple. When you examine it, there are many forces at work. Do you wonder, sometimes, whether we help create the psychological or maybe emotional atmosphere in which bad things, terrible things, take root, flourish, and then flower? We're like a hothouse for evil, all in ourselves. Seems that way sometimes, doesn't it?"

I didn't answer this. Instead, I watched her as she stared down into her cup of coffee, as if it could tell her something.

"Doesn't it seem to you that we live these incredibly diffuse, disjointed lives? Once upon a happier time, you grew up and stayed where you were. Probably bought the house down the street from your folks. Helped run the family business. So we all remained linked, in the same orbit. Naïve times. The Honeymooners and Father Knows Best on television. What a quaint idea: Father knows best. Now, we get educated and we depart."

She paused, then asked, "So, what would you do then, when it became clear to you that someone had decided to ruin your life?"

She added, "And don't you see? From our perspective, looking at the story from our safe spot in this world, it's easy to see that there is this person out there trying to ruin their lives. But they couldn't see that."

"Why not?" I blurted out.

"Because it's not reasonable. Because it made no sense. I mean, why? Why would he want to do this to them?"

"Okay, why?"

"Not yet. You need to find that out for yourself. But some things are clear: Michael O'Connell, with half their education, half their resources, half their prestige, had all the power. He had twice their smarts because they were like everyone else and he wasn't. There they were, caught up and entwined in the midst of all his evil, and yet, they couldn't see it. Not for what it was. What would you do? Isn't that the question? Awful things have happened, but what is the real threat?"

I didn't directly answer. Instead, I repeated myself, trying to get an answer, "But something changed?"

"Yes. A moment of lucidity."

"How so?"

She smiled. "A lucky phrase. In what was fast becoming a most unlucky situation."

19

A Change of Approach

At first, Ashley was overwhelmed by rage.

Seconds after Michael O'Connell's voice disappeared from the cell phone, she threw it across the room, where it exploded against a wall like a gunshot. She bent over at the waist, her fists clenched, her face contorted, flushed, teeth grinding. She picked up a textbook and threw it in the same direction, where it slammed on the plaster and thudded to the floor. She paced into her bedroom, seized a small throw pillow from the bed, then pummeled it, like a boxer in the last round, throwing rights and lefts recklessly. Seizing the pillow and sinking her hands into the fabric, she pulled it apart. Bits and pieces of synthetic stuffing flew into the air around her, landing in her hair and on her clothing. Her eyes were filling with tears, and she finally let out a wail of despair, sliding into a complete black depression.

Ashley threw herself down on the bed, curled into the fetal position, and cried piteously, giving in to everything that was flowing in torrents within her. Her body racked with frustration, she heaved and gasped, as if her frustration had stretched into every fiber of her body, like some errant infection.

When she had no more tears, she rolled over, staring up at the ceiling, clutching pillow shreds to her chest. She breathed in deeply. She understood that tears didn't solve any problem, but she felt a little better nevertheless.

When she could feel her heartbeat returning to normal, Ashley sat up.

"All right," she said out loud. "Let's get your shit together, girl."

She glanced over at the shattered cell phone and decided that her burst of anger was a blessing. She would have to get a new phone, and with it, a new number. One, she promised herself, that Michael O'Connell wouldn't have. She looked over at the desk, with the landline phone. "Cancel that."

Next to the telephone was her laptop computer. "All right," she said, again speaking to herself in the same way she would to a young child, "Change your Web service. Change your e-mail account. Cancel all bill-paying services. Start over."

Then she looked around the apartment. "If you have to move, you have to move."

She sighed deeply. She could go into the graduate-school registrar's office in the morning and get her transcripts corrected. She knew this would be a major hassle, but she had paper copies of her grades somewhere, and whatever mischief Michael O'Connell had managed, she could sort her way through it. The current course—and the nonexistent absences—might be impossible. But it was only one class, and although it was a setback, it wasn't fatal.

Getting fired was a bigger problem. She had no confidence that the assistant director wouldn't prove to be an ob-

stacle in the future. He was a rigid dilettante and a closet
sexist, and she would hate to have to deal with him again.
She decided that the best course of action would be to try to
get one of her undergraduate professors to write the assistant director a letter, simply telling him he'd been mistaken
in his assumptions about her, and that her employment
record should reflect this. She was pretty sure that she could
get someone to do this when she explained the circumstances. It might not correct her firing—but it might at least
neutralize the damage done.

After all, she told herself briskly, it wasn't as if the job at
the museum was the only job she could get. There had to be
others, filled with color and art, that would speak to who she
was and who she hoped to be.

The more Ashley planned, the better she felt. The more
she decided on, the more she felt in control, the more she felt
like herself, the stronger and more determined she believed
herself to be. After a moment or two, she got up, shook herself from head to toe, and walked into the bathroom.

She stared at herself in the mirror, shaking her head at her
swollen and red-rimmed eyes. "All right," she said as she
filled the sink with steaming-hot water and started to wash
her face, "no more damn tears over this son of a bitch."

No more getting scared. No more anxiety. No more
gnashing teeth and nervous frustration. She was going to get
on with her life, Michael O'Connell be damned.

She was suddenly hungry, and after washing away as
much of her sadness as she could, she went to the kitchen,
found a single pint of Ben & Jerry's Phish Food ice cream in
the freezer, and scooped out a large helping, letting the
sweet tastes improve her mood, before she went to her remaining telephone to call her father. As she crossed her
apartment, eating the ice cream out of the container, she
hesitated by the window, glancing out into the night with a
twinge of uncertainty. *No more staring into shadows.* Ashley turned away, seized her landline phone, and began dialing, unaware what pair of eyes were searching the wan light
of her home for a glimpse of her form, both satisfied and yet

dissatisfied with just the merest suggestions of her presence, completely at ease with the darkness, excited by how close he felt to her at that very moment. It was something that she would never understand, he thought to himself. How every step she took to try to separate herself only made him more excited and filled him with more passion. He turned the collar up on his coat and dropped back farther into a dark shadow. He could be warm right there all night if need be.

Hope was surprised to find Sally waiting for her when she arrived home that evening. They had fallen into the stiffest of patterns, marked by long silences.

She looked across at her partner of so many years and suddenly felt a surge of exhaustion and dismay cascade through her. This is it, she thought to herself. This is where we put words to an ending. A shapeless sadness filled her as she nervously looked over to Sally.

"You're back a little early tonight," she said as blandly as possible. "Hungry? I can put something together quickly, but it won't be real interesting."

Sally barely moved. Her hand was wrapped around another Scotch. "I'm not hungry," she said a little sloppily. "But we need to talk. We have a problem."

"Yes," Hope replied, slowly removing her jacket and setting down her backpack. "I would say so."

"More than one."

"Yes. More than one. Maybe I should get a drink, too." Hope went into the kitchen.

While Hope poured herself a large glass of white wine, Sally tried to sort through precisely where she was going to begin, and which of the multitude of troubles she would bring forth first. Some odd conflation was in her mind, joining the assault on her client account and the threat to her career with the unsettled coolness she felt toward Hope. Who am I? Sally asked herself.

She felt as she did in the days before she and Scott had separated. A sort of black, gray gloom coloring her thoughts. It took an immense force of will for her to remain seated. She wanted to rise up and run away. For a lawyer, accustomed to the world of solving sticky issues, she felt abruptly incompetent.

When she looked up, Hope was standing in the entrance.

"I need to tell you what has happened," Sally said.

"You've fallen in love with someone else?"

"No, no . . ."

"A man?"

"No."

"Then another woman?"

"No."

"You just don't love me anymore?" Hope continued.

"I don't know what I love. I feel as if I'm, I don't know, but fading, like an old photo."

Hope thought this an indulgent and overromantic statement. It made her angry, and it was all she could do, given all the tension she'd been under, to keep from bursting forth. "You know, Sally," she said with a coldness that surprised her, "I don't really want to discuss all the ins and outs of your emotional state. So things aren't perfect. What is it you want to do? I hate living in this minefield of a household. It seems to me that either we split up, or, I don't know, what? What would you suggest? But I sure as hell hate this psychological roller coaster."

Sally shook her head. "I haven't really thought about it."

"Like hell you haven't." Hope felt a little guilty about how good it felt to be angry.

Sally started to say something, then stopped. "There's another problem," she said. "One that impacts both of us, and how we live."

Sally quickly filled Hope in on the complaint from the state bar association and with the harsh financial reality that a good chunk of their savings had—at least for the time being—been wiped out, and that it would likely take some time for her to track down the money and file the necessary documents to get it returned.

Hope listened, aghast. "You *are* kidding, right?"

"I wish."

"But that wasn't *your* money, it was *our* money. You should have consulted me beforehand."

"I had to move with speed to avoid a real inquiry by the bar association."

"That's an excuse. But not one that explains why you didn't pick up the goddamn phone and tell me what was going on."

Sally did not reply.

"So, we're not only on the verge of divorce, but we're suddenly broke?"

Sally nodded. "Well, not completely, but until we get things sorted out . . ."

"Well, that's great. Just dandy. Just fucking terrific. What the hell are we supposed to do now?" Hope stood up and paced back and forth across the room. She was so angry with her partner that it seemed as if the room lights had dimmed and then brightened, like a power surge in the electricity.

Before Sally could reply, *I don't know,* the telephone rang.

Hope pivoted about, stared at the phone as if it were somehow to blame for misfortune, and stomped across the room to answer it. She was muttering obscenities to herself with every step, and the words managed to mark her pace.

"Yes?" she said rudely. "Who is it?"

From her spot in the armchair, and more or less miserable from the mess her life seemed to be in, Sally saw Hope's face abruptly freeze. "What is it?" Sally asked. "Is something wrong?"

Hope hesitated, obviously listening to the person on the other end of the line. After a moment, she nodded and said, "Jesus *effing* Christ. Hang on, I'll get her for you."

Then she turned to Sally.

"Yes. No. Here. You take it. It's Scott. The creep is back in Ashley's life. Big-time."

Scott arrived at their house about an hour later. He rang the doorbell, heard Nameless bark, and looked up to see Hope

opening the door. They had their usual second or two of
awkward silence, then she gestured for him to enter. "Hey,
Scott," she said. "Come on in." He was surprised that Hope
looked as if she'd been crying, because he had always assumed she was the tough one in the relationship with Sally.
One thing he did know for certain: his ex-wife was the
moody half of any relationship.

He dispensed with any greetings when he reached the living room. "Did you speak with Ashley?"

Sally nodded. "While you were driving over. She filled
me in on what she told you. Now she's stuck with no job and
a mess at school." Sally sighed. "I guess we underestimated
just how persistent Michael O'Connell might be."

Scott lifted his eyebrows. "That would seem to be an understatement. It was a mistake we probably couldn't have
avoided. But now we've got to help Ashley extricate herself."

"I thought that was what you went to Boston to do," Sally
said coldly, looking at her ex-husband with arched eyebrows. "Along with five thousand reasons in cash."

"Yes," Scott replied equally coolly, "I guess our bribe offer didn't work. So, what's the next step?"

They were all quiet for a moment, until Hope blurted,
"Ashley's in a bad situation. She clearly needs assistance,
but how? And what? What is it we can do?"

"There must be laws," Scott said.

"There are, but how do we apply them?" Hope continued.
"And, so far, what law do we think this guy has broken? He
hasn't assaulted her. Hasn't hit her. Hasn't threatened her.
He's told her he loves her. And he's followed her. And then
what he's done is screwed up her life with the computer.
Mischief, mostly."

"There are laws against that," Sally said, then stopped.

"Computer mischief," he said. "That hardly describes it."

"Anonymous," Sally said.

All three were thinking hard about what to say next. Then
Scott leaned back and said, "I had a really sticky problem of
my own the last week or so, generated anonymously by
computer. I think it's solved, but . . ."

Nobody spoke for a second, before Hope added, "So have I."

Sally looked up, surprised at what she'd heard.

But before she could say anything, Hope pointed directly at her. "And so has she."

Hope stood up. "I think everyone is going to need a drink." She headed off in search of another bottle of wine. "Maybe more than one drink," she threw back over her shoulder to where Scott and Sally were staring at each other in doubt.

•

The Massachusetts State Police detective seated across from me seemed at first like an oddly pleasant fellow, with little of the hard-bitten, world-weary appearance of a character in a police novel. He was of modest height and build, wore a blue blazer and inexpensive khaki pants, and had close-cropped sandy-colored hair with a disarming bushy mustache on his upper lip. If it weren't for the ice-black, nine-millimeter Glock pistol riding under his arm in a shoulder holster, he would have seemed more like an insurance salesman, or a high school teacher.

He rocked back in his chair, ignored a ringing telephone, and said, "So, you want to know a little bit about stalking, right?"

"Yes. Research," I replied.

"For a book? Or an article? Not because of some personal interest in the subject?"

"I'm not sure that I follow."

The detective grinned. "Well, it's a little like the guy who calls up the doctor and says, 'I've got this buddy at work who wants to know what the symptoms of, ah, a sexually transmitted disease like, ah, syphilis or gonorrhea are. And how he, ah, that's my friend, not me, might have gotten it, 'cause he's in a lot of pain.'"

I shook my head. "You think that I'm being stalked and want . . ."

He smiled, but it was a calculating grin. "Maybe you want to stalk someone and you're looking for tips on how to avoid arrest. That would be the crazy sort of thing a real intense stalker might try to pull off. It's always an error to underestimate them. And what they will do when it comes time for them to do it. A really dedicated stalker makes a science of his obsession. A science and an art."

"How so?"

"He not only studies his victim, but their world, as well. Family. Friends. Job. School. Where they like to eat dinner. Where they go to the movies or have their car serviced or buy their lottery tickets. Where they walk the dog. He uses all sorts of resources, both legal and illegal, to accumulate information. He is constantly measuring, assessing, anticipating. He devotes his every waking thought to his target—so much so that often he can think steps ahead, almost as if he is reading the victim's mind. He comes to know them almost better than they know themselves."

"What is all this driven by?"

"Psychologists are unsure. Obsessive behavior is always something of a mystery. A past that has, shall we say, rough edges?"

"Probably more than that."

"Yes, probably. My guess is, scratch the surface a bit, you'll find some pretty nasty stuff in their childhood. Abuse. Violence. You name it."

He shook his head. "Dangerous folks, stalkers. They aren't your ordinary type of low-rent criminal by any means. Whether you're a trailer-park checkout girl in the local supermarket being stalked by your biker ex-boyfriend, or a Hollywood star with all the money in the world being stalked by an obsessed fan, you're in a whole lot of danger, because, no matter what you do, if they want it enough, they *will* get to you. And law enforcement, even with temporary restraining orders and cyber-stalking laws, is designed to react to, not head off, an eventual crime. Stalkers know this. And the frightening thing is, they often don't care. Not a bit. They are immune to the usual sanctions. Embarrassment. Financial ruin. Prison. Death. These things don't necessarily frighten them. What they fear is losing sight of their target. It overcomes everything, and that single-minded pursuit becomes their entire rationale for living."

"What can a victim do?"

He reached into his desk and brought out a pamphlet titled "Are You Being Stalked? Advice from the Massachusetts State Police."

"We give you some material to read."

"That's it?"

"Until a felony is committed. And then, it's usually too late."

"What about advocacy groups and . . ."

"Well, they can help some people. There are safe spaces, secret housing, support groups, you name it. All can provide some assistance in some cases. And I would never tell someone not to contact those types—but you have to be cautious, because you might be bringing something to a confrontation that you really don't want. But it's usually too late, anyways. You want to know what's really crazy?"

I nodded.

"Our state legislature has been in the forefront of passing laws to protect folks, but the dedicated stalker finds his way around them. And, what's even worse, once you engage the authorities—like when you go file the complaint and have the case registered and obtain the court order requiring the stalker to stay away—that can just as easily trigger disaster. Force the bad guy's hand. Make him act precipitously. Load up all his weaponry and announce, 'If I can't have you, no one will.'"

"And . . ."

"Use your imagination, Mr. Writer. You know what happens when some guy shows up at a workplace or a home or wherever, dressed up like Rambo in cammy fatigues, with an automatic twelve-gauge shotgun, at least two pistols, and enough ammunition strapped to his chest to hold off a SWAT team for hours. You've seen those stories."

I was quiet. I had indeed. The detective grinned again.

"Here's something you should keep in mind: as best as we

can tell, both in law enforcement and forensic psychology, the closest profile we can arrive at for a truly dedicated stalker is more or less exactly the same as a serial killer."

He leaned back. "That kinda makes you think, doesn't it?"

20

Actions, Right and Wrong

Does anyone have any real idea what we're dealing with here?"

Sally's question hung in the air.

"I mean, other than what Ashley has told us, which admittedly isn't a hell of a lot, what do we know about this fellow who's screwing up her life?"

Sally turned toward her ex-husband. She was still nursing her way through the glass of Scotch and should have been drunk, but was far too much on edge to have lost her sobriety.

"Scott, you're the only one of us, outside of Ashley, of course, who has even seen this guy. I imagine that you drew some conclusions during your meeting in Boston. Got some sort of feeling for the man. Maybe that's where we can start."

Scott hesitated. He was far more accustomed to leading the conversation in a seminar room, and suddenly being asked his opinions took him a little aback. "He didn't seem like anyone any of us might be familiar with," he said slowly.

"What do you mean?" Sally asked.

"Well, he was well built, good-looking, and obviously smart enough, but he was also rough, sort of what you'd expect from a guy who maybe drives a motorcycle, works a blue-collar job punching a time clock somewhere, takes night classes at a community college after high school. My impression was that he came from a pretty deprived background—

not the sort of guy that you ordinarily find at my college, or at Hope's school, either, for that matter. And not anywhere like the sort of guy that Ashley usually drags in, professes undying love for, and breaks up with four weeks later. Those guys always seem to be artistic types. Thin-chested, long-haired, and nervous. O'Connell seemed tough and street-smart. Maybe you've run into a few like him in your practice, but my thinking is that you're a bit more high end."

"And this guy . . ."

"Low end. But that may not be a disadvantage."

Sally paused. "What the hell was Ashley doing with him in the first place?"

"Making a mistake," Hope said. She had been seated quietly, her hand on Nameless's back, seething inwardly. At first she felt unsure whether she deserved a place in the conversation, then decided that she sure as hell did. She did not understand why Sally seemed so detached. It was as if she were outside of what was happening—including their own finances being screwed up in a major fashion.

"Everyone makes bad choices every so often. Things we later regret. The difference is, we move on. This guy isn't letting Ashley move on." Hope looked over at Scott, then back at Sally. "Maybe Scott was your mistake. Maybe I am. Or maybe there was someone else that neither of us knows about and who you've kept secret for years. But regardless, you've moved forward. This guy is in a whole different world."

"Okay," Sally said cautiously, after an uncomfortable silence, "how do we proceed?"

"Well, for starters, let's get Ashley the hell out of there," Scott said.

"But Boston is where her studies are. That's where her life is. What, you think we should bring her back here, like she's some homesick camper at her first sleepaway camp?"

"Yes. Exactly."

"Do you think she'll come?" Hope interjected.

"Do we have that right?" Sally asked, speaking rapidly. "She's a grown-up. She's not a little girl anymore."

"I *know* that," Scott replied testily. "But if we are reasonable—"

"Is any of this reasonable?" Hope asked abruptly. "I mean, why is it fair for Ashley to run back to her home at the first sign of trouble? She has the right to live where she wants to, and she has the right to her own life. And this guy, O'Connell, doesn't have the right to force her to flee."

"True. But we're not talking about rights. We're talking about realities."

"Well," Sally said, "the *reality* is that we will have to do what Ashley wants, and we don't know what that is."

"She's my daughter. I think that if I ask her to do something, she damn well will do it," Scott replied stiffly, an edge of anger in his voice.

"You're her father. You don't own her," Sally said.

There was an unhappy silence in the room.

"We should determine what Ashley wants."

"That seems like a pretty wishy-washy, politically correct, and generally wimpy thing to do," Scott said. "I think we need to be more aggressive. At least until we really understand what we are up against."

Again they were quiet.

"I'm with Scott," Hope said abruptly. Sally spun in her direction, a look of surprise on her face.

"I think we should be, what? Proactive," Hope continued. "At least in a modest fashion."

"So, what are you two suggesting?"

"I think," Scott said slowly, "we should find out a bit about Michael O'Connell, at the same time that we get Ashley away from his immediate reach. So, we do what we're all capable of. Maybe one of us should start looking at him."

Sally held up her hand. "We should engage a professional. I know a private investigator or two who do this sort of inquiry routinely. Moderately priced, as well."

"Okay," Scott said, "you hire someone and let's see what they come up with. In the meantime, we need to get Ashley physically away from O'Connell."

"Bring her home? That seems juvenile and cowardly," Sally said.

"It also seems to make sense. Maybe what she needs right now is someone looking over her."

Scott and Sally glared at each other, clearly revisiting some moment from their past.

"My mother," Hope said, interrupting.

"Your mother?"

"Yes. Ashley has always gotten along well with her, and she lives in the sort of small town where a stranger coming to ask questions would be noticed. It would be tricky for O'Connell to follow her there. It's close enough, but far enough. And I doubt he could figure out where she was."

"But her school . . ." Sally said again.

"She can always repair a screwed-up semester," Hope said briskly.

"I agree," Scott said. "Okay, we have a plan. Now we just need to engage Ashley in it."

Michael O'Connell was listening to the Rolling Stones on his iPod. As Mick Jagger sang, "All your love is just sweet addiction . . . ," he half-danced down the street, oblivious to the stares of the occasional passerby, his feet tapping the drumbeat on the sidewalk. It was a little before midnight, but the music brought flashes of light into his path. He was letting the sounds guide his thoughts, imagining a rhythm to what his next step with Ashley would be. Something that she didn't expect, he thought to himself, something that underscored for her just how total his presence truly was.

He did not think she fully understood. Not yet.

He had waited outside her apartment until he saw the lights all go out and he knew that she had gone to bed. Ashley didn't understand, he thought, how it is far easier to see in the darkness. A light only carves out a specific area. Far wiser, he believed, to learn to pick shapes and movement out of the night.

The best predators work at night, O'Connell reminded himself.

The song came to an end, and he stopped on the sidewalk. Across the street, he saw a small, art-house-type cinema, showing a French film called *Nid de guêpes*. He slid back into a shadow and watched people come out of the theater. As he expected, they were mainly young couples. They seemed energized, not that uniquely somber, *I've just seen something meaningful* look that so often accompanies people emerging from what O'Connell contemptuously considered artsy cinema. His eyes settled on one young couple that came out arm in arm, laughing together.

They immediately irritated him. He could feel his heart rate accelerate slightly, and he watched them closely as they passed in front of a neon light on the sidewalk opposite him. His jaw clenched tightly and he had an acid taste on his tongue.

There was nothing remarkable about the couple, and yet, they were completely infuriating. He saw the young woman lean into the boy, taking his arm in hers and linking the two of them together, so that they became one walking down the street, their footsteps in unison, a moment of public intimacy. He picked up his own pace, moving parallel to the couple, assessing them more directly, as a misshapen anger within him grew unchecked.

Their shoulders rubbed together as they walked, and they were each hunched slightly toward the other. O'Connell could see that they alternated between laughter, smiles, and intense conversation.

He did not think that they had been together long. The language of their movements, their gestures toward each other, the way they listened and laughed at what each other said, spoke to a newness and an excitement, a courtship that was just taking root, where they were still coming to know each other. He saw the girl grip the boy's arm tighter, and he told himself that they had already slept together, but probably just once. Each touch, each caress, each moment of exploration, still had the electricity of adventure and the heady drug of potential.

He hated them utterly.

It was not difficult for O'Connell to imagine the rest of their night. It was late, so they would decide against sticking their heads into a Starbucks for coffee or Baskin-Robbins for a scoop or two of ice cream, although they would pause outside each and make a show of considering the decision, when, in actuality, what they wanted to devour was each other. The boy would keep up a chatter about movies, about books, about courses at whichever of the colleges he was at, while the girl listened, occasionally interjecting a word or two, while all the time listening more to who he was, and what he might mean to her. The boy would need no more encouragement than the pressure of her arm. They will get to the apartment laughing. And, once inside, it would only be seconds before they found the bed and threw their clothes aside, any fatigue from the long day instantly gone, overcome by the freshness of their lovemaking.

He was breathing hard, but quietly.

That's what they think will happen. That's what is supposed to happen. That's what is designed to happen.

He smiled. But not this night.

He moved in tandem with the couple, keeping his eye on their progress from the opposite sidewalk. At a corner, when the yellow WALK light flashed on, he instantly moved rapidly into the crosswalk, heading directly for them, his shoulders hunched forward, his head down, aiming just to their side. They started moving toward him, so that they were like a pair of ships in a channel, destined to come close, but slide past. O'Connell measured the distance, counting down the space in his head, noting that they were still conversing and not paying full attention to the surroundings.

As the space between him and the couple narrowed to only a few feet, O'Connell suddenly lurched sideways, just enough so that his shoulder came into hard contact with the boy's. The solid thump reassured him, and he abruptly spun toward the couple and shouted, "Hey! What the hell are you doing! Watch where you're going!"

The couple half-turned in O'Connell's direction.

"Hey, sorry," the boy said. "My fault. Sorry." They continued on after only a momentary glance in O'Connell's direction.

"Asshole," O'Connell said, loud enough for them to hear, but turning away from them rapidly. They had just gotten enough of a look.

The boy pivoted, still grasping the girl's arm, obviously thinking of replying, then choosing against it. He didn't want to say or do anything that might interrupt the mood and turned away. O'Connell counted to three slowly, giving the pair just enough time to put a little distance between them, their backs to him now, then he started following them. The sudden blare of a horn caused the girl to turn just barely, looking back over her shoulder and seeing him. He could see a small look of alarm on her face.

That's it, he thought. Walk a few more feet, assessing the surprise, imagining a threat.

As soon as he reached the sidewalk and saw that the girl was speaking rapidly to the boy, O'Connell ducked into a darkened storefront, shoving himself out of their sight line. Disappearing into the small space, he wanted to laugh out loud. Again, he counted to himself.

One, two, three . . .

Time enough for the boy to hear what the girl was saying and stop.

Four, five, six . . .

Turning in his place and peering back through the shadows and arcs of neon light.

Seven, eight, nine . . .

Straining against the darkness and night, but not seeing him.

Ten, eleven, twelve . . .

Turning back to the girl.

Thirteen, fourteen, fifteen . . .

A second glance, just to make sure.

Sixteen, seventeen, eighteen . . .

They start off again.

Nineteen, twenty . . .

An extra, unsettled look back over the shoulder to reassure himself.

O'Connell stepped out of the shadow and saw that the young couple had picked up their pace and were nearly halfway down the block. He followed quickly, crossing the street so that once again he was parallel to them, half-running until he came abreast of the two of them.

Once again, it was the girl who spotted him first.

He imagined the shaft of anxiety piercing her.

Across the street, the girl stumbled, twisting, and O'Connell fixed his eyes on her, so that when she looked in his direction, he was staring hard. With nothing but anger on his face, their eyes met across the road.

The boy turned toward him, but O'Connell had anticipated this, and he abruptly started to run forward, toward the end of the block, moving ahead of the pair. The sudden, abrupt, erratic behavior delighted him. It was not something they would have expected, and he knew it would throw them into confusion.

Behind him, the young woman and the young man would be debating. Go forward, in the direction of their apartment, or turn back, find a different route. Once again, he pushed himself back into a shadow and caught his breath. He took a quick survey of his surroundings and saw that the side street behind him was lined with small apartment buildings, not unlike Ashley's street, where tree branches stretched out into the ambient city light, giving them a ghostly appearance. Cars were parked tightly in every available space, and wan light flowed from building entranceways.

He slid from the shadows and rapidly walked three-quarters of the way down the street, taking up a position in another dark space, waiting. There was a streetlight at the beginning, and he guessed they would pass through its arc as they closed in on their apartment.

O'Connell was right. He saw the young couple come

around the corner, pausing momentarily, then moving rapidly forward.

Scared, he thought. Not certain that they were actually safe. But starting to relax.

He pushed himself out, hunched his shoulders forward, and, moving at a quick march, angled across the street to intersect them.

They saw him almost simultaneously. The girl gasped, and the boy, gentleman that he was, pushed her slightly behind him and squared himself toward O'Connell. The boy clenched his fist and positioned himself like a fighter ready for the bell to sound.

"Stay back!" he said. The young man's voice had risen, high-pitched with uncertainty. O'Connell heard the girl choke.

"What do you want?" the boy demanded, trying to keep himself between O'Connell and the girl.

O'Connell stopped and looked at the boy. "What are you talking about?"

"Stay away!" the boy said.

"Just chill, buddy," O'Connell said. "What's the problem?"

"Why are you following us?" This was the girl speaking, her voice a panic-laced half shriek.

"Following you? What the hell are you talking about?"

The boy kept his hands clenched, but looked surprised and even more confused.

"You folks are crazy." O'Connell quickly began to move past them. "Nut jobs."

"Leave us alone," the boy said. Not very convincing, O'-Connell thought. When he was about a half dozen paces past, he stopped and turned. As he suspected, they were still wrapped together, defensive, staring after him.

"You two are lucky."

They eyed him with astonishment.

"Do you know how close you came to dying tonight?"

Then, not giving them a chance to reply, he spun about and moved as swiftly as he could without running, from shadow to shadow, leaving the young couple behind him. He suspected they would remember their fear from this night far longer than they would remember the happiness that they'd started it with.

•

"I think I need to know more about Sally and Scott, and then, about Hope, too."

"Not Ashley?"

"Ashley seems young. Unfinished."

She frowned. "True enough. But what makes you think that Michael O'Connell didn't finish her?"

I didn't know how to answer, but I felt a distinct chill in her words. "You told me that someone dies. Surely you're not saying that it was Ashley . . ."

My question hung in the air between us. She finally said, "She was the one at greatest risk."

"Yes, but—"

She interrupted, "And I suppose you think you already understand Michael O'Connell?"

"No. Not fully. Not nearly enough. But I'm searching about for my next step, and I was wondering about the three of them."

She paused, fiddling with her glass of iced tea, again turning her head to stare out the windows. "I think about them often. Can't help myself."

She reached for a box of tissues. Tears were welling up in the corners of her eyes, but she wore a small smile. She took a long, slow breath of air.

"Do you ever consider why crime can be so devastating?" she asked abruptly.

I knew she would answer her own question.

"Because it is so unexpected. It falls outside ordinary routines of life. It takes us by surprise. It becomes totally personal. Utterly intimate."

"Yes. True enough."

She stared at me. "A history professor at a snobbish liberal college. A small-town attorney, expert in barely contested divorces and modest real-estate transactions. A guidance counselor and coach. And a head-in-the-clouds, young art student. Where were their resources supposed to come from?"

"Good question. Where?"

"That's what you need to understand. Not just what they figured out, and what they did, but where the intelligence and the strength came from."

"Okay," I replied slowly, drawing out the word.

"Because eventually they pay a heavy price."

I didn't say anything.

She filled the silence. "In retrospect, it always seems so simple. But when it is happening, it's never so clear-cut. And never quite as neat and tidy as we think it should be."

21

A Series of Possible Missteps

The more Scott read, the more terrified he became.

Immediately the following morning, after the less-than-satisfactory meeting with Sally and Hope, like any proper academician he had immersed himself in a study of the phenomenon represented by Michael O'Connell. Descending upon his local library, he started researching compulsive and obsessive behaviors. Books, magazines, and newspapers crowded his desk in a corner of the reading room. An oppressive, heavy quiet filled the space, and Scott suddenly felt that he could barely breathe.

He looked up in near panic, his heart moving quickly as if it were close to bursting.

What he had absorbed that morning was a litany of despair. Death had surrounded him. Over and over, he had read about this woman here, and that woman there, young, middle-aged, even elderly, who had been the object of some man's driven obsession. They had all suffered. Most had been killed. Even the survivors had been crippled.

It seemed to make no difference where the women were located. North or South, in the United States or abroad. Some were young, students like Ashley. Others were older. Rich, poor, educated, or impoverished, it was all irrelevant. Some had once been married to their stalkers. Some had been coworkers. Some had been classmates. Some had been lovers. All had tried all sorts of techniques, had turned to the law, turned to their families, friends, any possible source of help, to try to extricate themselves from the unwanted, relentlessly obsessive attention. He read *undaunted desire*.

All had found it useless to seek help.

They were shot, stabbed, beaten. Some managed to live. Many did not.

Sometimes children died alongside them. Sometimes coworkers or neighbors died, the collateral damage of rage.

Scott reeled under the onslaught of information. It made him dizzy as he began to see the trap Ashley was in. On page after page, in every book and article, the single common denominator was *love*.

Of course, he understood, it wasn't real love. It was something wildly perverse, emanating from the darkest part of a man's imagination and heart. It was something that deserved a spot in forensic psychiatric texts, not Hallmark cards. But the sort of love that he read about seemed to have found a foothold in each case, and this scared him even more.

Scott started to grab book after book filled with story after story, and tragedy after tragedy, searching for the one that would tell him what to do. His eyes raced over the words; he flipped pages in rapid succession, haphazardly tossing one book down and seizing another, driven by mounting anxiety, all the time searching for the one that would tell him the answer. As a historian, an academic, he believed that the answer was written somewhere, a paragraph on some page. He lived in a world of reason, of structured argument. Something in his world had to be able to help.

The more he insisted this to himself, the more he knew how fruitless his search was destined to be.

Scott rose, pushing back so hard from the desk that the heavy oaken library chair crashed back on the floor, sending a noise like a shot through the quiet space. He could suddenly feel the eyes of everyone in the room burning into his back, but he stumbled away from the table, as if he'd been wounded, dizzy, clutching at his chest. In that moment all he could do was panic. He gestured wildly at all the research, his throat closing, turned, abandoning all the papers. He ran, right through the card catalogs, past the reference desk and the librarians who watched him, shocked, never having seen a man thrust into so much fear by the printed word. One tried to call after him, but Scott could hear nothing as he burst out beneath an overcast sky, the air less chilled than his heart, knowing only that he had to get Ashley out of the path she was on, and do it quickly. He had no idea precisely how to achieve this, but he knew he had to act, and as fast as he could.

Sally, too, started that day filled with decisions she thought were eminently *reasonable*.

It seemed to her that the first order of business was to really measure what sort of individual her daughter had brought into their lives. That he was clever with a computer and had tampered with each of their lives seemed clear. She dismissed the instinct to take all the bits and pieces of information to the police, mostly because she wasn't yet sure that they would do any more than hear her complaint, and because she might jeopardize the integrity of her lawyer-client relations by doing so. Involving the police, she thought, would be a poor idea, right then.

What troubled her was that O'Connell, assuming he had pulled these things off, which she wasn't 100 percent sure was true, seemed to have an instinct for subtlety that was dangerous. He seemed to know how to hurt someone in ways that weren't defined by a blow or a gunshot, but by something more elusive, and this scared her. That he knew how to make their lives miserable was a danger that truly made her pause.

Still, she reminded herself, O'Connell wasn't really their match.

Or, more accurately, he wasn't a match for her. Scott, she was unsure of. Years of working in the polite society of a small liberal arts college had taken away the edgy toughness that she had been attracted to when they were first married. Back then, he'd been a veteran when it was unpopular to be one, and he'd approached learning and school with a tough-mindedness she'd found compelling. After he'd received his doctorate, and they were married and had Ashley and she had already decided to go to law school herself, she'd been aware that he was growing softer, somehow. As if the impending arrival of middle age affected not only his waistline, but his attitude as well.

"All right, Mr. O'Connell," she said out loud. "You've screwed with the wrong family. Now a little surprise or two for you."

She turned away and threw herself into her chair and reached for her phone. She had found the number she wanted in her Rolodex, and she dialed it rapidly. She was even patient when she was put on hold by a secretary. When she heard the voice come on the line, she felt reassured.

"Murphy here. What can I do for you, Counselor?"

"Hello, Matthew. I've got a problem."

"Well, Ms. Freeman-Richards, that's absolutely the only reason in the entire world that folks call this number. Why else talk to a private investigator? So, what's it to be on this occasion? A divorce case up there in that nice little city of yours? Something that has turned a tiny bit nastier than folks intended, perhaps?"

Sally could picture Matthew Murphy at his desk. His office was in a nondescript and slightly bedraggled old building in Springfield, a couple of blocks away from the federal courthouse, on the edge of a pretty run-down area. Murphy, she assumed, liked the anonymity that the place gave him. Nothing flashy and attention-grabbing for him.

"No, not a divorce, Matthew."

She could have called some considerably more upscale investigators. But Murphy had a far more checkered background, and a no-nonsense attitude that she thought might come in handy. Also, hiring someone from outside her own city was less likely to create any gossip in the county courthouse.

"Something else, then, Counselor? Perhaps something more, shall I say, *tricky*?"

He was, she thought, able to read much in the few words she'd spoken.

"How are your connections in the Boston area?" she asked.

"I still have some friends there."

"What sort of friends?"

He laughed before replying, "Well, some friends on both sides of the great divide, Counselor. Some not-so-nice types always looking for an easy score, and some of the guys looking to arrest them."

Murphy had been a state police homicide detective for twenty years before taking early retirement, and subsequently opening his own office. Rumors suggested that the severance package he'd received was part of an agreement to keep quiet about some activities of a Worcester narcotics squad that he'd taken an interest in while investigating a couple of drug-related murders. A questionable arena, Sally knew, if only by reputation, and Murphy had retired with a watch and ceremony, when the alternative might have been an indictment of his own or maybe even a bad night ending up at the end of some Latin King gang member's semiautomatic.

"Can you look into something in the Boston area for me?"

"I'm pretty busy with a couple of other cases. What sort of something?"

Sally took a deep breath. "A personal matter. It involves a member of my family."

He hesitated before saying, "Well, Counselor, that explains why you called an old warhorse down here, instead of one of those young, slick ex-FBI or -military-CID guys up there in the more rarefied atmosphere where you keep your practice. So, what exactly is it that you want me to, ah, do?"

"My daughter had gotten involved with a young man in Boston."

"And you don't like him much?"

"That's putting it mildly. He keeps telling her he loves her. Won't leave her alone. Pulled some computer crap that got her fired from her job. Screwed up her graduate-school work. Maybe more. Probably tailing her around. Maybe made some trouble for me, my ex, and a friend of mine, as well. More computer stuff."

"What sort of trouble?"

"Got into my accounts. Made some anonymous complaints. Generally speaking, screwed a lot of stuff up."

Sally thought that she was minimizing the damage that O'Connell had probably done.

"So, he's got some skills, this, what do you want to call him? Ex-boyfriend?"

"That's good enough. Although it appears that they only had one date."

"He did all this because of, what? A one-night stand?"

"Seems that way."

Murphy hesitated, and Sally's confidence was slightly shaken.

"Okay. I get it. Any way you slice it, sounds like this guy is a bad dude."

"Do you have any experience in this sort of case? An obsessive type."

Matthew Murphy was quiet once again. His silence made her feel increasingly uneasy.

"Yeah, Counselor, I do," he said slowly. "Ran into a couple of guys more or less like the guy you're describing to me. Back when I was in homicide."

This was a word that made her throat go dry.

*   *   *

Hope's mother had just come in from raking leaves when her phone rang. As was her custom, she reached for the receiver with a twinge of uncertainty.

"Hello, dear," Catherine Frazier said. "This is a surprise. It's been weeks and weeks since we spoke last."

"Hello, Mother," Hope said a little guiltily. "I've been busy with school and the team, and time has slipped away. How are you?"

"Why, just fine. Settling in and getting ready for winter. The locals all think we're in for a long one."

Hope took a single deep breath. Her relationship with her mother was marred by an underlying tension. While outwardly civil, it was as if it were constantly being tightened, like a knot holding a wind-filled sail, as the gusts around them increased. Catherine Frazier was a lifelong Vermonter, liberal almost to a fault in her political views— save one; the most important one to her daughter. She was a stalwart in the local Catholic church in the small town of Putney, which was adjacent to the more upscale, ex-hippie-populated, whole-wheat-and-granola town of Brattleboro— a woman who had survived the early death of her husband, never thinking about remarrying, who now enjoyed living at the edge of the woods alone. She still harbored considerable doubts about her daughter's relationship with Sally. She kept these to herself, living in a state that welcomed civil unions between women, but prayed fervently on Sunday mornings for some sort of understanding that had eluded her year in and year out, which had hardened the connections between them. Sometimes, in past years, she had bought up these feelings in the confessional, but she had grown tired of saying Hail Marys and Our Fathers because they rarely made her feel any more comfortable.

Hope thought her failure to be *normal* and to provide grandchildren was somehow at the root of the tension, which grew in volume both when they did talk and when they didn't, for the real subject that they should have addressed was never raised between them.

"I need a favor," Hope said.

"Anything, dear," Catherine replied.

Hope knew that this was a lie. There were more than a few favors that she might have asked for from her mother that might not have been granted.

"It has to do with Ashley. She needs to get out of Boston for a while."

"But what could possibly be the matter? She's not ill, is she? There hasn't been an accident?"

"No, not precisely, but . . ."

"Does she need money? I have lots of money and I'd be glad to help out."

"No, Mother. Let me explain."

"But what about her graduate studies?"

"Those can be put on hold."

"Dear, this is very confusing. What is the problem?"

Hope took a deep breath and blurted out, "It's a man."

When Scott first tried Ashley's cell phone that night, he got a *No longer in service* recording, which pitched him into a near panic as he dialed her landline. When she answered, he felt a surge of anxiety. As he greeted her, he concentrated on keeping fear out of his voice.

"Hey, Ash," he said briskly, "how are you doing?"

Ashley, for her part, was unsure what the answer to that question might be. She could not shake the sensation that she was being watched, that she was being followed, or that every word she spoke was being listened to. She was tentative when she left her apartment, wary when she walked down the street, leery of every shadow, every corner, every blind alleyway. Ordinary city sounds that she was so familiar with now penetrated her ears like some high-pitched whistle, almost painful in intensity.

She decided that she should partly lie. She did not want to upset her father.

"I'm okay. Things are just a bit of a mess."

"Have you heard from O'Connell again?"

She didn't exactly reply, except to say, "Dad, I've got to take some steps."

"Yes," he said far too quickly. "Yes. Absolutely."

"I've canceled the cell phone," she said, which explained the recording.

"Yes, and cancel this line as well. In fact, I think you're going to have to do far more than we ever anticipated."

"I've got to move," she said sullenly. "I like this place, but . . ."

"I think," Scott began tentatively, "that you're going to have to do more than just move."

Ashley didn't immediately respond.

"And there are some other steps—"

"What are you saying?" Ashley blurted out.

Scott took a deep breath and adopted his most reasoned, most flat and academic tone, as if he were discussing the flaws in a senior's paper. "I've done some reading and research, and I don't want to leap to conclusions here, but I'm thinking that there exists the potential for O'Connell to get, well, even more aggressive."

"*Aggressive.* That's a euphemism. You think he might hurt me?"

"Others, in similar circumstances, have been hurt. I'm just saying we should take some precautions."

More silence, before she responded, "What are you suggesting?"

"I think you need to disappear. That is, exit Boston, go someplace safe, hide for a while, and then resume things when O'Connell has finally moved on."

"What makes you so sure he will *move on*? Maybe he will just wait it out."

"We have resources, Ashley. If you have to leave Boston behind for good, move to L.A. or Chicago or Miami, well, that can be done. You're still young. Plenty of time to get where you want. I think we just need to take some significant steps, so that O'Connell can't find you again."

Ashley could feel anger surging within her. "He doesn't have the right," she began, raising her voice. "Why should it be me? What have I done wrong? Why does he get to screw up my life?"

Scott let his daughter fully vent before answering. This was a quality left over from her childhood, when early on he'd learned that letting Ashley bluster and complain would settle her down, and that ultimately she would listen if not to reason, then at least to something close to it. A father's trick.

"He doesn't have the right. He just has the ability. So, let's try to make some moves that he won't anticipate. And, first among these, is getting you away from him."

Again, Scott could sense Ashley measuring things on the other end of the phone. He had little idea that much of what he'd said had already occurred to her. Still, what he was suggesting seemed to discourage her, and Ashley found her eyes welling with tears. Nothing was fair. When she did speak, it was with resignation.

"All right, Dad. Time for Ashley to vanish."

•

"So, they hired a private investigator?"

"Yes. An extremely competent and well-trained fellow."

"That makes sense. It also seems like the sort of reasonable thing that any modestly well-educated and financially sturdy couple would arrange. Like bringing in an expert. I should go speak with him. He must have prepared some sort of report for Sally. That's what private investigators always end up doing. It must be available, somewhere."

"Yes. You are correct about that," she said. "There was a report. An initial one. I have the copy that was sent to Sally."

"Well?"

"Why don't you try to speak with Matthew Murphy first. And then, afterwards, I'll give it to you, should you think you still need it."

"You could save me some trouble here."

"Perhaps," she replied. "I'm not sure that saving you time and effort is precisely my task in this process. And, equally, I think visiting the private investigator will be . . . how shall I put it? An education."

She smiled, but humorlessly, and I had the distinct impression that she was teasing me with something. I stood up to leave, shrugging my shoulders. She sighed, seeing the discouraged look I had on my face.

"Sometimes, it's about impressions," she said abruptly. "You learn something, you hear something, you see something, and it leaves an imprint on your imagination. Eventually, that is what happens to Scott and Sally and Hope and Ashley, as well. A series of events, or moments of time, all taken together accumulate into a fully formed vision of what their future might be. Go see the private detective," she said with a brisk tone. "It will add immeasurably to your understanding. And then, if you think it necessary, I'll give you his report."

22

Vanishing

Punk was the first word that came to Matthew Murphy's mind.

He was staring down at an extremely unimpressive police record for Michael O'Connell, which showed a life of penny-ante and mostly insignificant run-ins with the law. Some credit card fraud, which Murphy assumed was using stolen cards, a car theft when O'Connell was slightly more than a teenager, one assault, which looked to be a bar fight that O'Connell apparently won. Of the various minor crimes that O'Connell had been charged with, none had resulted in anything more than probation, although O'Connell had spent five months in one county's jail when he'd been unable to make a modest bail. It took his court-appointed public defender that much time to get the assault charge downgraded to a simple battery. A fine, time served, and six months' probation on that one, Murphy read. He reminded himself to call the probation officer, though he doubted the man would be of much assistance. Probation officers tend to spend the bulk of their time on more significant criminals, and as best as Murphy could see, Michael O'Connell wasn't significant—at least in the eyes of the legal system.

Of course, Murphy thought, there was another way of looking at everything he had accumulated: O'Connell would do anything; he just hadn't been caught.

Murphy shook his head. Not precisely your master criminal.

He looked back down at the sheaf of papers on his lap. Five months in the county lockup. Not enough time to be more than inconvenienced, if you were a small-timer like O'Connell. Just the opportunity to pick up some valuable and useful skills from some of the more experienced inmates, if you kept your eyes and ears open and managed not to get preyed upon by the tough guys in the system. Crime, Murphy believed, like any advanced degree, took some studying.

There were black-and-white front- and side-view mug shots of O'Connell. Is that where you got your start? he wondered.

He doubted it. Those five months were just a little graduate work. He guessed that O'Connell had already learned much.

The state police detective who'd given him the rap sheets hadn't been able to access O'Connell's sealed juvenile records. This made Murphy wary. No telling what might be there. Still, as he looked over the printouts, he saw only the smallest suggestions of violence, which reassured him. Just a bad guy, he thought. Not a bad guy with a nine-millimeter.

He could glean a little background from the police documents: O'Connell was a trailer-park, coastal–New Hampshire kid. Probably didn't have much growing up. No white clapboard house with an apple pie baking in the oven and children playing touch football in the front yard; his childhood probably consisted of dodging blows. Good enough record in high school—when he was there. There were some

apparent gaps in the process. Some time in juvenile deten-
tion? he wondered. Managed to graduate from high school.
Bet you gave the guidance counselors a workout, he
thought. Smart enough to get into the local community college. Dropped out. Went back. Didn't finish. Transferred
credits to UMass Boston. Clever with tools—a mechanic
with some expertise. Had obviously used the same capabilities to learn computers. Plenty for him to look into, he
thought, if that was what Sally Freeman-Richards wanted.
He knew, more or less, what he was going to find. Abusive
father. Drunk mother. Or maybe absent father and seductive
mother. Divorce, blue-collar menial or domestic jobs, and
too-much-beer-on-Saturday-night violence.

Matthew Murphy was parked outside Michael O'Connell's grimy apartment on a bright, promising afternoon.
Slivers of bright sky seemed to pass between the run-down
apartment buildings, and from the corner he could make out
in the distance the CITGO sign hanging above Fenway Park.
He looked up and down the block and shrugged to himself.
It was like many Boston streets, he realized. Filled with
young people on their way up and old people on their way
down from something better. And a few, like O'Connell, using it as a way station on the road to something worse.

It had been easy to get a friend in the state police to run
O'Connell's name, which had provided the printout that he
had in his lap, along with the modest background material
and known addresses. Now he merely wanted to get a good
picture of the subject. On the seat next to him was a modern
digital camera with a long lens. The private investigator's
primary tool.

Murphy was in his midfifties, right in that age that arrived
before facing the anxiety of turning elderly. He was child-
less and divorced, and what he missed the most were the
tight-collar uniformed days when he was young and had
been out on the Mass. Pike behind the wheel of a cruiser,
routinely working high-speed, back-to-back shifts on coffee
and adrenaline. He also missed his time in the homicide division, but he was wise enough to understand that with the

enemies he'd made, making it to old age might have been problematic. He smiled to himself. All his life, he'd always had the knack for getting out of whatever trouble he was in, one step ahead of the hammer coming down. A year after he'd joined the state police, when he totaled his cruiser in a high-speed chase, he'd walked away with only a scratch or two, while the EMTs fruitlessly worked on the rich and drunk kids in their dad's BMW he'd been pursuing. In a firefight one midnight with a drug dealer coked out of his skull, the man had emptied a nine-millimeter in Murphy's direction, only to have every shot smash the wall behind him. The sole shot he'd fired with his eyes shut had found the other man's chest. He'd talked his way out of so many dicey situations, he could no longer recall them all, including a face-to-face with a multiple killer holding a butcher knife in one hand and a nine-year-old girl in the other, the body of his ex-wife at his feet and his mother-in-law's on the floor of the kitchen pooling blood. He'd received a commendation for that arrest. A commendation and a threat from the killer, who had vowed to make him one of his next projects, if he ever got free, which wasn't too damn likely. Matthew Murphy considered the number of threats he'd accumulated to be the most accurate measurement of achievement. He'd had too many to count.

He looked down at the papers again.

Michael O'Connell wasn't much more than an inconvenience.

He took a deep breath and let his eyes race through the documents one more time, searching for some indication that O'Connell couldn't be intimidated. He couldn't see any. That was the course that he would suggest Sally Freeman-Richards follow. A late-night visit from himself, buttressed by a couple of his off-duty state police buddies. An informal visit, but one with as much menace as they could muster, which was considerable. Rough him up a little bit at the same time they presented him with a restraining order signed by a judge. Let O'Connell think that pursuing Freeman-Richards's daughter would be far more trouble than it could ever be worth. And make absolutely certain that O'Connell understood that trouble, in this case, was pretty much defined by Murphy.

He smiled. Should do the trick, he thought.

He'd seen some pretty crazed stalkers in his day, the types that wouldn't be deterred by threats, the law, or even by brandished weapons—pit-bull types who would walk through a firestorm to get at the person they were obsessed with—but O'Connell seemed to him to really just be a petty criminal, and he had years of experience dealing with his type. What he couldn't see, the more he read about Michael O'Connell, was why this particular piece of minor-league garbage thought he could screw around with people like Sally Freeman-Richards and her daughter. He shook his head. He'd handled more than one homicide where an estranged boyfriend or husband had taken out his anger on some poor woman just trying to make her way. Murphy had a natural affinity for anyone seeking a way out of an abusive relationship. What he didn't understand was where the passion came from. In the cases he'd handled over the years, it seemed to him that love was perhaps the stupidest reason for throwing away one's freedom, one's future, or, in some cases, one's life.

Murphy took another look toward the apartment door. "Come on, kid," he said out loud. "Come on out where I can get a look at you. I've got better things to be doing."

As if on cue, he saw a movement in the sally port to O'-Connell's apartment building and, when he craned forward, immediately recognized O'Connell from the three-year-old mug shots.

He grabbed the camera and focused on O'Connell's face. To his surprise, O'Connell lingered for a moment, almost facing in his direction. He rapidly snapped off a half dozen frames.

"Got you," he said out loud, but to himself. Grinning. "You weren't hard to make."

What Murphy failed to realize at that moment was that the same was true of him.

*   *   *

It had been an easy call for Scott to make, although the arrangements were a little more complicated. The football coach had been in his office, going over game plans with his defensive coordinator. Scott had met the man on several occasions socially and made a point of attending as many games as he could.

"Coach Warner? It's Scott Freeman."

"Scott! Great to hear from you. But I'm a bit tied up right now . . ."

"Some unbelievably sophisticated defensive plan, designed to befuddle the enemy, rendering him into an ineffectual knot of incompetence?"

The coach laughed. "Yes. Absolutely. We won't accept anything less than a total emotional meltdown by the opposition. But surely that's not why you called?"

"I need a small favor. Some muscle."

"Muscle we have in abundance. But we also have classes and practice. The boys are pretty busy."

"How about on Sunday? I need two, maybe three guys. A very modest amount of heavy lifting, for which I will pay well and in cash."

"Sunday? That would be okay. What do you have in mind?"

"Actually, Coach, I need to move my daughter out of her apartment in Boston and get her things put in storage. In a hurry."

"This is the sort of blessedly simpleminded task that we football types are more than capable of performing," the coach said with a laugh. "Okay. I'll ask for a couple of volunteers today after practice, send them around tomorrow."

The three young men who showed up at Scott's office door the following morning were all huge and eager to make some extra cash. He rapidly explained that the job would consist of picking up a rental truck on Sunday morning, driving to Boston, packing everything in the apartment into cardboard boxes, and putting all the stuff in a storage facility just outside the city that he'd already arranged for.

"Need to get this done right away," Scott said. "No delays."

"What's the rush?" one of the boys asked.

Scott had anticipated the question. He had spent some time thinking precisely about what he wanted the three young men to know. Not the truth, certainly.

"My daughter is a grad student in Boston. Some time ago, she applied for some sort of grant to study abroad. Didn't think anything of it, but lo and behold, it just showed up the other day. But there's some sort of time restriction. Anyway, the upshot of the whole deal is that she's off to Florence to study Renaissance art for six to nine months. She's got to be on a plane in the next few days. And I don't want to end up paying for her apartment any longer than I already have to. I'm going to lose the security deposit, as is. Ah, well," he sighed with exaggerated drama. "If you like all those pictures of martyred saints and beheaded prophets, I guess that's where you've got to go. But I'm not imagining that the word *job* or the word *career* currently has much to do with my daughter's approach to life."

This caused the young men to laugh because it was something they could identify with. They made the final arrangements, and Scott told them he'd see them Sunday morning.

As the door closed, he thought, if anyone asks them, they will answer, gone. Out of the country. A credible story. Florence. They will remember that.

It was just a guess on his part, but he suspected a good one, that there would be one person who, assuming he spotted the three movers, would be most interested in the story Scott had so carefully planted.

Ashley felt a little ridiculous.

She had jammed a week's worth of clothing into a black duffel bag and a second week's worth into a small suitcase with rollers. The day before, the Federal Express deliveryman had arrived with a package for her from her father. It included two different guidebooks to cities in Italy, an English-Italian dictionary, and three large books about Renaissance art. Of these three, she already owned two. There was also a handbook put out by his own college called *A Student's Guide to Study Abroad.*

He had written up a brief letter, using his computer to make up an impressive masthead from the fictional Institute for the Study of Renaissance Art welcoming her to the program, and giving the name of a contact when she arrived in Rome. The contact was actually real—a professor at the University of Bologna whom Scott had once met at a historical conference, and whom he knew was on a yearlong sabbatical, teaching in Africa. He didn't think Michael O'Connell would ever be able to find him. And, even if he did, Scott had decided that mixing something fictional with someone real would at the very least be confusing. This, he had thought, was clever.

This letter was to be left behind by Ashley, as if forgotten by accident.

His directions for what she was supposed to do beyond leaving the fictional letter behind were detailed and, she thought, a little over-the-top. But he had made her promise that she would do precisely as he instructed. Nothing he was suggesting was truly out of line, and it all made eminently good sense, because to achieve what he wanted, some deception was in order.

One of the guidebooks was to be placed in an outside pocket on the duffel bag with the title protruding out, so that anyone who saw her carrying it couldn't help but notice it. The other books were to be left around the apartment, so that they would be packed, although Scott urged Ashley to arrange them prominently on her desktop and bedside table.

The next-to-last call she should make, before calling the telephone company and canceling her landline service, was to a taxi company.

When the cab arrived, she was to lock her apartment and place the key on the lintel above the outside door, where the football movers could easily find it.

Ashley looked around at the place that she'd come to regard as a sort of home. The posters on the walls, the potted
plants, the dingy orange shower curtain, had been her own,
and her first, and she was surprised by how emotional she
suddenly felt about the simplest of items. She sometimes
thought that she wasn't yet sure who she was, and who she
was going to become, but the apartment had been a first step
toward those definitions.

"God damn you!" she said out loud. She did not even have
to form the name in her mind.

She looked down at her father's handwritten note. All
right, she said to herself. Might as well play it out.

Then she went to the phone and dialed a cab.

She waited nervously right inside the apartment-building
door until the taxi arrived. Following her father's suggestions, she was wearing dark sunglasses and a knit hat pulled
down over her hair. Her jacket collar was turned up. *Look
like someone who doesn't want to be recognized and is in
the process of running away,* he had written her. She was a
little unsure whether she was acting, as if on a stage, or behaving reasonably. As the taxi rolled to a stop in front of her
building, she hurriedly stepped through the doorway and
placed the key where her father had told her to. Then, head
down, looking neither right nor left, she burst forward, acting as rapidly and as furtively as she could, still assuming
that Michael O'Connell was watching from some location.
It was early in the afternoon, and glare from the sun shredded the cool air around her, casting odd shadows into alley-
ways. She tossed her suitcase and duffel onto the seat, then
threw herself in behind them.

"Logan," she said. "International departures terminal."

Then she lowered her head, scrunching down in the seat
as if hiding.

At the airport, she gave the driver a modest tip and made a
point of saying, "Italy. I'm going to Florence. Going to
study abroad." She was unsure whether he understood anything she said.

She rolled her bags into the departures arena, her steps

punctuated by the constant roar of jets taking off above the harbor waters. There was excitement in the lines of people checking in. A hum of conversation, in all sorts of languages, filled the space. She glanced toward the exit gates, then she abruptly turned and headed to her right, to a bank of elevators. She fell in close with a crowd that had come off an Aer Lingus flight from Shannon, all redheads, white-skinned, speaking rapidly in accented tones, wearing the distinctive green-and-white-striped Celtic jerseys, on their way to a big family reunion in South Boston.

Ashley found a little space in the back of the elevator and quickly opened up her duffel bag. She stuffed her knit cap, fleece jacket, and sunglasses inside, removed a maroon Boston College baseball cap and a brown leather overcoat, changing swiftly, thankful that the other passengers, if they did notice what she was doing, seemed to think nothing of it.

She exited at the third-story walkway to the central parking garage. In the gray, shadowy parking area, smelling of oil and punctuated by high-pitched squealing sounds from tires on the circular ramps, she rapidly made her way across to the domestic terminals. She followed the signs toward the bus connecting to the T station.

Only a half dozen people were in the subway train compartment, and none of them were Michael O'Connell. There was no chance, she thought, that she was being followed. Not any longer. She began to feel excitement and a heady sense of freedom. Her pulse increased and she realized that she was smiling, probably for the first time in days.

Still, she elected to follow her father's instructions, thinking, They may be crazy, but I think they've worked so far. She got off the train at Congress Street and, still dragging her two bags, walked the few short blocks to the Children's Museum. Inside the entrance, she was able to check her bags and buy a single ticket. Then she rose up into the meandering maze of the museum, wandering from LEGO room to science exhibit, constantly surrounded by giggling squads of fast-moving children, teachers, and parents. She stood in the midst of all sorts of happy, excited noises and immediately understood the logic behind her father's plan: Michael O'Connell would have been unable to hide in the museum, despite the angles, stairs, and slides that filled it. He would instantly have stood out as wrong, where Ashley immediately became no different from any preschool teacher or mother's helper, making her slow and exhausted way through the crowds in the museum.

She checked her watch, still keeping to her father's schedule. At precisely 4 p.m. she retrieved her bags and exited directly into one of the cabs waiting outside. This time she inspected the street carefully for any signs of O'Connell. The museum was located in a onetime warehouse district, and the broad street was open in both directions. She recognized the genius in their choice of the location: no place to hide, no alleys, trees, dark places.

Ashley smiled and asked the cab to take her to the Peter Pan bus station. The driver grumbled—it was only a short ride— but she didn't care; for the first time in days it seemed, she had lost the sensation of being watched. She even hummed a little as the cab cut through the downtown Boston streets.

She purchased a ticket for Montreal on a bus leaving in less than ten minutes. The bus stopped in Brattleboro, Vermont, before going on to Canada; she would merely exit well before the destination on her ticket. And she was looking forward to seeing Catherine.

The stench of exhaust and grease filled her nostrils as she climbed onto the bus. It was already dark, and shafts of neon blended with the gleaming silver shape of the bus. She found a seat in the back, next to a window. For a moment, she stared out into the growing night and was a little amazed that instead of feeling uncertain and unsettled, she felt almost free. And when the driver slammed the door shut and ground the gears as he backed the bus out of its loading dock, she closed her eyes, listening to the rhythm of the engine, as it accelerated through downtown streets, heading toward the highway, and leaving the city behind. Although it was only early in the evening, she fell into a deep, dreamless sleep.

•

The sun was unrelenting. It was one of those Valley days where the stagnant air seemed trapped between the hills, obese with heat, when I parked a few blocks away from Matthew Murphy's office. A film of wavy, unapologetic warm air hung just above the sidewalk.

In many older New England cities, it is easy to see where the reconstruction dollars ran out and the local politicians counted up votes and saw little return. In the space of a single block or two, upscale businesses give way to a seedier, more decrepit look. It is not precisely decay, the way a tooth rots from the inside out, but more a sort of resignation.

The block where I expected to find his office was perhaps a little more run-down than some of the others. A dark and cavernous bar on the corner advertised TOPLESS ALL DAY ALL NITE on a handwritten sign stuck beneath a bright red BUD-WEISER neon light in the window. Across from that was a small bodega with stacks of chips, fruits, Tecate malt drink, and canned foodstuffs cluttering the aisles, and a Honduran flag hanging by the front door. The rest of the buildings were the ubiquitous redbrick of almost every city. A police car rolled past me.

I found the entrance to Murphy's building midblock. It was an unremarkable place, with a single elevator inside next to a directory that listed four offices on two floors.

Murphy was across from a social services agency. A cheap black wooden plaque by the door had his name and the phrase *Confidential Inquiries of All Natures* underneath in gold script.

I put my hand on the door to enter the office, but it was locked. I tried a couple of times, then reached up and knocked loudly.

There was no answer.

I knocked again and swore a couple of times under my breath.

When I stepped back, shaking my head and thinking that I had wasted the entire day driving down to the office, the door to the social services agency opened, and a middle-aged woman carrying an armful of dossiers emerged. She sighed when she saw me and offered up quickly, "No one's there anymore."

"Did they move?" I asked.

"Sort of. It was in the papers."

I looked surprised, and she frowned. "You have business with Murphy?"

"I have some questions for him."

"Well," she said stiffly, "I can give you his new address. It's just a half dozen blocks from here."

"Great. Where about are we talking?"

She shrugged. "River View Cemetery."

23

Anger

He reminded himself to remain calm.

This was difficult for Michael O'Connell. He generally functioned better on the edge of rage, where streaks of fury colored his judgment, reliably steering him into places where he was comfortable. A fight. An insult. An obscenity. These were all moments that he enjoyed almost as much as he did when he was making plans. There were few things, he thought, more satisfying than predicting what people would do, then watching them do it, just as he'd imagined they would.

He had observed Ashley's furtive dash from her building to the taxi, noting the cab company and identifying number. He wasn't surprised that she was going somewhere. Running came naturally to people like Ashley and her family, he had told himself. He considered them cowards.

He called the dispatcher for the cab service, gave the taxi's

ID number, and said he'd found some prescription glasses in a case that the young lady had apparently dropped on the sidewalk. Was there any way he could return them to her?

The dispatcher had hesitated for a moment while he went over his log of radio calls.

"Ah, I don't think so, fella."

"Why not?" O'Connell had asked.

"That trip was to the international departures terminal at Logan. You might as well just chuck 'em. Or drop 'em in one of those eyeglasses-for-charity boxes you see."

"Well," O'Connell said, trying to make a joke, "somebody's not gonna see too many sights in wherever they're going on vacation."

"Tough luck for her."

That was an understatement, Michael O'Connell thought, seething inwardly.

Now he was perched a half block from her apartment, watching three young men move boxes out of her apartment building. They had a midsize U-Haul truck double-parked in the street outside, and they seemed to be hustling to get the job done and get on their way. Once again, O'Connell told himself to remain calm. He shrugged his shoulders to try to loosen the tension that had built up in his neck, and he clenched and unclenched his fists a half dozen times, trying to relax himself. Then he slowly sauntered down the block toward where the three young men were working.

One of the boys was carrying two boxes of books, with a lamp precariously balanced on top, when O'Connell arrived at the front stoop. The boy was a little unsteady under the weight.

"Hey, coming or going?" O'Connell asked.

"Just moving out," the boy replied.

"Let me grab that for you," O'Connell said, reaching out for the lamp before it fell to the sidewalk. He had an electric sensation as he wrapped his fingers around the metallic base, as if the mere touch of Ashley's belongings were the same as stroking her skin. His hand caressed the lamp, and in his mind's eye he recalled precisely where it had been in the apartment, on the bedside table. He could sense the light throwing an arc over her body, illuminating curves and shapes. His breathing accelerated, and he almost felt dizzy when he handed it to the moving boy.

"Thanks," the boy responded as he wedged the lamp unceremoniously into the truck. "Just got the damn desk and the bed and a rug or two to go."

O'Connell swallowed hard and gestured toward a pink bedspread. He remembered that one night he had kicked it aside, before bending over her form. "This isn't your stuff?"

"Nah," the boy responded, stretching his back. "We're moving a professor's daughter's stuff. Getting paid pretty well."

"Not bad," O'Connell said slowly, as if biting off each word, working hard to keep anything other than idle curiosity out of his voice. "This must be the girl that lives on the second floor. I live down there." He gestured toward a couple of other buildings. "She's pretty hot. She leaving town?"

"Florence, Italy, the man says. Got a scholarship to study."

"Not bad. Sounds like a good deal."

"No shit."

"Well, good luck with the stuff." O'Connell gave a small wave and continued walking. He crossed the street and found a tree trunk to lean against.

He breathed in rapidly, letting an icy cold compulsion build up inside him. He watched Ashley's furniture disappear into the back of the truck and wondered if what he was watching was really happening. It was like standing in front of a movie screen, where everything seemed real, but not. A taxi driver with a fare to Logan International Airport. A trio of college kids packing and moving on a quiet Sunday morning. A private detective with an address in Springfield taking his picture from a car parked across from his own apartment. Michael O'Connell knew it added up to something, but precisely what, he wasn't yet certain. He was sure of one thing, however. If Ashley's folks thought that buying her a plane ticket would get her away from him, they were genuinely mistaken. All they had managed was to make things far more interesting for him. He would find her, even if he had to fly all the way to Italy.

"No one steals from me," he whispered to himself. "No one takes what's mine."

Catherine Frazier pulled her fleece jacket a little closer and watched her breath like smoke curl in front of her. The night air had an edge that predicted the evenings to come. Vermont is like that, she thought, it always gives a warning about what is coming, if one is only careful enough to pay attention. A cold taste of the dark sky on her lips, a sensation of numbness on her cheeks, above her a rattle of tree branches, a thin edge of ice on the ponds in the morning. There would be flurries in the next few days. She made a mental note to check her store of split wood piled up behind her house. She wished she could read people with the same accuracy as she did the weather.

The Boston bus was a little late, and instead of waiting inside the bowling alley and restaurant where it made its stop before heading on to Burlington and Montreal, she had stepped outside. Bright lights made her strangely nervous; she was more comfortable in shadows and fog.

She was looking forward to seeing Ashley, although, as always, she was a little nervous about how precisely she was to refer to her during her visit. Ashley wasn't her granddaughter, nor was she a niece. She wasn't related through adoption, although that was closest to what she was. Vermonters, as a rule, rarely butted into anyone else's business, having that Yankee sensibility that the less said, the better. But Catherine knew that the other ladies of her church, and the folks behind the counter at the general store, the Ace Hardware, and other places where she was well-known, would have their questions. Like many in New England, they all had fined-tuned radars for any small act that suggested hypocrisy. And something about welcoming her daughter's partner's child into her home, while silently but obviously condemning that relationship, put some feelings on edge.

Catherine put her head back and let her eyes sweep over the canopy of night sky. She wondered if one could have as many conflicted feelings as there were stars in the heavens.

Ashley had been a child when she had first entered Catherine's life. She remembered her first meeting with Ashley and found herself smiling in the darkness at the memory. I was wearing too many clothes. It was hot, but I had on a woolen skirt and sweater. How silly. I must have seemed like I was a hundred years old.

Catherine had been stiff, almost arch, stupidly formal, holding out her hand for a handshake, when she had been introduced to the eleven-year-old Ashley. But the child had disarmed her immediately, and so, in some respects, what truce she had with her own daughter, and the civility she displayed outwardly toward her daughter's partner—Catherine hated that word; it made their relationship seem like a business—stemmed from her affection for Ashley. She had attended raucous birthday parties and dismally wet soccer games, watched Ashley play Juliet in a high school production, although she hated it when the character Ashley played died on the stage. She had sat on the edge of Ashley's bed one night while the fifteen-year-old had sobbed uncontrollably at the breakup with her first boyfriend, and she had driven fast, far faster than ordinary, to get to Hope and Sally's home in time to snap pictures of Ashley in her prom dress. She had nursed Ashley through a bout with the flu, when Sally had been preoccupied with a court case, sleeping on the floor next to her, listening for her breathing throughout the night. She had hosted Ashley when she'd shown up, camping gear in tow, with a couple of college friends, heading toward the Green Mountains, and entertained her at dinner in Boston on a couple of happy occasions and one truly wonderful time in the bleacher seats at Fenway, when Catherine had found an excuse to go to the city and had offhandedly called, although she had inwardly known that seeing Ashley was the real reason for the trip.

She pawed at the gravel in the parking lot, waiting for the bus, and thought to herself that life had not delivered to her the grandchildren that she had wanted and expected, but instead fate had delivered Ashley. She believed that in the first moment that she had met Ashley, and the child had peered out shyly and asked, "Would you like to see my room? Maybe we can read a book together?" that she had entered into a wholly different realm, where Ashley was exempted from all the disappointment and difficulty that Catherine and Hope experienced.

"Damn it," Catherine said out loud. "How late can a bus be?"

In that moment she heard the wheezing noise of a big diesel engine, slowing to make a turn, and she saw headlights cutting across the darkness of the parking lot. She stepped forward quickly, already waving her arms above her head in greeting.

Sally's secretary buzzed her and said, "I have a Mr. Murphy on the phone who says he has some information for you."

"Put him through," Sally said.

"Hello, Mr. Murphy. What have you got for me?"

"Well," he said, speaking in a world-weary, cynical tone, "not as much as I can get, and will get, assuming you want me to continue, but I was figuring that you'd want an update sooner rather than later, given the, ah, personal nature of this particular inquiry."

"That would be correct."

"You want the bottom line? Or details first?"

"Just tell me what you know."

"Well, I don't think you've got too much to worry about. You've got something to worry about, that's for sure, don't get me wrong, but let me put it this way: I've seen worse."

Sally felt a surge of relief. "Okay, that's good. Why don't you fill me in?"

"Well, he's got a record. Not a real long one, and not one with a whole lot of red flags, if you know what I mean, but enough to be concerned."

"Violence?"

"Some. Not too much. Fights, that sort of thing. No weapons that I can see from the charges filed against him. That's good. But it can also mean he just hasn't been caught."

"Look," Murphy continued, "this guy O'Connell seems like a bad guy. But I've got the feeling that he's a lightweight. I mean, I've seen his type a million times, and with a little no-nonsense pressure, they fold up like a stack of chairs. You want to put up the cash, I can arrange for a couple of my buddies and me to go pay him a little visit. Put the fear of God into him. Make him understand that he's screwing around with the wrong sort of folks. Maybe help him to understand that a different approach to life will be healthier for him, all around."

"Are you saying threaten him?"

"No, ma'am. And I would certainly not advocate violence in any regard." Murphy paused, letting those words sink in, and letting Sally understand that he was saying exactly the opposite. "Because that would be a crime. And, as an officer of the court, I know, Counselor, that you would never hire me to injure someone. No, ma'am. I understand that. What I'm saying is that he can be, ah, *intimidated.* That's it. Intimidated. All well within the absolute letter of the law. As you and I understand the law to be. But something that definitely will make him think twice about what he's doing."

"That's a step maybe we should consider."

"Be happy to. Won't cost too much, either. Just the usual per diem and travel for me. A little something for my, ah, companions."

"Well," Sally said, letting a little hesitancy creep into her voice, "I'm not sure that I'm too comfortable with involving anyone else. Even friends whose, well, whose *discretion* in these sorts of matters you have confidence in. Especially a state policeman who might be forced, at some much later point, to testify in court, ah, truthfully. I'm just trying to think ahead here. Get a grasp on future eventualities and possibilities. Need to cover all bases, so to speak."

Murphy thought all lawyers failed to understand the lines between reality as it took place on the street and what was subsequently described by utterly reasonable people in the cool tones of a court of law. These were distinctions lost on almost all of them. Sometimes bloody distinctions. He sighed a little, but hid it from his voice.

"You make a good point, Counselor. But my guess is that I could handle this part of the, ah, arrangement, on my own, without involving anyone currently in a law enforcement job. If that was what you wanted."

"That would be wise."

"I should go ahead, then?"

"Why don't you design an approach, Mr. Murphy? And we'll go from there."

"I'll be in touch."

The telephone line went dead in her hand. Sally sat back in her chair feeling unsettled at the same time that she was reassured, which, she understood, was a complete contradiction.

•

It was a typical urban cemetery, tucked into a neglected corner of the small city, with a black wrought-iron fence surrounding it. My eyes swept the rows of gray headstones marked with name after name. They grew in stature as they marched up the slope of the hill. Simple slabs of granite gave way to more elaborate shapes and forms. The messages carved on the gravestones grew more elaborate as well. Lengthy testimonials to BELOVED WIFE AND MOTHER or DEVOTED FATHER. I didn't think Matthew Murphy, from what I already knew of him, was likely to be interred beneath horn-playing cherubs.

I started to walk up and down the rows, feeling my shirt stick to my back, and a thin line of sweat break out on my forehead. Right about the time I was about to give up, I saw a single, modest headstone with the name MATTHEW THOMAS MURPHY above a set of dates. Nothing else.

I wrote down the dates and stood for a moment. "What happened?" I asked out loud.

Not even a wisp of breeze or a ghostly vision replied.

Then I thought, with more than a small twinge of irritation, I knew who could answer that question.

There was a filling station a couple of blocks from the cemetery with a pay phone. I plugged some coins into the machine and dialed her number.

I didn't identify myself when she picked up the line. "You lied to me," I said, irritation in my voice.

She paused and I heard her take a deep breath. "How so? *Lie* is such a strong word."

"You told me to go see Murphy. And I find him not in some office, but in a graveyard. Turning himself into food for earthworms and maggots. Seems like a *lie* to me. What the hell is this all about?"

Again she hesitated, measuring cautiously. "But what did you *see*?"

"I saw a grave. A cheap headstone."

"Then you haven't seen enough."

"What the hell else was there to see?" I demanded.

Her voice was suddenly cold, distant. Almost wintry. "Look harder. Look much harder. Would I have sent you there for no reason? You see a slab of granite with a name and some dates. I see a *story*."

Then she hung up the phone.

24

Intimidation

He figured one more day spent on Michael O'Connell would be more than adequate.

Matthew Murphy had other, far more critical cases crying out for attention. Photographs of illicit affairs to be taken, records of tax evasion to be checked, people to be followed, people to be confronted, people to be questioned. He knew that Sally Freeman-Richards wasn't one of the better-heeled lawyers in the area; no BMW or Mercedes sedan for her, and he knew that the modest bill he would send her way would reflect some sort of courtesy discount. Maybe just the opportunity to play a little head game on the punk was worth 10 percent. He didn't get the chance to strong-arm too many folks anymore, and it brought back memories that he found enjoyable. Nothing like playing the tough guy to get one's heart pumping and adrenaline flowing.

He parked his car two blocks away from O'Connell's apartment in an enclosed lot. He drove up several flights of spaces until he was certain that he was alone, stopped, then went to the trunk of his car. He kept several weapons locked in the back, each in a worn duffel bag of its own. A long, red bag contained a fully automatic Colt AR-15 rifle with a twenty-two-shot banana clip. He considered it his get-out-of-big-trouble-fast weapon, because it was capable of blowing the hell out of just about any problem. In a smaller, yellow duffel, he kept a .380 automatic in a shoulder holster. In a third, black duffel, was a .357 revolver with a six-inch barrel loaded with the Teflon-coated bullets called cop killers because they would penetrate the body armor used by most police forces.

But, for the current assignment, he thought the .380 the right choice. He wasn't sure he would have to do anything more than let O'Connell know he wore it, which an unbuttoned suit coat would display easily enough. Matthew Murphy was practiced in all the methods of intimidation.

He slipped into the shoulder harness, pulled on a pair of thin, black leather gloves, and then, in a familiar fashion, practiced removing the weapon rapidly once or twice. When Murphy was satisfied that his old skills were as sharp as ever, he set out. A small breeze swirled some debris around his feet as he walked. Just enough light remained in the day for him to find a convenient shadow across from O'Connell's building, and as he slid his back up against a brick wall, he saw the first streetlights blink on. He hoped he wouldn't have to stand there too long, but he was patient and practiced at the art of waiting.

*   *   *

Scott felt a rush of self-congratulatory pride.

He had already received a message on his answering machine from Ashley, who had successfully followed his maze of directions and linked up with Catherine in Vermont. He was delighted with the way things had gone so far.

The football boys had returned after unloading Ashley's things into a self-storage facility in Medford. Scott had ascertained that, as he'd suspected, a fellow fitting O'Connell's description had indeed asked some questions before giving a transparently phony story and disappearing down the street. But he'd been left clutching air, Scott thought. Grabbing at a phantom. All his answers would lead nowhere.

"Didn't see this one coming, did you, you son of a bitch?" he said out loud.

He was standing in the small living room of his house, and he broke into a small jig on the worn Oriental carpet. After a second, he picked up the remote control that operated his stereo and punched buttons until Jimi Hendrix's "Purple Haze" crashed through the speakers.

When Ashley had been little, he'd taught her the old twenties' phrase *cut a rug* for dancing, so that she would come to him when he was working and interrupt him by asking, "Can we go cut a rug?" and the two of them would put on his old sixties' music and he would show her the Frug and the Swim and even the Freddy, which was, to his adult mind, the most ridiculous series of motions ever created probably in the entire history of the world. She would giggle and imitate him until she would tumble to the floor with childish peals of laughter. But even then, Ashley had owned a kind of grace of movement that astonished him. There was never anything clumsy or stumbling about any step Ashley took; to his mind, it was always a ballet. He knew that he was smitten in the way that fathers with daughters often are, but he'd applied his critical, academic approach to his perceptions and come away reinforced with the notion that nothing else could ever be as beautiful as his own child.

Scott breathed out. He couldn't imagine how Michael O'Connell would ever guess that she was in Vermont. Now it was simply a matter of letting some time pass, designing a new set of studies in a different city, then having Ashley pick up more or less where she had left off. A minor setback, a six-month delay, but bigger trouble averted.

Scott picked up his head and looked around the living room.

He felt suddenly alone and wished there was someone that he could share his feelings of elation with. None of his current crop of go-to-dinner-and-have-occasional-sex dates really fit the bill. His real friends at the college were truly professional in nature, and he doubted that any of them would understand. Not for one instant.

He frowned. The only person that he had really shared with was Sally. And he wasn't about to call her. Not at that moment.

A wave of black resentment passed through him.

She had left him to take up with Hope. It had been abrupt. Sudden. A collection of bags packed and waiting in the hallway while he tried to think of the right thing to say, knowing that there wasn't one. He had known she was unhappy. He had known she was unfulfilled and filled with doubts. But he'd assumed these things were about her career, or perhaps the way looking at middle age becomes frightening, or maybe even boredom with the complacent academic, liberal world that they occupied together. All these things he could wrap his imagination around, discuss, assess, comprehend. What he couldn't understand was how everything that they'd once known could suddenly be a lie.

For a moment, he imagined Sally in bed with Hope. What can she give her that I didn't? he demanded of himself, then, just as quickly, realized that that was an extraordinarily dangerous question to ask. He didn't want to know that particular answer.

He shook his head. The marriage was a lie, he thought.

The *I do*s and *I love you*s and *Let's make a life together* were all lies. The only true thing that came out of it was Ashley, and he was even unsure about that. When we conceived her, did she love me? When she carried her, did she love me? When she was born, did Sally know then it was all a lie? Did it come on suddenly? Or was it something she knew all along, and as she was busy lying to herself? He put his head down for an instant, flooded with images. Ashley playing at the seashore. Ashley going to kindergarten. Ashley making him a card with flowers drawn all over it for Father's Day. He still had that taped to the wall of his office. Did Sally know, during all those moments? At Christmas and on birthdays? At Halloween parties and Easter egg hunts? He did not know, but he did understand that the détente between them after the divorce was a lie, too, but an important one to protect Ashley. She was always seen as the fragile one, the one with something to lose. Somewhere in all those days, months, and years together, Scott and Sally had already lost whatever it was that they were going to lose.

He repeated to himself, She's safe now.

Scott went to a small cabinet and took out a bottle of Scotch. He poured himself a stiff drink, took a sip, let the bitter amber liquid slide slowly down his throat, then raised his glass in a mock, solitary toast: "To us. To all of us. Whatever the hell that means."

Michael O'Connell, too, was thinking about love. He was at a bar and had dropped a shot glass of Scotch into a mug of beer, making a boilermaker, a drink designed to dull the senses. He could feel himself seething within and realized that no drug and no drink would be sufficient to cover up the tension building inside him. No matter how much he drank, he was resigned to a nasty sobriety.

He stared at the mug in front of him, closed his eyes, and allowed rage to reverberate inside him, pinging off all the walls of his heart and imagination. He did not like being outmaneuvered or outthought or out-anythinged for that matter, and punishing the people who had done it was his immediate number one priority. He was angry with himself for believing that the modest Internet troubles he'd already delivered to them would be adequate. Ashley's family needed a far harsher series of lessons. They had cheated him out of something he was owed.

The more O'Connell raged at the indignity and insult to him, the more he found himself picturing Ashley. He imagined her hair, falling in red-blond strands to her shoulders, perfect, soft. He could draw in his mind's eye every detail of her face, shading it like an artist, finding a smile for him on the lips, an invitation in the eyes. His thoughts cascaded down her body, measuring every curve, the sensuousness of her breasts, the subtle arc to her hips. He could imagine her legs stretched out beside him, and when he looked up into the dim light of the bar, he could sense himself getting aroused. He shifted on his bar stool and thought that Ashley was ideal, except that she wasn't because she had engineered this slap across his face. A blow to his heart. And as the liquor loosened his feelings, he could sense his reply; no caress, no gentle probing, he thought coldly. Hurt her, the way she'd hurt him. It was the only way to make her understand completely how much he loved her.

Again he twitched in his seat. He was fully aroused now.

He had once read in a novel that the warriors of certain African tribes had become engorged with passion in the moments before battle. Shield in one hand, killing spear in the other, an erection between their legs, they had charged their enemies.

He liked that.

Making no effort to hide the bulge in his pants, Michael O'Connell pushed away his empty glass and stood up. He hoped for a moment that someone would stare or comment. More than anything in that second, he wanted a fight.

No one did. A little disappointed, he crossed the room and walked out onto the street. Night had descended, and a cold chill touched his face. It did nothing to cool his imagination. He could picture himself looming over Ashley, thrusting at her, penetrating her, using every inch, every crevice, every space on the body for his own pleasure. He could hear her responding, and to him there was little difference between moans and cries of desire, and sobs of pain. Love and hurt. A caress and a blow. They were all the same.

Despite the cold, he undid his jacket, unbuttoned his shirt, letting the cool air slide over him as he marched along, head back, gulping in huge breaths. The chill did little to erase his desires. Love is like a disease, he thought to himself. Ashley was a virus that coursed along unchecked in his veins. He understood in that second that she would never leave him alone. Not for a single waking second, for the rest of his life. He walked on, thinking that the only way to control his love for Ashley was to control Ashley. Nothing had ever seemed so clear to him before.

Michael O'Connell rounded the corner to the block to his apartment, his mind churning with images of lust and blood, all mingling together in a great dangerous stew, and not paying quite the attention that he should have paid when he heard a low voice behind him.

"Let's go have a little talk, O'Connell." An iron-hard grip seized him by his upper arm.

Matthew Murphy had easily spotted O'Connell as he passed beneath the glow of a streetlamp. It had been a simple matter to sweep out of his shadow and come up behind him. Murphy had been trained in these techniques, and all his instincts over twenty-five years of police work told him that O'Connell was a novice at true criminality.

"Who the hell are you?" O'Connell stammered.

"I'm your biggest fucking nightmare, asshole. Now open up the door and let's go up to your place nice and quiet like, so I can explain the world and the way it works to you in a civilized manner, without beating the shit out of you or far worse. You don't want worse, do you, O'Connell? What do your friends call you? OC? Or maybe just plain Mike? What is it?"

O'Connell started to twist, which only made the pressure on his arm tighten, and he stopped. Before he could answer, Murphy thrust another rapid series of questions at him.

"Maybe Michael O'Connell doesn't have any friends, so no nickname. So, tell you what, Mike-y boy, I'll just make it up as we go along. Because, trust me, you want me to be your friend. You want that more than you've ever wanted anything in this world. Right now, Mike-y boy, that's your absolute, top, number one need on this planet: making sure that I remain your friend. Do you get that?"

O'Connell grunted, trying to turn enough to get a good look at Murphy, but the onetime trooper stayed right behind him, leaning in, whispering into his ear, while all the time keeping a steady pressure on his arm and in the small of his back, pushing him forward.

"Inside. Up the stairs. Your place, Mike-y boy. So we can have our little chat in private."

Half-pushed, half-forced, O'Connell was steered through the entranceway and up to the second floor by the constant pressure from Matthew Murphy, who kept up a cold, mocking banter with each step.

Murphy increased his grip, squeezing at the muscle as they reached O'Connell's door, and he could feel O'Connell react to the sharp pain. "That's another thing about being friends, Mike-y boy. You don't want me angry. You just don't want me losing me temper. Might force me to do something you'd later regret, if you had a later in which to regret it, which I would sincerely doubt. You understand? Now open your door slowly."

As O'Connell managed to get the key out of his pocket and into the lock, Murphy looked down the hallway and saw the neighboring old lady's cat collection scurrying about. One even arched its back and hissed in O'Connell's direction.

"Not too popular with the locals, are you, Mike-y boy?" Murphy said, twisting the younger man's arm again. "You got something against cats? They got something against you?"

"We don't get along," O'Connell grunted.

"I'm not surprised." Murphy gave the younger man a vicious shove, sending him stumbling ahead into the apartment. O'Connell tripped over a threadbare rug on the floor, sprawling forward, thudding hard into a wall, twisting around to try to get his first real look at Murphy.

But the detective was on top of him with surprising quickness for a middle-aged man, looming over O'Connell like a gargoyle hanging from a medieval church, his face set in a half-mocking grin, but his eyes wearing a look of harsh anger. O'Connell scrambled to rise at least to a half-sitting position, and he stared up at Murphy, locking his eyes on the ex-detective's.

"Not too happy, are you, Mike-y boy? Not accustomed to being tossed around, are you?"

O'Connell didn't reply. He was still assessing the situation, and he knew enough to keep his mouth shut.

Murphy took that moment to slowly pull back his suit coat, revealing the .380 in its shoulder harness. "I brought a friend, Mike-y boy. As you can see."

The younger man grunted again, shifting his eyes between the weapon and the private investigator. Murphy swiftly reached inside his jacket and removed the automatic. He had not been intending to do this, but something in O'Connell's defiant stare told him to accelerate the process. With a rapid movement, he chambered a round and rested his thumb up against the safety catch. Slowly, he moved the pistol down toward O'Connell, until he finally rested the barrel up against the younger man's forehead, directly between the eyes.

"Fuck you," O'Connell said.

Murphy tapped the gun barrel against O'Connell's nose. Just hard enough so it would hurt, not hard enough to break anything. "Poor choice of words," Murphy said. With his left hand, he reached down and grasped O'Connell's cheeks, pinching them between his fingers, squeezing tightly. "And I thought we were going to be friends."

O'Connell continued to stare at the ex-detective, and Murphy abruptly slammed his head back against the wall. "A little more politeness," he said coldly. "A little more civility. Makes everything go much smoother." Then he reached down, grabbed O'Connell's jacket, and lifted him up, keeping the handgun firmly planted on O'Connell's forehead. Murphy maneuvered the younger man into a chair, half-tossing him so that O'Connell crashed back, the chair lifting on its back legs, and he had to struggle to keep his balance. "I haven't even really been bad, yet, Mike-y boy. Not at all. We're still just getting to know one another."

"You're not a cop, are you?"

"You know cops, do you, Mike-y boy? You've sat across from a cop more than once or twice, haven't you?"

O'Connell nodded.

"Well, you're absolutely fucking one hundred percent correct," Murphy said, smiling. He had known this question was coming. "You should wish I was a cop. I mean, you should be praying right now to whatever God it is that you think might just listen to you, praying, 'Please, Lord, let him be a cop,' because cops, they've got rules, Mike-y boy. Rules and regulations. Nope. Not me. I'm a lot more trouble than that. Much worse. Much much worse. I'm a private investigator."

O'Connell sneered, and Murphy slapped him hard across the face. The sound of his palm striking O'Connell's cheek resounded through the small apartment.

Murphy smiled. "I shouldn't have to explain these things to you, not someone who thinks he knows his way around like you do, Mike-y boy. But, just for the sake of our little discussion this evening, let me explain a few items. One, I was a cop. Put in more than twenty years fucking with folks a whole lot tougher than you. Most of those tough guys are sitting in stir, cursing my name. Or else they're real dead, and not thinking too much about yours truly because they probably have much more significant problems in the hereafter. Two, I am duly licensed by the Commonwealth of Massachusetts and the United States federal government and fully authorized to carry this weapon. Now, you know what those two little things add up to?"

O'Connell didn't reply, and Murphy slapped him again.

"Shit!" The word burst out of O'Connell's lips.

"When I ask you a question, Mike-y boy, please respond."

Murphy pulled back his hand again, and O'Connell said, "I don't know. What do they add up to?"

Murphy grinned. "What it means is that I've got friends— real friends, not like our little play friendship here tonight, Mike-y boy, but real friends who owe me all sorts of real favors, whose butts I might just have pulled out of one fire or another over all those years and would be more than willing to do absolutely fucking anything for me, and who are gonna believe everything I say about our little get-together here tonight if it comes to that. They aren't going to give a damn about a punk like you, no matter what happens. And when I tell them that you came at me with a knife or just about any sort of weapon that I can plant in your dead and lifeless hand, and I tell 'em it was just some damn tough luck, but I just had to blow your sorry little ass away, they're going to believe me. In fact, Mike-y boy, they're gonna congratulate me for cleaning up this world a little bit, before you had a chance to make any really big trouble. They'll file it away under *preventative maintenance*. So, that's the situation you're currently in, Mike-y boy. In other words, I can do just about anything I fucking well want to, and you can't do a thing. Is that clear?"

O'Connell hesitated, then nodded when he caught sight of Murphy pulling back his hand for another slap.

"Good. Understanding, they say, is the path to enlightenment."

O'Connell could taste a little blood on his lips.

"Let me just repeat this so that we are completely clear: I am free to do anything I might think right, including send your sorry little life straight to kingdom come or more likely hell. You get this, Mike-y boy?"

"I get the picture."

Murphy started to walk around the chair. He kept the barrel of the automatic in contact with O'Connell's skin, occasionally tapping it painfully against his head, or digging it into the soft space between O'Connell's neck and his shoulders.

"This is a really crummy place you've got here, Mike-y boy. Pretty run-down. Dirty." Murphy stared across the room and saw a laptop computer on a table, making a mental note to take a handful of O'Connell's backup discs with him.

So far, things were going more or less as Murphy had anticipated. O'Connell was as predicted. He could sense the younger man's discomfort, knew that the insistent rapping of the weapon against his head was creating indecision and doubt. In all moments of confrontation, Murphy thought, at some point the skilled interrogator simply takes over the subject's identity, controlling, steering him to compliance. We're on track, Murphy thought to himself. We're definitely making progress.

"Not much of a life, is it, Mike-y boy? I mean, I'm not seeing much of a future here."

"It suits me."

"Yes. But what is it about this that makes you think for a single second that Ashley Freeman would want to be a part of it?"

O'Connell remained quiet, and Murphy whacked him from behind with his free hand. "Answer the question, asshole."

"I love her. She loves me."

Murphy slapped him again. "I don't think so, you low-life, bottom-dwelling slug."

A thin line of blood came from O'Connell's ear.

"She's a class act, Mike-y boy. Unlike you, she's got possibilities. She comes from fine folks, and she's well educated and filled with all sorts of big-time potential. You, on the other hand, come from shit." Murphy accentuated the last few words by smacking the younger man hard. "And you're going to end up in shit. What? Prison? Or do you think you can manage to stay out?"

"I'm okay. I haven't broken any laws."

The repeated blows were taking effect. O'Connell's voice cracked slightly, and Murphy thought he could hear a little quaver behind the words.

"Really? You want me looking at you any closer?"

Murphy had come full circle, and once again he tapped the gun barrel against the bridge of O'Connell's nose, demanding a response.

"No."

"Didn't think so."

He grabbed O'Connell's chin and twisted it painfully. He could see some tears in the corners of the younger man's eyes. "But, Mike-y, don't you think you ought to be asking me a little more politely to stay out of your life?"

"Please stay out of my life," O'Connell said slowly and quietly.

"Well, I'd like to. I'd genuinely like to. So, Mike-y boy, just looking at it all, objective-like, don't you think it would be a really, really good thing for you to absolutely make sure that I'm not in your life anymore? That this little get-together, friendly as it might be, is the absolute last time you and I ever see each other? Right?"

"Right." O'Connell wasn't sure which question to answer, but he was sure that he didn't want to be hit again. And while he didn't think that the man in front of him would shoot him, he wasn't totally sure.

"I need to be persuaded, don't I?"

"Yes."

Murphy smiled. Then he patted O'Connell on the head. "Just so we truly understand each other, what we're doing here is negotiating our own private, special, one-on-one temporary restraining order. Just as if we'd gone to court. Except ours is fucking permanent, got it? I know you know what one of them means: stay away. No contact. But ours, because it is a special one, just between you and me, Mike-y boy, well, because ours isn't any wimpy old sort of eminently forgettable piece of paper issued by some old-fart judge that you're not gonna pay any attention to, ours comes with a real guarantee."

With the final word, Murphy slammed his fist into O'Connell's cheek, sending him sprawling on the floor. Murphy was over him, automatic in hand, before the younger man had a chance even to collect his thoughts.

"Maybe I should just stop fucking around and end this right now." With an audible click, Murphy released the safety catch on the pistol with his thumb. He held up his left hand as if to shield himself from the blowback of brains and blood.

"Give me a reason. One way or the other, Mike-y boy. But give me a reason to make a decision."

O'Connell tried to twist away from the gun barrel, but the ex-detective's weight pinned him to the floor. "Please," he suddenly pleaded, "please, I'll stay away, I promise. I'll leave her alone."

"Good start, asshole. Keep going."

"I'll never have any contact whatsoever. She's out of my life. I'll stay away. What do you want me to say?"

O'Connell was nearly sobbing. Each phrase seemed more pitiful than the last.

"Let me think about it, Mike-y boy."

Murphy lowered his shielding hand and pulled his weapon back from O'Connell's face.

"Don't move. I just want to look around."

He walked over to the cheap table where the computer rested. A handful of unmarked rewritable discs was spread about. Murphy grabbed them and slipped them into his coat pocket. Then he turned back toward the younger man, who remained on the floor. "This where you keep your Ashley file? This where you screw around with folks who are a whole lot better than you?"

O'Connell simply nodded and Murphy smiled. "I don't think so," he said briskly. "Not anymore." Then he smashed the butt of the pistol down onto the keyboard. "Whoops," he said as the plastic splintered. Two more blows to the screen and the mouse left the machine in pieces.

O'Connell simply watched, saying nothing. Using the barrel of the gun, Murphy poked at the shattered computer. "I think we're just about finished, Mike-y boy." He walked back across the room and stood above O'Connell. "I want you to remember something," he said quickly.

"What?" O'Connell's eyes were filled, as Murphy expected them to be.

"I can always find you. I can always run you to ground, no matter what nasty little rathole you crawl into."

The younger man just nodded.

Murphy looked closely at him, staring hard, searching his

face for signs of defiance, signs of anything other than compliance. When he was persuaded that there were none, he
smiled.

"Good. You've learned a lot tonight, Mike-y boy. A real
education. And it hasn't been too bad, has it? I've pretty
much enjoyed our little get-together. Almost fun, wouldn't
you say? No, probably you wouldn't. But there's just one last
thing . . ."

He suddenly bent over and dropped to his knees, once
again pinning O'Connell to the floor. In the same movement, he abruptly shoved the barrel of the automatic into
O'Connell's mouth, feeling it smash against his teeth. He
could see terror in the younger man's eyes, exactly what he
was looking for.

"Bang," he said quietly.

Then he slowly removed the weapon from O'Connell's
mouth, rose, gave him a grin, then pivoted abruptly and exited.

The cool night air hit Matthew Murphy in the face and he
wanted to put his head back and laugh out loud. He replaced
the .380 automatic in the shoulder holster, adjusted his coat
so he would look presentable, and started off down the street,
moving along rapidly, but not in any particular hurry, enjoying the darkness, the city, and the sensation of success. He
was already calculating how long it would take him to drive
back to Springfield and wondering whether he would get
there in time to catch a late dinner. He took a few strides and
started to hum to himself. He had been right. The opportunity
to deal with a punk like O'Connell was worth the 10 percent
discount he was going to give Sally Freeman-Richards. Now
that wasn't so damn hard, was it? he said to himself. He was
delighted to remind himself that none of his old skills had
dissipated, and he felt decidedly younger. First thing in the
morning, he would do up a small report—leaving out the
parts where the automatic had figured most prominently—
and send it along to Sally, accompanied by his bill and his as-

sessment that she would not have to worry about Michael
O'Connell again. Murphy prided himself on knowing precisely what fear can do to the minds of weak people.

O'Connell's ear throbbed and his cheek stung. He figured that
one or more of his teeth might be loose because he could taste
blood in his mouth. He was a little stiff when he rose from the
floor, but he went directly to the window and just managed to
catch a glimpse of the ex-detective as he turned the corner of
the block. Michael O'Connell wiped his hand across his face
and thought, Now that wasn't so damn hard, was it? He understood that the easiest way to make a policeman believe
him was always to take the beating. It was sometimes painful,
sometimes embarrassing, especially when it was some old
guy, whom he knew he could easily have handled anytime except the time when the guy had a gun and he did not. Then he
smiled, licking his lips and letting the salty taste fill him. He
had learned a great deal that night, just as Matthew Murphy
had told him. But mostly what he had learned was that Ashley
wasn't in some foreign country in some graduate program. If
she were in Italy, thousands of miles away, why would her
family send some big-talking ex-cop around to try to intimi-
date him? That made no sense at all, unless she was close by.
Far closer than he'd imagined. Within reach? He believed so.
O'Connell inhaled sharply through his nose. He did not know
where she was, but he would find out soon enough, because
time no longer meant anything to him. Only Ashley did.

•

    The News-Republican building was on a desultory tract of
downtown land, adjacent to the train station, with a depressing view of the interstate highway, parking lots, and vacant
spaces filled with trash. It was one of those spots that aren't
exactly blighted. Instead, it seemed simply ignored, or perhaps exhausted. Lots of chain-link fences, swirling debris
caught by wayward gusts of wind, and highway underpasses
decorated with graffiti. The newspaper office was a rectangu-
lar, four-story edifice, a cinder-block-and-brick square. It

seemed more like an armory or even a fortress than a newspaper office. Inside, what was once quaintly called the morgue was now a small room with computers.

Once a helpful young woman had shown me how to access the files, it did not take me long to find the record of Matthew Murphy's last day. Or, perhaps, *last moments* might be more accurate.

The front-page headline read EX–STATE POLICE DETECTIVE SLAIN. There were two subheads: BODY FOUND IN CITY ALLEY and POLICE CALL KILLING "EXECUTION-STYLE."

I filled several pages in my notebook with details from the spate of stories that day, and several follow-up pieces that appeared in the next few days. There was, it seemed, no end to possible suspects. Murphy had been involved in many high-profile cases during his time on the force and, in retirement, had continued to make enemies with a daunting regularity as he worked as a private investigator. There was little doubt in my mind that his murder had been given top priority by the Springfield detectives working the case, and by the state police homicide unit that had undoubtedly taken over. There would have been significant pressure on the local district attorney, cop killings being the sort of make-or-break cases that define careers. Everyone in law enforcement would want to be involved. Killing one of their own slices a small part from each of them.

Except as I went through the stories, they seemed too thin, and what should have happened did not.

Details began to be repetitious. No arrest was made. No grand jury indictment announced to great fanfare. No criminal trial scheduled.

It was a story where the big dramatic ending evaporated into nothing.

I pushed myself away from the computer, staring at a blinking *no further entries found* to my final electronic request.

That wasn't right, I thought. Someone had brutally killed Murphy. And it had to connect to Ashley.

Somehow. Some way.

I just couldn't see it.

25

Security

The office secretary knocked on Sally's open door, an overnight envelope in her hand. "This just came for you. I'm not sure who it's from. Do you want me to handle it?"

"No. I'll take it. I know what it is." Sally thanked her assistant, grasped the envelope, and closed the door. She smiled. Murphy was an overly cautious man. She guessed that he kept a number of post office boxes handy for mail of a more sensitive nature. Prominent letterheads and return addresses were often inconvenient for people in his line of work.

He had called her from the road, coming back from Boston several nights earlier. "I think your problem will pretty much disappear from now on, Ms. Freeman-Richards."

She had been at her home, sitting across from Hope. Both of them had been reading, Hope immersed in Dickens's *A Tale of Two Cities,* while she had been glancing through leftover sections of the Sunday *New York Times.*

"That's good news, Mr. Murphy. I'm delighted to hear that. But tell me, how precisely did you reach that conclusion?" She easily slipped into her practiced, reasonable attorney tones.

"Well, I don't know how *precise* you want me to be. But our mutual *friend*"—he laughed at the use of the word—"well, he and I had a talk. A good talk. A lengthy discussion of the pros and cons of his, shall we say, *behavior.* And after this conversation completed its predictable course, Mr. O'Connell allowed as to how it might indeed be a significant problem to continue pursuing Ashley. He was helped to see the light of reason and stated unequivocally that he would remove himself from her life from that point further."

"You believed him?"

"I had every reason to believe him, Ms. Freeman-Richards. His sincerity was evident."

Sally had paused, trying to read between Murphy's words. "No one was hurt?"

"Not permanently. Unless, perhaps, Mr. O'Connell now has a broken heart, but I kinda doubt that. He was, however, deeply impressed with the recklessness of continuing his course of action, and he reached an enlightened conclusion, after I explained certain realities to him. Forcefully. I'm not sure that you really want much more detail, Ms. Freeman-Richards. It might make you uncomfortable."

Sally thought their conversation had an odd gentility, as if she were somehow incapable of hearing certain things. It had a Victorian sensibility, as if she might get pale and faint with a case of the vapors.

"I wouldn't want that."

"I didn't think so. I will send you a disposition report in the next day or so. And should you have any reason to suspect anything or see something suspicious, please call, night or day, and I will see it taken care of. I mean, there's always the slim chance that Mr. O'Connell might have a change of heart once again. But I doubt that. He seems like a weak person, Ms. Freeman-Richards. A very small man, and I don't mean how tall he is. But I believe he's now out of your lives one hundred percent. And, so, if you have any investigatory needs in the future, I hope you will keep me in mind."

Sally was a little surprised at Murphy's description of O'Connell. It didn't exactly jibe with her conclusions to that point. But it was reassuring to hear, and so she shunted away any contradictions she might have felt.

"Of course, Mr. Murphy. It seems like you took care of things exactly as I'd hoped. And I can't tell you how pleased I am to hear this."

"It was my pleasure, ma'am."

She hung up the phone, then turned to Hope. "Well, that's that."

"What's what?"

"I sent a private detective I know over to explain the facts of life to the creep. Like you'd think, when confronted by someone substantially stronger and significantly tougher and more experienced, he folded up like a cheap card table. Guys like him, they're cowards from the get-go. Just let them know that you can't be bullied, and they tuck their tails between their legs and disappear."

"You think so?" Hope replied. "I don't know. My impression is that the creep is a little more determined than that, although I sure as hell don't know why. And a little more capable than you're giving him credit for. Look what a mess he made for all of us with a little computer access."

"Look, Hope, we tried to negotiate fairly with him. We tried to give him a chance to walk away, didn't we? We even paid him a substantial sum of money. How could we have been more fair? How could we have been more direct?"

"I'm not sure."

"We were totally straightforward, right?"

"I suppose so."

"And he didn't get it, did he? *He* didn't want to make things easy for everyone, did he? So now he's gotten a little lesson in how tough *we* can be. And just like that, it's all over."

Hope didn't shake her head outwardly. But she had her doubts. Sally had seen this in her eyes, had opened her mouth to say something, then stopped and allowed the two of them to return to silence.

"Well, that's that," she had said with a touch of finality, a little irritated with Hope for not being more supportive.

Sally took the envelope from Murphy and sat down at her desk, replaying the conversation with Hope. She had the curious thought that things were oddly reversed: it should have been Hope, who was younger and often more headstrong, who should have been satisfied, and not Sally.

Sally tore open the flap and dropped the contents onto her desktop.

There was a cover letter, a sheaf of papers stapled together, several photographs, and a set of computer discs.

The pictures were of Michael O'Connell, taken outside his apartment. The sheaf of papers contained his modest police record and what work and school history Murphy had unearthed, along with some family information, including the names and address of his mother and father. A notation said the mother was deceased. A yellow note pasted to the computer discs said, *These have been encrypted. An expert can probably unravel them, no problem. They probably contain info about your daughter. Maybe pictures. I took them from OC's apartment, but I'd guess he has copies hidden somewhere. I did not know if you wanted to spend extra $ to have them professionally examined. The computer that he was using was accidentally destroyed during our session, so any info on the hard drive is likely ruined.*

Murphy's cover letter briefly described meeting O'Connell outside his apartment, but gave no real details about their "conversation." At the bottom was a bill for services, which included a courtesy discount.

Sally immediately grabbed a checkbook and wrote out a draft to Murphy. She sealed this in a plain envelope, along with a note that said merely, *Thank you for your help. We will call you if there is any follow-up necessary.*

She pushed all the material, including the computer discs, into a manila envelope, wrote *Ashley's Creep* in large letters on it, and with a sense of relief walked over to her large file cabinet and slid it into the back of the bottom drawer, where she thought it would happily remain untouched for years to come.

*   *   *

There is a clarity to late-afternoon light at the edge of the Green Mountains, as if things become sharper, more defined, as the day fades into night in the last weeks before winter. Catherine was poised by the window above her kitchen sink, looking westward, her eyes on Ashley. The younger woman was out back, bundled up in a bright yellow fleece, seated at the edge of a flagstone patio. Beyond her was a grassy field, which led up to the edge of the forest. They had gone into Brattleboro the day before and purchased sheets of paper, an easel, and brushes and watercolors, and Ashley was now immersed in a painting of her own, trying to capture the last streaks of day as they moved across the ridges and lingered in the pine branches. Catherine tried to read Ashley's body language; it seemed to contain both frustration and excitement simultaneously. She was relaxed, enjoying her moment with the brush in her hand and the colors unfolding in front of her. Catherine was struck by the thought that the young woman and the painting were much the same; in the process of design.

They had spent much of the night Ashley had arrived on the bus drinking tea and talking about what had happened. Catherine had listened with both astonishment and a growing sense of unease.

She looked out her window and saw Ashley commit a long, pale blue stroke of watercolor sky to the paper in front of her. "It isn't right," she said out loud.

She feared that Ashley would somehow be—she wasn't sure exactly—*infected* by Michael O'Connell. It was as if, in that moment, she was afraid that Ashley would turn against all men because of the actions of one man.

She gripped the edge of the sink to steady herself. She was not quite able to articulate within herself the dark edge of her thoughts. She didn't want to think, *I don't want Ashley to become like Hope.* And when some clouds of this fear worked into her heart, she grew upset with herself, for she loved her daughter. Hope was smart. Hope was beautiful. Hope was graceful. Hope inspired others. Hope brought out the best in the kids she worked with and the kids she coached. Hope was everything that a mother could possibly want in a daughter, except one thing, and that was the mountain that Catherine didn't seem able to scale. And as she stared out the window watching her—what? Niece? Adopted grandchild?—she was trapped between fears. The problem was—although Catherine didn't recognize this right at that moment—they were the wrong set of fears altogether.

•

"How did Murphy die?" I demanded.

"How? Surely you can figure out the how. Bullet. Knife. Colonel Mustard in the library with the candlestick. Whatever," she replied.

"No. Correct . . ."

"It's the why that concerns us. Tell me," she continued suddenly, "did they ever arrest someone for Murphy's murder?"

"No. Not that I can tell."

"Well, it seems to me that in your hunt for answers, you're looking in the wrong places. No one was arrested. That tells you something, doesn't it? You want me—or some detective or prosecutor somewhere—to say 'Well, Murphy was killed by . . . but we didn't have enough evidence to make an arrest.' Because that would be nice and neat and tidy." She hesitated. "But I never said this was a simple story."

What she said was true.

"Can you think as creatively as Scott and Sally and Hope and Ashley?"

"Yes," I replied far too quickly.

"Good." She huffed the word out. "Easy to say. Hard to do."

I didn't respond to what she said. To answer might have been to insult myself.

"But tell me, can you do the same for Michael O'Connell?"

26

The First Intrusion

From the center of the Longfellow Bridge he could see up the Charles toward Cambridge. It was brisk in the early morning, but crews were rowing down the center of the river, their oars sweeping through the inky dark in unison, making small swirls in the placid surface. A sheen was on the water as the rising light scoured the liquid. He could hear the crews grunting in syncopation, their rhythm defined by the steady beat of the coxswain's voice. He particularly liked the way the smallest man set the pace, how the slightest of the team ordered the larger, stronger men to his command. The least was the most important; he was the only one who could see where they were going, and he controlled the steering. O'Connell liked to think that even though he was strong enough to pull an oar, he was also smart enough to sit in the stern with the rudder.

Michael O'Connell often went to the walkway across the bridge when he needed to think through a complicated problem. The traffic moved recklessly on the roadway. Pedestrians kept up their get-to-the-office pace across the sidewalk. Beneath him the water flowed seaward, and in the distance, T trains filled with commuters emerged from beneath the streets. It seemed to O'Connell that he was the only one standing still. A hundred things common to the city morning should have distracted him, but he found that where he stood, he could concentrate fully on whatever dilemma was in his life.

He thought: I have two.

Ashley.

And the ex-cop Murphy.

Clearly, the route to Ashley passed through either Scott or Sally. It was simply a matter of finding it, and he was confident he could do so. The obstacle, however, was the ex-cop, who posed a far more significant problem. He licked his lips, still tasting the blood in his mouth, feeling the swelling from where he'd been slapped. But the redness and welts faded much faster than his memory. As soon as O'Connell surfaced close to the parents, they would sic the private eye on him. And he was uncertain just how dangerous the ex-cop would be. Somewhat less dire than his threats, O'Connell thought. He reminded himself of a simple, critical fact: In all his dealings with Ashley and her family, he needed to be the one capable of power. If there was to be violence, it had to be in his control. Murphy's presence shifted that balance, and he didn't like it.

He reached out and gripped the ornate concrete barrier with both hands, to steady himself. Fury was like a drug, coming on him in waves, turning everything in his sight into a kaleidoscope of emotions. For an instant he stared down at the dark river passing beneath his feet and doubted that even its near-freezing temperatures could cool him down. He breathed out slowly, controlling his rage. Anger was his friend, but he couldn't let it work against him. He told himself, Stay focused.

The first order of business was to remove Murphy from the picture.

He did not think this would be difficult. A little dicey, but not impossible. Not as easy as what he had done with a few computer strokes to Scott and Sally and Hope, just to let them know who they were dealing with. But not beyond him by any means.

Michael O'Connell looked out across the water and saw one of the crews come to a rest. The shell sliced through the water, driven by momentum, while each rower slumped slightly over his oar, dragging the blades behind them. He liked the way the shell continued, driven by exertion, propelled by nothing more than the memory of muscle. It was like a razor slicing across the surface of the river, and he thought he was much the same.

He spent much of the day and the first part of the evening keeping watch on the office building where Murphy had his practice. Michael O'Connell had been pleased from the first moment that he'd set eyes upon it; the building was shopworn and shabby and lacked many of the modern security devices that might have made what he had in mind more difficult. O'Connell smiled to himself; if this wasn't his first rule, it should have been: Always use their weaknesses and make them into your strengths.

He had used three different locations for his surveillance. His car, parked midway down the block; a Spanish grocery store on the corner; and a Christian Science Reading Room almost directly across from the building. He'd had one bad moment when he had emerged from this last location and Murphy had stepped that moment out the front door of his office.

Like any detective, practiced in safety, he had instantly turned right and left, peered up and down the street and across the roadway. O'Connell had felt a single fear pierce him, a cold sensation that he would be recognized.

He had known, in that instant, if he turned away, if he ducked into a building, if he froze and tried to hide, Murphy would make him instantly.

So, instead, he forced himself to idly walk down the street, making no effort of any sort to conceal himself, heading toward the corner store, just hunching his shoulders up, turning his head a little to the side so that his profile wouldn't be obvious, not looking back once, only lifting his right hand and adjusting his jacket collar, to obscure his face until he reached the bodega door. As soon as he was inside, however, he shoved himself to the side and peered out the window, to see what Murphy was doing.

Then he laughed softly. The detective was walking steadily away.

As if he didn't have a care in the entire world, O'Connell thought, as he watched a seemingly unconcerned Murphy pace down the block and turn toward a parking lot. Or maybe he's just walking along with all the arrogance of someone who knows he can't be touched.

Recognition, O'Connell thought, is about context. When you *expect* to see someone, you will. When you don't, you won't. He or she becomes invisible.

Murphy would never imagine that O'Connell had rather easily tracked the detective to his workplace. Murphy would never imagine that in his pocket Michael O'Connell had the detective's home address and telephone number. Murphy would never imagine that after delivering a beating that O'Connell would follow him out to western Massachusetts. All these things were beyond him, O'Connell thought. And that is why he couldn't see me, even though I was standing barely twenty yards away from him.

He thought he was finished with me.

O'Connell went back to his car, where he waited and watched, taking time to note when the other few office workers emerged from the building for the evening. One of them was probably Murphy's secretary. He watched this woman heading in the same direction as the detective had earlier, toward the parking lot. Not nice, O'Connell thought, making the wage slave do the locking up in the evening. Especially someone not really trained in the art of making doors truly secure. After a moment, he turned on the ignition of his car and carefully pulled out, timing his exit to match with hers.

Within forty-eight hours, Michael O'Connell felt he'd acquired enough information to take the next step, which he knew was going to bring him much closer to the freedom to pursue Ashley.

He now knew, within reason, when each of the other offices in Murphy's building closed up for the night. He knew that the last person to leave each day was the office manager for the counseling center across from Murphy, who merely locked up the front door with a single key. The lawyer who occupied the ground floor had only one paralegal. O'Connell suspected the lawyer was cheating on his wife, because he and the paralegal left together arm in arm, wearing the unmistakable glow of a couple who'd engaged in something illicit. O'Connell liked to think that they were having sex down on the floor, writhing away on some dirty, threadbare carpet. Fantasizing about the locations, the positions, and even the passion helped him pass time.

He didn't know much about Murphy's secretary, but he'd acquired a few bits and pieces about her. She was in her early sixties and widowed. She lived alone, a dowdy woman in a dowdy life, accompanied only by two pugs, whom he'd learned were named Mister Big and Beauty. She was devoted to the dogs.

O'Connell had trailed the secretary into a Stop & Shop supermarket. It had been easy enough to engage her in a little conversation when she stopped in front of the dog food section.

"Excuse me, ma'am, I wonder if you might help me out. . . . My girlfriend has just adopted a small dog, and I wanted to get some real gourmet pet food, but there are so many to choose from. Do you know much about dogs?"

He suspected that she walked away a few minutes later, thinking, *What a nice, polite young man.*

Michael O'Connell had parked two blocks away from Murphy's building, in the opposite direction from the parking lot that all the people who worked there seemed to frequent. It was a quarter before five and he had everything he needed packed in a cheap duffel bag concealed in the trunk. He breathed in and out rapidly, a little like a swimmer preparing to mount the starting block, calming himself.

One tricky moment, he told himself. Then the rest should be easy.

O'Connell exited the car, double-checked to make sure

that the meter he had parked at was filled to capacity, then quick-marched toward his target.

At the end of the block, he paused, letting the first shafts of darkness creep around him. The New England night drops abruptly in the first days of November, seeming to pass from day to midnight in a matter of moments. It is an unsettled hour of the day, the time when he was most comfortable.

It was just a matter of getting inside without being seen, especially by Murphy or his secretary. He took another deep breath, placed Ashley firmly in his mind, reminded himself that she would be much closer by the end of the night, and moved rapidly down the street. A lamp blinked on behind him. He considered himself invisible; no one knew, expected, or imagined that he would be there.

When he reached the front door, O'Connell saw the small hallway inside was empty. Within a second, he was inside.

He could hear a whooshing sound as the elevator descended toward him. He immediately walked across the hallway into the emergency stairwell, closing the door behind him just as the elevator arrived. He pushed himself against a wall, trying to imagine the people on the other side of the solid steel. He thought he could hear voices. As sweat ran down under his arms, he imagined Murphy's unmistakable tones, then his secretary's.

Need to feed those pugs, he said to himself. Time to get going.

He heard the front door close.

O'Connell looked down at his watch. Come on, he whispered. Day is done. Counseling-center office manager, it's your turn.

He pushed himself back against the wall and waited. The stairwell wasn't a particularly good place to hide. But he knew this night it would serve his purposes. Just another sign, he thought to himself, that he was destined to be with Ashley. It was as if she were helping him to find her. We were meant to be together. He moderated his rapid breathing

and closed his eyes, letting the patience of obsession over-
whelm him, his mind blank except for memories of Ashley.

In his life, Michael O'Connell had broken into a number of
empty stores, an occasional house, more than a few factories,
and other places of business. He was confident in his expertise as he sat on the cold stairs and waited. He had not even
taken the trouble to prepare some sort of wild-eyed story
should someone have found him there. He knew that he was
safe. O'Connell understood that love was protecting him.

It was nearly seven when he heard the last creaking noise
from the elevator. He paused, bending his head toward the
sound, and suddenly the world around him descended into
darkness. The office manager had hit the master light
switches next to the elevator. He heard the front door open,
close, then click as the single lock was fastened. He glanced
down at his watch, the illuminated face glowing just bright
enough to read.

He waited another fifteen minutes before pushing through
the door to the stairwell and reentering the vestibule. He was
almost surprised by how easy it was all turning out to be.

He peered carefully through the glass front door, up and
down the empty street. Then he quickly turned the single
dead-bolt lock and let himself out.

Moving quickly, he walked the two blocks to his car and
opened the trunk, removing the duffel bag that he'd concealed there.

It took him only a few minutes to return to the office
building.

First, he reached inside his bag and removed several pairs
of surgical gloves. These he rapidly pulled on, one on top of
the other, a double thickness of protection. He took out a
spray bottle of ammonia-based disinfectant and generously
sprayed the lock handle that he'd touched. As soon as he'd
finished that, he once again locked the door. He then
sprayed the door handle to the stairwell and any place else
he might have put his hands. Next, he climbed the stairs to

the second floor, removing a small flashlight on the way up. He had covered the lens with a piece of red tape, cutting the light in half, making it next to impossible to spot from outside, through a window. He took his time, searching the hallway for any signs of exterior security devices, but found none. Michael O'Connell shook his head. He would have imagined that Murphy would select a more secure location. But infrared cameras and video-monitoring systems cost cash. What the building offered was probably the lowest of rents, and therein lay its attraction.

He smiled to himself.

Plus, what was there to steal?

No cash. No jewelry. No art. No portable electronic items.

Any self-respecting crook would have found significantly easier and considerably more valuable pickings elsewhere. Hell, the corner bodega probably had more than a thousand bucks in a metal drop box, and a useful twelve gauge on the shelf beneath the register. It would be a far more inviting target.

But ripping off a corner store junkie-style wasn't what he had in mind. O'Connell looked around. What did this building have that was valuable?

He grinned again. *Information.*

The key to his adventure that night was to make sure the information he was seeking wasn't quite what anyone would expect.

O'Connell took his time picking the lock to Murphy's office, and when he finally let himself in, he was alert to possible secondary security devices, such as a motion detector or a hidden camera. As the door swung open, he pulled a thin balaclava over his head. The high-tech garment, designed to keep someone warm on some windy ski slope, covered everything except his eyes. He gritted his teeth, half-expecting to hear an alarm.

When he was greeted with silence, he could barely contain his delight.

Maneuvering cautiously through the office, he took a moment to assess what was there. He wanted to laugh.

There was a threadbare waiting room, with a desk for the secretary and a cheap, lumpy couch and armchair and a single inner office, where Murphy did business. A more solid door guarded this, and more than one dead-bolt lock.

O'Connell hesitated, reaching out with his hand to the doorknob, then stopped. He thought to himself, The cheap bastard probably has whatever security system he thinks he needs right in there.

He turned away and looked over at the secretary's desk. She had her own computer station.

Sitting himself down at her chair, he clicked on the computer. A welcome screen came up, followed by an access prompt, demanding a password.

He took another deep breath and typed in the name of each of her dogs. Then he tried a few combinations of the two, blending them unsuccessfully. He considered possibilities for an instant, then smiled as he punched the keys for *Pug Lover*.

The machine whirred and clicked and O'Connell found himself looking at what he presumed were almost all of Murphy's case files. He scrolled down and found *Ashley Freeman*. He fought off the urge to open that one instantly. Holding himself back would increase the pleasure. Then he systematically began going through every other file on the secretary's machine, lingering on more than one occasion on the provocative digital pictures stored alongside some of the cases. Carefully, he began to copy everything onto some new rewritable computer discs that he had purchased. He did not think that he was getting everything that the ex-detective had on his own computer. Surely, O'Connell thought, Murphy had to be smart enough to keep some material concealed where only he could access it. But for his purposes, he had more than enough.

It took him a couple of hours to finish. He was a little stiff, and he stepped away from the secretary's desk and stretched. He dropped to the floor and quickly did a dozen push-ups, feeling his muscles loosen. He went over to the inner door to

Murphy's office. He reached inside his duffel bag and removed a small crowbar. He made a couple of desultory efforts, scratching the door's surface, digging into the wood, before giving up. Then he went over to the secretary's desk, pried open the drawers, and tossed about the contents, strewing paper, printer cartridges, and pencils around the floor. He found a framed portrait of the two pugs, which he dropped, shattering the glass. As soon as he felt that enough of a mess had been made, he left, locking the door behind him. As soon as the dead bolt slid into place, he once again took his crowbar and broke out the doorjamb, leaving splinters of wood throughout the area, and the door ajar.

Next he went over to the counseling office and broke in there, using the same bash-and-batter technique. Once inside, he ransacked drawers and file cabinets quickly, spreading as much debris around as he could in a few minutes.

He went back down the stairwell and did the same to the attorney's space. He tossed open file cabinets and dashed papers around the floor. He jimmied open the attorney's desk, finding several hundred dollars in cash, which he stuffed into his duffel bag. He was about to leave when he decided to take a single whack at the drawers on the paralegal's desk. She would probably feel left out if he didn't trash her space as well, he thought, laughing to himself. But he stopped when he saw what was resting in the bottom of the last drawer.

"Now what's a good girl like you doing with one of these?" he whispered.

It was a .25-caliber semiautomatic pistol. Small, easily concealed, a favorite of hit men and assassins because it was already quiet when fired, and because it was easy to fit with a homemade silencer. When loaded with expanding-head bullets in the nine-shot clip, it was more than adequate for the tasks it was designed for. A lady's gun, unless it was in the hands of an expert.

"I'll just be taking you along," he hissed. "Did you get a permit for this? Did you register it with the Springfield police? I'm guessing you didn't, honey. A nice, illegal street gun. Right?"

Michael O'Connell slipped the weapon into his bag. A most profitable night, he thought, as he stood and looked at the mess he'd made.

In the morning, the office manager in the counseling center would call the police. A detective would come and take a statement. He would tell them to go through their things and determine what was stolen. And they would then conclude that some half-fried junkie had broken in, looking for an easy score, and, frustrated by how little there was to steal, had resorted to angrily throwing things around. Everyone would have to spend the day cleaning up, calling in a couple of workmen to repair the ripped doors, a locksmith to install new locks. It would all just be an inconvenience to everyone, including the attorney and his lover, who sure as hell wouldn't report the loss of an illegal gun.

Everyone, except Matthew Murphy, who would determine that his extra locks and heavy door had saved his office. He would first congratulate himself, conclude nothing was taken, and probably wouldn't even bother to call his insurance company.

All he would do would be to buy his secretary a new frame for her pictures of her dogs.

A cheap frame, at that, O'Connell thought, as he exited into the night.

•

The chief investigator for the Hampden County District Attorney's Office was a slight man in his early forties, with tortoiseshell eyeglasses and sandy-colored, thin hair that he wore disarmingly long. He promptly placed his feet up on his desk and rocked back in a red leather desk chair as he looked intently across the room toward me. He had an off-putting style that seemed both friendly and edgy at the same moment.

"And so, it is Mr. Murphy's death and our subsequent failure to bring the investigation to a respectable conclusion that has brought you here?"

"Yes," I said. "I presume that a number of different agencies ultimately looked at the case, but if anyone had been close to an arrest, it would have been your job to steer that case through the system."

"Correct. And we did not indict anyone."

"But you had a suspect?"

He shook his head. "Suspects. That, in a nutshell, was the problem."

"How so?"

"Too many enemies. Too many people who would not only be served by his death, but a significant number of folks who would genuinely be pleased. Murphy was killed, his body tossed into an alleyway like a piece of trash, and there was more than one glass around this state raised in celebration."

"But surely you were able to narrow the field down?"

"Yes. To some extent. It is not as if the people we were entertaining as suspects were naturally inclined to assist the police. We still hope that someone, somewhere, maybe in a jailhouse, or a bar, will let something slip and we will be able to focus our attention on one or two individuals. But until that happy time arrives, the murder of ex-detective Murphy remains an open case."

"But you must have some leads . . ."

The chief investigator sighed, removed his feet from the desktop, and swung about.

"Did you know Mr. Murphy?"

"No."

"He was not a particularly likable fellow," he said, shaking his head. "He was the sort of person that walked some pretty narrow lines. Legally speaking, that is. One cannot be sure on which side this killing fell until one actually knows something about the murder. Beyond, of course, what the body told us, which, alas, was not much."

"But something?"

"The killing had all the earmarks of a professional."

The chief investigator stood up, walked behind me, and placed his index finger to the back of my head. "Pop. Pop. Two shots in the head. A twenty-five, probably silenced. Both slugs were soft-tipped bullets and significantly deformed upon removal, making an eventual match impossible. Then the body was dragged into an alleyway, pushed behind some garbage cans, and remained undiscovered until a garbage truck arrived the following morning. The person who shot him was someone with the expertise to catch Murphy unawares. Very little in the way of workable forensics. Not even an ejected shell casing, which lends further credence to the notion that this was someone well trained in killing, because they stopped and retrieved those before leaving. It rained the night he was killed, pretty hard, which further compromised the crime scene. No witnesses. No immediate leads. A very difficult case from the start, without someone helpfully pointing us in the right direction."

He circled around and this time perched on a corner of his desk. He smiled with a slight barracuda look.

"What was this murder? Revenge? Payback for something in his past? Maybe it was simply a robbery. His wallet was cleaned out. But the credit cards were left behind. Curious that, right?" He paused. "And your own interest in this case? It stems from precisely what?"

"Murphy was peripherally involved in a case that I'm looking into." I guarded my words carefully.

"An investigator spoke to every client he had. Someone took a look at every case he was working. Every case he'd ever worked. Which interests you?"

"Ashley Freeman," I said cautiously.

The chief investigator shook his head. "That is most interesting. I wouldn't think there is much of a story there. That was one of his smaller jobs. A couple of days invested, no more. And resolved, I think, sometime before the murder. No, the person who killed Murphy was connected to either one of the drug rings he helped put away when he was a cop, or one of the organized-crime types he was looking at in his private business. Or maybe one of the police officers who were engaged in messy divorces. All those are better suspects."

I nodded.

"But, you know, the one thing that really intrigues me about the case?"

"What is that?" I asked.

"When we started looking under rocks and pulling back curtains, it seemed like everyone we spoke with was expecting us."

"Expecting you? But why would that be unusual?"

The chief investigator smiled again. "Murphy tried to keep things very confidential. That is, after all, the nature of the business. He kept everything close to the vest. He was secretive; didn't share much. Didn't let anyone in on his business. The only person who had even the vaguest idea what he was up to on a day-to-day basis was his secretary. She did all his typing, billing, and filing."

"She was unable to help you?"

"Clueless. Utterly clueless. But that wasn't the issue." He paused, eyeing me closely. "So how is it that all those people *knew* he was looking at them? Now, certainly some of the subjects he was engaged with were bound to have figured out in some way or another that he was snooping around their lives. But that would be the smaller percentage. Yet, somehow, that wasn't the situation. I repeat: People *knew*. Everyone. When we showed up at their doors, they were waiting, alibis and excuses all intact. That's wrong. One hundred percent wrong. And there lies the real question, does it not?"

I stood up.

"You want a real mystery story, Mr. Writer?" the chief investigator said as he shook my hand and returned to his side of the desk. "Well, answer that question for me."

I kept my mouth shut. But in that moment, I knew the answer.

27

The Second Intrusion

Hope hated the quiet.

She found herself walking across campus, attending the final practices of the season, getting ready for the winter, anxious. She was constantly on edge, but unable to get a grasp on her feelings. She would find herself pacing down the campus pathways as if in a hurry when she wasn't. She would suddenly feel her throat parched, her lips dry, and her tongue thick, and she would gulp away at bottles of water. In the midst of conversation she would realize that she hadn't heard much of what was said. She was distracted by fear, and as each day went by in benign silence, she imagined that much worse was happening somewhere.

She did not, for a single second, imagine that Michael O'Connell was out of their lives.

Scott, as best she could tell, had thrown himself wholeheartedly back into his teaching schedule. Sally had returned to her upcoming divorce settlements and house closings, with a certain smug satisfaction that she had figured things out and taken the necessary steps to bring the situation to a conclusion. And Hope and Sally had once again retreated into the cold-war détente that marked their relationship. Even the smallest of affections had dissipated. There was never a caress, a compliment, nor a laugh, and certainly not a touch inviting sex. It was almost as if they had become nuns, living under the same roof, occupying the same bed, but married to some ideal beyond them. Hope wondered whether Sally's last months with Scott had been the same. Or had she kept up appearances, sleeping with him, faking passion, fixing meals, cleaning up, carrying on conversations, while all the time slipping away at odd hours to meet with Hope and telling her that that was where her heart truly lay?

In the distance, Hope could hear voices from the playing fields. Play-off time, she thought. One more game. Two to the semifinals. Three to the championship. She could barely concentrate on the challenges. Instead, she was caught up in some morass of feelings, about Ashley, about Michael O'-Connell, about her mother, and mostly about Sally, where they mixed together in a stew of impossibility.

As she walked along, she remembered meeting Sally. Love, she thought, should always be so simple. Meet at an art gallery opening. Talk together. Tell a joke and hear each other's laughter. Decide to have a drink. Then a meal. Then another meeting, this time in the middle of the day. And finally a small touch on the back of the hand, a whisper, a glance, and it fell together, just as Hope had known it would from the first minute.

Love, she thought. That was the word that Michael O'-Connell used over and over, and one Hope hadn't used in weeks. Perhaps months. Ashley had told her, *He says he loves me.* Hope knew that nothing he had done had anything to do with love.

She hunched her shoulders forward.

He was gone, she told herself.

Sally says he's gone.

Scott says he's gone.

Ashley thinks he's gone.

She did not believe this.

But she could not see one piece of concrete evidence that he had returned.

She heard voices, and she saw the girls on her team waving, running drills, and talking together, gathered in the center of the practice field. She reached for the whistle on a lanyard around her neck, then decided to let the fun continue for a minute or two longer. Being young goes by so fast, they should enjoy every moment. Except she knew that it was not in the nature of the young to ever understand this.

She sighed, blew her whistle, and decided that she would speak with her mother and with Ashley daily, just to make sure everything was all right. She wondered why Sally and Scott were not doing the same.

Sally stared at the headline in the afternoon paper and felt the blood drain from her face. She devoured every word of the series of stories, then reread them all, memorizing details. EX-COP FOUND MURDERED ON CITY STREET. When she placed the paper down, she noticed that her hands were covered with black newsprint. She eyed them, as if surprised, then realized that her palms had grown so sweaty while she was reading that the ink on the pages had melded onto her fingers.

KILLING CALLED "EXECUTION-STYLE." The words seemed to trail after her, shouting for attention. POLICE EYE ORGANIZED CRIME CONNECTION.

The first thing she told herself was, This has nothing to do with Ashley.

She rocked back, as if someone had slammed her hard in the stomach. It has everything to do with Ashley.

Her first instinct was to call someone. As a lawyer, she had met any number of other attorneys connected with the county prosecutor's office. Surely one of them would have more details. Some inside information that would tell her what she needed to know. She reached for her Rolodex with one hand and the phone with the other, then stopped herself. What are you doing?

She took a deep breath. Do not invite someone to scrutinize your life. Any prosecutor even vaguely connected to Murphy's murder would ask her far many more questions than he would provide answers to her questions. By making that call, she would inject herself and her troubles into a mix that she wasn't at all sure she wanted to be part of.

Sally coughed. She had sent Murphy off to *deal* with Michael O'Connell. He had reported back successfully. Problem solved. Everyone safe. Ashley could get on with her life. And then, a short time later, Murphy is dead. It didn't make sense to her. It was like seeing a famous mathematician, an Einstein, write $2 + 2 = 5$ on a chalkboard and not hear a single voice raised in correction.

She seized the newspaper and reread every word for a third time.

Nothing suggested that Michael O'Connell had had anything to do with it.

It was professionally handled. Clearly some really bad guys that had crossed paths with Murphy were to blame. The killing went far beyond the capacity of a mechanic, computer nut, occasional college student, and minor-league criminal like Michael O'Connell, Sally insisted to herself. Really, it had nothing to do with them in the slightest, and for her to imagine otherwise was a mistake.

She leaned back in her desk chair, breathing hard.

No, we're all safe. It's just a coincidence. His death had nothing to do with their situation. After all, she had selected Murphy in the first place because of his willingness to skirt the niceties of the law. And he had undoubtedly done far worse, in his other cases, creating enemies wherever he went. One had finally caught up with him. That had to be it.

She exhaled slowly. No, the real problem was that whatever threats Murphy had made to O'Connell to keep him in line had now evaporated. That was the biggest danger they faced. That was assuming that Michael O'Connell even knew about Murphy's murder and would then see it for the opportunity it presented.

Big assumptions, she told herself. Still, she reached for the phone again.

She hated to do it, hated that it would make her seem somehow inadequate, that she had failed to handle her part of the job properly, but she realized that she still needed to call her ex-husband.

Sally dialed Scott's number and realized that she was sweating once again.

"Have you seen the paper?" Sally asked abruptly.

When Scott heard Sally's voice on the line, his first reaction was irritation.

"The New York Times?" he replied briskly, knowing that that wasn't the paper she meant.

This was the sort of oblique answer that made Sally want to strangle Scott.

"No. The local paper."

"No. Why?"

"There is a front-page story, stories actually, about the murder of an ex–police detective in Springfield."

"Yes. Tragic, I'm sure. So what?"

"He's the private investigator I sent to see Michael O'-Connell, right when you were arranging to get Ashley out of Boston. He did his thing a few days after you managed her disappearance."

"His *thing* . . . ?"

"I didn't ask too many questions. And he didn't volunteer any. For obvious reasons."

Scott hesitated. "And this has precisely what to do with us and Ashley?"

Sally was quick to reply, "Probably nothing. Probably just coincidence. Probably just a really bad but totally unconnected series of events. The detective reported that he'd met with O'Connell and we wouldn't have any more troubles. And then he gets himself killed. It has taken me aback, a bit. I can't be certain that it has anything to do with anything. But I thought you should at least be aware. I mean, it probably changes the situation, somehow."

"So," Scott said, speaking in well-modulated classroom tones, "are you suggesting that we might have a problem? Damn it, I thought we had worked this whole thing out. I thought we'd put that son of a bitch behind us for good."

"I don't know. Do we have a problem? I doubt it. I was just trying to inform you of a detail that might be relevant."

"Well, look, Ashley's still up in Vermont, safe and sound with Hope's mother. It seems to me that her next step—our next step—is to get her into a new graduate program, down in New York City, or maybe across the country in San Francisco, someplace new. I know that she has this affection for Boston, but we've agreed that starting fresh is the right idea. So she whiles away some time in Vermont, watching the leaves turn and getting snowed on, and then gets started anew in the spring semester. End of story. We should be proceeding with that sort of scenario, and not getting terribly bent out of shape at every little thing."

Sally gritted her teeth. She hated being lectured to.

"Chimera," she said.

"I beg your pardon?"

"A mythological beast of terrifying proportions that wasn't really there."

"Yes. And?"

"Just a way of looking at this. An academic way," Sally said, to irritate Scott, something she knew she shouldn't do, but found herself doing. Relationships that fail have certain addictions, and this was one of those for the two of them.

"Well, perhaps. Regardless, let's just move ahead. We need to collect Ashley's academic records so she can reapply to graduate schools, even if she has to start on a part-time basis. Best if you or I do that, not her. Better to have them mailed to us than to Vermont."

"I will do that. I'll use the office address." Sally hung up the phone, as irritated as ever, reminded that she knew her ex-husband perfectly. He had not changed in years, not since she'd first met him and not by anything that had happened since. He was as predictable as ever.

She was still at her desk. She looked out and saw that darkness had overcome the last light of the day, and even the shadows had turned black.

*   *   *

Michael O'Connell watched the same shadows lengthen from his vantage point beneath a wide oak tree less than half a block from Sally and Hope's house. He could feel a quickening within him, almost as if he could sense how much closer he was to Ashley. Up and down the block, he could see lights start to blink on. Every few moments a car would swing up the roadway, its headlights sweeping across the lawns. He could see some activity in kitchens, as dinners were prepared, and the softer, metallic glow of television sets turned on.

I have only a short time. He did not think he would need much.

Sally and Hope lived on a meandering, older street. It was an odd mixture of architecture, some newer ranch-type houses, mingling with stately Victorians that dated back to the turn of the century. It was a curious neighborhood, in much demand because of its leafy streets and solid, middle-class outlook. Doctors, lawyers, professors, for the most part lived there. Lots of lawns and hedges and small gardens and Halloween parties. Not the sort of neighborhood where people invested heavily in security devices and state-of-the-art protection systems.

O'Connell moved swiftly up the block. He knew that Sally usually stayed late in her office and Hope held soccer practice until it was too dark to see the ball. This would delay them just long enough.

He cut across the block from tree trunk to tree trunk and, without hesitating, slid into the dark spaces adjacent to their house. There was an old wooden fence behind a driveway, which led into their backyard. He stopped for a moment when kitchen lights blinked on in their neighbor's house, pushing himself back against the exterior wall.

The house had been built on a small hill, so that the main living area was above his head. But, like many older houses, it had a large basement, with an old door framed in neglected, rotting wood that was rarely, if ever, used. It took him less than ten seconds to jimmy it open and let himself in.

He left the door slightly ajar behind him and reached into his pocket and removed his red-taped flashlight. He took a deep breath as he realized that somewhere, within feet of the dank, musty space where he was standing, was some bit of information that would tell him precisely where Ashley was. An envelope with a return address. A telephone bill. A credit card statement. A piece of paper with her name taped to the refrigerator door. He licked his lips, excited, his hands nearly shaking with anticipation. Breaking into Murphy's office had been a familiar job. It was simply a piece of the puzzle into Ashley's whereabouts. He thought he had handled it carefully and professionally.

This break-in was different. This was a chore of love.

He took a second to breathe in the thick air of the basement. If she could only see what I've had to do to find her, to bring us together, he thought, then she would understand why we are meant to be together. Someday, he fantasized, he would be able to tell her that he had endured beatings, broken laws, risked his safety and freedom, all on her behalf.

And then he told himself, If she can't love me then, then she doesn't deserve to love anyone.

He could feel a twitch, a muscle spasm, running through his body, and he had to fight to keep control. He could feel his breathing getting shallow, coming in gasps. For a second, he told himself to remain calm. He pictured Sally. Hope. Scott. And as he did that, he was almost overcome by anger. He could no longer separate the entwined feelings of love and hate. When he managed to calm himself down, he started to move gingerly through the basement, heading toward some rickety old stairs that would carry him up to the living areas. He wasn't sure what precisely he was searching for, although he knew whatever it was, it was nearly within reach.

He pushed open the door at the top of the stairs and immediately figured he was in a pantry, just off the kitchen. He wanted to douse the flashlight as quickly as possible—even covered in red, the glow was far more likely to attract a curious neighbor's interest than the overhead light. He spotted a bank of switches on the wall and flicked the first, which lit up the kitchen. Michael O'Connell smiled and switched off the flashlight.

He told himself, Stay away from the windows and start looking. It's here. Somewhere. What you need to know. I can feel it. I'm coming, Ashley.

He took another step forward before a low, mean growl came from the darkness of a nearby vestibule.

•

I suppose, like most people, I've had my sense of fear mostly defined by Hollywood, which likes to provide a steady diet of aliens, ghosts, vampires, monsters, and serial killers; or those electric, unforeseen moments in life when the other car runs a red light and you pound on the brakes in panic. But real, debilitating fear comes from uncertainty. It gnaws away at one's defenses, never fading, and never far from the heart. As I sat across from the young woman, I could see every line fear had carved on her face, aging her far too fast, every tic it had delivered, to her hands, which she rubbed nervously, to the corner of her eyelid, which twitched uncontrollably, to the tremors in her voice, clearer than the words she whispered.

"I shouldn't have agreed to meet with you," she said.

Sometimes, it's not so much a fear of dying as it is a fear of going on living.

She wrapped both hands around a cup of hot tea and slowly lifted it to her lips. It was brutally hot outdoors, and everyone else in the mall coffee shop was drinking iced drinks, but she seemed unaware of the heat.

"I appreciate it," I replied. "I won't take much of your time. I just want to confirm something."

"I have to go. I can't stay. I can't be seen speaking with you. My sister has the kids, and I can't leave them with her for too long. We're moving. Next week, going to..." She stopped, shook her head. "No, I'm not saying where we're going. You understand, of course?"

She bent forward slightly and I could see a thin, long white scar up near her hairline. "Of course. Let me make this really quick," I said. "Your husband, he was a police captain, and you hired Matthew Murphy during divorce proceedings, right?"

"Yes. My ex-husband was hiding income and stiffing me and the three kids. I wanted Murphy to find out where he was putting the money. My attorney said Murphy was good at that sort of thing."

"Your ex, he was a suspect in Murphy's murder, correct?"

"Yes. State police detectives questioned him several times. They spoke with me, too."

She shook her head, then added, "I was his alibi."

"How so?"

"The night Murphy was killed, my ex-husband showed up at my house nice and early. He'd been drinking. He was morose, suicidal. Insisted on coming in, seeing the kids. I couldn't get him to leave."

"Didn't you have a court order?"

"Yes. Keeping him away. One hundred yards at all times. That's what the judge's order said. Lot of good that did. He's six four and two hundred forty pounds and he knows every cop in the Valley. They're all buddies. What was I supposed to do? Fight him? Call for help? He did what he wanted to do."

"I'm sorry. The alibi . . ."

"So, he started drinking. Then he started beating on me. Kept it up for hours. Until he passed out. Woke up in the morning and apologized. Said it would never happen again. And it didn't, for a whole other week."

"You told this to the state police detectives?"

"I didn't want to. I wish I'd had the guts to say to them, 'Sure, he did it. He told me he did it,' and maybe get him out of my life that way. But I wasn't able to."

I hesitated. "The thing I'm interested in is—"

"I know what you're interested in." She reached up and touched her forehead, running her finger along the small ridge of the scar. "When he punched me, his class ring from Fitchburg State—that's where we met—cut me pretty badly. Gave me this to remember him by. You want to know how he knew about Murphy. Right?"

I nodded.

"He threw it in my face during an argument. Screamed at

me, 'So you figured I wouldn't find out about the private eye you hired?' "

I could see tears in the corners of her eyes.

"He got an anonymous letter. A plain manila envelope. It had a copy of everything Murphy had uncovered about him. All the confidential stuff that was supposed to just go to me and my attorney. Postmarked from some place in Worcester. I don't even know anybody in that city. So, who would send this to my ex? It cost me two teeth when he knocked them out. It should have cost Murphy his life, if only I'd been lucky enough to have it be my ex-husband who got so enraged that he went after him with a gun instead of someone else. Maybe it did cost Murphy his life. Maybe somebody else got the same envelope. I don't know. I wanted it to be my ex who did it. It would have made things so much easier."

She pushed back from the table. "I have to go." She glanced around nervously, then turned, head down, shoulders scrunched forward. She pushed through the coffee shop doors and raced through the mall, dodging shoppers as if fear itself hovered in some black cloud, right behind her ear, whispering dangers.

I watched her and wondered whether I had just seen what Ashley's future might have been.

28

A Fast Drive

Hope was standing on the short redbrick pathway up to their front door when the headlights from Sally's car swept across the lawn. She waited, a little unsure what to do. Once she would have walked back to Sally's car to give her an end-of-the-workday hug, but now she was uncertain whether she should even hesitate so they could enter together. She shuffled her feet and stared down the neighborhood into the darkness. It seemed to Hope that the two of them had quietly taken to coming home later and later in the day, so that the silences that awaited them through the evening had less time to weigh on them.

"Hey," she said as she heard Sally's car door slam shut.

"Hey," Sally said back, her voice exhausted.

"Tough day?"

Sally walked slowly across the lawn toward her. "Yes," she said cryptically. "Let me tell you about it inside."

Hope nodded and stepped up to the front door. She stuck her key in the lock and opened the door wide. It was black inside, and it seemed that the night flowed right past her into the house, like a dark and dangerous current. Hope stopped right inside the entrance vestibule and instantly knew something was terribly out of place. She inhaled sharply.

"Nameless!" she called out.

The overhead lamp flicked on, and Sally stood beside her.

"Nameless!" Hope called out again.

Then: "Oh my God . . ."

Hope dropped her backpack to the floor and stepped forward. Fear had outstripped all other emotions, filling her with ricocheting sensations: a burst of cold, a flash of heat, a wash of damp. "Nameless!" she cried out again. She could hear the panic in her voice. Behind her, Sally was turning the lights on, throwing illumination into the living room, the hallway, the downstairs television room. And finally the kitchen.

The dog was spread out on the floor, motionless.

Hope groaned, something deep, from some place within her that she had never felt before and threw herself onto Nameless's body. She sank her hands into his fur, trying to feel for some warmth, then pressed her ear up against his chest, listening for a heartbeat. Behind her, Sally stood, frozen, in the doorway. "Is he . . ."

Hope let out another moan, her eyes already blinded with tears. But in the same moment, she reached beneath the dog's body and, in a single motion, lifted him up in her arms. She turned to Sally, and without speaking the two of them raced back out into the darkness.

Sally drove fast, faster than she could ever remember, as they headed south on the interstate, driving toward the animal hospital in Springfield. As she wove between cars, the speedometer touching 100 mph, she heard Hope say, "It's okay, Sally. You can slow down."

Hope might have said something else, but Sally understood only that Hope had lowered her head into the dog's muzzle, which muffled what she said. It only took them a few more minutes to make the final miles, and as they cut through the sullen city streets, Sally found herself unable to say anything, but listening to each ravaged sob coming from Hope in the backseat was a little like being sliced by a knife.

She saw the red-and-white EMERGENCY ENTRANCE sign and swerved the car to a stop in front. The sound of the car tires got the attention of the nurse attendant at the triage desk right inside the sliding glass doors. Before Hope had carried Nameless more than a couple of feet, the attendant had helped her to put the dog's limp form on a stretcher.

By the time Sally had parked the car and come inside, Hope was already huddled in the waiting room, her head in her hands. She barely looked up when Sally sat beside her.

"Hope it's . . . ," Sally started, then stopped.

"He's dead. I know it," Hope said. "I couldn't hear a heartbeat. Feel a pulse. Couldn't feel him take a breath. He was old, but . . . We shouldn't have rushed down here. It just happens, you know, you get old and it happens."

Sally sat and glanced up at the clock. She did not think it would take long for the veterinarian on duty to emerge and tell Hope what she already knew. But to Sally's surprise, five minutes passed, then ten. At twenty, they were still waiting. At the half-hour mark, a tall young man, wearing a white laboratory jacket over pale green hospital scrubs, emerged. "Miss Frazier?" he said in a quiet, well-modulated voice that Sally knew instantly came from experience at handling bad news. He looked at Hope.

"Yes." Her voice quivered.

"I am sorry," he said slowly. "We tried to revive him, but he was already gone by the time you arrived."

"I know," Hope said. "I just had to try . . ."

"There was nothing else you could have done," the vet said. "And we did our best."

"Yes. I know that. Thank you." It was as if each word she spoke had to be pulled out of an icy region deep within her.

"He was not a young dog," the vet said slowly.

"Fifteen years," Hope said.

The vet nodded. He seemed to hesitate momentarily, before asking, "And how did you find him tonight?"

"When we came home, he was in the kitchen. On the floor."

The vet took a deep breath. "Would you care to come in, say a final good-bye? And there's something I'd like to show you."

"Yes," Hope said, trying unsuccessfully to hold back her tears. "I'd like that. I'd like to see him one more time." She followed the vet through a pair of swinging doors, while Sally trailed a couple of feet behind her.

The exam room was bathed in bright white light from an overhead fixture. It was like any typical emergency room, with ventilators on the wall, blood-pressure monitors, equipment cabinets. In the center of a shiny steel table that remorselessly reflected the light, Nameless was stretched out, his light fur matted. Hope reached out and stroked his side. His eyes were closed, and Hope thought he looked peaceful and merely asleep.

The vet remained silent for a moment, letting Hope run her hands over her dog's fur. Then he cautiously said, "Was there anything unusual in the house tonight, when you got home?"

Hope turned. "I'm sorry? Unusual?"

"What do you mean?" Sally said.

"Were there any signs of a break-in?"

Hope looked confused. "I'm not sure that I follow."

The vet stepped to her side. "I'm sorry if this is hard, but when we were examining Nameless, a few things seemed out of place."

"What are you saying?" Hope asked.

The vet reached down and pulled back the fur around Nameless's throat. "See the red striations? Bruising marks. We would typically see those from choking. And here, look." He gently lifted Nameless's lips, exposing his teeth. "This appears to be flesh. And some blood, as well. We also found what appears to be some cloth strands and blood on his paws. Near the nails."

Hope looked up at the vet as if she could not quite see what he was driving at.

"When you get home, check your doors and windows for signs of forced entry." The vet looked over at Sally, then at Hope, and smiled, in a wry, offset manner. "It's pretty obvious who he thought he needed to protect, no matter how old he was," the vet said slowly. "I can't be certain, not without an autopsy, of course, but it seems to me that Nameless died fighting."

•

"Who murdered Murphy?" I asked. "Do you believe Michael O'Connell shot him?"

She looked at me oddly, as if the question were somehow out of place. We were at her home, and as she hesitated, I found myself distracted, my eyes sweeping the living room. I realized suddenly that there were no photographs.

She smiled. "I think you should ask yourself, did Michael O'Connell *need* to kill Murphy? He might have *wanted to*. He had a weapon. He had the chance. But had he not done enough, already, by mailing all that confidential information to so many different people to achieve the desired end? Could he not be reasonably confident that someone, in that list of people, would react violently? Wasn't that O'Connell's *style*, to act obliquely? To create events and situations? To manipulate the environment? He needed Murphy out of his way. Murphy came from a world that Michael O'Connell knew, and knew intimately. He was well aware of the threat that he posed. Murphy was not unlike O'Connell in his predictable reliance on violence to achieve results. He *had* to excise Murphy from the situation. And that happened, didn't it?"

She looked at me and lowered her voice, almost to a whisper. "What do we do? How do we act? It's not hard to know what to do when the enemy levels his weapon at you. But aren't we often our own biggest enemies because we do not want to believe what our eyes are telling us? When the storm gathers, do we not just as often think that it won't thunder? The flood won't burst the dam, will it? And so, it catches us, doesn't it?"

She took another deep breath and once again turned to stare out the window.

"And after it catches us, will we drown?"

29

A Shotgun on the Lap

Hi, Michael. I miss you. I love you. Come save me.

He could hear Ashley's voice speaking to him, almost as if she were sitting in the passenger seat of his car. He replayed the words over and over in his mind, giving them different inflections, one time pleading and desperate, another time sexy and inviting. The words were like caresses.

O'Connell imagined himself on a mission. Like a soldier maneuvering through mine-infested territory, or a rescue swimmer diving into turbulent waters, he was heading north, crossing the Vermont border, drawn inexorably toward Ashley.

In the darkness, he ran his fingers over the gashes on the back of his hand and his forearm. He had managed to staunch the bleeding from the bite in his calf with gauze from a cheap first-aid kit he kept in the glove compartment. He was really goddamn lucky that the dog hadn't grabbed his Achilles tendon and shredded it. His jeans were ripped, and, he suspected, they were streaked with dried blood. He would have to replace them in the morning. But all in all, he thought, he had come out on top.

O'Connell reached up and flicked on the car's overhead light.

He looked down at his map and tried to do the calculations in his head. He knew that he was less than ninety minutes away from Ashley. This estimate even allowed for a wrong turn or two when he got onto the rural roads leading to Catherine Frazier's home.

He smiled inwardly and again heard Ashley calling to him. *Hi, Michael. I miss you. I love you. Come save me.* He knew her better than she knew herself.

Cracking open the window slightly, he let some crisp air into the car, trying to cool himself down. O'Connell believed there were two Ashleys. The first was the Ashley who had tried to get rid of him, who had seemed so angry, so scared, and so elusive. That was the Ashley that belonged to Scott and Sally and the freak, Hope. He frowned when he thought of them. There was something truly sick and perverted about their relationships, and he knew that Ashley would be far better off when he had rescued her.

The real Ashley had been the Ashley across the table from him, drinking and laughing at his jokes, but mesmerizing as she slid along the route of loose invitation. The real Ashley had connected with him, both physically and emotionally, in a way far deeper than he had ever thought possible. The real Ashley had invited him into her life, even if only briefly, and it was his duty to find that person again.

He would set her free.

O'Connell knew that the Ashley her parents and lesbian stepmother thought existed was a shadow Ashley. The student, artist, museum-drone Ashley was all fiction, created by a bunch of wimpy, liberal, middle-class nonentities who only wanted her to be like them, to grow up and have the same stupidly insignificant lives they did. The real Ashley was waiting for him to arrive like some fairy-tale knight and show her a different life. She was the Ashley who longed for adventure, an existence on the edge. The Bonnie to his

Clyde, an Ashley who would operate right beside him, outside the rules of life. That she was reluctant, afraid of the freedom that he represented, was only to be expected. The excitement that he was bringing to her was bound to be frightening.

It was just a matter of showing her.

Michael O'Connell smiled to himself. He was confident. It might not be easy. It was likely to be tricky. But she would eventually see.

Feeling a renewed sense of excitement, O'Connell punched at the gas and felt the car leap forward. Within a few seconds he was out in the left-hand lane, accelerating hard. He knew there would be no one to stop him. Not that night.

Not far to go, he thought. Not far to go, at all.

Hope let the night wrap around her, cloaking her misery in shadows. She had let Sally drive home. Hope's silence seemed pale, ghostlike, as if she were only some spectral part of herself.

Sally had the good sense to simply steer the car and leave Hope alone with her thoughts. She felt a little guilty that she didn't feel as bad as she probably should have. But thoughts were rushing toward her, and as awful as the loss of Nameless might be, how he died and what that all meant were far greater considerations. She had an undeniable need to take some action, as she tried to piece together what had really taken place that night.

The car crunched to a halt in their driveway, and Sally said, "I am so sorry, Hope. I know what he meant to you."

It seemed to Hope that those were the first soft words she'd heard from her partner in months. She breathed in deeply and wordlessly got out of the car and walked across the lawn, fallen leaves kicking up around her feet. She stopped at the front door and took a second to examine it before she turned back to Sally. "Not here," she said with a deep sigh. "Unless whoever it was can pick a lock, which he probably can. But someone, like one of the neighbors or a delivery guy or someone, would have seen him out front."

Sally had joined her. "Around back. By the basement. Or maybe one of the side windows."

Hope nodded. "I'll check the back. You check the windows, especially over by the library."

It did not take Hope long to find the shredded doorjamb. She stood for a moment, simply staring at the shards of wood that littered the cement basement floor. "Sally, down here!"

There was only a single bare overhead bulb, which cast odd shapes into the musty corners of the old house's basement. Hope remembered that when Ashley was young, she was always scared to come downstairs alone to do her laundry, as if the corners and cobwebs hid trolls or ghosts. Nameless had been her preferred companion on those occasions. Even as a teenager, when Ashley knew she was far too sophisticated to believe in such things, she would collect all her too-tight jeans and skimpy underwear she didn't want her mother to know she was wearing, then grab a dog biscuit and hold the basement door open for Nameless. The dog would clatter eagerly down the stairs, making enough of a racket to scare away any lingering demon, and wait for Ashley, already sitting, his tail sweeping half-moons of enthusiasm on the floor.

Hope turned when Sally came down the stairs. "This is where he got in."

Sally eyed the splinters and nodded. She stepped aside as Hope moved past her.

"Then he would have come up the stairs. He probably had one of those little mini-flashlights. Then into the kitchen."

"That's where Nameless must have heard him. Or smelled him," Sally said.

Hope took a breath. "Nameless liked to wait for us in the vestibule, so he would have reacted to the sound behind him and known right away it wasn't you or me or even Ashley coming home."

Hope glanced around the kitchen. "This is where he made his stand," she said softly. Last stand, she thought to herself. She could see the old dog, the gray hairs on the back of the neck raised, worn teeth bared. His home, his family. No one was getting past him, even if his eyesight was weak and his hearing almost gone. Not without paying a price, this she knew. She coughed back some more tears and dropped down to the floor, inspecting the area carefully. "See," she said after a few seconds. "Right here."

Sally looked down. "What is it?"

"Blood. Got to be blood. And not Nameless's either."

"I think you're right," Sally said. Then softer: "Good dog."

"But whoever it was that broke in, what was he looking for?"

This time it was Sally who inhaled sharply. "It was him," she said quietly.

"Him? You mean . . ."

"The creep. O'Connell."

"But I thought . . . you said he was out of our lives. The private eye told you . . ."

"The private eye, Murphy, was killed. Murdered. Yesterday."

Hope's eyes widened.

"I was going to tell you, right when we got home." Sally didn't need to continue.

"Murdered? How? Where?"

"On a street in Springfield. Execution-style, or so the paper said."

"What the hell does 'execution-style' mean?" Hope asked, her voice rising.

"It means someone walked up behind him and put two small-caliber bullets into the back of his brain." Sally's voice was cold, mingling detail with fear.

"You think it was him? Why?"

"I don't know. I don't know for sure. I can't tell. A lot of people hated Murphy. Any one of them . . ."

"We're not interested in anyone else. I mean, do you

think . . ." Hope stared down at the splatters of blood on the floor. "So, it might have been anybody in Springfield. But you think this break-in was . . ."

"Who else?"

"Well, it could have been any burglar. It's not like it's unheard-of in this neighborhood."

"It's still pretty unusual. And even when there is a break-in, it's usually just teenage kids, anyway. This doesn't feel like that. Do you see anything stolen?"

"No."

"Then who else?"

"If it was O'Connell, that means . . ."

"He's back after Ashley. Obviously."

"But why here?" Hope finally said.

Sally shuddered. "He was searching for information."

"But I thought Scott had invented this story and sold it to the creep. You know, Italy. Studying Renaissance art. Long gone and out of reach."

Sally shook her head. "We don't know," she said coldly. "We have no idea what O'Connell knows, or what he thinks, or what he's learned. Or what he's done. We know Murphy was killed and we know Nameless was killed. Are the two the same? We're the ones in the dark." She sighed, then clenched her fists and pushed one up against her head in frustration. "We don't know anything for sure."

Hope looked down at the floor and thought she saw another droplet or two of blood, by the door leading into the house. "Let's look around for a minute, see if we can trace his steps."

Sally closed her eyes and leaned back against the wall for a moment. She gave out a long, slow breath. "At least there's nothing here that would tell him where she is. I was really careful about that." Opening her eyes, she continued, "And Nameless, just fighting him, you know, the way he did, that was probably more than enough to chase the son of a bitch out of here."

Hope nodded, but inwardly she was less sure. "Let's just look around."

Another splatter of blood was in the hallway leading into the small library and television room.

Hope let her eyes sweep about, searching for telltale signs that O'Connell had been in here. When her eyes fell on the telephone, she gasped and took a step forward. "Sally," she said quietly, "look there."

Several crimson blood drops were on the telephone.

"But it's just the phone . . . ," Sally started. Then she realized that the red message light was blinking. She pushed the playback button.

Ashley's cheerful voice filled the room.

"Hi, Mom, and, hi, Hope. I miss you. But I'm having a great time with Catherine. We're heading out to dinner, and I was just wondering if I could sneak down there in the next couple of days. Catherine will let me borrow her car, you know, maybe pick up some warmer clothes? Vermont is beautiful during the daytime, but at night, it's getting chilly, and I'm going to need a parka and maybe some boots. Anyway, that's the idea. I'll talk to you later. Love ya."

"Oh my God," Sally blurted. "Oh no."

"He knows," Hope said. "He knows. For sure."

Sally rocked back and spun around, her face stricken, her heart frozen in fear.

"That's not all," Hope said softly. Sally followed her eyes to a bookcase. The second shelf was filled with family pictures—of Hope and Sally, of Nameless, and of all of them with Ashley. There was also an elegant shot of Ashley, caught in profile, hiking in the Green Mountains, just as the sun was setting, the luckiest of pictures. It was a favorite of theirs because it captured her right at that wondrous transition from child to adult, from braces and bony knees to grace and beauty.

The picture usually occupied the center of the shelf.

It was no longer there.

Sally choked and grabbed at the phone. She dialed Catherine's number, then stood helplessly as it rang over and over, without answer.

*   *   *

Scott had chosen that night to drive over to one of the other nearby colleges and attend a speech by a constitutional rights scholar from Harvard Law School, who was giving a presentation as part of a lecture series. The topic had been the history and evolution of the rights to due process. The speech had been genuinely lively. He was energized, and when he stopped on his way home to pick up some chicken lo mein and beef and snow peas at a Chinese restaurant, Scott was looking forward to the remainder of the evening, alone with student papers.

He reminded himself to call Ashley at some point that evening, just to check in, see how she was, see if she needed some cash. He was a little uncomfortable that Catherine was footing the bill for Ashley's stay. He thought he should find some equitable financial understanding, especially because he was a little unsure how long Ashley would have to be there. Not much longer, surely. But still, she was probably something of a burden. He didn't really know whether Catherine was wealthy. They had only met once or twice, on blessedly brief, overly polite occasions. He did know that she was fond of Ashley, which made her basically okay in his book.

The lo mein had started to drip through the paper bag when he came through the door and heard the telephone ring. He dumped it on the kitchen counter and grabbed the phone.

"Yeah, hello?" he said abruptly.

"Scott, it's Sally. He was here, he killed Nameless, and now he knows where Ashley is and I can't reach them on the phone."

Her voice burst over the line, the words rushing toward him.

"Sally, calm down," he said. "One thing at a time."

He could hear his own tones. Calm. Reasonable.

Inside, he could feel his heart, his breathing, his head, all spinning and accelerating, as if he were dropping suddenly through a sullen, windswept sky.

*   *   *

Ashley and Catherine walked slowly through Brattleboro back to Catherine's car, coffees in hand, observing a row of artisans' studios, hardware stores, outdoor-gear outlets, and bookstores. It reminded Ashley of the college town where she had grown up, a place defined by the seasons and their modest pace. It was hard to feel uncomfortable or even threatened in a town that bent over backward to accommodate differing points of view.

It was a twenty-minute drive from the town out into the countryside where Catherine's house was nestled between hills and fields, isolated from the neighbors. Catherine made Ashley drive, complaining that her eyesight wasn't nearly as sharp at night as it once was, although Ashley figured that she just wanted to enjoy her latte in peace. Ashley was happy to hear the older woman go on this way; there was something fierce about Catherine. She wasn't willing to allow any of the aches and pains of aging limit anything she did, as long as she got to rail against the process.

As they drove, Catherine gestured toward the road ahead. "Don't nail some deer. Bad for the deer. Bad for the car. Bad for us."

Ashley dutifully slowed the car and took a glance in the rearview mirror. She could see a set of headlights coming up fast behind them. "Someone seems to be in a hurry."

She tapped her brakes once, just to make sure that the car behind them saw their lights.

"Jesus Christ!" she burst out.

The car behind them had roared up to their rear bumper, closing the distance with a screech, tailgating them, only inches back.

"What the hell?" Ashley shouted. "Hey, get back!"

"Stay calm," Catherine said coldly. But she had dug her fingernails into the seat.

"Stop it!" Ashley shouted as the car behind them suddenly flicked on its high beams, filling up the interior with light. "God damn it, what are you doing?"

She could not see who was in the car, nor could she make out the make and model. She seized hold of her steering wheel as they maneuvered down the isolated country road.

"Let him pass," Catherine said, keeping as much alarm out of her voice as she could. She pivoted in her seat, trying to look out the back, but she was blinded by the headlights and restricted by her seat belt. "Just pull to the side, first place you see. The road gets a little wider up ahead." She was trying to remain calm at the same moment that her head was calculating rapidly. Catherine knew the roads in her community well; she was trying to think ahead, trying to envision how much space they might have.

Ashley tried to speed up, just to gain some separation, but the road was too narrow and twisted. The car behind them accelerated, keeping pace. She started to slow down.

"What the hell does he want?" she shouted again.

"Don't stop," Catherine said. "Whatever you do, don't stop. Son of a bitch!"

"What if he hits us?" Ashley asked, to prevent herself from screaming.

"Just slow down enough so he goes by us. If he hits us, hang on. The road forks right, a mile ahead, and we can take that turn and head back toward town. It'll take us toward the fire station, and maybe the cops, too."

Ashley grunted in agreement.

Catherine did not tell Ashley that nearby Brattleboro might have twenty-four-hour police, ambulance, and fire service, but her little town relied on the state police after 10 p.m. or volunteers, who had to be summoned by radio. She wanted to check her watch, but was scared to release her grip on the handholds.

"Up there, on the right!" Catherine cried out. She knew there was a small turnoff a quarter mile ahead, designed to give school buses just enough room to turn around. "Head for that!"

Ashley nodded and pushed down on the gas once again. The car behind them jumped with them, sticking close as Ashley swerved the car onto a small dirt patch by the road.

She tried to move suddenly enough so that the car behind them would have no choice but to pass.

Except it didn't.

Both women heard the squealing sound of brakes, and the screeching noise of tires complaining against the highway.

"Hang on!" Ashley shouted.

Both braced for impact, and Ashley crunched her foot down on the brake. The car was immediately enveloped in a cloud of dirt and dust, and they could hear gravel pinging off the undercarriage and spitting into the nearby trees.

Catherine threw one hand up to shield her face, and Ashley thrust herself back in the seat as the car skidded on the loose-packed dirt. Ashley spun the wheel into the skid, just as her father had taught her, seizing control before they slammed into an embankment. The rear end fishtailed for an instant, but Ashley was able to subdue it, wrestling with the wheel. She looked up, expecting to see the car behind them roar past, but she saw nothing.

The car shuddered and stopped, and Ashley pivoted, expecting headlights and collision.

Catherine slammed back in the passenger seat, bumped her head against the window, grunting hard. "Hang on!" she yelled again, expecting another impact.

But all that greeted them was silence.

Scott listened to the empty ringing, knowing no one was picking up the line.

The first thing he told himself was not to read too much into the failure to connect. They were probably just out for a meal and not yet home. Ashley was something of a night owl, he reminded himself, and more than likely she'd enlisted Catherine in a late showing at a movie theater, or maybe a drink at a bar. There were dozens of reasons why they could still be out. Do not panic, he told himself. Getting hysterical for no real reason wouldn't help anyone or anything and would only irritate Ashley when they did manage to reach her. And probably irritate Catherine, as well, because she wasn't the sort that ever liked being thought of as incompetent.

He breathed in sharply and called his ex-wife back.

"Sally? There's still no answer."

"I think she's in danger, Scott. I really think so."

"Why? Why this time?"

Sally's head was filled with some perverse equation: dead dog times dead detective, divided by splintered doorjamb, multiplied to the missing photograph power. And it equals . . . But instead she said, "Look, a bunch of things have happened. I can't fill you in, but—"

"Why can't you fill me in?" Scott asked, as pedantic as ever.

"Because," Sally spoke between gritted teeth, "every second we delay could prove—"

She didn't finish. For a moment, the two of them were silent, the gulf between them cavernous.

"Let me speak with Hope," Scott said abruptly.

This took Sally by surprise. "She's right here, but—"

"Put her on."

There was a momentary telephone fumbling before Hope picked up the line. "Scott?"

"I can't get through, either. Not even the answering machine."

"She doesn't have one. She believes in making people call her back."

"Do you think—"

"Yes, I do."

"Should we call the police?" Scott asked.

Hope paused. "I will. I know most of the cops up there, sort of. Hell, a couple of them were high school classmates of mine. I can get one of them to drive over there and check on things."

"Can you do this without making too much of an alarm?"

"Yes. I can simply say I can't reach my mother and she's elderly. They all know her, and it shouldn't be a problem for them."

"Okay. Do it," Scott said. "And tell Sally I'm on my way up there. If you reach Catherine, tell her I'm going to show up there later tonight. But I'll need directions."

As Hope spoke, she saw that Sally was pale, her hands shaking. She had never seen Sally so scared, and this unsettled Hope almost as much as the shapeless night that engulfed them.

Catherine was the first to speak. "Are you okay, Ashley?"

And Ashley nodded, her lips dry and throat almost closed, not trusting her voice. She felt her racing heartbeat return to normal, and she said, "I'm fine. What about you?"

"A knock on the head. That's it."

"Should we go to the hospital?"

"No. I'm okay. Although I seem to have spilled my six-dollar cup of coffee all over myself."

Catherine unfastened her safety belt and opened her door. "I need a breath of air," she said briskly.

Ashley reached over and shut off the engine. She, too, stepped out into the night. "What happened? I mean, what was that all about?"

Catherine was staring back down the road, then she turned and looked up in the direction they were traveling. "Did you see that bastard go by us?"

"No."

"Well, I didn't see what happened to him either. I wonder where the hell he went. I hope he spun out into the trees, or over some cliff."

Ashley shook her head. "I was trying to keep control."

"And a fine job you did," Catherine said, her voice regaining a steadiness that reassured Ashley. "Indeed, NASCAR quality. Those guys have nothing on you, Ashley, if I may point out the obvious. Very dicey situation, handled expertly. We're still here, and there's not even a dent in my nice, almost new car."

Ashley smiled, despite the anxiety that still echoed within

her. "My father used to take me down to Lime Rock in Connecticut and book us time on the big track in his old Porsche. I learned a lot from him."

"Well, not exactly the standard father-daughter outing, but one that has turned out to be valuable."

Ashley took a deep breath. "Catherine, has something like that ever happened to you before?"

The older woman was standing by the side of the road, her eyes searching through the darkness. "No. I mean, sometimes when you putter around on these narrow, winding roads, some high school kid will get frustrated and zoom past on a blind turn. But that guy seemed to have something else in mind."

They climbed back into the car and strapped themselves in. Ashley hesitated, then coughed out a few words.

"I wonder if, you know, the creep who was pursuing me . . ."

Catherine leaned back hard in the seat. "You think the young man that caused you to leave Boston . . ."

"I don't know."

Catherine snorted. "Ashley, dear, he doesn't know you're here, and he doesn't know where I live, and it's damn hard to find anyway out in the middle of nowhere. And it seems to me that if you go through life looking over your shoulder and assigning every bad thing that is out of the norm to this creep O'Connell, or whatever his name is, then you won't have much of a life at all."

Ashley nodded. She wanted to be persuaded, told herself to be persuaded, but agreement came slowly.

"Anyway, the young man professes to love you, Ashley, dear. *Love.* I fail to see what nearly driving us off the road has to do with love."

Again, Ashley remained silent, although she thought she knew the answer to that question.

They drove the remainder of the trip in relative silence. There was a long gravel-and-dirt drive up to Catherine's place. She hoarded her privacy within her four walls, while she blustered and badgered everyone in the community outside her home. Ashley stared at the dark house. It had once been a farm, dating back to the early 1800s, and Catherine liked to joke that she had updated the plumbing and the kitchen but not the ghosts. Ashley stared at the white clapboard and wished they'd remembered to leave some lights on inside.

Catherine, however, was accustomed to the dark welcome and launched herself from the car. "Damnation," she said abruptly. "I hear the phone ringing."

She grunted loudly and added, "Too damn late for phone calls."

Ignoring the night, confident in her understanding of every dip and ridge on the walkway to her front door, Catherine left Ashley scrambling behind her. Catherine never locked her doors, so she burst inside, flicking on the lights as she made her way to an ancient rotary-dial phone in the living room.

"Yes? Who is it?"

"Mother?"

"Hope! How nice. But you're calling late."

"Mother, are you okay?"

"Yes, yes, why?"

"Is Ashley with you? Is she okay?"

"Of course, dear. She's right here. What is the matter?"

"He *knows*! He may be on his way there."

Catherine inhaled sharply, but kept her wits about her. "Slow down, dear. Let's take this one step at a time."

As she said this, she turned toward Ashley, who was standing frozen in the doorway. Hope started to speak, but Catherine heard little. For the first time, she could see abject fear in Ashley's eyes.

Scott drove red-line hard.

The small car leapt with enthusiasm, easily pushing past one hundred miles per hour. He could hear the engine roaring behind him as the night swept past, a blur of shadows, stately pine trees, and black, distant mountains. What should have taken close to two hours from Scott's house to Catherine's he expected to do in half that time. He was unsure whether this would be fast enough. He was unsure what was happening. He was unsure what O'Connell was doing. And he was unsure what the night held. He knew only that some odd, misshapen danger was directly in front of him, and he was determined to throw himself between the threat and his daughter.

As he drove, hands gripping the wheel tightly, he was almost overcome with images from their past. All the memories of raising a child flooded him. He felt an utter cold, crippling chill within him, and as each mile slid behind him, he could hardly fight off the sensation that he was a mile per hour too slow, that whatever was about to happen, he was going to miss it by just seconds. And so, he jammed his right foot down on the accelerator, oblivious to anything except the need to move quickly, perhaps more quickly than he had ever moved before.

Catherine hung up the telephone and turned toward Ashley. She kept her voice low, steady, and extraordinarily calm. She selected her words carefully, giving them an antique formality. Concentrating on her words helped her fight her growing panic. She breathed in slowly and reminded herself that she came from a generation that had fought much bigger battles than those presented by this fellow O'Connell, and so she layered her words with a Roosevelt determination.

"Ashley, dear. It appears that this young man who seems most unhealthily attracted to you has actually learned that you are not in Europe, but here, visiting with me."

Ashley nodded, unable to respond.

"I think that what might be wisest is if you were to go upstairs to your bedroom and lock the door. Keep the telephone handy. Hope informs me that your father is driving up here, even as we speak, and that she is also intending to summon the local police."

Ashley took a step toward the stairs, then stopped.

"Catherine, what are you going to do? Maybe we should just get back in the car and get out of here."

Catherine smiled. "Well, I doubt it makes sense to give this fellow another shot at us on the road. I imagine he already tried once tonight. No, this is my home. And *your* home, as well. If this fellow means you any harm, well, I think we'd be better off dealing with it here, where we are familiar with the territory."

"Well, then I won't leave you alone," Ashley said with a burst of false confidence. "We'll both sit and wait together."

Catherine shook her head. "Ah, Ashley, dear, that is most kind of you to offer. But I believe I would be far more comfortable waiting here, knowing that you were behind a locked door upstairs and out of the way. Regardless, the authorities should be here shortly, so let us be cautious and sensible. And sensible, right now, means please to do what I ask you."

Ashley started to protest, but Catherine waved her hand.

"Ashley, allow me to defend my home in the manner I see fit."

The impact of Catherine's sturdy use of language was immediate. Ashley finally nodded. "All right. I'll be upstairs. But if I hear anything I don't like, I'll be down here in a flash." She wasn't exactly sure what she meant by *anything I don't like.*

Catherine watched as Ashley bounded up the single central stairway. She hesitated until she heard the distinctive sound of an old-fashioned key in a door lock clicking shut. Then she walked over to a small wood closet, built right into the wall next to the large open-hearth fireplace. Jammed behind fire logs in an old leather case was her late husband's shotgun. She had not brought it out in years, not bothered to clean it in as long a time, and was not completely certain that the half dozen shells rolling free in the bottom of the case were still capable of being fired. Catherine imagined that there was about an equal chance that the old weapon might explode in her hands if she had to pull the trigger. Still, it was a large, intimidating weapon, with a gaping hole at the end of the barrel, and Catherine hoped that that might be all that was necessary.

She took the shotgun out and sat down hard in a wing chair beside the fireplace. She fed all six shells into the magazine, then cocked the weapon and sat back, waiting, the gun across her lap. The weapon was greasy, and she rubbed her fingertips against her slacks, smearing them with dark streaks. She didn't know much about guns, although she knew enough to click the safety catch off.

Catherine rested her hand on the stock as she heard the first small sounds of movement, just beyond the windows, closing in on the front door.

•

She continued to stare out the window, and I could imagine that she was chewing over one thought or another, then she abruptly turned back toward me and asked, "Have you ever actually thought you could kill someone?"

When I hesitated before answering, she shook her head. "That's probably the answer right there. Maybe a better question for you to consider is how we romanticize violent death."

"I'm not sure what you mean," I said slowly.

"Think of all the ways we express ourselves through violence. On the television, or in movies. Video games for kids. Think about all those studies that show that the average kid grows up witnessing how many thousands of deaths? Many thousands. But the truth is, despite all that education, when we are actually confronted by the sort of rage that could be fatal, we rarely know how to respond."

I let her step away from the window and move back across the room to where she took a seat without replying.

"We like to imagine," she said coldly, "that we will always know what to do in the most difficult of situations. But in reality, we don't. We make mistakes. We fall prey to errors in judgment. All our flaws come flooding out. What we think we can do, we can't. What we need to do is beyond us."

"Ashley?"

She shook her head. "Don't you think fear cripples us?"

30

A Conversation about Love

Catherine took a single deep breath and lifted the shotgun to her shoulder, tracking the sounds from outdoors. She counted the steps to herself. From the window, to the corner of the house, past the flowerpots arranged so carefully in a row, to the front door. He will try the front door first, she told herself. Although her tongue seemed swollen, she shouted out roughly:

"Just come on in, Mr. O'Connell."

She did not have to add, *I'm waiting for you.*

There was a momentary quiet in which Catherine listened to her own labored breathing, which was nearly drowned out by the throbbing of her heart. She kept the shotgun lifted to her shoulder and tried to calm herself down as she sighted down the barrel. She had never shot anything in her life. Indeed, she had never fired a gun, even in practice. She had grown up a doctor's daughter. Hope's father had grown up on a farm and served as an enlisted man in the marines during the Korean War. Not for the first time, she wished he were at her side. After a second or two, she heard the front door open and a set of footsteps in the hallway.

"Right in here, Mr. O'Connell," she spat out hoarsely.

There was nothing tentative in the sound of his steps as O'Connell came around the corner and stood in the entranceway. Catherine immediately leveled the shotgun, pointing it at his chest.

"Hands up!" She couldn't really think of anything else to say. "Freeze, right where you are."

Michael O'Connell neither stayed completely still nor did he raise his hands.

Instead, he took a small step forward and gestured at the weapon.

"You mean to shoot me?"

"If I have to."

"So," he said slowly, eyeing her carefully, then letting his vision sweep around the room, as if he were memorizing every shape, every color, and every angle. "What would make you *have to*?" He spoke as if they were sharing a joke.

"You probably don't want to have me answer that," she replied archly.

O'Connell shook his head, as if he understood, but disagreed. "No," he said slowly, edging a little farther forward, "that's exactly what I need to know, isn't it?" He smiled. "Are you going to shoot if I say something you disagree with? If I move somewhere? If I get closer? Or if I step back? What will make you pull the trigger?"

"You want an answer? You can get one. Probably the hard way."

O'Connell moved a step closer. "That's far enough. And I would like you to raise your hands." Catherine coughed out the words calmly, hoping that she sounded determined. But her voice felt flimsy and weak. And perhaps, for the first time, genuinely old.

O'Connell seemed to be measuring the distance between them.

"Catherine, right? Catherine Frazier. You are Hope's mother, correct?"

She nodded.

"Can I call you Catherine? Or do you prefer something more formal. Mrs. Frazier? I want to be polite."

"You can call me whatever you wish, because you aren't staying long."

"Well, Catherine—"

"No, I changed my mind. Make it Mrs. Frazier."

He nodded, again as if there were a joke.

"Well, *Mrs. Frazier,* I won't have to stay long. I would just like to speak with Ashley."

"She is not here."

He shook his head and grinned.

"I'm sure, Mrs. Frazier, that you were brought up in a proper household, and then later taught your own child how wrong it is to lie, especially directly to another person's face. Lying to someone's face makes a person angry. And angry people, well, they do terrible things, don't they?"

Catherine kept the gun trained on O'Connell. She made an effort to control her breathing, swallowing hard.

"Are you capable of *terrible things,* Mr. O'Connell? Because, if so, perhaps I should just shoot you now and end this evening on a sour note. Mostly sour for you, however."

Catherine had no idea whether she was bluffing. She concentrated hard on the man in front of her and did not have the ability to see much past the space between them. She could feel sweat dripping beneath her arms and wondered why O'Connell wasn't acting more nervously. It was as if he were immune to the sight of the weapon. She had the unsettling thought that he was enjoying himself.

"What I am capable of, what you are capable of—those are real questions, are they not, Mrs. Frazier?"

Catherine drew a deep breath and squinted as if taking aim. O'Connell moved about the room, continuing to familiarize himself with the layout, apparently unconcerned.

"Intriguing questions, Mr. O'Connell. But now it is time for you to leave. While you are still alive. Leave and never return. And mainly, leave Ashley alone."

O'Connell wore a smile, but Catherine could see his eyes moving about the room. She could see that behind his grin there was something far blacker, far more turbulent, than she had ever imagined.

When he spoke, his voice was low. "She's close, isn't she? I can tell. She's very close."

Catherine didn't speak.

"I don't think you understand something, Mrs. Frazier."

"What is that?"

"I love Ashley. She and I are meant to be together."

"You are mistaken, Mr. O'Connell."

"We are a pair. A set. A matched set, Mrs. Frazier."

"I don't think so, Mr. O'Connell."

"I will do whatever it takes, Mrs. Frazier."

"I believe you will. Others might say the same."

This was the bravest thing she could muster, right at that moment.

He paused, eyeing her. She imagined that he was strong, muscled, and athletic-quick. He would be as fast as Hope, she thought, and probably far stronger. There was little between them that might slow him down, if he made a move for her. She was seated, vulnerable, only the ancient shotgun in her arms preventing him from whatever he was going to do. She suddenly felt desperately old, as if her eyesight were fading, her hearing diminished, her reactions dulled. It seemed to her that he had all the advantages, save one. And she had no idea whether he had a weapon with him, beneath his jacket, in his pocket. Gun? Knife? She breathed in hard.

"I don't think you understand, Mrs. Frazier. I will always love Ashley. And the idea that you or her parents or anyone can keep me from her side is really pretty laughable."

"Well, not this night. Not in my house. Tonight, you're going to turn around and walk out. Or else you're going to get carried out minus your head, thanks to my shotgun here."

He paused again, still smiling. "An old bird gun. It fires small-caliber shot that's barely more painful than a BB."

"You'd like to test that?"

"No," he said slowly. "I don't think I would."

She was quiet while O'Connell seemed to think hard about something.

"Tell me something, Mrs. Frazier, while we're having this friendly conversation, why is it that you think I'm not right for Ashley? Am I not handsome enough? Smart enough? Good enough? Why is it that I shouldn't be allowed to love her? What do you really know about me? Who do you think might love her more than I do? Isn't it possible that I might be the best thing that ever happened to her?"

"I doubt it, Mr. O'Connell."

"Don't you believe in love at first sight, Mrs. Frazier? Why is one sort of love acceptable, but another all wrong?"

This hit a nerve within her, but she kept her mouth closed. O'Connell paused, then stiffened.

"Ashley!" O'Connell shouted. "Ashley! I know you can hear me! I love you! I will always love you! I will always be there for you!"

His words echoed through the house.

O'Connell turned back to Catherine. "Did you call the police, Mrs. Frazier?"

She didn't reply.

"I think you did," he said quietly. "But what law have I broken here tonight? I can tell you: none."

He gestured at the shotgun. "Of course, the same is not true for you."

She tightened her grip on the stock of the rifle and pressed her finger against the trigger. Don't hesitate, she told herself. Don't panic. It was as if the familiar world of her own home, her own living room, surrounded by her own pictures and mementos, was suddenly alien. She wanted to say something that might remind her of normalcy. *Shoot him!* A voice shouted out deep within her. *Shoot him before he kills all of you!*

In that second of indecision, O'Connell whispered, "It's not easy to kill someone, is it? It's one thing to say, 'Take another step and I'll shoot,' and another altogether to actually do it. You might think about that. Good night, Mrs. Frazier. I will see you again. I will be back."

Shoot him! Shoot him! Kill him now! As she tried to understand the voice within her head, O'Connell turned, and with surprising speed abruptly disappeared from her sight. She gasped. Ghostlike. One second he was there in front of her, the next he was gone. She could hear his footsteps on the planks of the wooden floor in the hallway, then the thudding of the front door opening and slamming shut.

Catherine exhaled slowly and sat back hard. Her fingers around the shotgun seemed frozen, and it took some force of will to peel them from the weapon. She lowered it into her lap. She suddenly felt exhausted, tired in a way that she had not experienced in years. Her hands shook, her eyes filled with tears, and she had trouble stealing breath from the air around her. She remembered a similar moment in the hospital ward years earlier, when her husband's hand had slipped from hers, and just like that, he was gone. The same sensation of helplessness that had filled her then.

She wanted to call out for Ashley, but she could not. She wanted to rise up and lock the front door, but she was frozen. We have no chance.

Catherine remained in her chair for several minutes. She had no idea how many. She only stirred, regaining some grip on her circumstances, when the flashing blue and red lights of a police cruiser suddenly filled the room around her.

Thoughts raced like power surges through Ashley.

She had remained huddled, behind the locked bedroom door, aware that Catherine and O'Connell were speaking, but unable to make out the words, except those that Michael O'Connell had shouted out, each of which had speared her with fear. When she'd heard the front door slam, she remained frozen in position on the floor, behind the bed, a pillow clutched to her chest, her head facedown in the center, as if she were trying to prevent herself from hearing, seeing, and even breathing. The pillowcase was damp where she had gripped it with her teeth to prevent herself from crying out. She could feel tears racing down her cheeks, and she was terrified. And terrified of being terrified. She was ashamed that she had left Catherine alone to confront Michael O'Connell, despite the older woman's insistence. She was well past the *why can't he leave me alone* stage and knew that she was lost on a much larger sea than she'd ever imagined.

"Ashley!" Catherine's voice penetrated the walls and her fears.

"Yes . . ." She gulped out her reply.

"The police are here. You can come down."

When she left the bedroom and stood at the top of the stairs, she looked down and saw Catherine standing in the hallway across from a middle-aged local police officer wearing a Smokey the Bear hat. He held a notepad and pencil and was shaking his head.

"I understand, Mrs. Frazier." The policeman was speaking slowly, a little densely, and Ashley could see Catherine was clearly frustrated. "But I can't put out an all points bulletin on someone *you* invited into your home, simply because he seems to be obsessively in love with Miss Freeman. . . . Good evening, Miss Freeman, if you could come down . . ."

Ashley descended the stairs.

"Now, did this fellow strike you, or threaten you?"

Catherine snorted. "Everything he said was a threat, Sergeant Connors. It was not in the words he said, but in the manner he spoke them."

The policeman looked over at Ashley. "You were upstairs, miss? So you didn't witness anything?"

Ashley nodded.

"So, other than his presence, he didn't *do* anything to you, did he, miss?"

"No," Ashley said. The word seemed impotent.

He shook his head, closed the notebook, as he turned back toward Catherine. "What you should have said, Mrs. Frazier, is that he struck you and put you in fear for your life. Some physical contact. That would give us something to go on. You could have said that he brandished a weapon. Even that he was trespassing. But we can't arrest someone for telling you that he loves Miss Freeman."

The policeman smiled and tried to make a little joke. "I mean, I bet just about all the boys fall in love with Miss Freeman."

Catherine stamped her foot. "This is useless. You say you cannot help at all?"

"Unless we're pretty darn certain a crime has been committed."

"What about stalking? That's a crime!"

"Yes. But that's not what happened here tonight, is it? But if you can prove a pattern of behavior, well, then you should have Miss Freeman here go before a judge and get a restraining order. That means that if this guy came within a hundred yards of her, we could arrest him. It would give us some ammunition, so to speak. But absent that . . ."

He looked over at Ashley.

"You haven't got any such order, like in Boston, where you live?"

She shook her head.

"Well, you ought to consider it. Of course . . ."

"Of course what?" Catherine demanded.

"Well, I don't like to speculate . . ."

"What?"

"You have to be cautious. Don't want to trigger some real nasty behavior. Sometimes a restraining order does more harm than good. Talk to a professional, Miss Freeman."

"We *are* talking to a professional!" Catherine interrupted. "After all, Sergeant, isn't this what your job is?"

"I mean someone who is expert on these sorts of domestic issues."

Catherine shook her head, but had the good sense not to say anything else. It would do no good to insult the local police.

"If he comes back, Mrs. Frazier, call the substation and I'll send someone around. Day or night. That's the least we can do. He knows there's a cop around, he's not likely to try much. That's the best offer I can make."

The policeman made a show of replacing his pencil and notebook in his shirt pocket as he turned and walked to the door. He paused and, to Ashley, seemed a little embarrassed.

"Our hands are sort of tied," he said. "I'll make a report about this call, in case you do go to a judge for an order."

Catherine merely snorted again. "Well, that's a comfort," she said angrily. "That's truly reassuring. This is all like saying we need to wait for the entire house to burn down before we call the fire department."

"I wish I could be more helpful. I really do, Mrs. Frazier, because I understand these sorts of things are difficult. But, like I say, call us if he shows up again. We'll be out here in a jiffy."

The policeman suddenly lifted his head, listening.

"Jesus," he said abruptly. "Someone's going real fast."

Both Catherine and Ashley leaned forward and heard the distant noise of an engine howling with speed. Ashley, of course, recognized the sound. As they stood there, it grew closer, louder, and they all saw headlights cutting through the nearby stands of trees.

"That's my father," Ashley said. She thought she should at least be relieved to see him and feel safe, because he would know what to do. But those feelings eluded her.

•

"I have become a student of fear," she said. "Physiological reactions. Psychological stresses. Behavioral issues. I read psychiatric textbooks and social science treatises. I read books about how people respond under all sorts of difficult situations. I keep notes, go to lectures, whatever I can, just to try to understand it better."

She turned away, staring back out the window at the benign suburban world beyond the glass.

"This doesn't seem like much of a clinic," I said. "Things seem pretty quiet and safe around here."

She shook her head. "All illusion. Fear just takes different forms in different locations. It's all based on what we expect to happen in the next few seconds, versus what actually occurs."

"Michael O'Connell?"

A wry smile creased her face. "Do you ever wonder how it is that some people simply innately understand how to deliver terror? The hit man. The sexual psychopath. The religious fanatic. It just comes naturally to each of them. He was one of those types. It's as if they aren't tethered to life in the same way that you or I or Ashley and her family were. The ordinary emotional bonds and restraints we all feel were some-how absent in O'Connell. And they were replaced by some-thing truly unsettling."

"What was that?"

"He loved who he was."

31

Running from Something Unseen

Catherine stood outside, staring up into the canopy of stars that filled the midnight sky above her house. It was cold enough to see her breath, but she was far more chilled by what had just occurred. The one place that she expected to be safe was in her own home, on land that she had occu-pied for better or for worse for so many years, where every tree, every shrub, every breeze that clattered through the eaves spoke to some memory. It was what was supposed to be solid about life. But this night, the safety of her home had thinned from the moment she had heard the words *I will be back.*

Catherine turned back toward the front door. It suddenly seemed to her that it was too cold to stand outside, trying to sort out what to do, which surprised her a little. She had of-ten stood beneath the Vermont sky and considered many questions, in all seasons. But this night, the black sky didn't provide clarity, just a quick chill that worked its way down her back, and she shivered. She had the terrible thought that Michael O'Connell wouldn't feel the frost. His obsession would keep him warm.

She glanced over at the line of trees on the edge of her property, out past a flat area beside the house, where her hus-band had borrowed a tractor and smoothed out a section, then planted it with athletic turf grass and erected a set of goalposts, all as a birthday present when Hope turned eleven. Usually staring at the minifield recalled so many happy moments, it comforted Catherine. But this night, her eyes went past the faded white frame of the goal. She imagined that O'-Connell was out there, just beyond her sight, watching them.

Catherine gritted her teeth and went back inside, but not before making a single obscene gesture to the shadowy line of trees. Just in case, she thought to herself. It was well past midnight, but there was still packing to do. Her own bag was ready, but Ashley, still shaken, was taking longer.

Scott sat in the kitchen, drinking black coffee, the old shotgun on the table in front of him. He ran a finger along the length of the barrel and thought to himself that they would be much better off if Catherine had just pulled the trigger. They could have spent the rest of the night dealing with the local police and a coroner, and hiring her an attorney, although he suspected that she wouldn't even have been arrested. If she had just shot the bastard as O'Connell came through the front door, he thought, he would have arrived and then helped sort everything out. And life would have gone back to normal within days.

He heard Catherine come through the door and enter the kitchen.

"I think I will join you," she said as she poured herself a cup.

"It's going to be a long night," Scott said.

"Already is."

"Ashley about set?"

"She'll be ready in a minute," Catherine said. "She's just pulling a few things together."

"She's still pretty shaky."

Catherine nodded. "Don't blame her. I'm still a little shaky, as well."

"You hide it better."

"More experience."

"I wish . . ." he started, then stopped.

Catherine smiled out of the side of her mouth wryly. "I know what you wish."

"I wish you'd blown him straight to hell."

She nodded. "So do I. In retrospect."

Neither said what both were thinking: having O'Connell standing at the wrong end of a shotgun had been an opportunity they doubted they would have again. As quickly as this thought came into Scott's head, he tried to dismiss it. The educated, rational part of him insisted, violence is never the answer. Then, just as smoothly, the reply rose up: Why not?

Ashley entered, hovering in the doorway.

"All right," she said. "I'm ready."

She stared at her father and Catherine. "Are you sure leaving is the right thing?"

"We're pretty isolated out here, Ashley, dear," Catherine said cautiously. "And it seems very hard to predict what Mr. O'Connell will do next."

"It's not fair," Ashley said. "Not fair to me, not fair to you, not fair to anybody."

"Being fair, I think, is no longer much of an issue," Scott said.

"Being safe is the first concern," Catherine said, still speaking gently. "So let's err on the side of caution." Ashley clenched her fists together, battling tears.

"Let's just go," Scott said. "Look, at the very least it will make your mother feel a whole lot better when you're home. Hope, too. And Catherine, she sure as hell doesn't want to be up here alone, dealing with the son of a bitch after he realizes out that we've moved Ashley out."

"Next time," Catherine said stiffly, "I don't think I will bother with conversation."

She gestured at the shotgun, which made Scott and Ashley both smile.

"Catherine," Ashley said, wiping away at her eyes, "you would make a fine professional killer."

Catherine smiled. "Thank you, dear. I will take that as a compliment."

Scott rose from the table. "Does everyone understand how this is going to work tonight?"

Both Ashley and Catherine nodded. "Seems elaborate," Catherine said.

"Better elaborate than sorry. It's best to assume he's watching the house, don't you think? And that he might try to follow us. And we don't know what he might try to pull. He's already run you off the road once tonight."

"If that was him," Ashley said. "We never got a good look at the guy. Or his car. It doesn't make sense. Why would he try to kill us one minute, then stand in the hallway and shout out he loves me?"

Scott shook his head. It didn't make sense to him, either. "Anyway, we shall give him something to think about, if he is watching."

He collected the bags and arranged them all by the front door. Behind him, Catherine was turning off every light in the house. Leaving the two women in the hallway, he walked out into the nighttime. He scanned the night shapes, flashing back to when he was Ashley's age, in Vietnam, staring out through spyglasses into the jungle, the battery of howitzers behind him, silent for once, the damp, stale smell of closely packed sandbags close to his chest, wondering if they were being observed from the vines and tangled, thick undergrowth.

Scott slid behind the wheel of the Porsche, fired up the engine, and backed into a space next to Catherine's small four-wheel-drive station wagon. He left his car running, stepping out after popping the hood. He reached in and started Catherine's car. He went to the right-hand side of each vehicle, opened the door, and adjusted the passenger seat, so that they were lowered as far as they could go.

Scott went back inside, seized all the bags, and went out again into the night.

He placed Catherine's bag in his car, and Ashley's in Catherine's, closing the trunks, but leaving all four car doors open.

He walked back swiftly to the front door. "Ready?"

Both women nodded.

"Then let's go. Fast, now."

All three of them moved together, in a single dark lump. Ashley slipped into the passenger seat in the Porsche, and Catherine behind the wheel of her own car. As she took her place, Ashley immediately dove down, so that she could not be seen. She had tucked her hair up under a dark navy watch cap.

Scott ran around, slamming all the car doors, before jumping into his own seat. He gave Catherine a thumbs-up signal, and she accelerated hard, her wheels spitting gravel. Scott pulled in, barely inches away. Fast now, he thought. But Catherine was already jamming her foot down on the gas, and the two of them headed quickly for the highway, in tandem.

Scott scanned the road behind him, on the lookout for headlights. But the twists in the highway made it difficult. He thought, There's a full moon tonight. If I were chasing someone, I'd be driving without lights.

Beside him, Ashley remained scrunched down. He accelerated, keeping up with Catherine.

She was heading to a spot she knew, right before the entrance to the interstate highway. It was a drive-in bank that had a small parking lot in the rear. When she spotted the entrance, she waited until the last second to flick on her blinker and tugged the wheel sharply. She could hear the tires squeal briefly as she zipped between the dual drive-in windows, pulling into the rear, where there were no lights. She could hear the roar of the Porsche's engine directly behind her. She stopped and breathed in.

Scott pulled in beside her, then leapt from his car and ran to the edge of the building.

A single car went past on the main road, then a second. He couldn't make out the driver of either car.

But neither car slowed; instead they disappeared down the road, neither one turning for the interstate. Nor did they seem hesitant and suspicious. He waited for another car to go past, which took nearly a minute. Then he returned to where the two women were waiting.

"All right, switch time," he said. "No sign of him."

Wordlessly, Ashley slid from her seat in the Porsche and jammed herself into the passenger seat of the wagon, tucking an old plaid fleece blanket around herself. Catherine nodded, then put the car in gear and headed out toward the entrance ramp of the interstate heading south.

Scott pulled behind her, but instead of taking the ramp south, toward their destination, he stopped by the side of the road. He watched the small car's taillights disappear. He waited, determined to get a look at any car that might be heading south behind Catherine, but none came along. There was no one else around that he could see. He paused again and, after counting to thirty, suddenly floored the Porsche and, with tires screeching, ducked the nose of the sports car onto the northbound ramp. By the time he was at the bottom of the ramp, he was already doing close to ninety. He saw a tractor-trailer in the right-hand lane, blocking his access, but instead of braking, he punched the gas and flew past the trucker in the breakdown lane. The truck's air horn blasted the night behind him, and the driver flashed all his lights in irritation. Scott ignored him, looking hard for the illegal U-turn coming up on his left. He just hoped no trooper was hanging out in it. His high beams caught a FOR AUTHORIZED USE ONLY sign, and he slammed on the brakes. In the same motion, he cut all his lights.

The Porsche bumped on the dirt and bottomed out once as he went from the northbound side to the south. A quick glance told him the road was empty, and accelerating hard, he flung the Porsche back onto the highway, flicking on his headlights once again. He saw a pair of deer's eyes lighting up red in the median.

He took a deep breath. Try following that, he said to himself.

Scott figured it would take less than ten minutes for him to come up behind Catherine and Ashley, checking every car before he reached their tail. Then he would escort them the rest of the way home.

He pursed his lips together tightly.

I've got a few tricks left, he thought. He could feel the car engine throbbing with speed and, for the first time that night, felt some control over the situation.

He was smart enough, however, to remind himself that this sensation was not likely to last long.

The need for sleep, after so much tension, prevented them all from gathering together until much later that day. Ashley, in particular, had dissolved into sobs upon hearing all the details of Nameless's death and had cried bitterly in bed, before finally tumbling into a deep but dire sleep, her dreams marred by black images of death. On more than one occasion, she cried out, bringing either Sally or Hope to her door to check on her as if she were still a little girl.

Scott had gone back to the college. He had stolen some ninety minutes of sleep in his chair in his office before waking, feeling that the entire day was somehow misshapen. In the men's room, washing up, he spent a few seconds staring at himself in the mirror. History, he thought, is the study of men and women who rise to extraordinary events. It is, over and over, an examination of one person's bravery, another's cowardice, a third's prescience, and a fourth's failures. It is emotion and psychology, played out on a field of action. He felt a kind of cold sickness inside, wondering whether he had spent all his adult life studying what others did without learning how to *do something* himself.

Michael O'Connell, he believed, was simply a moment in his own history. And how he acted in the next few days, Scott thought to himself, would define him forever.

Sally struggled with anger.

It seemed to her that everything they had tried had failed. They had tried to be reasonable, polite. They had tried to be forceful. They had tried to bribe their way out. They had tried intimidation. They had tried deception. They had tried flight. And for all the various schemes they had come up with, they had gained nothing but failure. Their own lives had been roiled and thrust into turmoil, their own careers threatened, their privacy invaded, their lives upset and truly pushed into some other realm.

A world of fear, she thought. That was what awaited them.

She was seated in the living room, alone. She found herself grimacing, shaking her head, waving her hands in the air, pointing angrily, gesticulating, frowning, as if she were in the midst of some furious conversation, but no one else was in the room to hear the words that she was forming in her head. Upstairs, Ashley was still asleep, but Sally intended to awaken her soon. Hope and Catherine had gone outside for a walk to pick up some sort of take-out for dinner. In all likelihood they were discussing what had descended upon them. She had been left behind, on guard.

Sally could feel her pulse racing. They were at some crossroads moment, but she was as yet unsure what paths were available.

She leaned her head back and closed her eyes.

I have screwed everything up, she thought to herself. I have made a mess of everything.

She sighed and went across the room to a desk where they kept scrapbooks and old photos, memorabilia too valuable to throw out, not significant enough to frame. She opened a large drawer and pawed through the piles until she found what she was looking for: a picture of her mother and father. They both had died far too young, one in a car accident, the other from a heart condition. Sally wasn't sure why she needed to look at them, but she was almost overcome with the need to see their eyes, looking toward her, as if to reassure her. They had left her alone, and she had seized upon Scott—with all her misgivings about who she was and what she was going to become—because she had told herself that he would be *consistent*. It was probably the same sense that had driven her to law school, filled with a determination to make sure that she was never a victim of events again. She shook her head at this thought and reminded herself how foolish this was. Anyone can be victimized. At any time.

As this rancid thought coursed around inside her, she heard Ashley stirring upstairs.

She took a deep breath. There is one truth, she thought: a mother will do anything to protect her child.

"Ashley! Is that you? Are you up?"

There was a momentary pause, then a reply, preceded by a long, drawn-out groan. "Yeah. Hi, Mom. I'll be down right after I brush my teeth."

She was about to respond when the telephone rang.

The sound chilled her.

She checked the caller identification, but it merely said *private caller*.

Sally reached out, bit down on her lip, and picked up the receiver.

"Yes, who is it, please?" she said with as much lawyer frost as she could manage.

There was no reply.

"Who is it!" she demanded sharply.

The line remained quiet. She couldn't even hear breathing.

"God damn it, leave us alone!" she whispered. Her words drove like nails into the silence and she slammed down the phone.

"Mom? Who was it?" Ashley called out from upstairs. Sally could hear a momentary tremble in her daughter's voice.

"Nothing," she called back. "Just a damn telephone solicitor, pitching magazine subscriptions." As quickly as the words were out of her mouth, she wondered why she had failed to tell the truth. "You coming down?"

"Be right there." Sally heard the bedroom door close. She picked up the receiver and dialed *69. In a moment, a recorded voice came on the line. "The number 413-555-0987 is a pay telephone in Greenfield, Massachusetts."

Close, she thought. Less than an hour's drive away.

When Michael O'Connell hung up the pay phone, his first instinct was to head south, where he knew Ashley was waiting for him, and try to take advantage of the moment. Every word he'd heard from Sally had told him how weak she was. He leaned back, closing his eyes, envisioning Ashley. He could feel blood racing through his body, almost as if every vein and artery had become electric. He breathed in slow, shallow breaths, like a swimmer hyperventilating before taking a plunge, and told himself that following her to her own home would be precisely what *they* would expect.

They will be preparing, he thought. Inventing some scheme to prevent him from getting close to her. Designing a defense, building walls. They cannot beat me.

This was the simplest, most obvious, nonnegotiable fact.

Again he breathed in. *They* will think that I'm on my way there.

But then, what's the rush?

Let them worry. Let them lose some sleep. Let them startle at every night noise.

And, he thought, when their defenses were thin from exhaustion and tension and doubt, he would arrive. When they least expected it.

O'Connell tapped his foot against the sidewalk, like a dancer finding the rhythm.

I am there, at their side, even when I'm not there, he told himself.

Michael O'Connell decided that on this day, he wasn't in any hurry. The love he felt for Ashley could also be exceedingly patient.

•

This time she told me to meet her at midnight outside the emergency room of a hospital in Springfield. When I asked her why midnight, she informed me that she did volunteer work at the hospital two nights a week, and that the witching hour was when she customarily took her break.

"What sort of volunteer work?" I asked.

"Counseling. Battered wives. Beaten children. Neglected elderly. They all show up at the hospital, and someone has to be on hand to steer them into the right channels for the state to help out." Her voice had seemed coldly patient, despite the images that she suggested. "What I do is find the

proper paperwork to accompany broken teeth, black eyes, razor slashes, and fractured ribs."

She was waiting for me, smoking a cigarette, taking deep
drags, down to the filter. I pointed at the cigarette as I walked
through the parking-lot shadows toward her.

"I didn't know you smoked."

"I don't." She took another long pull. "Except here. Two
nights a week. One cigarette at the midnight break. No more.
When I return home, I throw the rest of the pack away. Buy a
new pack each week."

She smiled, her face partially hidden by shadow. "Smoking
seems like a modest sin, compared with what I see here. A
child, perhaps, with his fingers systematically fractured by a
cracked-out stepfather. Or a mother in her eighth month,
beaten with a metal coat hanger. That sort of thing. Very routine. Very ordinary. Very cruel. Just the usual sort of ugliness
that passes for life. Remarkable, isn't it, how cruel we can be
to one another?"

"Yes."

"So, what more do you need to know?" she asked.

"Scott and Sally and Hope weren't willing to risk uncertainty, were they?"

She shook her head. A high-pitched, caterwauling ambulance siren cut through the night. Urgency arrives with many
different sounds.

32

The First and Only Plan

When they gathered, later that evening, a sense of helplessness was in the air. Ashley, in particular, seemed crippled by events. She huddled beneath a blanket in an
armchair, her feet tucked up under her, clutching an ancient

stuffed brown bear whose ear had been partially shredded by Nameless.

Ashley looked around the room and realized that she had created the mess she was in, but then, she couldn't exactly see what she had done to have it reach this point. Long forgotten was the single, slightly drunken night that had landed her in bed with Michael O'Connell. Even more distant was the conversation when she'd agreed to go out with him that one time, thinking then that O'Connell was different from all the college boys that she had come to know.

Now, she only thought herself naïve and stupid. And she had absolutely no idea what she was going to do. When she looked up and let her eyes fasten on Catherine and Hope and her mother and father, one after the other, she realized that she had endangered all of them; in different ways, certainly, but still, they were all in jeopardy. She wanted to apologize, and so, that was where she started.

"This is all my fault. I'm to blame."

Sally responded quickly, "No you're not. And punishing yourself won't do any of us any good."

"Well, if I hadn't—"

Scott stepped in. "You made a mistake. We've been all over this before, and we should leave that mistake behind. We all managed to compound that mistake by thinking we were dealing with someone reasonable. So, perhaps you were wrong once, Ashley, but O'Connell managed to get all of us involved pretty quickly, and we're all guilty of underestimating what he is capable of. Recriminations and blame are really stupid avenues to pursue now. Your mother is right; the only issue in front of us is, what do we do next?"

"I think," Hope said slowly, "that's not really it, Scott."

He turned toward her. "How so?"

"The issue is, how far are we willing to go?"

This quieted the room.

"Because," Hope continued, her voice even, but her words reverberating with authority, "we have only the vaguest idea of what Michael O'Connell is willing to do. There are plenty of indications. We know he is capable of just about anything and everything. But what are his limits? Does he even have any? Where will he draw the line? I think it would be unwise for any of us to think that he has any restraints."

"I wish I'd—" Catherine started, then stopped. "Well," she said with customary briskness, "Scott knows what I wish I'd done."

"I suppose," Sally said, "that now it is time for us to engage the authorities."

Catherine coldly added, "Well, that's what the local policeman told me outside my house, after my little get-together with Mr. O'Connell."

"You don't sound like you think much of that idea," Hope said.

"I don't." Beneath her breath, Catherine added, "When the hell have 'the authorities' ever helped anyone?"

Scott turned to Sally. "Sally, you're the lawyer. I'm sure that in your professional life, you've run into these sorts of problems. What would be involved in the process? What could we expect?"

Sally paused, running through details in her head before speaking.

"Ashley would have to go before a judge. I suppose I could handle the legal work, but it's always wiser to hire outside counsel. She would have to testify that she was being stalked, that she was in fear for her well-being. She might be required to prove that there was some systematic behavior on O'Connell's part, but most judges are pretty understanding, and they would be likely to accept what Ashley said without requiring much outside corroboration. They would issue a restraining order that would allow the police to arrest O'Connell if he came within some specified distance—usually it's one hundred feet to one hundred yards. The judge would also, in all likelihood, order O'Connell to not have any contact with her, either by telephone or by computer. These orders are generally pretty complete and would effectively remove him from Ashley's life, given one rather large *if*."

"What's that?" Ashley asked.

"*If* he complies with the order."

"And if he doesn't?"

"Well, then the police can get involved. Technically, he could be arrested and held in violation of the order. That would put him away for some time. The standard sentence is up to six months. But that's assuming the judge gives him the maximum. In reality, there's more give-and-take. Judges are reluctant to put people in jail for what they often imagine is merely a dispute between a couple."

Sally took a deep breath. "That's the way it is all supposed to work. The real world is never quite as clear-cut as all that."

She looked around at the others in the living room. "Ashley makes a complaint and testifies. But what real proof do we have of anything? We don't know that he cost her her job. We don't know that he was the one who made all the trouble for us. We don't know that he broke in here. We can't prove that he killed Murphy, although maybe he did."

Sally took a deep breath. The others remained absolutely quiet.

"I have been thinking about this," she said, "and it's not an obvious call, by any means. Not in the slightest. I bet Michael O'Connell has experience with restraining orders and has them figured out. In other words, I think O'Connell knows what he can and can't get away with. But to get something beyond that simple restraining order, to actually get O'Connell accused of a crime, Ashley would be required to prove that he is behind everything that has happened. She would have to be persuasive in a court of law, and under cross-examination. It would also put her within arm's reach of Michael O'Connell. When you accuse someone of a crime—even of stalking—it creates a secondary intimacy. You are connected to that person in a profound way, even if there is an order keeping him at a distance. She would have to confront him in court, which would, I guess, feed his obsession. He might even enjoy it. But one thing is certain: Ashley and O'Connell would be forever linked. And it also means that Ashley would be looking over her shoulder forever, unless she flees. Goes someplace new. Becomes someone different. And, still, that isn't a sure thing. If he decided to devote his life to finding her . . ."

Sally was rolling now, picking up momentum. "But being frightened and proving there is a real foundation for that fear in a court of law are different things. And then, there is a secondary consideration entirely."

"What's that?" Scott asked.

"What will he do if Ashley does get the order? Just how angry will he be? How incensed? And what will he do then? Maybe he will want to punish her. Or us. Maybe he will decide that it is time to do something drastic. *If I can't have you, no one will.* What do you think that really means?"

They were all quiet, until Ashley said, "I know what it means."

None of them wanted to ask her what they all understood.

But Ashley spoke out, her voice trembling.

"He means to kill me."

Immediately Scott blustered and interrupted, "No, no, no, Ashley, you mustn't say that. We don't know that, not at all."

Then he stopped, because he realized how ridiculous each word he spoke had sounded.

For an instant, Scott felt dizzy. It was as if everything that was crazy—that this man might kill Ashley—made sense, and everything that should have made sense was turned upside down. He felt a complete coldness enter him and found himself rising out of his chair.

"If he comes close again . . ."

This threat seemed as hollow as everything else.

"What?" Ashley suddenly blurted out. "What will you do? Throw history books at him? Lecture him to death?"

"No, I'll . . ."

"What? What will you do? And how will you do it? Are you going to watch me twenty-four hours a day, seven days a week?"

Sally tried to remain even-keeled. "Ashley," she said quietly, "don't get angry—"

"Why not?" she shouted. "Why shouldn't I get angry? What right does this creep have to ruin my life?"

The answer to that question, of course, was obvious to all of them.

"So what do I have to do?" she said, her voice filled with tears, emotion coloring every word. "I guess I have to leave. Start over. Go someplace far away. Hide out for years and years, until something happens so I can come out? It's like some great big game of hide-and-seek, huh? Ashley hides and Michael O'Connell seeks. How will I ever know I'm safe?"

"I suppose," Sally said, still speaking as cautiously as she could manage, "that's all that we can hope for. Unless . . ."

"Unless what?" Scott asked.

She was choosing her words carefully. "We can think up some other plan."

"What do you mean?" Scott demanded abruptly.

Sally spoke slowly, "What I'm saying is that there are two routes here. One is to work within the legal system. It might be inadequate, but it is what we have. It has worked for some people. But not for others. The law can make one person safe, and kill another. The law guarantees nothing."

Scott leaned forward. "There is an alternative?"

Sally was almost shocked by what she was saying. "The alternative would be working on this problem outside the law."

"What would that include?" Scott asked.

"I think," Sally said coldly, "you might not want to ask that question quite yet."

This reply plunged the room into silence.

Scott spent what he thought was a long time staring at Sally. He had never heard her sound so cold-blooded before.

"Why not," Catherine blurted out, "just invite the bastard over here for dinner and then shoot him when he walks through the front door? Bang! A mess in the front parlor. I volunteer to clean it up. End of story."

Again there was some silence in the room. Each of them could feel a certain appeal in this idea. But it was Sally, dropping into her most pragmatic, practiced legal tones, that immediately saw the problem.

"That might remove one dilemma—Michael O'Connell—but in its stead, a zillion other problems would arrive."

Scott nodded. "I think I see what you're saying, but go on."

Sally actually mustered a smile at her ex-husband and Catherine. "First off, what you say—inviting him over and shooting him—is first-degree murder, even if he does deserve it. In this state it is punishable by twenty-five years to life, without parole. And the mere fact that we have all discussed it makes us all conspirators, so none of us, including Ashley, would walk away. I suppose one can always argue for an acquittal—*jury nullification* is the legal term, where the jury actually decides you were justified in taking the action you did—but that is a rarity. And not something anyone should count on."

"There are other problems, as well," Scott added. "What makes you think that we wouldn't ruin all of our lives in the process? Our own careers, who we are, all would disappear. And we'd become the fodder for Court TV or *The National Enquirer*. Every bit of our lives would be exposed publicly. And even if we did this—and managed to insulate Ashley from the event—she would spend the rest of her life visiting us in prison and refusing interviews from *Hard Copy*, or watching her life turned into some Lifetime network movie of the week."

Hope, who had been quiet, interjected, "The way you describe it, it would mean that O'Connell had won. He might be dead, but Ashley's life—all our lives—would be ruined. And what he said—*if I can't have her*—would turn out to be true, in a perverse way. She would be branded forever."

Catherine snorted, as if disagreeing, but in actuality she could see the entire scenario, and beyond. She clapped her hands together and spoke out briskly, "Well, there must be some way to remove Michael O'Connell from Ashley's life before something worse happens."

Scott's mind was churning. The word *remove* triggered a series of thoughts within him.

"I think," he said slowly, "I have an idea."

The others looked toward him. He stood up and took a few quick paces back and forth.

"For starters," he said carefully, "it seems to me that we should take a page from his own book."

"What do you mean?" Sally said.

"What I mean," Scott replied carefully, "is that we learn to outstalk the stalker. Let's find out everything—and I mean everything—we can about the son of a bitch."

"Why?" asked Hope.

"Because he must be vulnerable somewhere. And it is what he would least expect."

Catherine nodded her head vigorously. Somewhere in all of them there had to be a mean streak; it was simply a matter of finding it and employing it.

"All right," Sally replied, "I suspect we could do that. But to what end?"

Scott was measuring his words cautiously. "We cannot kill him ourselves, but we must *remove* him. Who can do this for us? And do it in a way where all of us—especially Ashley—walk away without a scar. In fact, barely a scratch, if we do it right."

"I don't know who you mean," Sally answered for the rest of them.

"You said it yourself, Sally," Scott replied. "Who *removes* someone from society for five, ten, twenty years right up to life?"

"The State of Massachusetts."

Scott nodded. "It is simply a matter of finding a way to have the state *remove* Michael O'Connell. They will do this happily and enthusiastically, won't they? All we have to do is provide one small item for them."

"What's that?" Ashley asked.

"The right crime."

•

"Do you not see the genius in Scott's plan?" she asked.

"I don't know that *genius* is the word I would choose," I replied. "*Stupid* and *risky* come immediately to mind."

She paused. "All right, fair enough, on first impression. But here is what is unique in Scott's thinking: it goes utterly and completely against the grain. Just how many tenured history professors at small, prestigious liberal arts colleges become criminals?"

I didn't reply.

"Or a guidance counselor and prep-school coach? A small-town lawyer? And Ashley, the art student? What could be more out of character than for that well-heeled group to decide to commit a crime? And to choose something that might lead to violence?"

"Still, I don't know..."

"Who better to step outside the law? They knew better than almost anyone what they were doing, thanks to Sally and her expertise in the court system. And Scott, he was far better equipped to become a criminal than he'd ever imagined, thanks to his military training. He was disciplined. Wasn't their biggest problem the moral prohibitions against crime that accompany their status in society?"

"I still would have thought they would call the police."

"What guarantee did they have that the system would work for them? How many times have you picked up the morning paper and seen some tragedy unfold, fueled by an obsessive love? How often have you read of policemen complaining, 'Our hands were tied'?"

"Still..."

"The words you surely don't want carved into your own headstone are *If Only...*"

"I agree, but..."

"Their position was hardly unique. Movie stars know about stalking. Secretaries in busy offices. Trailer-park, stay-at-home mothers. Television personalities. Obsession can cut across any sort of economic and social background. But their response to it all was unique. And what was their goal? To keep Ashley safe. How much purer could their motive be? Put yourself in their shoes for an instant. What would you do?"

And there was the simplest, most unanswerable question.

She took in a deep breath. "In reality the only issue was, could they get away with it?"

33

Some Hard Decisions

Scott was energized, driven to his feet. He looked at the women gathered around him and feverishly began to imagine plots and plans, all fueled by the rage he harbored toward Michael O'Connell. Sally was shifting about, and he could see the lawyer in her starting to gnaw through what he'd said, shredding his words, unraveling his ideas. She will see all the dangers in what I am proposing, he thought. He wondered whether she would see that those dangers might be less than the single threat faced by Ashley.

But to his surprise, Sally abruptly nodded her head. "Whatever it takes," she said coldly. "We should be prepared to do whatever it takes."

Then she turned toward Catherine and Hope. "You know, I think we are about to step over a line, and perhaps the two of you might want to reconsider whether you want to be involved. Ashley is, after all, Scott's and my daughter, and our responsibility. Hope, admittedly, you've been her second mother, maybe even more, and Catherine, her only real grandparent—but still, you're not blood, and—"

Hope snarled at her, "Sally, shut the fuck up."

The room was immediately silenced, and Hope rose to stand with Scott. She gathered herself and said, "You know, I have been involved in Ashley's life, for better or for worse, since the day you and I first met. And even if our last days haven't been so good, and our future is questionable, that doesn't diminish my feelings for Ashley. So, to hell with you. I will make up my own mind as to what and what not I'm willing to do."

Catherine quietly added, "Me, too."

Sally reeled back in her seat. I have screwed everything up. What the hell is wrong with me? she thought to herself.

"Don't you understand anything about love?" Hope asked.

This question floated around the living room. After letting the silence creep around all of them, Hope turned to Scott.

"Okay, Scott, maybe you ought to outline exactly what you have in mind."

Scott stepped forward. "Sally's right. We are about to cross a line. Things are going to get doubly dangerous from this moment on." He suddenly saw risk in everything, and it made him hesitate. "It's one thing to talk about doing something illegal. It's another thing to actually take that risk."

He turned toward Ashley.

"Honey," he said slowly, "this is the point where you are to get up and leave the room. I would like it if you went upstairs and waited for Mom or me to call you back down."

"What?" Ashley nearly shouted, instantly irate. "This involves me. This is my problem. And now, when you think you're going to do something, something that involves me intimately, I'm supposed to exit? Forget it, Dad, I'm not being excluded. This is my life we're all talking about."

Again silence gripped all of them, until Sally spoke.

"Yes, you are. Ashley, honey, listen. We need to know that you are isolated—legally—from whatever we do. So you can't be a part of the planning. You'll probably have to *do* something. I don't know. But it won't be part of a criminal conspiracy. You need to be protected. Both from O'Connell, and from the authorities if whatever we come up with blows up in our faces." Sally used her clipped, efficient lawyer voice. "So, don't ask any damn questions. Do what your father says. Go upstairs. Wait patiently. Then do whatever it is we ask, without question."

"You're treating me like a child!" Ashley blurted.

"Precisely," Sally said calmly.

"I won't stand for that."

"Yes, you will. Because that's the only way I will proceed."

"You can't do this to me!"

"What are we doing?" Sally persisted. "You don't know what we are going to do. Are you suggesting that we have no right to act unilaterally on behalf of our own daughter? Are you complaining that we shouldn't take steps to help you?"

"What I'm saying is that this is my life!"

"Yes." Sally nodded. "You said that. We heard it. And that is precisely why your father asked you to leave the room."

Ashley glared at her parents, tears forming in her eyes. She felt utterly helpless and impotent. She was about to refuse again when Hope interrupted.

"Mother," she said cautiously, "I'd like it if you went upstairs with Ashley."

"What?" Catherine demanded. "Don't be absurd. I'm not a child that can be ordered about."

"I'm not ordering you." Hope paused. "Actually, yes, I am. And I would say the same to you as Scott and Sally just said to Ashley. You will be called upon to do something. I am sure of that. It's hard for me to act in other ways if I'm constantly worried about you all the time. Simple as that."

"Well, that's nice of you to worry, dear, but I'm far too old and set in my ways to have my only child turn into my guardian. I can make up my own damn mind."

"That's what concerns me." Hope looked fiercely at her mother. "Why is it that you can't see that if I worry about you—just as Sally and Scott will worry about Ashley—that we will be constrained by what we might do? Are you so self-centered that you can't allow me to choose my own path?"

This question stifled Catherine's reply. She thought that in her many years with her daughter, it was the same question that had been posed to her over and over. Each time, she had acquiesced, even when Hope was unaware that she had. Catherine snorted and sat back hard in her chair, angry with what her daughter was suggesting, and also angry that she could see the sense in it. She steamed for a moment, then stood up.

"I think you're wrong," she said. "About me. And you"—she pivoted toward Sally—"are perhaps wrong about Ashley." Catherine shook her head. "We are, both of us, perfectly capable of taking all sorts of chances. Tough chances, I daresay. But this is just the first step, and if you need me to absent myself, right at this moment, I will." She turned toward Ashley. "That might change. I hope it does. But for now, okay. Come, dear, you and I will go upstairs and trust that these folks will see the light when they see the complete foolishness of excluding us."

She reached out and grasped Ashley, half-lifting her out of her seat.

"I don't like this. Not at all," Ashley said. "I don't think it's in the slightest bit fair. Or right." But she and Catherine trudged up the stairs.

The three remaining behind were quiet, watching them exit. Sally said, "Thank you, Hope. That was a pretty smart move."

"It's not chess," Hope said.

"But it is," Scott said. "Or, at least, it's about to be."

It took a little time, but they were able to hash out the initial division of responsibilities.

From the bare bones they had acquired in Murphy's report, Scott was to delve into Michael O'Connell's past. See his home, investigate where he grew up, uncover whatever possible about O'Connell's family, work history, education. It would be up to Scott to ascertain who they were really up against. Sally was to spend the weekend examining the law. They did not know what crime they wanted to assign to Michael O'Connell, not yet, although they suspected it would have to be a major felony. They avoided the word *murder* throughout their conversation, but it lurked in everything they said.

Creating a crime out of whole cloth requires some planning, which was Sally's job. She was to ascertain not merely what the best crime would be—that is, what would remove O'Connell most certainly from their lives for the longest period—but also what crime would be the easiest for the state to prove. What would quickly and efficiently lead to

O'Connell's arrest. What would be least likely to be pled out or result in some sort of bargain with prosecutors. It had to be a crime that he could not trade away by testifying against other, more culpable people. He had to be in whatever it was absolutely alone. And she had to uncover what elements the state would need to prove their case in a court of law, beyond a reasonable doubt.

Hope, who they believed was the only one of them that O'Connell might not immediately recognize, was given the task of finding him and following him. She was to examine as much of his day-to-day life as she could.

They assumed that in what each of them was doing were the answers.

It was hard to see who faced the most danger. Probably Hope, Sally thought, because she would be physically closest to O'Connell. But Sally knew that as soon as she opened her first law book, she was guilty of a crime. And Scott, she recognized, was heading off into the least certainty, because there was no telling what he might find when he first dropped the name Michael O'Connell in the neighborhood where he grew up.

It was decided that Catherine and Ashley would stay in the house. Catherine, who still regretted not shooting O'-Connell when she had the chance, was in charge of designing some sort of protective system, in case O'Connell should arrive at their door again.

This was Sally's single greatest fear: that before they had a chance to act, he would.

She did not use the word *race* with Hope or Scott.

She simply assumed they were thinking along the same precise lines.

•

She eyed me for a moment or two, as if expecting me to say something, but when I remained silent, she announced, "Have you thought much about the concept of the perfect crime? I've been spending a good deal of my time these days considering some questions. What is right, what is wrong? What is just, what is unjust? But what I have come to believe is that the perfect crime, the true perfect crime, is not only the crime that one gets away with—that would be the absolute minimal standard—but also one that results in some psychological sea change. A life-altering experience."

"Stealing a Rembrandt from the Louvre wouldn't qualify?"

"No. That merely makes one rich. And doesn't really make you something other than an art thief. Not much different from the gun-wielding punk who holds up a convenience store. I think the perfect crime—maybe *ideal* crime—is actually something that exists on a more moral plane. It rights some mistake. It creates justice, not defies it. It establishes opportunity."

I rocked back in my seat. I had dozens of questions, but letting her speak made more sense.

"And something else," she added coldly.

"What is that?"

"The crime restores innocence."

"Ashley, right?"

She smiled. "Of course."

34

The Woman Who Loved Cats

The semifinal game went to penalty kicks.

Sports, she thought, devises many cruel endings, but this was certainly among the harshest. Hope's team had clearly been outmanned, but had found some reserve of determination that had allowed them to hang in against their opponent. The girls were obviously exhausted, their exertion worn in their eyes. They were all streaked with sweat and dirt, and more than one sported bloody knees. The goalie was pacing back and forth nervously, apart from the others. Hope considered going over to say something, but she understood that this was a moment when her player had to stand alone, and that if she had not prepared her properly in all the practices that had led to this moment, then nothing she might add in that second would make up for that deficit.

Luck was not with them. Hope's fifth shooter, her captain, all-league and all-region, who had never missed a penalty in four years on varsity, rang her shot off the crossbar, and with that single evil noise of ball resounding against metal, the season ended. Just like that, as sudden as a heart attack. The girls on the other team all squealed with unbridled joy and rushed forward to embrace their keeper, who had not once touched the ball in the entire shoot-out. Hope saw her own player fall to her knees in the muddy field, before dropping her head into her hands and bursting into tears. The other girls were equally stricken, and Hope could feel her own emotions stretched thin, but she still managed to tell them, "Do not leave your teammate alone out there. You win as a team, you lose as a team. Go remind her."

The girls all ran—Hope had no idea where they got the energy—to surround their captain. Hope was proud of all of them in that moment. Winning, she thought, brings out the happiness in all of us, but losing brings out the character. Hope watched the team gather in the field. She remembered that she would have another battle to fight in the days to come. She shivered and felt cold; there was nothing left between that moment and the winter. This game was over. Time now to play another.

Although she didn't know it, the parking spot on the street that Hope slid her car into was precisely the spot Matthew Murphy had chosen to keep watch on Michael O'Connell's apartment building. She leaned back in her seat and pulled her knit ski cap a little lower on her head. Then she adjusted a pair of new, clear eyeglasses on her nose. She did not routinely wear glasses, but she imagined that some disguise was necessary. Hope wasn't certain that Michael O'Connell had actually ever seen her in person, but she suspected so. She believed that he had done to all of them more or less what she was doing at that moment. She wore jeans and a old navy peacoat against the late-afternoon chill. Hope might have fifteen years on most of the students in the area, but she could look young enough to be on their outer fringes. She had picked out her clothes with the same nervous intensity of someone going out on a first date, desperate to make an impression by not making an impression. She simply wanted to blend in on the Boston streets, like a chameleon taking on the color and hue of everything that surrounded her, and become invisible.

She guessed that if she stayed put in the car that after a few minutes he would undoubtedly spot her.

Assume he knows everything, she reminded herself. Assume he knows what you look like and has memorized every detail of your four-year-old compact car, right down to the license plate number.

Hope remained frozen in her seat, until she imagined she appeared so obvious that wearing fake glasses would be irrelevant. She glanced down at Murphy's report, took another long look at the photograph of O'Connell that accompanied it, and wondered whether she would actually be able to recognize him. Not knowing what else to do, she pushed open the car door, stepping out onto the street.

She stole a look toward Michael O'Connell's address, wishing that it would become dark enough so that she could see him turn on a light in his apartment, then realized that by staring she was far more likely to allow him to see her than she was to see him. She turned and rapidly walked down to the end of the block, imagining a set of eyes boring into her back. She turned the corner and stopped. What precisely was the purpose of staking out his apartment if the first thing she did was quick-march directly away from it?

She took a deep breath and felt utterly incompetent.

Useless, useless, she said to herself. Go back, find some spot in an alley or behind a tree, and wait him out. Have as much patience as O'Connell does.

Shaking her head, she turned and walked back around the

corner, her eyes scanning the block for some spot to hide, and saw O'Connell exiting his building. He had his head back, and he was grinning, exuding a jauntiness and evil that infuriated her. She was angry; it seemed that he was mocking her, when, of course, there was no indication that he even knew she was there. She slid sideways, trying to huddle against a wall, hoping to avoid making eye contact, but still watching him. At the same moment, she saw a small, wizened elderly woman weave her way down the block, on the same side of the street as Michael O'Connell. As soon as he spotted her, Hope saw him scowl. The look on his face frightened Hope; it was as if O'Connell had transformed himself in a split second, going from devil-may-care nonchalance to intensely furious.

The old woman seemed the very definition of *harmless*. She was moving along painfully slowly. She was short and stumpy, and wore a dowdy black wool overcoat that was probably twenty years old and had a multihued knit hat on her head. Both her hands were gripping white plastic grocery bags, weighed down with foodstuffs. But Hope could see the old woman's eyes flash as she spotted Michael O'Connell, and she swayed slightly in her path to block his route.

Hope clung to a tree across the narrow street from where O'Connell and the old lady confronted each other.

The woman tried to lift a hand, still clutching the grocery bag, and waggled a finger in his direction.

"I know you!" she said loudly. "I know what you're doing!"

"You don't know shit about me," O'Connell replied, his own voice raised.

"I know you're doing something to my cats. I know you're stealing them. Or worse! You are a nasty, evil man, and I should call the police on you!"

"I haven't done anything to your damn cats. Maybe they've found some other crazy old woman to feed them. Maybe they don't like the food you leave out. Maybe they just found better accommodations elsewhere, you old bitch.

Now leave me alone, and be careful that I don't call the health authorities on you, because they will sure as hell seize all those mangy goddamn cats, take them all out, and kill them."

"You are a cruel, heartless man," the old woman said stiffly.

"Get out of my way and go screw yourself," O'Connell said as he pushed past the woman, and continued to saunter down the street.

"I know what you're doing!" the old woman repeated, shouting after him.

O'Connell turned, staring back at her. "Do you now?" he answered coldly. "Well, whatever it is you think I'm doing, you're lucky I don't decide to do the exact same thing to you."

Hope saw the old woman gasp and step back as if she'd been struck. O'Connell grinned again, clearly satisfied with his response, and pivoted, heading rapidly down the street. Hope did not know where he was heading, but knew she should follow him. When she turned back to the old woman, frozen in position on the sidewalk, she got an idea. As Michael O'Connell turned the street corner at the end of the block, Hope launched herself toward the woman.

Glancing to make certain that Michael O'Connell had disappeared, Hope gestured toward the elderly woman. "Excuse me, ma'am," she said as gently as she could while still getting the old woman's attention. "Excuse me . . ."

The woman turned warily toward Hope. "Yes?" she asked cautiously.

"I'm sorry," Hope said rapidly. "I was on the other side of the street and I couldn't help but overhear the words you had with that young man."

The woman continued to eye Hope as she closed the distance between them.

"He seemed very rude and disrespectful."

The old woman shrugged, still not sure what Hope was getting at.

Hope took a deep breath and launched her lie.

"My cat, a really cute calico, with two white front paws—I call him Socks—has been missing for a couple of days. He's lost and I just don't know what to do. It's driving me crazy. I live just a block or two over." Hope waved in a general direction indicating virtually all of greater Boston. "And maybe you've seen him?"

In truth, Hope didn't like cats. They made her sneeze, and she disliked the way they looked at her.

"He's such a cutie, and I've had him for years and it's not like him to be gone this long." The lies tripped easily off her tongue.

"I don't know," the old woman said slowly. "There are a couple of calico cats in my collection, but I don't recall any new ones. But then . . ."

The woman's eyes slipped off Hope and stared in the direction that Michael O'Connell had disappeared. She hissed, almost like one of her charges.

"I can't be sure *he* hasn't done something evil."

Hope adopted a stricken look. "He doesn't like cats? What sort of person . . ."

She didn't need to finish. The old woman took a small step back and looked Hope up and down, sizing her up. "Perhaps, you would like to come in, have a cup of tea, and meet my children?"

Hope nodded as she reached down to carry the woman's grocery bags. I'm in, she thought. It felt like being invited to stand next to a dragon's lair.

Scott sighed and stared out at the faded cinder-block and redbrick, low-slung high school and imagined that the same person who had designed it probably also designed prisons. A line of yellow school buses parked in front, engines running, filled the air with a distinctly harsh diesel smell. A frayed American flag had twisted around the flagpole, tangling up with the state flag of New Hampshire. Both flapped spastically in the stiff breeze. To the side was a high, rusty chain-link fence. A marquee out front carried two messages:

GO WARRIORS! and SAT/ACT TESTS SING UP NOW. No one seemed to have noticed the misspelling.

Scott, too, had a copy of Matthew Murphy's report stuffed inside his suit coat. It only hinted at the bones of Michael O'Connell's past, and Scott was determined to put flesh to those few words. O'Connell's high school had been as logical a place as any to start, even if their information would be ten years old.

He had spent a depressing morning surveying the world where O'Connell had grown up. Coastal New Hampshire is a place of contradictions; the Atlantic Ocean gives it great beauty, but the industry that leeched near the land where rivers empty into the sea was stolid and heartless, all smoke-stacks and rail stations, warehouses and smelting plants that worked around the clock. It was a little like staring at a far-too-old stripper working a down-and-out club in the middle of the day.

Much of the area where Michael O'Connell grew up was dedicated to the construction of large ships. Huge cranes capable of moving tons of steel outlined the gray sky. Hot in the summer, cold in the winter, it was the sort of place where people wore hard hats throughout the day, coveralls, and sturdy, battered boots. The people who worked in the yards were sturdy and steady, as essential as the heavy equipment they operated. The place valued toughness over almost everything.

Scott felt completely out of place. As he sat in his car, watching the swarms of high school kids emerge from the shopworn school building, he felt as if he came from a dif-ferent country. He lived in a world where his job was push-ing students toward all the trappings of success that America likes to trumpet: big cars, big bank accounts, big houses. The teenagers he watched filing onto the waiting buses had lesser dreams, he guessed, and were far more likely to end up in a factory, working long hours and punching a time clock.

If I grew up here, I would do anything to get out, he thought.

As the loaded buses started to roll out, he emerged from

his car and walked swiftly toward the school's main entrance. A security guard hanging by the door pointed him to the main office. Several secretaries were behind a counter. He could see past them to where the principal was dully lecturing some female student with purple-spiked hair, a black leather jacket, and ear and eyebrow studs. "Can I help you?" a young woman asked.

"I hope so," Scott replied. "My name is Johnson. I work for Raytheon; you know, we're from the Boston area. We are about to offer a young man a position. His résumé says he graduated from this high school ten years ago. You see, we have some government contracts, so we have to double-check things."

The secretary turned to her computer. "The name?"

"Michael O'Connell."

She clicked some keys. "Graduated, class of 1995."

"Is there anything else that might help us out?"

"I can't give out grades and other records without written permission."

"Yes, of course," Scott said. "Well, thank you."

He hesitated as the young woman turned back to filing papers electronically. Scott's eyes caught a glance from an older woman, who had emerged from a vice principal's office just as he'd spoken O'Connell's name. She seemed hesitant. Then, with a little shrug, she walked over to where he was standing.

"I knew him," she said. "He's going to get a job?"

"Computer programming. Data filing. That sort of thing. It's not crucial, but because some of the information is connected to Pentagon contracts, we have to do some routine background checks."

She shook her head, surprised. "I'm glad to hear that he's straightened his life out. Raytheon. That's a big corporation."

"His life back then. Was it that bent?"

The woman smiled. "You might say so."

"You know, everybody has some trouble in high school. We try to look past the typical teenage things. But we need to be on the lookout for anything more serious."

The woman nodded again. "Yes. Petty stuff." She hesitated. "O'Connell?"

"I'm reluctant. Especially if he's turned things around. I wouldn't want to mess up his chances."

"It would be a help, really."

The woman hesitated a second time, then said, "He was bad news, when he was here."

"How so?"

"Smart. Far smarter than most. Significantly so. But troubled. I always thought he was a Columbine-type kid, except Columbine hadn't happened yet. You know, quiet, but plotting something. The thing about him that always upset me was, if he got it into his head that you were a problem, or you were in his way, or if he wanted something, then that was the only thing he would focus on. If he got interested in a class, well, he'd get an A. If he didn't like a teacher, well, then strange things would happen. Bad things. Like the teacher's car getting trashed. Or his class records getting screwed up. Or a phony police report filed suggesting some sort of illegal behavior. He always seemed connected somehow. But never close enough so that anyone could prove anything. I was delighted when he left this school."

Scott nodded. "Why—" he started, but the woman finished for him.

"If you came from that household, something would be wrong with you, too."

"Where—"

"I shouldn't." She took out a piece of paper and wrote down an address. "I don't know if this is still accurate. It might not be."

Scott took it. "How is it you remember this? It's been ten years."

She smiled. "I've been waiting all that time for someone to come walking through the door and start asking questions about Michael O'Connell. I just never thought it would be someone considering giving him a job. Figured it would be the police."

"You seem very certain."

The woman smiled. "I was once his teacher. Eleventh-grade English. And he made a distinct impression. Over the years, there have been a dozen or so whom one never forgets. Half of those for the right reasons, half for the wrong. Will he be working in an office with young women?"

"Yes. Why?"

"He always seemed to make the girls here uncomfortable. And yet, they were drawn to him, as well. I could never quite figure it out. Why would you be attracted to someone you knew would cause you trouble?"

"I don't know. Maybe I should talk with some of them?"

"Sure. But after all this time, who knows where they might be? Anyway, I doubt you can find too many people willing to talk about Michael. As I said, he made an impression."

"His family?"

"That's his home address. Like I said, I don't know if his father still lives there. You can check."

"Mother?"

"She was out of the picture years ago. I never got the full story, but . . ."

"But what?"

The woman stiffened abruptly. "I understand she died when he was little. Ten maybe? Maybe thirteen? I don't think I should say anything else. I've already said too much. You don't need my name, do you?"

Scott shook his head. He had heard what he needed to hear.

"Earl Grey, dear? With a little bit of milk?"

"That would be fine," Hope replied. "Thank you very much, Mrs. Abramowicz."

"Please, dear, call me Hilda."

"Well, Hilda, thank you very much. This is most kind of you."

"Be with you in a second," the old woman continued. Hope could hear the kettle start to sing. She cast her eyes about, taking in as much of the apartment as she could. A crucifix was on the wall, beside a vibrantly colored painting of Jesus at the Last Supper. This was surrounded by faded black-and-white photographs of men in stiff collars and women in lace. They were juxtaposed with pictures of a dark but green landscape, streets filled with cobblestones, and a church with pointed spires. Hope added it all together: long-dead relatives in an Eastern European country not visited in decades. It was a little like papering the walls of the apartment with ghosts. She kept searching for the old woman's story; paint peeling near the windowsill; a row of vials and containers of medications. There were stacks of magazines and newspapers, and a television set that had to be at least fifteen years old adjacent to an overstuffed red armchair. It all spoke of emptiness.

There was only a single bedroom. She looked around and spotted a basket with knitting needles near the armchair. The apartment smelled of age and cats. Eight or more were perched on the couch, on the windowsill, and by the radiator. More than one came over and rubbed up against Hope. She guessed there were double the number hiding in the bedroom.

She took a deep breath and wondered how people could end up so lonely.

Mrs. Abramowicz entered with two cups of steaming tea. She smiled down at the collection of cats, who immediately began rubbing her and trailing after her. "Not quite dinnertime yet, loveys. In a minute. Let Mother have a little talk, first." She turned to Hope. "You don't see your Socks in my little menagerie, do you?"

"No," Hope said, adopting a sad tone. "And I didn't see him in the hallway, either."

"I'm trying to keep my darlings out of the hallway. I can't, all the time, because they like to come and go, that's the way cats are, you know, dear. Because I believe *he* is doing something very bad to them."

"What makes you think—"

"He doesn't realize it, but I recognize each and every one. And every few days, one will be missing. I want to call the police, but he's right. They will probably take the rest of my little friends away from me, and I couldn't stand that. He's a bad man, and I wish he would move out. I should never—"

Mrs. Abramowicz stopped, and Hope leaned forward. The old woman sighed and looked around her apartment.

"I'm afraid, dear, if your little Socks came to visit, then that bad man might have taken him. Or hurt him. I cannot tell."

Hope nodded. "He sounds terrible."

"He is. He scares me and I usually won't talk to him, except when we have words, like today. I think he scares some of the others who live here, as well, but they won't say anything either. And what can we do? He pays his rent on time, doesn't make any noise, doesn't have wild parties, and that's all the ownership cares about."

Hope sipped at the sweet tea. "I wish I could be certain. About Socks, that is."

Mrs. Abramowicz sat back. "There's one way," she said slowly. "You could be certain. And it might help answer some of my questions, too. I'm old and I'm not very strong anymore. And I'm scared, but I've got no place else to go. But you, dear, you seem much stronger than me. Stronger even than I was, when I was your age. And I will wager that you're not scared of much."

"Yes."

The old woman smiled again, almost coyly. "When my husband was alive, our apartment was larger. In fact, it included all the space that Mr. O'Connell now occupies. We had two bedrooms and a sitting room, a study and a formal dining room, and this entire end of the building. But after my Alfred died, they cut it up. Made our one big apartment into three. But they were lazy when they did it."

"Lazy?"

Mrs. Abramowicz took another sip. Hope saw her eyes flash with an unexpected anger. "Yes. Lazy. Wouldn't you think it lazy to not bother to change the locks on some of the doors to the new apartments? The apartments that were once *my* apartment."

Hope nodded. She felt a sudden, electric tension within her.

"I do so want to know what he's done to my cats," Mrs.

Abramowicz said slowly. Her eyes narrowed, her voice deepened, and Hope realized that there was something formidable about the woman. "And I imagine you'd like to know about Socks, too. There's only one way to be sure, and that's to look inside." She leaned forward, putting her face only a foot or two away from Hope, and whispered, "He doesn't know it, but I have a key to his front door."

•

"So," she said as a shadow slipped across her face, "do you now see what was in play?"

Any reporter knows there is a necessary seduction between subject and writer. Or maybe it's instinctively knowing how to cajole the most difficult of stories out of a source. Still, I knew she was steering the conversations, had been since the beginning. Our meetings were trysts for information, but by telling the story, I would be using her as much as she had used me.

She paused, then said, "How often do you hear amongst your middle-aged friends the desire to change things? To be something other than who they are? They want something to happen that turns their life upside down, so they no longer have to face the dreary, deadly routines of life."

"Often enough," I replied.

"Most people lie when they say they want a change, because change is far too terrifying. What they really want is to regain their youth. When you are young, all the choices are adventures. It's when we reach middle age that we begin to second-guess our decisions. We stepped upon a path, and we have to walk it, no? And it all becomes problematic. We don't win the lottery. Instead, the boss calls us in and tells us we're being downsized. The husband or the wife of twenty years announces, 'I've met someone new and I want out.' The doctor looks up from the sheet of test results with a frown and says, 'These numbers aren't good. I'm going to order some additional exams.' "

"Scott and Sally . . ."

"For them, Michael O'Connell had created that moment.

Or, perhaps, that moment was fast approaching. Could they protect Ashley?"

She suddenly put her hand to her lips, and I heard a gasp escape from her throat. She took a second to regain her composure. "Because, although no one had quite articulated it, not yet, they all knew somewhere deep within, that what they hoped to purchase would come at a high price."

35

A Single Boot

Hope stood uncomfortably outside the door to Michael O'Connell's apartment with the key in her hand. Behind her, Mrs. Abramowicz lurked in her own doorway, cats circling at her feet. She gestured eagerly for Hope to go ahead.

"I'll keep watch. It will be all right. Just hurry," Mrs. Abramowicz whispered.

Hope took a deep breath and slipped the key into the lock. She wasn't sure about what she was doing or what she was looking for, nor did she know precisely what she hoped to learn. But she had the key in her hand, and as it turned the lock with only the quietest of clicks, she imagined O'Connell walking down the sidewalk, turning the corner to his street, closing in on her as the night fell. She could sense his breath behind her ear, imagined the hiss of his voice. She gritted her teeth and told herself that she would fight hard, if it came to that.

"Quick, dear," Mrs. Abramowicz said, still urging her forward. "Find out what he's doing to my cats."

Hope pushed the door open and stepped inside.

She did not know whether to shut the door behind her or leave it ajar, so that—what? she thought. If he comes back,

I'm trapped here. No back door. No fire escape. No way to flee. She took a deep breath and closed the door almost all the way. At least, she thought, she would be able to hear a warning from Mrs. Abramowicz, if the old lady was capable of issuing one.

Hope surveyed the apartment. It was dingy and neglected. Clearly, O'Connell didn't care about his immediate surroundings. No colorful posters on the walls, no plants in the window, no multihued throw rug on the floor. No television or stereo. Only a few tattered computer-course textbooks stuffed into a far corner. The apartment was decrepit and austere; a monk's hideout. This unsettled Hope, the recognition that all the passion in Michael O'Connell's life rested in his imagination. He lived in a different world from the one where he put his head down and slept.

She moved swiftly into the apartment, took a deep breath, and in that instant invented a plan.

Memorize, she told herself. Remember everything.

She reached inside her jacket pocket and found a scrap of paper. On a small desk she spotted a cheap pen. She immediately sketched a rough floor plan, then turned back to the desk.

It was a cheap wooden tabletop stretched across two black metal filing cabinets. A single wooden, stiff-backed chair was drawn up in front of a laptop computer. The setup had a naked simplicity; she could imagine Michael O'Connell seated across from the screen, its metallic light bathing his face, as he concentrated on the images in front of him. The laptop appeared new. It was open, plugged in, and the power light was lit.

Hope took a deep breath, listened for any sounds from the hallway, then sat down in front of the computer. She wrote down the computer make and model on her scratch paper. Then she eyed the black screen. Like a workman reaching for an exposed wire, she touched the mouse pad in the center. The machine whirred, then flashed as the screen saver came up.

Hope felt her lips go dry and her throat constrict.

The screen saver was a picture of Ashley.

It was a little out of focus and had clearly been hurriedly taken from a few feet away. It caught her as if she were turning suddenly, surprised at some noise that had burst from behind her. Her face was creased with fear.

Hope stared at the picture and heard her breathing grow short and shallow. The picture O'Connell had chosen for his screen saver told her several things, none of them good. O'Connell worshipped that moment when Ashley had been caught unawares and was filled with terror.

It was love, she thought. The very worst kind.

Biting down on her lip, she moved the cursor over to the *My Documents* file and clicked on it. There were four different listings: *Ashley Love. Ashley Hate. Ashley Family. Ashley Future.*

She clicked on the first, only to see a box come up: *Password Required.*

She moved the cursor to *Ashley Hate.*

The machine blinked back *Password Required.*

Hope shook her head. She thought she might come up with the password if she sat and considered it, but she was already worrying about the amount of time she'd spent in the apartment. Still breathing fast, she closed everything down on the computer, returning it to its original state. Then she pulled open the file drawers, but discovered they were empty, other than for a couple of stray pencils and some printer paper.

When she stood up, she was a little dizzy. Hurry, she told herself. You're pushing your luck.

She looked about. Check the bedroom, she thought.

The room smelled of sweat and neglect. She moved quickly to a battered chest of drawers and rifled through them as quickly as she could. A single mattress was on a frame, sheets and blanket tossed haphazardly on top. She dropped to her knees and checked under the bed. Nothing. She turned to the small closet. A few jackets and shirts hung inside. A single black blazer. Two ties. One button-down shirt and a pair of gray slacks. Nothing of any note. She was about to turn away when she saw, alone in the farthest corner of the closet, a single battered work boot, with a stiff gray athletic sock crusted with dirt stuffed in the top. It was partially obscured by a pile of sweat-streaked workout clothes.

A single boot didn't make any sense to her.

She looked around for the companion, but couldn't spot it anywhere.

This bothered her, and she froze in position, staring hard at the boot, as if it could tell her something. Then she reached into the back, and carefully moved aside the clothing, taking hold of the boot. It was heavy, and she thought instantly that something might be inside. Like a surgeon peeling back a flap of skin, she removed the sock and looked down.

She heard herself groan.

Inside the boot was a gun.

She started to reach for it, then told herself, Don't touch it. She did not know why.

A part of her wanted to seize it, steal it, just take it away from Michael O'Connell. Is this the gun he will use to kill Ashley?

Hope felt trapped, as if she were being held underwater. She knew if she took the gun, O'Connell would know that one of them had been here. And he would take action. Maybe it would trigger a violent response. Maybe he had another weapon stashed somewhere. Maybe, maybe. Questions and doubts warred within her. She wished there were some way she could render the gun harmless, like removing a firing pin. She had read about that once in a thriller novel, but she had no idea how to do it. And taking the bullets would be useless. He would know someone had been there and simply replace them.

She stared at the gun. She could see on the side of the barrel the brand and the caliber, .25.

The weapon's ugliness almost overcame her.

Not sure that she was doing the right thing, she carefully replaced the boot in the corner of the closet and rearranged the clothes so that things looked exactly as before.

She wanted to run. How long had she been inside the apartment? Five minutes? Twenty? She thought she could hear footsteps, voices, and realized that she was hallucinating. Leave now! she told herself.

Hope rose and started to exit, walking past the bathroom, which she didn't bother to check, and the small kitchen, which made her stop.

Cats, she thought to herself. Mrs. Abramowicz will want to know.

She peered into the tiny area. No table, just a refrigerator, a small four-burner stove, and a couple of shelves filled with canned soups and stews. No cans of cat food. No box of rat poison to mix into a lethal meal.

Hope went to the refrigerator and pulled the door open. Some sandwich fixings and a couple of cold beers were all that O'Connell kept inside. She closed the door, then, almost as an afterthought, opened up the freezer, expecting to see a couple of frozen pizzas.

What she saw was like a blow, and she was barely able to stifle a scream.

Staring back at her were the frozen bodies of at least a half dozen cats. One of them had its teeth exposed, gargoylelike, a terrifying ice grin of death.

Panic filled Hope, and she stepped back, hand over her mouth, her heart racing, nauseous, dizzy, feeling as if her temperature had spiked. She needed to scream, but nothing could choke past her tightened throat. Every fiber of her being told her to run, to flee, to get away and never look back. She tried to tell herself to remain calm, but it was a losing battle. When she reached out, to close the freezer door, her hand shook.

From the hallway, she suddenly heard a hiss. "Hurry, dear! Someone is at the elevator!"

Hope turned away, running for the front door.

"Hurry!" she heard Mrs. Abramowicz whisper. "Someone is coming!"

The old lady was still perched in her own entranceway when Hope burst out into the hallway. She could see the elevator counter starting to rise, and she closed the door to O'-Connell's apartment. She fumbled with the key, nearly dropping it, while she tried to slide it into the lock.

Mrs. Abramowicz shrank back, taking refuge in her own place. The cats by her feet were scurrying back and forth, as if they caught the sense of fear and panic in the old woman's voice. "Hurry, hurry, we must get away!"

Hope saw that the old woman had nearly disappeared into her own flat, retreating from sight, leaving her door only open a crack. She felt the key drive the dead-bolt lock home and she stepped back, turning toward the elevator. She could see a light from inside the compartment when it reached the floor.

She froze, unable to move.

The elevator seemed to pause, then rose past the floor without stopping.

Her ears were ringing with adrenaline, and every sound seemed distant, like an echo across a wide canyon.

She assessed herself, conducting an inventory of her heart, her lungs, her mind, trying to see what still functioned, what had been shut down by fear.

Behind her, Mrs. Abramowicz cracked her door open a little wider and stuck her head out into the hallway.

"False alarm, dear. Did you find out what happened to my cats?"

Hope inhaled deeply, trying to calm her racing heart. When words came to her, they were cold. "No," she lied. "No sign of them anywhere."

She could see some disappointment in the old woman's eyes.

"I think I should be leaving now," she said stiffly. But she had the good sense to slide the key to Michael O'Connell's apartment into her jacket pocket as she turned and headed rapidly for the emergency stairs. She knew that waiting for the elevator would require a patience she no longer owned.

Hope lurched down the stairs, moving as quickly as she could, the pit of her stomach still clenched with tension. She barreled ahead, shoulders hunched forward, needing desperately to get outside. When she looked up, she suddenly saw a form in the lobby doorway, looming in the darkness ahead of her. She nearly froze with crushing fear, until she saw that it was only two other tenants entering. One of them snorted, "Hey!" as she pushed past them, out into the night cold, welcoming the darkness that surrounded her. She nearly jumped down the last stairs to the sidewalk and, without a look back, cut across the small street toward her car, fumbling with her keys, before thrusting herself into the driver's seat. Inwardly, she could hear a voice insisting, *Escape! Get away now!* She was about to pull out when she looked up and once again froze.

Michael O'Connell was sauntering down the sidewalk opposite her.

She tracked him with her eyes as he paused outside the building, dug in his pocket for his keys, and then, not even glancing in her direction, stepped up and disappeared inside. She waited and then, a few moments later, saw lights flash on in his apartment.

Hope feared that he would somehow know that she had been there. That she had disrupted something, left something out of place. She put her car in gear and pulled out of the parking spot. Without looking back, she drove to the corner, then turned and continued down a wide street for several blocks, until she saw another spot where she could pull to the side. She slid the car in and thought to herself, What was it? Three minutes? Four? Five? How many seconds existed between her break-in and his return?

Her stomach clenched, and the nausea of fear finally overcame her. Hope opened the door to her car and was quietly and privately sick, vomiting into the gutter all of Mrs. Abramowicz's Earl Grey tea.

Scott got an early start the following morning, rising in his cheap motel room just before dawn and driving in the dreary gray November half-light to a spot just across from the house where Michael O'Connell had grown up. He shut down the car and sat, waiting, feeling the first hints of winter seep into the compartment. It was a sad street, a step above a trailer park, but not much of one. The houses were all low-slung, and all in need of repair. Paint peeled from eaves, gutters had pulled free from rooflines, broken toys, abandoned cars, and dismantled snowmobiles littered more than one front yard. Screen doors flapped in the wind. More than one window had been patched with a sheet of heavy-duty plastic. It seemed a place abandoned by options. It was a place for six-packs, lottery-ticket and motorcycle dreams, tattoos and Saturday-night drunks. The teenagers probably worried about pregnancy and hockey in equal doses, and the older folks were more likely consumed by whether their small pensions would keep them off food stamps. It was one of the least friendly spots Scott had ever seen.

As at the school the afternoon before, he knew he was completely out of place.

Scott watched the morning ebb and flow of children heading to school buses and men and women carrying lunch pails heading to work. When things quieted down, he stepped out of the car. He had a roll of $20 bills in his pocket and figured perhaps more than a few would be spent that morning.

Turning his back on O'Connell's home, Scott headed to the nearest house, directly across the street.

He knocked loudly and ignored a dog's frantic deep-throated barking. After a few seconds, a woman angrily shouted at the dog to quiet down, and the door opened.

"Yes?" A woman in her late thirties with a cigarette hanging from her lip, dressed in a pink coat with a grocery-store logo on it, answered the door. She struggled to hold a cup of coffee in one hand while grasping the dog's collar with the other. "Sorry, he's pretty friendly, really, but just scares the hell out of folks, jumping all over them. My husband keeps saying I need to train him better, but . . ." She shrugged.

"It's okay," Scott said, speaking through the screen of the exterior door.

"How can I help you?"

"I'm with the Massachusetts State probation department," Scott lied. "We're just doing a presentencing check on a first-time offender. A Michael O'Connell. Used to live across the street here. Did you know him?"

The woman nodded. "A little. Haven't seen him in a couple of years. What did he do?"

Scott thought for a moment, then said, "It's a robbery charge."

"Stole something, huh?"

Yes, Scott thought. "Seems that way."

The woman snorted. "And got his damn fool self busted, huh? I always figured him for something a little more clever."

"Smart guy, right?"

"Acted smart. I'm not sure the two are the same."

Scott smiled. "Anyway," he said slowly, "what we're really interested in is background. I've still got to interview his father, but, you know, sometimes the neighbors . . ." He didn't need to finish because the woman nodded vigorously.

"Don't know too much. We've only been here a couple of years. But the old man—well, he's been here since the Ice Age. And he ain't particularly popular around here."

"Why is that?"

"He's on disability. Used to work at one of the shipbuilders over in Portsmouth. Had some kind of accident. Said he hurt his back. Collects a check every month from the company, from the state, and from the Feds, too. But for a guy that says he's hurt, he seems to get around okay. Moonlights as a roofer, which is kinda odd work for a guy who claims to be crippled. My husband says he gets paid in cash under the table. I always figured it would be some tax guy snooping around here, asking questions."

"That doesn't say why people don't—"

"He's just a mean-ass drunk. And when he gets drunk, he gets abusive. Makes a racket. You can hear him screaming all sorts of language in the middle of the night, except, odd thing is, there ain't no one there for him to scream at. Sometimes he comes out and shoots off some old gun he keeps in that mess he calls home. There's kids around, but he don't care. Took a shot at one of the neighborhood dogs once, too. Not mine, luckily. Anyway, opened fire for no real reason at all, just because he could. Just a bad dude, all around."

"And the son?"

"Like I said, I hardly knew him. But the apple, as they say, don't fall far from the damn tree. At least, don't sound like it."

"What about the mother?"

"She died. I never knew her. It was an accident. Or so the story went. Some people think she took her own life. Others want to blame her old man. Police looked pretty hard at the whole thing. It was pretty suspicious. But then, it got dropped. Maybe something in the papers back then, I don't know. It happened before I got here."

The dog barked once more, and Scott stepped back.

"Thanks very much," he said. "One thing. Please keep this confidential. It sort of screws up any questions we might ask if people start talking."

"Ah, sure." The woman pushed at the dog with her foot and took a drag from the cigarette. "Hey, can you folks down in Massachusetts put the old man in jail alongside the kid? It sure would make things quieter around here."

Scott spent the rest of the morning working his way around the neighborhood, pretending to be a variety of investigators. Only once did he get asked for some identification, and he backed his way out of that conversation quickly. He didn't learn much. The O'Connell family had predated most of the other folks in the neighborhood, and the impressions they had made limited their contact with their neighbors. Their lack of popularity helped Scott in one regard: folks were willing to talk. But what people said merely reinforced what Scott had already heard or presumed.

There had been no sign of the elder O'Connell emerging from the house, although Scott told himself that the man might have slipped away when he was talking with one person or another. Still, a small, black Dodge pickup truck hadn't moved all day. Scott assumed this was the older O'-Connell's vehicle.

He knew he would have to knock on that door, but he was as yet unsure exactly who to pose as. He decided he would make one more effort, at the local library, to find out about the circumstances surrounding O'Connell's mother's death.

The town's library, in contrast to the bedraggled buildings on side streets and former farmland, was a two-story, glass-and-brick building, adjacent to a new police department and town offices complex.

Scott approached the main desk, and a slight, thin woman, maybe a half dozen years older than Ashley, looked up as she was sliding library cards into the backs of books and asked him not unpleasantly, "May I help you?"

"Yes. Do you keep high school yearbooks on file? And could you direct me to where you would keep local newspapers on microfilm?"

"Sure. The microfilm room is over there." She gestured with her hand toward a side room. "And the collection is pretty clearly marked. Do you need help with the machine?"

Scott shook his head. "Think I can manage. The yearbooks?"

"In the reference section. What year were you hunting down?"

"Lincoln High, class of 1995."

The young woman made a small face of surprise, then grinned. "My class. Maybe I can help you?"

"Did you know a young man named Michael O'Connell?"

She froze. For a second she didn't reply.

Scott watched the young woman's face race through bad memories.

"What has he done?" she finally whispered.

Sally pored over an array of legal texts and law review articles, searching for something, but precisely what, she was unsure. The more she read, the more she assessed, the more she analyzed, the worse she felt. It was one thing, she thought harshly to herself, to be on the intellectual side of crime, where actions were seen in the abstract world of the courtroom, involving arguments and evidence, search and seizure, confessions, forensics—and then the system took over. The criminal justice system was designed to bleed the humanity out of actions. It neutered the reality of a crime, turning it into something theatrical. She was familiar and comfortable with the process. But what she was doing was a step in a far different direction.

Find a crime.

Figure out how to assign it to Michael O'Connell.

Put him in jail. Go on with their lives. It sounded simple. Scott's enthusiasm had been encouraging, until she had actually sat down and tried to work her way through all the various possibilities.

The best she had come up with so far were fraud and extortion.

It would be tricky, she thought to herself, but they could probably take all of O'Connell's actions up to that point and re-form them so they would look like some sort of scheme to blackmail her and Scott out of cash. She thought she could probably make it appear to a prosecutor that everything O'Connell had done—especially his harassment of Ashley—was an aggressive plot. The only thing they would have to manufacture was some sort of threat unless they paid some sum of money. Scott could claim under oath that when he'd handed over $5,000 to O'Connell in Boston, O'-Connell had demanded more, and that he'd stepped up his pursuit when they had been reluctant. They could even explain away their failure to engage the police up to this point, saying that they were scared what he might do.

The problem—or, Sally thought ruefully, the first problem of what were likely to be many—was what she remembered Scott saying after he'd handed over the $5,000. He thought that O'Connell had been wearing a hidden microphone that had recorded the entirety of their conversation.

If that were true, suddenly they would be seen as the liars.
O'Connell would skate free, they might face charges, and
her practice and Scott's job might be in jeopardy. They
would be back at square one, they would be in trouble, and
there would be nothing standing between O'Connell, his
anger, and Ashley.

And, she realized, even if they were successful, there was
no guarantee that O'Connell wouldn't get some sort of re-
duced sentence. A couple of years? How long would it take
with him behind bars to allow Ashley to reinvent herself, to
get free of his obsession? Three? Five? Ten? Could she ever
be 100 percent certain that he wasn't going to arrive on her
doorstep?

Sally rocked back in her seat.

Kill him, she thought.

She gasped out loud. She could not believe what her own
voice was saying to her.

What is it about your life that is so great that it shouldn't
be sacrificed?

This made some sense to her. She didn't really love her
work, she was filled with doubts about her relationship with
Hope. It had been weeks, maybe months, since she'd felt joy
about who she was, and what she stood for. Meaning in life?
She wanted to laugh, but couldn't bring herself to do so. She
was a middle-aged, small-town lawyer, growing old, watching the lines of worry take root in the skin of her face every
day. She thought the only mark she'd ever made in life was
Ashley. Her daughter might have been the result of a lie of
love, but there was no denying that she was categorically the
best thing that Sally and Scott had managed in their brief
time together.

Her future is worth dying for. Yours isn't.

Again Sally was shocked at what her imagination insisted.
This is madness. But it was madness that made sense.

Kill him, she told herself.

And then she had another, even more bizarre thought.

Or find a way to make sure he kills you.

And then pays for it.

She leaned back and stared at the books and texts surrounding her.

Someone had to die. Of this she suddenly became completely convinced.

•

I had nightmares for the first time since I'd started in on the story.

They arrived unbidden and kept me spinning in my bed, sweat-drenched in sleep. I awakened once deep in the night, staggered into the bathroom for a drink of water, and stared at myself in the mirror. I slipped from the room, padding down the carpeted hallway and peering in on my children, reassuring myself that their sleep wasn't as troubled as my own. When I returned, my wife muttered, "Everything okay?" but had dropped off again before I could answer. I dropped my head to the pillow and peered up into the endless edges of darkness.

The next day, I called her on the phone.

"I think I need to speak with some of the principals in this little drama now," I said roughly. "I've been putting that off for far too long."

"Yes. I've been expecting that eventually you would make that demand. I'm just not sure who would be willing to speak with you at this point."

"They are willing to have their story told, but not willing to speak with me?" I asked incredulously.

When she spoke, I could sense some distant turmoil within her; some events in the story were turning more critical. I was getting closer.

"I'm afraid," she said.

"Afraid of what?"

"So many things are in balance. A life balances a death. Chance balances against despair. So much is at stake."

"I can find them," I said abruptly. "I don't have to play this cat-and-mouse game with you. I could hunt down faculty lists. Search legal databases. Go to student websites. Gay-women websites. Psychopath chat rooms. I don't know. One of them will have enough information so that I'll be able to assign real names, real places, and truths to what you've told me."

"You don't think I have been telling you the truth?"

"I do. I'm just saying that I know enough so that I could pursue all this on my own."

"You could do that, but that would cause me to stop taking your calls. And perhaps you would never know what really happened. You might know some fact, or you might be able to piece together the details, so that you had the flesh of the story. But not the bones. Never the organs beneath the surface, telling you the why. Would you risk that?"

"No." I said. "I would not."

"I did not think so."

"I will play by your rules. But not much longer. I'm reaching the end of my rope."

"Yes. I can hear that in your voice." But it did not sound as if this had the slightest impact on her. And with that, she hung up the phone.

36

The Pieces on the Board

Ashley was still angry, and sulking about being excluded from the most crucial decision she would ever have to make. Catherine was a little less stymied by Hope, Scott, and Sally's unreasonable exclusions. She spent an hour on the telephone, dialing numbers, speaking in low tones, before collecting Ashley and saying, "There's something you and I need to do."

Ashley was standing in the kitchen with a cup of coffee, staring over at the corner where Nameless's bowl—now empty—remained. No one had had the heart to move it. She felt knotted, tied to a mast while around her things were happening that she was intimately involved in, but she could not see.

"What?"

"Well," Catherine said softly, "I don't exactly like being on the outside looking in."

"Neither do I."

"I think we should take a few steps. Steps I'm not sure anyone in this family has ever considered before." Catherine held up her car keys. "Let's get going," she said briskly.

"Where are we headed?"

"Going to meet a man," Catherine replied breezily. "A most unsavory character, I suspect."

Ashley must have looked slightly surprised, because the older woman smiled. "That is what we need. Someone distasteful." She turned and, with Ashley in tow, headed out to her car. "We won't be telling your parents or Hope about this trip," she said as she pulled out onto the street. Ashley remained quiet as Catherine accelerated the car, checking the rearview mirror repeatedly, to make sure they were not being followed. "We need some help from someone from a different world. With different values. Luckily," she sighed, "I know a few folks up near my home who knew someone who filled that particular bill."

Ashley had several more questions but sat back, assuming she would find out what she needed to know soon enough. She lifted her eyebrows when Catherine steered the car out of the side streets onto a main boulevard, then turned toward the entrance ramp to the interstate, heading back in the direction they had fled from only a few days earlier.

"Where are we going?"

"A little spot just about forty-five minutes north of here," Catherine said breezily. "Perhaps two hundred yards from the line separating the Commonwealth of Massachusetts from the great state of Vermont."

"And what will we find there?"

Catherine smiled. "A man, like I said. The sort of man I doubt either of us has ever met before." Her smile faded, and she spoke a little more harshly. "And perhaps some security."

She did not explain this, nor did Ashley ask her to, although the younger woman doubted *security* was so easily found, even just over the border in Vermont.

Scott left the town library hurriedly.

What he had heard was an unsettling story—a small-town-America story that mixed rumor, innuendo, jealousy, and exaggeration together with some truths, some facts, and some possibilities. Stories such as the one he'd just heard have a certain radioactivity. They may not be clear to the naked eye, but they generate infectious power.

"The thing you need to know," the librarian had told him, "was just how messy the death of Michael O'Connell's mother truly was."

Messy, in Scott's mind, hardly captured the situation.

Some relationships are volatile from the start and should never form, but for some curious and hellish reason, take root and create a deadly ballet. That was the home life that Michael O'Connell was born into: a father who was abusive, more often than not drunk, who maintained a household riveted together by bolts of anger; and a mother who had once been a high school valedictorian, who had tossed away her promise on the man who'd seduced her in her first year at community college. His Elvis good looks, dark hair, muscled body, good job in the shipyards, fast car, and ready laugh had all hidden his harsher side.

The police visits at the O'Connell household had been a regular Saturday-night event. A broken arm, teeth knocked out, bruises, social workers, trips to the emergency room, had been her wedding gifts. In turn he'd received a broken nose that spoiled his handsome face when it was set improperly and more than once had to stare down his wife when she waved a kitchen knife in his direction. It was a steady and all-too-familiar pattern of abuse, violence, and forgiveness that would have continued forever, except for two events: the father fell, and the mother grew sick.

The senior O'Connell slipped from a work spot thirty feet

in the air, slamming into a steel girder when he tumbled. He should have died, but instead spent six months in the hospital, recovering from a pair of fractured vertebrae, managing to gain an addiction to painkillers and a substantial insurance and disability settlement, the majority of which he wasted buying rounds of drinks at the local VFW hall and falling prey to a couple of get-rich-quick schemers. Meanwhile, O'Connell's mother had a bout with uterine cancer. Surgery and her own dependence upon painkillers led to a life filled with greater uncertainty.

O'Connell was thirteen on the night his mother died. One day past his birthday.

What Scott had learned from the librarian and a quick search of the local newspaper's files was both troubling and confusing. Both parents had been drinking and fighting; it had been going on for some time, according to some neighbors, but it was not all that unusual and was not a 911 level of violence. But in the early evening, just after dark, there had been a sudden eruption of loud noises, followed by two gunshots.

The gunshots were the questionable part of the story. Some of the neighbors distinctly remembered a significant space of time—thirty seconds, perhaps as much as a minute or a minute and a half—between the shots.

O'Connell's father himself had called the police.

They arrived to find the mother dead on the floor, a close-contact gunshot wound to her chest, a second bullet in the ceiling, the barely teenage boy huddled in the corner, and the father, face covered with red scratch marks, holding a snub-nosed .38 pistol in his hand. This was the senior O'Connell's story: They'd been drinking and then they'd fought, as usual, only this time she had pulled out the revolver that he kept locked in his bureau drawer. He didn't know how she'd managed to find the key. She threatened to kill him. Said he'd punched her once too often, and that he should get ready to die. Instead he'd charged across the kitchen like an enraged bull, screaming at her, daring her to

fire. He'd seized her hand. They'd grappled. The first dis-
charge went into the roof. The second went into her chest.

A fight. Too much alcohol. An accident.

That was his story, or so the librarian told Scott, shaking
her head as she did.

Of course, Scott understood, the police immediately wondered whether it had been O'Connell's father who had brandished the weapon, and the mother who had been the one
fighting for her life. More than one detective looked at the
crime-scene photos and thought it was just as likely that
she'd refused his drunken advances and had grabbed the gun
barrel in a fatal attempt to prevent him from shooting her.
The shot in the ceiling was an afterthought, conveniently
provided to make his version of events seem truthful.

And in that confusion—where two stories of equal possibility had presented themselves, the one of self-defense, the
other of the cheapest sort of drunken murder—the only answer could be provided by the teenager.

He could tell one truth—and send his father to prison and
himself to a foster-care home. Or he could tell another, and
the life he knew—the only life he knew—would more or
less continue, absent his mother.

Scott thought that this was perhaps the only moment that
he would feel any sympathy for O'Connell. And it was a
retroactive sympathy, because it stretched back almost fifteen years.

For an instant, he wondered what he would have done. And
then he understood that a terrible choice is no choice. The
devil you know is better than the devil you don't know.

So the young O'Connell had backed up his father's history.

Scott wondered, Did he see his mother being shot in his
nightmares? Did he see her fighting for her life? Did every
morning when he awoke and saw the way his father eyed
him with distrust brand some terrible lie into him?

Scott drove across town and pulled his car up in front of
the O'Connell house. It's all right there. All the ingredients
necessary to become a killer.

Scott did not know much about psychology—although like any historian he understood that sometimes great events turned on emotions. But he knew enough to know that even the most armchair Freudian could see how his past made O'Connell's future dangerous. And, as Scott found himself breathing in rapidly, he knew the one thing standing square in O'Connell's life was Ashley.

Will he kill Ashley just as easily as his father killed his mother?

Scott lifted his head and once again focused on the house where O'Connell grew up. As he watched, he was unaware of the shape that emerged from the shadow of a nearby tree, so that when a set of knuckles knocked suddenly against his window, he turned in surprise, feeling his heart abruptly quicken.

"Get out of the car!"

This was a demand without compromise.

Scott, confused, looked up and saw the face of a dark-haired man with a crooked nose nearly pressed up against the window. In one hand, the man held an ax handle.

"Get out!" he repeated.

Scott's panicky first instinct was to put the car in gear and then to punch the gas, but he did not, just as he saw the man pull the ax handle back like a batter eyeing a hanging curve. Instead, he took a deep breath, undid his safety belt slowly, and pushed open the door.

The man eyed him dangerously, still brandishing the ax handle as a weapon.

"You the one asking all the questions?" he demanded. "Just who the hell are you? And why don't you tell me why you're so goddamn interested in me before I knock your head clean off?"

Sally turned to her computer and realized that what she had been about to do was potentially incriminating. She reached into her desk drawer and removed an old yellow legal pad. Opening a computer file with the details of an as-yet-unspecified crime would be a mistake. She reminded herself to think backward—more or less the same way a detective does. A piece of paper can be destroyed. It was a little like walking across a beach; footprints above the high-tide mark could last forever. Below, they were quickly erased by the never-ending waves.

She bit down on her lip and seized a pencil.

At the top of the page she wrote, *Motive*.

This was followed by a second category: *Means*.

And, by necessity, the third: *Opportunity*.

Sally stared at the words. They formed the holy trinity of police work. Fill in those blanks, and nine times out of ten you will know who to arrest and charge. And just as often, who can be convicted in a court of law. As a criminal defense attorney, the job was simple: attack and disrupt one of those elements. Like a three-legged stool, if one side was cut, the entirety would tumble. Now she was planning a crime of her own and trying to anticipate how the undetermined crime would be investigated. She kept using euphemisms in her mind. *Crime* or *incident* or *event*. She shied away from the word *murder*.

She added a fourth category to her sheet: *Forensics*.

This she could work on, she thought. Sally started to list the various ways that they could be tripped up. DNA samples—that meant hair, skin, blood—all had to be avoided. Ballistics—if they needed to use a gun, they had to find one that wasn't traceable to them. Or else, they would have to dispose of it in a way that it could never be found, and short of dropping it into the ocean, that was hard to accomplish. And then there were other issues. Fiber from clothes, telltale fingerprints left behind, shoe prints in soft earth, tire prints from car tracks. Witnesses who might see someone coming or going. Security cameras. And she couldn't even be sure that seated in a stiff chair under some harsh overhead light, across from a pair of detectives—one inevitably playing the good cop, the other, the bad—that Scott or Ashley or Hope or Catherine wouldn't say something. They might try to tell some story or, worse, simply lie—the cops always caught the lies—and they would all be sunk.

Of course, if any of them was seated in that chair in an interrogation room, everything that they had ever hoped for was already lost.

They had to do whatever they were going to do completely anonymously. It had to appear, even to someone looking hard at it, that it stemmed from something other than Ashley.

The more Sally considered it, the harder it seemed. And the more impossible the task, the more desperate she felt. She could sense things unraveling around her; not just her job, which she'd neglected, but her relationship and ultimately her entire life. It was as if the uncertainty over Ashley's safety made everything else impossible.

Sally shook her head. She looked down at the paper in front of her. She was abruptly reminded of taking tests in law school. In a way, this was the same. The only difference was this time failure wasn't about a grade. It was about their future.

She made a note: *Purchase multiple sets of surgical gloves.*

That would at least limit their DNA and fingerprint exposure, whenever they figured out what they were going to do.

She made a second note: *Go to the Salvation Army store and purchase clothing. Don't forget shoes.*

Sally nodded to herself. You can do this, she told herself. Whatever it is.

The *distasteful* man that Catherine and Ashley were going to meet was standing by the door of his battered Chevy sport utility vehicle, puffing on a cigarette and pawing the gravel of the parking lot with his right foot, like an impatient horse. Catherine immediately spotted his red-and-black hunting jacket, and the NRA stickers adorning the back of the SUV. He was short, with a receding hairline and a barrel chest, a beer-and-a-shot sort of guy, Catherine thought. He once worked in a mill or a manufacturing plant, but had discovered a far more consistent source of income.

She pulled her car across from his and told Ashley, "Stay here. Keep your head down. If I need you, I'll give a wave."

Ashley, for her part, wasn't sure what to make of the situation. She nodded and pivoted about, so that she could keep her eyes on Catherine.

Catherine got out of the car. "Mr. Johnson, I'm guessing?"

"That's right. You must be Mrs. Frazier?"

"Indeed."

"I don't usually like coming out like this. I prefer to do my business at regular shows."

Catherine nodded. She doubted that this statement was true, but it was part of the charade.

"I appreciate your taking the time," she said. "I wouldn't have called if the situation weren't pressing."

"Personal use? Personal protection?"

"Yes. Absolutely."

"You see, I'm a collector, not a dealer. And usually I merely trade and sell at authorized gun shows. Otherwise, I'd have to have a federal permit, you understand."

She nodded. She recognized that the man was speaking in a sort of code, to skirt the law.

"Again, I'm appreciative," she said.

"You see, a regular gun dealer has to fill out all sorts of paperwork for the Feds. And then there is the three-day waiting period. But a gun collector can swap and trade without those requirements. Of course, I've got to ask: You are not planning anything illegal with this weapon?"

"Of course not. It's for protection. You can't be safe enough these days. So, what do you have for me?"

The gun dealer moved to the back of his truck and opened the hatch. Inside there was a steel-sided suitcase with a combination lock, which he rapidly opened. On a bed of black Styrofoam there was an array of handguns. She stared down at them with little comprehension. "I'm not much of a gun person."

Mr. Johnson nodded. "The forty-five and the nine-mill are probably way more than you need. It's these two that you want to consider: the twenty-five automatic and the thirty-two revolver. The thirty-two short barrel is probably what you're searching for. It's more, ah, feminine-sized. Six shots in the cylinder. Just point and shoot. Very dependable, reliable, small, not heavy, anyone can handle it. Fits in a purse. A real popular gun with the ladies. Drawback is it doesn't pack the biggest punch, you know? Bigger gun. Bigger payload. That's not to say that a shot from a thirty-two won't kill you. It will. But you see what I'm saying?"

"Of course. I think I'll take the thirty-two."

Mr. Johnson smiled. "Good selection. Now, I'm required by law to ask you whether you plan to take this gun out of state."

"Of course not," Catherine lied.

"Or transfer it to another person."

Catherine didn't even glance toward Ashley waiting in the car. "Absolutely not."

"Nor do you intend to use the weapon for any illegal purpose?"

"Again, negative."

He nodded. "Sure." He stared at Catherine, then over at her car. "I already have your contact information. And I've got the serial numbers. If someone, like an ATF agent, were to come asking questions, you know they would find answers with me. I wouldn't be pleased to provide them, but I would. Otherwise it would be me looking at doing some time. You understand what I'm saying? You got a husband you want to shoot, well, that's your business. I'm just saying that—"

Catherine held up her hand. "My husband passed away some years ago. Please, Mr. Johnson, be reassured. This is merely protection for an older woman who lives alone in the countryside."

He smiled. "Four hundred dollars. Cash. And I'll throw in a box of extra shells. Find some place to practice. It can make all the difference in the world."

He took the weapon and placed it in a cheap leather case. "That's free," he said and handed the gun to Catherine as she handed over the money.

"One other thing you might want to keep in mind. When you decide to pull that trigger," he said slowly, lifting his own hands into a shooter's position, "make sure you use both hands to steady yourself, assume a comfortable stance, take a deep breath, and then one more thing . . ."

"Yes?"

"Empty it. All six. You decide to shoot something, or someone, Mrs. Frazier, well, there's no such thing as going halfway, you know. It's only in Hollywood that the good guy can shoot a gun out of some bad dude's hand, or wing 'em in the shoulder. Not in real life. You make that choice, aim dead center in the chest and then make sure you don't leave any questions behind. You want to shoot something? Then you kill it."

Catherine nodded. "Words to live by."

•

The assistant dean of the Art History Department only had a few moments, she told me. It was her regularly scheduled office hours, and there was usually a backlog of students out-side her door. She grinned as she outlined the panoply of stu-dent excuses, complaints, inquiries, and criticisms that awaited her that day.

"So," she said, leaning back in her chair, "what is it that has brought an actual adult to my door this day?"

I explained, in the vaguest terms I thought would manage to keep her talking, what I was interested in.

"Ashley?" she said. "Yes. I do remember her. A few years ago, no? A most curious case, that one."

"How so?"

"Excellent undergraduate grades, a real artistic streak, a hard worker—she had an excellent part-time position at the museum—and then it all seemed to fall apart for her in a most dramatic fashion. I always suspected some sort of boy trouble. Usually that's the case when promising young women suddenly go into a tailspin. In most cases, these sorts of problems can be solved with copious amounts of tissue for the tears, and several cups of hot tea. In her case, however, there was all sorts of talk, rumors mostly, throughout the department, about how she got fired from that job, and the integrity of her academic work. But I'm not comfortable speaking about these things without her authorization. In writing. You don't by any chance have a document such as that with you, do you?"

"No."

The dean shrugged, a small, wry smile on her lips. "I am limited then in what I can tell you."

"Of course." I got up to leave. "Still, thanks for your time."

"Say," the dean asked, "maybe you can tell me what happened to her? She seems to have dropped off our radar completely."

I hesitated, not exactly sure how to answer her question. The pause caused the dean to look up in concern.

"Did something happen to her?" she asked, suddenly all jocularity vanishing from her tones. "I would hate to hear that."

"Yes, I suppose you could say something did happen to her."

37

An Enlightening Conversation

Scott emerged slowly from his car, staring at the man he knew was O'Connell's father. The father brandished the ax handle menacingly. Scott stepped back out of the weapon's reach and took a deep breath, wondering why he oddly felt so calm. "I'm not sure you want to be threatening me with that, Mr. O'Connell."

The older O'Connell twitched and grunted, "You've been up and down this neighborhood asking about me. So I'll put it down when you tell me who you are."

Scott fixed his eyes on the father's. He narrowed his gaze, remained silent, poker-faced, until the man said, "I'm waiting for an answer."

"I know you are. I'm just wondering what sort of answer you're going to get."

This confused O'Connell's father. He stepped back, then forward again, lifting the ax handle as he repeated, "Who are you?"

Scott continued to stare, slowly looking O'Connell senior up and down, as if he had absolutely nothing to fear from the ax handle aimed at his head. The man's build was both soft and hard—beer belly hanging over his stained jeans, thick, muscled arms sporting a variety of entwined tattoos. He wore only a black T-shirt with the Harley-Davidson logo above his jeans and boots, seemingly oblivious to the cold November air. His dark hair was streaked with gray, cropped close to his head. A tattoo with the name *Lucy* prominently displayed on his forearm was probably all that remained of his marriage, other than his son and the house. Scott thought the man had probably been drinking, but his words weren't slurred, nor was his step unsteady. He had probably drunk just enough to loosen inhibitions and cloud his thinking, which, Scott hoped, was a good thing. He slowly folded his arms and shook his head at O'Connell, a motion to underscore the idea that he was in charge of the situation. "I could be more trouble than you've ever seen. And I mean the worst sort of trouble, Mr. O'Connell. The kind of trouble that has significant pain attached to it. On the other hand, I could also be a big help to you. That would be an opportunity to make some money. Which is it going to be?"

The ax handle came down partway.

"Keep talking."

Scott shook his head. He was making things up as he went along.

"I don't negotiate on the street, Mr. O'Connell. And the man I represent surely wouldn't want me spilling his business all over the place where anyone might take notice of it."

"What the hell are you talking about?"

"Let's go inside your place, and then we can have a little private conversation. Otherwise, I'm going to get back in my car, and you will never see me again. But you might be visited by someone else. And that someone, or even a couple of someones, Mr. O'Connell, I assure you, will not be nearly as reasonable as I am. Their sort of negotiation is significantly different from mine."

Scott thought O'Connell had probably spent much of his life either making threats or receiving them, and so this was all a language the man was likely to understand.

"What did you say your name was?" O'Connell asked.

"I didn't say. And I'm not likely to, either."

O'Connell hesitated, the ax handle dropping farther.

"What's this about?" he demanded. But the tone his words carried contained some interest.

"A debt. But that's all I'm saying right now. This could be valuable for you. Make some money. Or not. Up to you."

"Why would you pay me anything?"

"Because it is always easier to pay someone than the alternative." Scott let O'Connell's father mull over what *the alternative* might mean.

Again, O'Connell's father paused, then the ax handle swung down to his side. "All right. I'm not buying any of this bullshit. Not yet. But you can come inside. Tell me what this is all about. Make your pitch, whatever it is."

And with that, he gestured across the street to his home, using the ax handle to direct their path.

There is a place in the woods beyond the dirt road that parallels the Westfield River, below a spot called the Chesterfield Gorge, where either side of the stream is protected by sixty-foot-high sheets of gray rock, carved by some prehistoric seismic shift, that is favored in the colder months by hunters, and in warmer times by fishermen. In the hottest days of summer, Ashley and her friends would sneak up to the river and go skinny-dipping in the cool pools.

"I think you should use both hands," Catherine said sternly. "Steady the weapon in your right hand, grip them both with your left, take aim, and then pull the trigger."

Ashley moved her feet slightly apart, cupped her left hand over her right, and tightened her muscles, feeling the trigger with her index finger. "Here goes," she said quietly.

She pulled the trigger and the gun bucked in her hand. The shot resounded through the forest, and a piece of tree bark splintered off the oak she had aimed at.

"Wow. I can feel it tingle right through my forearm."

Catherine nodded. "I think what you want, dear, is to pull the trigger five or six times, while you are holding the gun steady, so that all six shots will be clustered together. Can you do that?"

"It feels like it wants to jump around. Go all over the place. Almost like it's alive."

"I guess you could say that it has a personality all its own."

Ashley nodded, and Catherine added, "And not a particularly nice one."

"Let me try again."

Again she assumed the firing position, and this time tightened her left hand's grip to steady herself. "Here we go."

She fired the remaining five shots. Three hit the tree trunk, spaced about two or three feet apart. The other two spun off into the forest. She could hear them whistling into oblivion, snapping through branches and the few remaining low-hanging leaves. The sound of the gun echoed in the bare trees around them and filled her ears. She let out a long, slow whistle of breath.

"Don't close your eyes," Catherine said.

"I think I should try again."

Ashley clicked open the cylinder and dropped the spent shells on the pine-needle floor. She slowly took another half dozen bullets and loaded them into the weapon. "Only going to use this thing one time."

"Yes. True enough. And only then if you really have to."

"That's right." Ashley turned and took aim at the tree trunk once again. "Only if I really have to."

"If you have no choice."

"If I have no choice."

Both of them had much to say about that, but didn't actually want to use the words out loud, not even in the silent anonymity of the forest.

Scott moved slowly up the half-gravel, half-dirt driveway that led to O'Connell's house, a distance of perhaps thirty yards from the quiet street. It was a single-story, white-framed building, with a battered television antenna hanging from the roof like a bird's broken wing, next to a newer, gray satellite dish. In the front yard, a faded red Toyota was missing one door, one wheel up on a cinder block. Large brown rust stains marred the sheet-metal surface. There was also a newer black pickup truck, parked by a side door, partway beneath a flat roof constructed out of a single sheet of corrugated plastic. The roof made the space into a carport, but it was littered with a beaten red snowblower and a snow-mobile missing its treadmill. As Scott walked past the pickup, he noticed an aluminum ladder, a wooden tool kit, and some roofing materials had been thrown haphazardly in the bed. O'Connell was pointing him toward the side door, but Scott noted a main entrance in the front. He doubted it was used much.

Probably a back entrance, he thought. Check to make sure.

"Through there. Don't mind the mess. I wasn't expecting company," O'Connell's father said gruffly.

Scott let himself in the aluminum screen door, then through a second, solid-wood door, into a small kitchen. *Mess* was an accurate description. Pizza boxes. Microwavable dinners. Three cases of Coors Light in silver boxes. A bottle of Johnnie Walker Black Label on the table to accompany the array of cans.

"Let's go into the living room. We can have a seat, Mr.—okay, Mr. whatever your name is. What should I call you?"

"Smith works," Scott said. "And if you have trouble keeping that straight, Jones will do just as well."

O'Connell's father snorted a small laugh.

"Okay, Mr. Smith or Mr. Jones. Now that I've invited you

in here, why don't you sit right over there where I can keep an eye on you, and you can explain yourself nice and quick, so that I don't go back to thinking that my friend the ax handle is the better way of dealing with you. And you might get to the how-I-make-some-money part real quick. You want a beer?"

Scott walked into a small living room. There was a threadbare sofa, a recliner with a large red-and-white cooler next to it that served as a table, across from an oversize television set. Newspapers and pornographic magazines littered the floor, along with piles of grocery-store circulars and catalogs from various hunting stores. On one wall there was a stuffed deer head, which stared out blankly from behind glass eyes. A T-shirt hung from one of its antlers. He tried to imagine the house when O'Connell had been growing up here, and he could see in its bones the potential for a kind of normalcy. Get the debris out of the yard. Remove the interior clutter, fix up the couch. Replace the chairs. Hang a couple of posters on the walls, and spruce everything up with paint, and it would have been almost acceptable. The random piles of litter told him much about the father and little about the son; O'Connell's father had probably replaced his dead wife and absent son with much of the mess.

Scott slid into a chair that creaked and threatened to give way and turned toward O'Connell's father.

"I've been asking questions because your son has something that belongs to the person I represent. My client would like it back."

"You a lawyer, then?"

Scott shrugged.

O'Connell slipped into the lounge chair, but kept the ax handle in his lap. "Who might this boss of yours be?"

Scott shook his head. "Names are really irrelevant to this conversation."

"Okay, then, Mr. Smith. Then tell me what he does for a living."

Scott smiled, as evil a grin as he could muster. "My client makes a great deal of money."

"Legally or illegally?"

"I'm unsure whether you want to ask that question, Mr. O'Connell. And I would probably lie anyway, if I were going to respond." Scott listened to the words tumbling out of his mouth, almost shocked at the ease he felt in inventing a character, a situation, and leading the older O'Connell on. Greed, he thought, is a powerful drug.

O'Connell smiled. "So, you'd like to get in touch with my wayward kid, huh? Can't find him in the city?"

"No. He seems to have disappeared."

"And you come snooping around here."

"Just one of a number of possibilities."

"My kid don't like it here."

Scott raised his hand, cutting O'Connell's father off. "Let's get past the obvious," he said stiffly. "Can you help us find your son?"

"How much?"

"How much can you help?"

"Not sure. He and I don't talk much."

"When did you see him last?"

"A couple of years. We don't get along too good."

"What about at holidays?"

O'Connell shook his head. "I told you, we don't get along too good. What's he taken?"

Scott smiled. "Again, Mr. O'Connell, information like that would render your position, shall I say, precarious? Do you know what that means?"

"I'm not stupid. Of course. And how precarious, Mr. Jones?"

"Speculation is useless."

"Just how much goddamn trouble is he in? The type of trouble that gets you beat up? Or the type of trouble that gets you killed?"

Scott took a breath, wondering just how far to push the fiction.

"Let's just say that he can repair the damage he's done. But it will require cooperation. It is a sensitive matter, Mr.

O'Connell. And much more delay could prove problematic." Scott felt utterly cold inside.

"What, drugs? He steal some drugs from somebody? Or money?"

Scott smiled. "Mr. O'Connell, let me put it to you this way. Should your son try to get in touch with you, and you were to advise us of that action, there would be a reward."

"How much?"

"You asked that already." Scott rose out of his chair, letting his eyes roam over the room, seeing a single hallway, leading to the rear bedrooms. It was a narrow space, he thought, that wouldn't allow much maneuvering. "Let's just say that it would be a pleasant Christmas gift."

"So, if I can find the kid, how do I get ahold of you? You got a phone number?"

Scott put on the most pompous voice he could manage. "Mr. O'Connell, I really dislike telephones. They leave records, they can be traced." He gestured toward the computer. "Can you send e-mail?"

O'Connell wheezed out rapidly, "Of course. Who can't? But I got to have a promise, Mr. fucking Jones or Smith, that my kid ain't going to get himself killed over this."

"Okay," Scott said, lying with ease. "An easy promise to make. You hear from your kid, you send an e-mail to this address." He walked over to the table and found an unpaid phone bill and the stump of a pencil. He made up a completely bogus e-mail address and wrote it down.

He handed the paper to O'Connell. "Don't lose that. And the phone number where I can reach you?"

The father rattled off his telephone number as he stared at the address. "Okay," O'Connell's father said. "Anything else?"

Scott smiled. "We won't be seeing each other again. And, should anyone ask you, I presume you will have the sense to say that this little meeting never took place. And, should that someone be your son, well, then that admonition would go double. Do we understand each other?"

O'Connell's father looked at the address a second time, grinned, and shrugged. "Works for me."

"Good. Don't get up. I can show myself out."

Scott's heart was moving rapidly as he slowly made his way back out. He knew that somewhere behind him was not only the ax handle, but a gun, which the neighbors had told him about, and probably a heavy-caliber rifle, as well; the glassy-eyed deer head mounted on the wall said as much. He had to trust that O'Connell's father hadn't had the simple good sense to write down his license plate number, although it was doubtful that he would fail to recognize the distinctive old Porsche if he saw it again. Scott told himself to take note of every detail on the way out; he might return to the house again, and he wanted to be familiar with the arrangement of the furniture. He took note of the flimsy locks on the door, then exited. Greed was an awful thing, and someone who would sell out his own child owned a cruelty that went somewhere beyond his own emotional reach. He felt a sudden wave of nausea nearly overcome him. But he had the sense to poke his head around the back side of the house, revealing the extra doorway that he had expected. Then he turned and hurried down the driveway. He could see gray clouds scudding across the horizon.

Michael O'Connell thought that he had been far too quiet and far too absent over the past few days.

The key to forcing Ashley to understand that no one— other than him—could actually protect her lay in underscoring everyone's vulnerability. What prevented her from fully recognizing the depth of his love and the overwhelming need he had for her to be at his side was the cocoon that her parents had erected around her. And when he thought about Catherine, he got a bilious taste in his mouth. She was old, she was fragile, she was out there alone, and he had had the opportunity to remove her from the equation, but had failed to, even when she'd been within his reach. He decided that he would not make that mistake again.

He was seated at his computer, idly toying with the cursor, oblivious to the quiet that surrounded him. The machine was new. After Matthew Murphy had smashed his old one, he had almost instantly gone out and acquired a replacement. After a moment, he turned away, shutting down his machine with a couple of quick clicks.

He felt an overwhelming urge to do something unpredictable, something that would get Ashley's attention, something that she couldn't ignore and that would let her know it was useless to run from him.

He stood up and stretched, raising his arms above his head, arching his back, unconsciously mimicking the cats in the hallway. Michael O'Connell felt a surge of confidence. It was time to visit Ashley again, if only to remind them all that he was still there and still waiting. He picked up his overcoat and car keys. Ashley's family was unaware how close the parallels between love and death really are. He smiled and believed that they didn't understand that in all of this *he* was the romantic one. But love wasn't always expressed with roses or diamonds or a saccharine Hallmark greeting card. It was time to let them know that the picture of his devotion had not changed. His mind churned with ideas.

The phone was ringing as Scott returned to his house.

"Scott?" It was Sally.

"Yes," he said.

"You sound out of breath."

"I heard the phone ringing. I was outside. I just got home and had to dash inside. Is everything okay?"

"Yes. Sort of."

"What do you mean?"

"Well, nothing overt has happened. Ashley and Catherine spent the day off doing something, but they won't say what.

I've been in my office trying to see our route out of this mess with mixed results, and Hope has hardly said a word since she got back from Boston, except she says we all need to talk once again and without delay. Can you come right over?"

"Did she say why?"

"I told you, no. Aren't you listening to me? But it has something to do with what she found out in Boston, when she was watching O'Connell. She seems very upset. I've never seen her so sullen. She's sitting in the other room, staring into space, and all she will say is that we all need to talk right away."

Scott hesitated, thinking about what might have turned Hope so quiet, which wasn't her usual style in the slightest. He tried not to react to the almost frantic tones he heard in Sally's voice. She was being stretched thin, he thought. It reminded him of their last months together, before he knew about her affair with Hope, but when, on some deeper, more instinctual level, he had known everything was wrong between the two of them. He found himself nodding and said, "All right. I found out a great deal more about O'Connell, as well. Nothing damn good, and . . ." He paused again. For the first time since he had driven across the state, the vaguest semblance of an idea had begun to form in his imagination. "I'm not sure how we should use it, but . . . Look, I'll be over shortly. How is Ashley?"

"She seems withdrawn. Almost distant. I guess some pop psychologist would say this is the start of a major-league depression. Having this guy in her life is like having some sort of really difficult disease. Like cancer."

"You shouldn't say that," Scott said.

"I shouldn't be a realist? I should be some sort of optimist?"

Scott paused. Sally could be tough, he thought, and she could be maddeningly direct. But now, with their daughter's situation, it frightened him. He was unsure whether his *we can get out of this* thinking or Sally's *we're in big trouble and it's getting worse* attitude was right. He wanted to scream.

Instead, he gritted his teeth and replied, "I said I'll be right over. Tell, Ashley . . ."

He stopped again. He could sense Sally breathing in hard.

"Tell her what? That everything's going to be okay?" she asked bitterly. "And Scott," she added after a small hesitation, "try to bring whatever our next step is. Or else a pizza."

•

"They are still reluctant," she said.

"I understand," I said, although I wasn't sure that I truly did. "But still, I need to speak with at least one of them. Otherwise the story isn't complete."

"Well," she said slowly, obviously thinking over her words carefully before speaking, "there is one who is willing, in fact, eager, to tell what they know. But I'm not sure that you are completely ready for that conversation."

"That doesn't make any sense. One wants to talk, but what? The others are preventing it and think they are protecting themselves? Or are you protecting all of them?"

"They're not sure that you fully understand their position."

"Don't be crazy. I've talked to all sorts of people, been all over this. They were in a quandary. I know that. Whatever they did to get out, it would seem justified. . . ."

"Really? You think so? The end justifies the means?"

"Did I say that?"

"Yes."

"Well, what I meant was—"

She held up a hand, cutting me off, and stood looking across the yard, out past some trees to the street. She sighed deeply. "They were at a crossroads. A choice had to be made. Like so many of the choices that people— ordinary people—are forced to make, it would have profound personal consequences. That's what you need to understand."

"But what choice did they have?"

"Good question," she replied with a small, haunted laugh. "Answer it for me."

38

A Measure of Evils

Scott walked up the pathway to his ex-wife's house filled with doubts and uncertainties, all warring within him. When he reached the entranceway, he lifted his hand to ring the doorbell, but hesitated. For an instant he turned back and stared into the edges of darkness that filled the street. He was much closer now to Michael O'Connell, yet he knew that O'Connell still hid from him. He wondered if he was being studied just as closely by their target. He did not know if it was possible to get ahead, to gain an edge. He doubted it. For all he knew, somewhere in that block, right then, right at that moment, O'Connell was standing, hidden by the completeness of the black, watching him. Scott felt a surge of rage within him; he wanted to scream out loud. He imagined that everything that he'd discovered on his research trip, that he'd thought was so unpredictable, was actually totally expected, totally foreseen, and totally anticipated. He could not shake the idea that somehow, as impossible as it would be, O'Connell had learned everything that Scott had done.

A short groan escaped his lips, and he could feel sweat beneath his arms. He took a sudden step away from the door, angry, trying to confront the man he believed was watching, and then he stopped.

Behind him the door opened. It was Sally.

She stared for a moment, out into the night, following the path of Scott's eyes. In that second, she understood what he was searching for.

"Do you think he's out there?" Her voice was flat and hard.

"Yes. And no."

"Well, which is it?"

"I think he's either right there, right in some shadow or another, watching every move we make. Or else he's not. But we can't tell the difference, and so we're screwed, one way or the other."

Sally reached out and put her hand on his shoulder. A small act of surprising tenderness, it felt strange to her, as she realized that she had not actually physically touched in years the man whose bed she'd once shared. "Come on in," she said. "We're just as screwed inside, but it's warmer."

Hope was drinking a beer, holding the cold bottle to her forehead, as if she were flushed with fever. Ashley and Catherine were dispatched to the kitchen, to put together some sort of meal—or, at least, that was Sally's explanation, as transparent as it was, to get them out of the room where whatever planning was going to happen. Scott could feel some residue of tension, as if the sensation he'd had on the front steps, staring back into the night, had lingered with him. Sally, on the other hand, was organized. She turned to Scott and gestured toward Hope. "She's barely said a word since she got back. But I believe she found out something."

Before Scott could say anything, Hope set her beer down hard on the table.

"I think it's worse than we imagined," she said, breaking her silence.

"Worse? How the hell could anything be worse?" Sally asked.

Hope had a sudden image in her mind: the grinning death mask of a frozen cat.

"He's a very sick, twisted guy. Likes to torture and kill small animals."

"How do you know?"

"I saw."

"Jesus H. Christ!" Scott exclaimed sharply.

"A sadist?" Sally asked.

"Maybe in part. Sure seems that way. But that's just a part of who he is. One other thing." Hope's voice was rigid, hard, granitelike. "He's got a gun."

"Did you see it, as well?" Scott demanded.

"Yes. I got into his apartment while he was out."

"How did you manage that?"

"What difference does it make? I did. I made friends with a neighbor. The neighbor happened to have a key. And what I saw inside only persuaded me that things will get worse. Not better. He's a really bad guy. How bad? I don't know. Bad enough to kill Ashley? I didn't see anything that might suggest that he wouldn't. He's got encrypted computer files all about her. One called *Ashley Love* and one called *Ashley Hate*. That right there probably tells you all you need to know. But it's worse. He's got some about us, too. I couldn't tell what was in them. But obsession probably doesn't begin to describe what we're up against. So, you tell me. He's sick. He's determined. He's obsessed. What does that add up to? Can we hide from that? Can anyone?"

"What are you saying, Hope?" Sally asked.

"I'm saying that nothing I saw suggested any outcome other than some inevitable tragedy. And you know what that means." Hope had difficulty shaking the images from O'-Connell's apartment from her imagination. Frozen dead cats, a gun in a shoe, stark, monastic walls, a grimy, unkempt place devoted to a single purpose: Ashley. She slumped back in her chair, thinking how hard it was to convey the simplest idea: O'Connell had nothing in his life other than his one pursuit.

Sally turned to Scott. "What about your trip? Did you learn anything?"

"A lot. But nothing that would contradict anything Hope just said. I saw where he grew up. And I actually spoke with his father. A meaner, nastier, more depraved son of a bitch would be hard to find."

They all considered this statement. There was a lot to say, but all three of them knew that it wouldn't amount to anything they didn't already know.

Sally broke the silence. "We have to . . ."

The more that was said, the colder she felt inside. She felt that if her heart were monitored, it would flatline. "Is he a killer?" she asked abruptly. "Are we sure?"

"What's a killer? I mean, how can we tell? For certain," Scott said. "Everything I learned told me the answer to your question is yes. But until he does something overt . . ."

"He might have killed Murphy."

"He might have killed Jimmy Hoffa and JFK, too, for all we know," Scott replied fiercely. "We need to focus on what we actually know for certain."

"Yes, well, certainty is not something we have in absolute abundance," Sally replied. "In fact, it's about the absolute least thing we have. We don't *know* anything, except that he's evil, and he's out there somewhere. And that he might or might not hurt Ashley. He might or might not pursue her forever. He might or might not do just about any damn thing."

Again, they were all silent. Hope thought they were some-how trapped in a maze, and that no matter what path they took, there was no exit.

Sally finally spoke in a whisper, "Someone has to die."

The word froze the room.

Scott spoke first, his voice raspy, as if sore. He looked at Sally. "The plan was to find a crime and assign it to O'Con-nell. That's what you were supposed to research."

"The only way to do that with any certainty—God damn it, I hate using that word—is to either create something com-plex, which we might not have the time to invent, or have Ashley lie. I mean, we could beat her up and then have her claim it was O'Connell. That would be an assault and would probably buy him some serious jail time. Of course, one of us would have to provide the bruises and knocked-out teeth and fractured ribs to make it into a real serious felony. How do you like that scenario? And, if it were to blow up when some detective started asking questions . . ."

"All right, but what—"

"We always have the old fallback alternative of going to

the authorities and getting a restraining order. Does anyone think for one instant that that piece of paper will protect her?"

"No."

"Based on what we now know about O'Connell, do we think he will make the mistake of violating the restraining order without harming Ashley, which would allow him to be prosecuted? Which, don't forget, is a lengthy process, during which time he would be out on bond."

"No, God damn it," Scott muttered.

Sally looked over at Scott. "The man you met . . . the father . . ."

"A bastard. First-degree evil."

Sally nodded. "And his relationship with his son?"

"He hates his child. His child hates him. They haven't seen each other in years."

"What do you know about that hatred?"

"He was abusive, both toward O'Connell's mother and O'Connell. He was the sort of guy that drank too much and then used his fists liberally. No one in the entire neighborhood likes him. And he was probably hell for any kid, much less one like O'Connell."

Sally inhaled sharply, trying to impress reason upon the words she was speaking when she knew they had a particular kind of insanity. "Would you say," she spoke cautiously, "would you say that this man was in some regards the reason, psychologically speaking, of course, that Michael O'Connell is who he is?"

Scott nodded. "Of course. I mean, even the most simple armchair Freud amongst us knows that."

"Violence breeds violence," Sally said.

"Yes."

"The reason Ashley is threatened is because this man years ago created in his own child an unhealthy, probably murderous and obsessive need to be loved, to possess someone else, I don't know, to ruin or be ruined, however you want to put it."

"That was my impression." Scott's own voice was gathering some momentum. "And there's something else. The mother—who wasn't any bouquet of flowers, either—died under questionable circumstances. He *might* have killed her. He just couldn't be charged."

"So, in addition to maybe creating a killer, maybe he is one, as well?" Sally asked.

"Yes. I guess you could say that."

"If you step back, for just a second here," Sally continued, weighting her language with desperation, "would you not agree that whatever danger Michael O'Connell threatens our Ashley with, it was established in his psyche by his father?"

"Yes."

"So," she said abruptly. "It's simple then."

"What's simple?" Hope said.

Sally smiled, but there was absolutely no humor in anything she said. "Instead of killing Michael O'Connell ourselves, we kill the father. And find a way to blame the son for the murder."

Silence again filled the room.

"It makes sense," Sally said quickly. "The son hates the father. The father hates the son. So, if they were brought together, death is not an unlikely result, right?"

Scott nodded slowly.

"Aren't the two of them, in a pretty clear way, the basis for the threat to Ashley?"

This time Sally turned to Hope, who also nodded.

"Can we be killers?" Sally asked. "Could we murder someone—even for the best of reasons—and then wake up the next day and start life up again just as if nothing of any great importance had taken place?"

Hope looked over at Scott. No easy answer from him right then, she thought.

Sally was harsh with every word. "Murder, you see, inevitably changes everything. But the point of killing is to restore Ashley's life to its pre–Michael O'Connell status. We can probably manage that—if she is excluded from almost the entirety of the process. Which is a difficult enough aspect to manage. But the three of us, we're the conspirators in this. It will change us, will it not? I think profoundly. Because right now, with this conversation right here, we're taking a step. Up to this point, we've been the good guys, trying to protect our daughter from evil. But we take this step—even a small one—and we're suddenly the bad guys. Because, no matter what Michael O'Connell *might* have done, or whatever Michael O'Connell *might* be planning to do, we are somewhere beyond him. He's being driven by recognizable psychological forces; his evil stems from his upbringing, his background, whatever. He's probably *not* to blame for the bad guy he's become. He's the unconscious product of deprivation and pain. So, whatever he's done to us, and whatever he might do to Ashley, it at the very least has some sort of moral or emotional basis. Maybe it's all wrong, but it has an explanation to it. Us, on the other hand, well, what I'm saying is that we're going to have to be cold-blooded, selfish, and without any redeeming aspects. Save perhaps one."

Both Hope and Scott had listened intently to Sally's speech. She had writhed about in her chair, as if tortured by every word she spoke, until finally coming to a frozen halt.

"What's that?" Hope asked cautiously.

"Ashley will be safe."

Again they were all silent.

Sally caught her breath with a sharp gasping sound.

"This is assuming one critical detail," she said almost in a whisper.

"What detail is that?" Scott demanded.

"That we can get away with it."

•

Night had descended, and we sat in two wooden Adirondack chairs on her stone patio. Hard seats for hard thoughts. I was flush with questions, more insistent than ever about speaking with the principals, or, at the very least, one of them who could fill me in on the moment when they changed from victims to conspirators. But infuriatingly, she wasn't willing to be bulldozed. Instead, she stared out into the humid summer darkness.

"Remarkable, isn't it, what one will consider doing, when pushed to a limit?" she said.

"Well," I replied cautiously, "when one's back is up against the wall..."

She laughed, but humorlessly. "But that's just it," she said abruptly. "They *thought* their backs were up against that proverbial wall. How can you be certain?"

"They had legitimate fears. The threat O'Connell posed was obvious. They just didn't know. And so given the choice between unknowns, they took charge of their own circumstances."

She smiled again. "You make it sound so easy and so convincing. Why don't you turn it around?"

"How?"

"Well, imagine looking at the problem from the law enforcement point of view. You have a young man who has fallen in love, pursuing the girl of his dreams. Happens all the time. You and I know that his pursuit is truly an obsession—but what could a police detective actually prove? Do you not think that Michael O'Connell effectively hid his computer sorties into all their lives so they couldn't be traced? And what had they done in response? Tried to bribe him. Tried to threaten him. Had him beaten up. If you were a policeman, coming upon this situation, which do you think would be the easier case to prosecute? My guess is, Scott, Sally, and even Hope. They have already lied. They have already been duplicitous. Even Ashley has skirted the law, with the revolver she obtained. And now they were conspiring to commit murder. Of an innocent man. Perhaps he wasn't innocent in some psychological or moral sense, but still... And they wanted to *get away with it*. What claim did they have for the ethical high ground?"

I didn't answer this question.

My own imagination was churning: How did they manage?

"Do you remember who told them that saying and doing are different things altogether? Who pointed out how hard it actually is to pull a trigger?"

I smiled. "Yes. It was O'Connell."

She laughed bitterly. "Yes. That was what he said to the

toughest of them all, the one with the least to lose by firing
that shotgun's load into his chest, who had seen most of her
life already pass by and would be risking the least by shooting. At that critical moment, she failed, didn't she?"

She paused, staring up into the darkness. "But someone
would have to be brave enough."

39

The Start of an Imperfect Crime

Sally spoke first. "We will need to identify and divide up
the responsibilities. We must create a plan. And then we
must stick to it. Religiously."

She was surprised by the words coming out of her mouth.
They were so harshly calculating, it sounded to her as if they
were being spoken by someone she didn't know. The three
of them seemed to be the least likely of murderers, she
thought. She had immense doubts whether they could actually pull off something like what she had proposed.

Hope looked up. "I don't know anything about this. I've
never even had a speeding ticket. I hardly ever read mystery
novels or thrillers, except back when I was in college I read
Crime and Punishment in one course, and *In Cold Blood* in
another."

Scott laughed a little uncomfortably. "Great," he said. "In
the first, the killer is driven near mad by guilt and finally
confesses, and in the other, well, the bad guys get caught because they are clueless and then they go to the gallows.
Maybe we ought to not use *those* books as models."

This, he thought, was probably funny, but no one even
smiled.

Sally waved a hand in the air. "You know, forget it," she

said archly. "We're not killers. We shouldn't even be thinking this way."

Scott broke the momentary silence. "In other words, wait
for something to happen, and then hope that it isn't a disaster?"

"No. Yes. I'm not sure." Sally was suddenly unsteady, both
in what she said out loud and what she felt inside. "Perhaps
we are not giving the legal channels enough credence. Maybe
we go get the restraining order. Sometimes they work fine."

"I fail to see how that is a solution," Scott said. "It resolves
nothing. It leaves us, and more critically Ashley, in a perpet-
ual state of fear. How can anyone live that way? And even if
it causes O'Connell to back off, every day that passes, every
day that he *appears* to be out of her life, all that reassurance
really just builds into more and more uncertainty. It solves
nothing! It creates an illusion of safety. Even if it were to
create real safety, how would we ever know? For sure?"

Sally sighed deeply. "You're very good at arguing things
that cannot be debated, Scott. Tell me, will you pull the trigger and kill someone?"

"Yes," he blurted out.

"Easy, quick answer. Passion speaking, not sense. How
about you, Hope? Would you kill someone, a stranger, to
protect Ashley—or maybe, at that crucial moment, wouldn't
you suddenly say to yourself, 'What am I doing? She's not
my child.'"

"No. Of course not," Hope replied.

"Again, we're awfully quick with our answers."

Scott felt a surge of frustration. "So, devil's advocate,
what about you? Will you do it?"

Sally frowned. "Yes. No. I don't know."

Scott leaned back in his seat. "Let me ask you this. When
Ashley was little, and when she got sick, do you ever remember praying 'I'd rather it was me. Make me sick. Make
her well.'"

Sally nodded. "Every mother, I guess, has felt that."

"Would you give your life for your child?"

Sally could feel her throat closing with emotion. She nodded. She swallowed hard, to regain control.

"I can do it," she said slowly. "I can design a crime. I know enough about it. And maybe it will work. Maybe it won't. But even if we all go to prison, we will at least have tried to defend her. And that's something."

"Yes, but not enough." Scott was a little surprised at how stiff he sounded. "Tell me what you are thinking."

Sally shifted about. "What do we suppose is O'Connell's greatest weakness?"

"It must have something to do with the father," Scott said.

"Actually," Sally continued, "their bad relationship. That sort of hate is something I suspect O'Connell won't be able to control."

Scott and Hope both went quiet.

"It's where he seems vulnerable. Just like he managed to find out things about us where we were vulnerable, that's what we need to use against him. Hasn't he taught us some of the things we need to know? He found out where we were weakest, and then he exploited that. He has done the same with Ashley. He turns everything upside down so that he can control things. Why are we here? Because we think he is going to hurt her. Maybe even kill her, if his frustration grows uncontrollable. So, if we step back, think a little, it seems to me that we merely do to him what he's been doing to us. We create havoc, without leaving a trail."

Again, the two others remained silent, but everything Sally said seemed to make sense. Both Scott and Hope stared at the woman that they had once loved or continued to love and saw someone they barely recognized.

"We must bring the father and son together. That would be crucial. They must face each other. Hopefully, they'll fight. That needs to be something a detective can prove. That they came together and they fought. And into that anger, we have to find a way to inject ourselves. Secretly. Leaving absolutely no marks behind and completely unseen by anyone—except the man we kill."

Sally stared across the room, but lifted her eyes toward the ceiling, no longer even facing Hope and Scott. Her voice took on a musing, almost speculative tone. "You see, it would make sense. They hate and distrust each other. There is a history of violence between the two. Unfinished business. What would make more sense than the son killing the father in a rage?"

"That's true," Scott said. "A Greek-tragedy sense of justice. But they haven't spoken in years. How do we—"

Sally held up her hand. She spoke softly. "If he thought Ashley was there at the old man's house . . ."

Scott burst out, "You mean to use her as bait?" He was shaking his head. "But that's impossible."

"What other bait do we have?" Sally asked coldly.

"I thought we agreed that Ashley was to be excluded from all this," Hope said.

Sally shrugged. "Ashley could make a phone call without knowing why she was making it. We could give her a script."

Hope leaned forward. "Assuming . . . but only just assuming, we can get them into the same room together. And then we show up . . . how do we kill him?" She was suddenly taken aback by the words she heard herself speak.

Sally paused, thinking. "We're not strong enough. . . ." Then her face froze. "You said Michael O'Connell has a gun?"

"Yes. Hidden in his apartment."

Sally nodded. "We have to use that gun. Not even a gun like it. That precise gun. His gun. The one with his fingerprints on it and maybe carrying his DNA."

"How do we get it?" Scott asked.

Hope, however, was reaching into her jeans pocket. She held up the key to O'Connell's apartment.

The other two stared at her. And in that moment, although neither Scott nor Sally said anything, both thought the same thing: This is possible.

Sally remained alone while the others went in to begin the dinner that Catherine and Ashley had whipped up. She thought she should feel awful, but she did not. A large part of her was energized, almost gleefully excited by the prospect of murder.

She wanted to laugh out loud at the irony of it all. We will do something that will change us forever so that we don't have to change forever. She overheard Hope's voice coming from the kitchen and imagined that the only route back to wherever it was where they had once loved one another traveled through Michael O'Connell and his father. She asked herself, Can death create life? Surely, she imagined, the answer had to be yes. Soldiers, firemen, rescue workers, policemen—all know they might face that choice one day. Sacrifice so that others can survive. Were they doing anything different?

She reached over and took up a yellow legal pad and a cheap pen.

Sally started to sketch ideas on the pad of paper. She began a list of items that might be needed, and details that would create a compelling portrait for the police investigators who would inevitably arrive. As she wrote down things to consider, she realized that the actual act of pulling the trigger was less crucial than how it would be perceived afterward. She leaned forward, like an anxious student taking an exam who suddenly remembers the answers, as she began to work backward through the crime.

Invent a killing, she said to herself.

She held up her hand in front of her face. We are about to become everything we've always hated, she thought. She slowly clenched her hand into a fist, although it wasn't a fist that she felt; it was as if she had suddenly wrapped her fingers around O'Connell's neck, choking off the air from his windpipe, imagining that she could abruptly, unexpectedly, strangle him into oblivion.

•

It was late, and I hesitated in the doorway.

You hear something. Someone tells you a story. Words spoken in a low-voiced whisper. And it suddenly seems as if there are far many more questions than there are ever answers. She must have sensed this, because she said, "Do you begin to see now where their reluctance to speak with you comes from?"

"Yes," I said. "Of course. They want to avoid prosecution. There's no statute of limitations on murder."

She snorted. "That's obvious. That's been obvious from the beginning. Try to look beyond that decidedly practical aspect of all this."

"All right, because they are frightened of the betrayals involved in the story."

She inhaled sharply, almost as if afraid of something. "And what, pray tell, were those betrayals, as you so elegantly put it?"

I thought for a moment. "Sally had been educated in the law, and she should have had more respect for its powers."

"Yes, yes," she said, nodding. "An officer of the court. She saw only the flaws in the law, not its strengths. Go on."

"And Scott, well, a professor of history. Perhaps more than any of the others, he should have had an appreciation of the dangers in acting unilaterally. He was the one with the sense of social justice."

"A man who disdained violence suddenly embracing it?" she asked.

"Yes. Even when he was young and went into the service, that was more a political act, or maybe, you might say, an act of conscience, than it was some sort of gung ho patriotism. That kept his hands if not exactly clean, at least not exactly dirty, either. But Hope . . ."

"What about Hope?" she asked abruptly.

"It seems that she was the least likely of them all to be, I don't know, wrapped up in criminality. After all, her connection was the least profound."

"Was it? Had she not risked the most of all of them? A woman who loved another woman, with all the societal baggage that carries, who took the biggest chance on love and who had, it would appear, given up on the desire to have her own family, to present a *normal* face to the world, and so had adopted Ashley as her own. And what did she see when she looked at Ashley? Did she see a part of herself? Did she see a life she might have chosen? Did she envy her, love her, feel some sort of immense internal connection that is different from what we ordinarily expect from a mother or father? And, as the athlete that she was, did she not prize a direct take-charge sort of approach?"

Her sudden volley of questions encapsulated me as swiftly as the dark of night.

"Yes," I said. "I can see all that."

"All of Hope's life was about taking chances and following her instincts. It was what made her so beautiful."

"I hadn't thought of it that way."

"Do you not think Hope was, in some regards, the key to all this?"

I shook my head, but just slightly. "Yes and no."

"How so?" she demanded.

"Ashley remained the key."

40

A Run through the Shadows

Ashley pushed against the headboard of her bed, placing her feet against the wood, so that she was back to front, feeling the muscles in her legs tighten until they began to shake with exertion. It was what she had done when she was young, when her body seemed to outdistance itself, and she was afflicted with "growing pains," feeling as if her bones no longer fit into her skin. Sports, running hard in the afternoons, while Hope watched, had helped, but many nights she had tossed and turned in her bed, waiting for her body to grow into whoever it was she was going to become.

It was early, and the house was still filled with the occasional sounds of sleep. Catherine in the next room snored loudly. There wasn't any stirring from either Sally or Hope, although late the night before, she had heard them talking. The words had been too distant for her to make out, but she presumed they had something to do with her. She hadn't heard any muffled, hidden noises of affection in some time, and this troubled her. She very much wanted her mother to stay with Hope, but Sally had grown so distant in the past years, she was unsure what would happen. Sometimes she didn't believe she could handle the emotional briars of another divorce, even one that was gentle. From experience she knew the "amicable divorce" doesn't really make the internal pain any less.

For a moment, Ashley listened, then slowly let a few tears well up in the corners of her eyes. Nameless had always slept at the end of the hallway on a tattered dog bed just outside the master bedroom, so that he could be close to Hope. But often, when Ashley was young, he had sensed in that magical dog way when something was troubling her, and he would come down, uncalled, nose open the door to her room, and without any fuss take up a position on the carpet by her bureau. He would watch her until she would tell him whatever was bothering her. It was as if by reassuring the dog, she could reassure herself.

Ashley bit down on her lip. *I'd shoot him myself, just for what he did to Nameless.*

She kicked her feet off the bed and rose. For a moment, she let her eyes meander slowly over all the familiar items of her childhood. On one wall, surrounding a poster board, were dozens of her own drawings. There were snapshots of her friends, of herself dressed up for Halloween, on the soccer field, and ready for the prom. There was a large, multi-hued flag with the word PEACE in its center above an embroidered white dove. An empty bottle of champagne with two paper flowers in it signified the night her freshman year in college when she'd lost her virginity, an event she had secretly shared with Hope, but not her mother and father. She slowly let out her breath and thought to herself that all the things she could see in front of her were signs of who she had been, but what she needed to imagine was what she was going to become. She went to the shoulder bag hanging from the doorknob to her closet, reached in, and removed the revolver.

Ashley hefted it in her hand, then turned and assumed a firing position, aiming first at the bed. Slowly, one eye closed, she rotated, bringing the weapon to bear on the window. Fire all six shots, she reminded herself. Aim for the chest. Don't jerk on the trigger. Keep the weapon as steady as possible.

She was a little afraid that she looked ridiculous.

He won't be standing still, she thought. He might be rushing forward, trying to close the distance between himself and death. She reassumed her stance, widening her bare feet on the floor, lowering herself a couple of inches. She did measurements in her memory: How tall was O'Connell? How strong was he? How fast would he move? Would he plead for his life? Would he promise to leave her alone?

Shoot him in the goddamn heart, she told herself, if he has one.

"Bang," she whispered out loud. "Bang. Bang. Bang. Bang. Bang."

She lowered the revolver to her side.

"You're dead and I'm alive. And my life gets to go on," she said softly, to make certain that no matter how troubled the sleep of the others was, they wouldn't hear her. "No matter how damn bad it might seem, it will be better than this."

Still gripping the gun, she sidled to the edge of the window. Concealing herself behind the curtains, she peered up and down the street. It was only a little past dawn, a weak half-light slowly bringing out shapes up and down the block of houses. It would be cold, she thought. There would be damp frost on the lawns. Too cold for O'Connell to have spent the night outside, keeping watch.

She nodded and replaced the gun in her satchel. Then she rapidly pulled tights, a black turtleneck, and a hooded sweatshirt from her drawers and grabbed her running shoes. She did not think that she would have many moments over

the next few days when she could be alone, but this seemed
to her to be one of them. As she tiptoed from the room, she
had a twinge of regret, leaving the pistol behind. But she
couldn't really run with it, she thought. Too heavy. Too
crazy.

The air was tinged with Canadian cold that had drifted
down through Vermont. She closed the front door quietly
and pulled a knit cap down over her ears, then took off fast
up the street, wanting to get away from the house before
anyone could tell her not to do what she was doing. Whatever risk was involved, it rapidly fled from Ashley's
thoughts as she accelerated hard, forcing her heartbeat to
warm her hands, going fast enough to leave even the cold
behind.

Ashley ran hard, seeming to keep up a rhythm to her
thoughts. She let the pounding of her feet turn her anger into
a sort of runner's poetry. She was so fed up with being restricted and ordered around and constrained by her family
and by her fears that she insisted to herself that she was willing to take a chance. Of course, she told herself, don't be so
stupid as to not make it difficult; she traveled an erratic,
zigzag path.

What she wanted, she thought, was the luxury of acting
rashly.

Two miles became three, then four, and the morning's
spontaneity dissolved into a steadiness that she hoped protected her. The wind was no longer cold and burning on her
lips and drawn into her lungs, and she could feel sweat around
her neck. When she turned and started back toward her home,
she felt some fatigue, but not enough to slow her down. Instead, what she felt was an unsettled heat that burned inside
her. She scanned the path ahead and suddenly saw movement. She was nearly overcome by the sensation that she was
no longer alone. She shook her head and kept moving.

Some eight blocks from her house, a car sliced dangerously close by. She gasped, wanting to shout an obscenity,
but kept running.

Six blocks from her house, a loud voice called out a name

as she ran past. She could not tell if it was hers, and she
didn't turn to look, but started to move faster.

Four blocks from her house, someone nearby honked a
car horn. The sound made her nearly jump out of her skin,
and she started to sprint.

Two blocks from her house, she suddenly heard tires
squealing behind her. She gasped for breath and, again,
didn't turn to investigate, but leaped from the roadway to the
uneven cement sidewalk, broken up by tree roots that had
pushed the surface into a ripple of cracks and breaks, like
the unsettled surface of the ocean before a storm. The pavement seemed to snap at her ankles, and her feet complained
with the difficulty. She ran harder. She wanted to close her
eyes and tried to shut out all sounds. This was impossible, so
she began humming to herself. She religiously kept her eyes
straight ahead, refusing to turn in either direction, like a
racehorse with blinders on, sprinting as fast as she could
manage toward her home. She jumped across a flower bed
and dashed across the lawn, almost slamming into the front
door, before she stopped and slowly turned around.

She stared up, then down the street. She saw a man back-
ing his car out of his driveway. Some laughing children
overloaded with bulging backpacks heading toward a school
bus stop. A woman with a long, bright green overcoat tossed
over her nightgown, reaching down for the morning paper.

No O'Connell. At least nowhere that she could see.

She leaned her head back, gasping in drafts of cold air.
Her eyes strayed across the morning normalcy and she
gasped back a sob. In that moment, she realized that he no
longer actually had to be present in order to be present.

From a spot a short ways down the street, Michael O'Connell feasted his vision upon Ashley as she stood hesitantly
on the front porch of her mother's house. He was sipping
from a large coffee cup, hunched down behind the wheel of
his car. He believed that if she knew how to look, she might

see him, but he made little other effort to conceal himself. He simply waited.

He had considered, then dismissed, trying to stop her as she ran. The surprise might cause her to panic, and it would have been too easy for her to flee. She was far more familiar with the side streets and backyards of the neighborhood, and as quick as he was, he was unsure whether he could have caught her. But, more important, she might have screamed, gotten the attention of neighbors, and somebody might have called the police. If she had made a scene, he would have had to back down before he had a chance to speak with her. More than anything, what he did not want was to have to make some sort of explanation to some skeptical police officer as to what he was doing.

He had to find the right moment. Not this one, on the street where she'd grown up. It resonated her past. He was her future.

Easier, by far, he thought, to drink in her vision. He particularly liked watching her legs move. They were long and supple, and he wished that in their sole night together, he'd paid even more attention to them. Still, he was able to picture them, naked, glistening, and he shifted about in his seat as he felt the first heat of being aroused. He wished that Ashley would remove her knit cap, so that he could see her hair, and when he looked up and she did this, he smiled and wondered if he could send her all sorts of subliminal messages, directly from his thoughts to hers. It just reinforced in his mind how linked they were.

Michael O'Connell laughed out loud.

He could simply look at Ashley from afar and feel her warmth throughout his body. It was as if she energized him. He reached out, as if driven by passion, unable to sit still, and opened his door.

A short ways away, Ashley turned at that same moment and, without seeing the movement, filled with despair, stepped back into the house.

Michael O'Connell stood up, half in the car, one leg on

the ground behind the door, staring at the spot where Ashley had disappeared. In his imagination, he could still see her.

Steal her, he said to himself.

It seemed so simple to him.

He smiled. It was just a matter of getting her alone.

Not exactly alone, he thought. But alone in his world. Not hers.

I am invisible, he thought, as he slid back into the car and pulled away from the curb.

He was wrong about this. From the window in her upstairs bedroom, Sally stood, watching. She gripped the window frame with white-knuckled fingers, close to breaking the wood, her nails digging into the paint. It was the first time she had seen Michael O'Connell in the flesh. When she'd first spotted the figure behind the wheel of the car, she had tried to tell herself that he wasn't who she thought he was, but, in the same thought, knew she was deluding herself. It was him. It could be no one else. He was as close as he'd always been, right beyond their reach, shadowing Ashley's every step. Even when she could not see him, he was there. She felt dizzy, enraged, and almost overcome by anxiety. Love is hate, she thought. Love is evil. Love is wrong.

She watched the car disappear down the street.

Love is death, she thought.

Breathing hard, she turned away from the window. She decided against instantly telling everyone that she'd spotted O'Connell on their street, only yards away from the front door, spying on Ashley. The family would be enraged, she thought. Angry people behave rashly. We need to be calm. Intelligent. Organized. Get to work. Get to work. Get to work. She turned back and found the pad of paper where she was making her notes. Notes for a murder. When she picked up her pencil, though, she noticed that her hand was quivering just slightly.

In the late afternoon, Sally went shopping for items she believed were integral to their task. It was not until early in the evening that she got back, checked once on Ashley, who appeared oddly bored, curled up on her bed reading, wondered where Hope was, as she listened to Catherine fiddle about in the kitchen, and then got around to calling Scott on the phone.

"Yes?"

"Scott? It's Sally."

"Is everything okay?"

"Yes. We got through the day more or less without incident," she said without mentioning that she had seen O'Connell lurking about their street that morning. "How much longer that will be the case, I have my doubts."

"I understand that."

"Good. I hope so. Because I think you should come over here now."

"All right . . ." He hesitated.

"It's time to act." Sally laughed, but without humor, as if pricked by some deep cynicism. "It seems to me that we've agreed more in the past few weeks than we ever did when we were actually married."

Scott, too, smiled ruefully. "That is a strange way of looking at things. Maybe. But when we were together, well, there were times it wasn't that bad."

"You weren't living a lie like I was."

"*Lie* is a strong word."

"Look, Scott, I don't want to fight over past fights again, if that makes sense."

For a moment they remained silent, then Sally added, "We're getting sidetracked. This isn't about where we were, it's about where we can go or even who we are. And most important, it's about Ashley."

"Okay," Scott said, feeling that some huge swamp of emotions was between them that was never spoken of and never would be.

"I have a plan," Sally blurted.

"Good," he said after taking a deep breath. He wasn't sure that he meant that.

"I don't know if it is a good one. I don't know if it will work. I don't know if we can pull it off."

"Let's hear it."

"We shouldn't be talking on the phone. At least not on these lines."

"Right. Of course not. That makes sense." He wasn't at all sure why this made sense, but he said it anyway. "I'll be over straightaway." He hung up the phone and thought that there was something awful in the routines of life. Teaching, living alone with all the ghosts of statesmen, soldiers, and politicians that made up his courses, his existence was completely predictable. He guessed that that was going to change.

Hope returned to the house before Scott arrived. She had been out walking, trying without much luck to sort through all that was happening. She found Sally in the living room, poring over some loose sheets of paper, pencil stuck in her mouth. She looked up when Hope entered.

"I have a plan. I'm not sure it will work. But Scott's coming over and we can go over it together."

"Where are my mother and Ashley?"

"Upstairs. Not at all pleased with being banned from the conversation."

"My mother doesn't appreciate being excluded from things, which is a curious position for someone who has spent much of her adult life living in the woods in Vermont, but there you have it. That's the way she is." Hope hesitated, and Sally looked up as if she heard a catch in Hope's voice.

"What is it?"

Hope shook her head. "I don't know exactly, but try to follow me on this. She's doing what we ask her to, right? Well, that's just not her style. Not in the slightest. She's always been a lone-wolf type, the *I don't give a damn what other people think* sort of person. And her seeming compliance . . . well, I'm not sure that we should rely on her ever doing exactly what we ask her to. She's just a bit of a loose cannon. It's what my dad always loved about her, and me, too, except, upon occasion, growing up, it made things, well, *difficult,* if you catch my drift."

Sally smiled. "Are you all that different?"

Hope shrugged, but laughed in response. "I guess not."

"And don't you think that I might have been attracted to those qualities, as well?"

"I never thought of *stubborn* and *unpredictable* as my best sides."

"Well, just goes to show what you know." Sally managed a small grin as she dipped her head to the paperwork spread out on her lap.

The two women were both silent. Oddly, Hope thought, it was the first affectionate thing Sally had said in weeks.

There was a knock on the door. "That will be Scott," Sally said. She gathered her papers together as Hope went to let him in. In the second or two of solitude, she put her head back and took in a deep breath. Once you start this thing moving, there will be no going back.

Catherine fumed inwardly. She looked across at the younger woman, until finally Ashley dashed her book to the floor after reading the same page for the third time and said, "I don't know if I can stand this much longer. I'm being treated like a six-year-old. Being sent to my room. Told to keep myself occupied while my parents map out my future. God damn it, Catherine, I'm not a baby! I can fight for myself."

"I agree, dear," Catherine said.

"You know, I should take that damn pistol and just solve this problem once and for all."

"I believe, Ashley, dear, that's in some ways what your parents are trying to avoid. And I didn't get you that gun so that you could go off and use it willy-nilly, just because you're pissed off. I got it so that you could protect yourself, if O'Connell came after you."

Ashley leaned her head back. "He has, you know."

"Has what, dear?"

"He's come after me. He's probably outside right now. Just waiting."

"Waiting, dear?"

"For the right moment. He's crazy. Crazy in love. Crazy obsessed. Crazy I don't know what. But he's there. He has only one thing of any importance in his life, and it is me."

Catherine nodded. She suddenly leaned forward. "Can you do it?"

Ashley opened her eyes and stared across the room, first fixing on Catherine, then on the shoulder bag that contained the pistol.

"Can you do it?" Catherine repeated.

"Yes," Ashley answered stiffly. "I can. I can. I know it."

"I couldn't. I should have. With the shotgun when he was right across from me. I should have. But I didn't. Can you be stronger than I was, dear? Can you be more determined? Are you braver?"

"I don't know. But, yes. I think so."

"I need to know."

"How can anyone know, until they actually do it? I mean, I'm angry enough. Maybe scared enough. But can I pull the trigger? I think so."

"I imagine you could," Catherine said. "At least maybe you could. The chances are, you could. It's dark out. Are you convinced he's out there?"

"Yes."

"Well, you could end it all by putting the pistol in your jacket pocket and taking a walk with me around midnight. And when he tried to stop us, you act. He might say he just wants to talk with you, that's what they always say. But instead of talking you just shoot him. Right there. Right then. The police will come and probably arrest you. And then we can have your mother hire the best attorney. Take your chances in a court of law. It's not exactly as if this community, where your mother and Hope live, is particularly predisposed to giving men—and especially men who have been stalking a young woman—much leeway. Or, for that matter, the benefit of any doubt whatsoever."

"You think . . ."

"I think you can do it if you're willing to pay the price."

"Prison?"

"Maybe. Notoriety. Being the poster child for every person with some other agenda, which will surely happen, just as your folks have predicted it would. But it might be worth it."

Ashley rocked her head back. "I can't stand this for much longer. One minute I'm terrified. The next I'm furious. I feel safe one second. Then threatened the next."

"Why can't we be violent before they are violent towards us?" Catherine said fiercely. "Why is that so goddamn unfair? Why do we have to wait to be a victim?"

"I'm not going to."

"Good. I didn't think so. So, let's consider what *we* can do."

Ashley nodded her head in agreement.

Scott looked at several small piles of items collected in the living room. "You've been shopping."

"Indeed," Sally said.

"You want to go over it for us?" Scott picked up and fiddled with a box of ammonia-based Handi Wipes. "Like these?"

Sally was quiet, even-toned. "If one thought they had left a DNA sample in a compromising location, they could swipe it down with these, eradicating any trace evidence."

Scott blew out his cheeks. He was almost dizzy. Handi Wipes, he thought. Part of a murder weapon.

Sally watched her ex-husband and could feel him wavering. She continued solidly, "As best as I can deduce, what we have agreed to do is bring O'Connell and his father together. We can do that. Scott more or less inadvertently has given us a way. And I think we can presume they will have words. We've been over that. Then we must find a way to steal O'Connell's own weapon, use it, as he presumably would, on his father, and return it to O'Connell's hideaway before he realizes it is missing."

"Why not just leave it at the, ah, crime scene?" Scott asked.

"I thought of that," Sally replied. "But it will be the crucial piece of evidence. The police and the prosecution just love finding the murder weapon. It's what they will build their theory around. It will be the item that is incontrovertible in a court of law. To be sure, it, more than anything else, needs to be discovered in his control."

"What are these other things?" Hope asked.

Sally looked over at the gathered items. There were several cell phones, a tube of Super Glue, a portable computer, a size-small men's coverall, two boxes of surgical gloves, several pairs of surgical bootees that could be pulled over a pair of shoes, two black, tight-fitting balaclava face and head cover-ups, and a Swiss Army knife. "They are what we need, as best as I can tell. There are some other things that would be really useful, as well, like some hair from a comb in O'Connell's apartment, maybe. I'm still fitting pieces together."

"What's the computer for?" Scott asked.

Sally sighed. She turned to Hope. "That's the same make and model that you saw in O'Connell's apartment, right?"

Hope examined the machine. "Yes. As best as I can tell. At least, that's what I remember."

"Well," Sally said, "you said that his computer contains encrypted material about Ashley. And about us. This one doesn't."

Hope nodded. "I think I see."

"The police will seize his computer. I'd rather have it be one that we'd prepared for that circumstance."

"Switch them?"

"Correct. It will just erase a link between us and him. He's probably got backup somewhere, with all the stuff about Ashley and us, but still . . . Timing will be critical."

She handed each of them a sheet of yellow legal-pad paper. At the top she had drawn a timeline.

Hope stared down at the paper. Sally had delineated tasks, events, actions, but had marked each with an *A, B,* or *C.* When she looked up, she saw that Sally was watching her.

"You haven't assigned roles," Hope said. "You've got three people doing interrelated things, but you haven't yet said who does what."

Sally leaned back in her chair, trying to remain composed. "I have tried to think of this from the position of a modern police officer," she said. "You have to consider what they will find, and how they will interpret it. Crimes are always about a certain logic. One thing should lead them to the next. They have modern techniques, like DNA analysis and forensic weapons studies and all sorts of capabilities that we only know about peripherally. I've tried to think of as many of these as I could and remember what screws up investigations. Fire, for example, makes a mess of things—but it doesn't necessarily destroy firearms forensics. Water compromises all sorts of wounds and DNA, ruins fingerprints. Our problem is that we want to commit a crime, a violent crime, but we want to leave a trail. Not a perfect trail, but enough of one that leads in the direction we want. The police will, if we're careful, do the rest, even without a confession from O'Connell."

"What if he points the police in our direction?"

"We must be prepared for that. We can, to some degree, create alibis for each other. But mainly, we must make it seem unreasonable. That's the trick. Far better that the police simply not believe anything he says—which is what they will be inclined to do—and try to ride out any attention that comes our way. Don't underestimate how unlikely it is that we are doing what we are about to do. And police, well, they really like simple answers to simple questions. Even simple questions about death."

Sally paused, staring first at Scott, then Hope.

"But I don't think he will," Sally said.

"Will what?"

"Point the police at us. If we do this right, he won't know."

Scott nodded. "But, you know, I was there, asking questions. Someone is likely to remember me."

"That's why at some key point you will have to be miles

away doing something in someone else's presence. Like using a credit card and making a complaint someplace where there is a video camera. But on the other hand, it's probably critical that you're close by, as well."

Scott sat back hard. "I see that, but . . ."

"The same is true for Ashley and Catherine. Although they will have a role to play."

Again the others remained silent.

Sally took a deep breath. "Which brings us to the crucial question. The actual crime. I've thought about this, and I think it will have to be me."

She waited for someone to say something, but no one did.

"I'll have to get the gun," Hope said. "I'm the one who knows where it is. I've got the key."

"Yes. But you were there once before. You have the same problem that Scott has. No, someone else has to get the gun. You can tell me where."

Hope nodded, but Scott shook his head.

"That's, of course, assuming it remains where you saw it. Which is a big assumption."

Sally coughed, then said, "Yes, but if we *cannot* recover the gun, we're only partially committed. We can still pull back, then come up with a secondary plan on a new day."

Scott was still shaking his head. "Okay, if we steal the gun. And then get it to you . . . what makes you think you can handle a weapon? Especially under these circumstances?"

"I'll just have to. It's my job, I think."

Hope shook her head. "I don't know about that. It seems to me that there is a certain danger—I'm trying to be like you, Sally, and think like a policeman—in Ashley's mother committing the crime. That might make sense to a cop, you know. Protecting your child. But I doubt that any cop would think that the mother's *partner* would perform this act. In other words, my distance from Ashley, her not being my own child, my own blood, protects me from inquiries, don't you think? And I'm younger, quicker, and stronger, in case there is some actual running involved in all this."

Both Scott and Sally stared at her. Both could see what

she was about to say, but neither could muster the words to prevent her from saying it.

Hope tried to smile through a cloud of her own doubt. "No," she said slowly, "it should be me with that gun in my hand."

•

This time, I was sure I could hear a catch in her voice.

"Do you ever wonder how much of life can change in a second? So many things seem small, yet they become large."

It was close to midnight, and she had surprised me by calling.

"Do you think," she asked abruptly, "that we make better choices in the dark, alone, at night, when we lie in bed and try to sort through a sea of troubles? Or is it wiser to wait until morning, when there is daylight and clarity? I wonder what sort of decisions they were making," she said slowly. "Night decisions? Day decisions? You tell me."

I didn't answer. I thought she wasn't really looking for a response, but she persisted.

"I mean, how would you characterize it? You're the writer. Was this wise? Were they taking steps that were difficult, but necessary? Or were they acting foolishly? What were the odds of success? Or of failure? They were all such *reasonable* people, about to embark on the least reasonable of courses."

I said nothing as she stifled a sob.

"I have a name for you," she said quickly, taking me by surprise. "It will, I suspect, bring you a little closer."

I waited, pen ready, saying nothing, imagining everything.

"The end," she said. "Can you see it? Let me put it to you this way: do you think they were prepared for the unexpected?"

"No. Who ever truly is?"

She laughed, but then the sound seemed to turn to tears. It was hard to tell over the phone line.

41

Unfolding

Sally looked across at Hope. They were in their bedroom, and only a single bedside table lamp threw wan yellow light across the room.

"I can't let you do this," Sally said.

"I'm not sure you have a choice," Hope said with a small shrug. "I believe the decision has been made. And anyway, it's probably the least dangerous part of the whole enterprise." This was a lie, but how much of one, Hope was unsure.

"Enterprise?"

"For lack of a better word."

Sally shook her head. "A bomb goes off in a marketplace, and we call it *collateral damage*. A surgery goes wrong, we call it *complications*. A soldier gets killed, he becomes a *casualty*. Seems to me that we live on euphemisms."

"And what about us?" Hope asked. "What word would you choose for the two of us?"

Sally frowned. She walked over to a mirror. Once upon a time she had been beautiful. Once upon a time she had been vibrant. She barely recognized the person staring back at her. "I guess the two of us don't know what the next day will bring. *Uncertainty*. There's a word."

Hope felt a crease of emotion. "You could say you loved me."

"I do. It's just myself that I no longer love."

They were quiet while Sally looked down at her sheets of paper.

"We do this, you know, and everything will be different."

"I thought the point was to restore everything to the same as it was before."

"Both," Sally said stiffly. "I think it will be both."

She picked up a handwritten series of instructions from the top of the pile. "This has to go to Ashley and Catherine. Do you want to come with me when I speak with them? Actually, no, don't. If you're not there, they can't ask you any questions."

"I'll wait for you here." Hope lay back on the bed, crawling beneath the comforter, feeling a shiver run down her back.

Sally found Ashley and Catherine in Ashley's room.

"I have some requests for you guys. Can you do the things listed here—it's not too much—without asking any questions? I need to know."

Catherine took the list from Sally's hand, read it through rapidly, then handed it over to Ashley.

"I think we can do that," she said.

"I wrote out a script and I'm giving you a disposable cell phone that I'd like you to lose after you contact him," Sally said. "You can ad-lib, of course, but you need to get the main point across. Do you see that?"

Ashley stared at the words on the page and nodded. "Do you think—"

"Sounds like the start of a question," Sally said with a wry smile. "The point is, you must, I repeat, you must, sell O'Connell on this trip. He has to be made to do this. And, it seems to all of us, anger and jealousy and perhaps a little indecision is precisely the concoction that will encourage him. If you can find a better set of words, by all means use them. But the end result absolutely must be the same. Do you get that? Hope, your father, and I will be counting on that. Can you act this part, Ashley, honey? Because much will ride on your powers of persuasion."

"Much of what?" she asked.

"Ah, another question. And it won't get answered. See there at the bottom. Bunch of phone numbers. I don't expect you to be able to memorize them all, but it is essential that by the end of the day, this paper, and everything else, be destroyed. That's it for now."

"That's it?"

"You're being asked to play a part. Just like you requested. But what the final act is, you are not being told. And what you are being asked to do limits, shall we say, your *exposure*. Catherine, I'm counting on you to see this through. And to accomplish the other elements on that list."

"I don't know that I like this," Catherine said. "I don't know that I like acting in the dark."

"Well, we're all in uncharted territory here. But I need to be one hundred percent sure about our roles."

"We will do what you ask. Although I don't see—"

"That's the point. You don't see."

Sally paused in the doorway. She looked over at Catherine, then to her daughter. "I wonder if you understand how much people love you," she said cautiously. "And what people might be willing to do for you."

Ashley didn't reply, other than to nod her head.

"Of course," Catherine injected, "the same might be said for Michael O'Connell, which is why we're all here."

Scott sat in the Porsche and dialed O'Connell's father on the cell phone that Sally had provided for him. The line rang three times before the man picked it up.

"Mr. O'Connell?" Scott said with a businesslike tone.

"Who's this?" The words were slightly slurred. A two-beer, maybe three, tone.

"This would be Mr. Smith, Mr. O'Connell."

"Who?" A momentary confusion.

"Mr. Jones, if you prefer."

O'Connell's father laughed. "Oh, yeah, hey, sure. Hey, that e-mail you gave me didn't work. I tried it and it came back undeliverable."

"A slight change in procedures precipitated by necessity, I assure you. I apologize."

Scott assumed that the only real reason that O'Connell's

father had a computer in the first place was to easily access pornographic websites.

"Let me give you a cell phone number." He quickly read off the number.

"Okay, got it. But I ain't heard shit from my boy, and I'm not expecting to."

"Mr. O'Connell, I have every indication that things might change. I believe that you might hear from him. And, if so, please call that number immediately, as we discussed previously. My client's interest in speaking with your son has, shall I say, increased in recent days. His need has, shall we say, grown more urgent. Therefore, as you can easily see, his sense of obligation to you, if you were to make that call, would be substantially more than I initially guessed. Do you understand exactly what I'm saying?"

O'Connell hesitated, then said, "Yeah. I get lucky, the kid shows up, and it's gonna turn out even better for me. But like I say, I ain't heard from him and I ain't likely to."

"Well, we can always hope. For everyone's sakes," Scott said as he disconnected the line. He leaned his head back and reached for the electric window switch. He felt as if he were choking. He was almost overcome with nausea, but when he tried to vomit, he could only cough dryly.

He breathed in rapidly and looked down at the yellow sheet of paper that Sally had given him, with its list of tasks. There was something deeply terrible about her ability to organize, and to think with mathematical precision about, something as difficult as they were about to do. For a moment, he could feel his temperature rising again, and a vile, bilious taste in his mouth.

All his life, Scott believed, he had performed on the periphery of importance. He had gone to war because he knew it was the defining moment of his generation, but then he had stepped back and kept himself safe. His education, his teaching, were all about helping students, but never himself. His marriage had been a humiliating disaster with the sole exception of Ashley. And now, here he was in middle age churning his way through the days of his life, and this threat was the first moment when he was being asked to do something truly unique, something outside all the careful boundaries and limitations he had placed on his life. It was one thing to act like a boisterous father and say, "I'd kill that guy," when there was really little chance of that happening. Now that their plan to cause a death was in place and starting to grind its gears inexorably forward, he wavered. He wondered whether he could do more than merely lie.

Lying, he thought. That I'm good at. Plenty of experience.

Again he looked at the list. Words were not going to be enough, he knew.

Another wave of nausea threatened his stomach, but he fought it off, put the car in gear, and headed first for the hardware store. He knew, later, perhaps at midnight, he had to make a trip to the airport. He did not expect to sleep much in the hours to come.

It was midmorning, and Catherine and Ashley were the only people remaining in the house. Sally had departed, dressed as she would for her office, other clothing stuffed into her briefcase. Hope, as well, had left the house as if nothing were out of the ordinary, her backpack thrown jauntily over her shoulder. Neither of the two women had said anything to Ashley and Catherine about what the day held.

And both Catherine and Ashley had seen a furtiveness in their eyes.

If Sally and Hope had slept much the night before, it was lost in their tense gestures and short-tempered words. Still, they had both moved with a singleness of purpose that had almost set Ashley back. She had never seen either of the two women behaving with such steel-eyed and iron movement.

Catherine came in, breathing hard. "Something is clearly afoot, dear." She held her yellow legal paper with instructions in her hand.

"That's putting it mildly," Ashley said. "God damn it. I can't stand being outside, trying to look in."

"We need to follow the plan. Whatever it is."

"When has any plan that my parents have come up with ever really worked out?" Ashley said, although she realized she sounded a little like a petulant teenager.

"I don't know about that. But Hope generally does exactly what she says she's going to do. She's as solid as a rock."

Ashley nodded. "Thick as a brick. After the divorce, my dad used to play that for me on his tape deck and we would dance around the living room. Common ground was hard to find, so he would start blasting all his sixties rock and roll. Jethro Tull. The Stones. The Dead. The Who. Hendrix. Joplin. He taught me the Frug and the Watusi and the Freddy." Ashley suddenly looked out the window, unaware that her father had recalled the same memory days earlier. "I wonder if he and I will ever dance again. I always thought we would, you know, just the one time, when I got married, when everyone was watching. He would just swoop in and we'd do a turn or two and everyone would clap. Long white dress for me. Tuxedo for him. When I was little, the only thing I wanted was to fall in love. Not a sad, angry mess, like my mother and father. Something more like Hope and my mother, except there would be a really, really good-looking, smart guy involved. And you know, when I would say this to Hope, she was always the first to tell me how great it would be. We would laugh and imagine wedding dresses and flowers and all the little-girl things." Ashley stepped back. "And now, the first man to say he loves me and truly mean it is a nightmare."

"Life is strange," Catherine said. "We have to trust them that they know what they're doing."

"You think they do?"

Catherine saw that in Ashley's right hand she held the revolver.

"If I get the damn chance . . ." Ashley said.

Then she pointed at the list. "All right. Act one. Scene one. Enter Ashley and Catherine, stage right. What's our opening line?"

Catherine looked down at her list. "First thing is the trickiest. We have to make sure that O'Connell isn't here. I guess we're taking that walk outside."

"Then what?" Ashley asked.

Catherine looked down at the paper. "Then it's your big moment. It's the bit your mother underlined three times. Are you ready?"

Ashley didn't answer. She was unsure.

They got their coats and walked out the front door together. Ashley and Catherine paused, standing on the front stoop, staring up and down the block. It was all family-neighborhood quiet. Ashley kept her fingers gripped around the pistol handle hidden deep in her parka pocket, her index finger rubbing against the trigger guard nervously. She was struck with the way her fear of Michael O'Connell had made her see the world as so many threats. The street where she had spent much of her childhood playing, as she shuttled between her parents' two houses, should have been as familiar to her as her own room upstairs. But it was no longer. O'Connell had changed it into something utterly different. He had sliced away everything that belonged to her: her school, her apartment in Boston, her job, and now the place where she had grown up. She wondered whether he really knew how much genius existed in his evil.

She touched the gun barrel. Kill him, she told herself. Because he is killing you.

Still scanning the neighborhood with their eyes, Catherine and Ashley proceeded slowly up the street. Ashley wanted to invite him to show himself, if he was there. Halfway down the block, despite the rain, she removed her knit ski cap. She shook her head, letting her hair fall to her shoulders, before stuffing the hat back upon her head. She wanted, for the first and only time in months, to be irresistible.

"Keep walking," Catherine said. "If he's here, he will show."

They sidled down the sidewalk, and from behind they heard a car start down the street. Ashley clutched the pistol and felt her heartbeat accelerate. She barely breathed in as the sound increased.

As the car drew abreast of them, she pivoted abruptly, swinging the weapon free and spreading her feet as she crouched into the shooting stance that she had practiced so diligently in her room. Her thumb slid over the safety switch, then to the hammer. She exhaled sharply, almost a grunt of effort, and then a whistle of tension.

The car, with a middle-aged man behind the wheel, rolled past them. The driver didn't even turn; his eyes were checking addresses on the opposite side of the street.

Ashley groaned. But Catherine kept her wits about her. "You should put that weapon away," she said quietly. "Before some nice stay-at-home mother spots it in your hand."

"Where the hell is he?"

Catherine didn't answer.

The two of them continued slowly. Ashley felt utterly calm, committed, ready to pull out her weapon and end it all with a rapid-fire answer to all his questions. Is this what it feels like to be ready to kill someone? But the real O'Connell, as opposed to the ghostlike O'Connell who had lurked just behind her every step for so long, was nowhere to be seen.

When they'd patiently made it around the block and sauntered back to Sally and Hope's home, Catherine muttered, "All right. We know one thing. He's not here. He has to be somewhere. Are you ready for the next step?"

Ashley doubted anyone could know the answer to that until they tried.

Michael O'Connell was at his makeshift desk in a darkened room, bathed in the glow of the computer screen. He was working on a little surprise for Ashley's family. Dressed only in his underwear, his hair slicked back after a shower, techno music pouring through the computer's speakers, he tapped his fingers on the keyboard in rhythm with the electric chords. The songs he listened to were fast, almost out of control.

O'Connell took delight in having used some of the cash that Ashley's father had given him in the pathetic effort to buy him off to purchase the computer that replaced the one that Matthew Murphy had smashed. And now, he was hard at work on a series of electronic sorties that he believed would make for significant trouble in their lives.

The first was to be an anonymous tip to the Internal Revenue Service suggesting that Sally was asking her clients to pay her fees half by check and half in cash. There is nothing, Michael O'Connell thought, that the tax people hate more than someone trying to hide big chunks of income. They would be skeptical when she denied it, and relentless as they pored over her accounts.

This made him laugh out loud.

The second was designed as an equally anonymous tip to the New England offices of the federal Drug Enforcement Agency alleging that Catherine was growing large quantities of marijuana on her farm in a greenhouse inside her barn. He hoped the tip would be enough to get a search warrant. And even if the search turned up nothing—as he knew it would—he suspected the heavy hand of the DEA would wreck all her precious antiques and memorabilia. He could picture her house strewn with her items.

The third was a little surprise that he'd planned for Scott. Surfing around the Internet, using the log-on *Histprof,* he had discovered a Danish website that offered the most virulent pornography, prominently featuring children and underage teenagers in all sorts of provocative poses. The next step was to buy a phony credit card number and simply have a selection sent to Scott at his home. It would be a relatively simple matter to tip the local police to its arrival. In fact, he thought, he might not even have to do that. The local police would probably get a call from U.S. Customs, whom he knew monitored such imports into the States.

He laughed a little to himself, imagining the explanations that Ashley's family would try to come up with when they found themselves enmeshed in all sorts of bureaucratic red tape, or sitting across a table in a bright, windowless room from either a DEA agent, an IRS agent, or a police officer who had nothing but contempt for the sort of smug middle-class folks they were.

They might try to blame him, but he doubted it. He just couldn't be sure, which held him back. He knew that pressing the proper keys on his three entries would undoubtedly leave an electronic footprint that could be traced to his own computer. What he needed to do, he thought, was break into Scott's house one morning while he was teaching and send the request to Denmark from Scott's computer. It was also critical to create an untraceable electronic path for the other tips. He sighed. These would require him to travel to southern Vermont and western Massachusetts. Inventing screen personae wasn't a problem, he thought. And he could send the tips from computers either in Internet cafés or local libraries.

He leaned back in his chair and once again laughed out loud.

Not for the first time, Michael O'Connell wondered why they thought they could compete against him.

As he was grinning, working over each of these unpleasant surprises for Ashley's parents and family in his head, the cell phone on his desk corner rang.

It surprised him. He had no friends who would call. He'd quit his mechanic's job, and no one at the school where he was occasionally taking classes had his number.

For a second, he stared at the small window on the outside of the phone that gave the incoming identification. He saw only a single heart-stopping name: *Ashley*.

•

Before giving me the detective's name, she had made me promise to guard my words.

"You won't say anything," she had said. "You won't tell him anything that will set him on edge. You must promise me that, or else, forget it, I won't give you his name."

"I will be cautious. I promise."

Now, in the waiting room of the police station, seated on a threadbare couch, I was less sure of my capabilities. To my right, a door opened and a man about my own age, with salt-

and-pepper hair, a garishly pink tie around his neck, a substantial stomach, and an easygoing, slightly twisted smile on
his lips, emerged. He stuck out his hand, and we introduced
ourselves. He showed me back to his desk.

"So, how can I help you?"

I repeated the name I had given him in an earlier phone
call. He nodded.

"We don't get too many homicides around here. And when
we do, they're usually boyfriend-girlfriend, husband-wife. This
was a little different. But I don't get your interest in the
case."

"Some people I know suggested taking a look at it. Thought
it might make a good story."

The detective shrugged. "I wouldn't know about that. I will
say this, it was a hell of a crime scene. A real mess. Sorting
through it was quite a task. We're not exactly Hollywood
Homicide in here." He gestured around the room. It was a
modest place, where every bit of equipment, including the
men and women who worked there, showed the fraying of
age. "But even if people think we're all dumb as logs, eventually we were able to figure it all out."

"I don't think that," I said. "The dumb as logs part."

"Well, you're the exception, rather than the rule. Usually
folks don't get the big picture until they're sitting across from
one of us in handcuffs, we've got 'em nailed six ways to Sunday, and they're looking at doing some serious prison time."

He paused, eyeing me carefully. "You're not working for a
defense attorney, huh? Someone who jumps into a case and
tries to find some mistake that they can crow about in an ap-
pellate court?"

"No. Just looking for a story, like I said."

He nodded, but I wasn't sure he completely believed me.

"Well," the detective said slowly, "I don't know about that at
all. It might be a story. But it's an old one. Okay. Here you go."

He reached down beneath his desk, brought up a large
accordion-style file, and opened it on the desk in front of us.
There were a stack of eight-by-ten color glossy photographs,

which he spread out on top of all the paperwork. I leaned forward. I could see debris and ruin were strewn throughout the pictures. And a body.

"A mess," he said. "Like I told you."

42

The Gun in the Shoe

At about the same time that Catherine and Ashley were walking around the block wondering where Michael O'Connell was, Scott was parked in the far corner of a thickly wooded rest area off Route 2. The virtue of the rest area was that it was almost entirely blocked by trees and brush from the highway. That, in part, was why they had chosen Route 2 as the way to travel to Boston. It wasn't as quick as the turnpike, but it was less patrolled and less traveled. He was alone in his beaten old truck, having left the Porsche in his driveway.

Scott could hear the shallowness of his breathing, and he told himself that he was being crazy. Whatever tension there was at this moment, it would undoubtedly get far worse by the end of the day. His patience was rewarded a few minutes later when he saw a late-model white Ford Taurus pull into the rest area. It came to a stop about twenty feet away. He recognized Hope behind the wheel.

He reached down to the leg well beside him and pulled up a small, cheap red canvas gym bag. It rattled with a metallic sound when he picked it up. He got out of the truck and swiftly walked across the parking area.

Hope rolled down the window.

"Keep watch," Scott said briskly. "You see anyone pulling in, let me know pronto."

She nodded. "Where did you—"

"Last night. After midnight. I went down to long-term parking at the Hartford airport."

"Good thinking. But don't they have security cameras in the parking garage?"

"I went to the satellite lots. No pictures. This will only take a second. This a rental?"

"Yes," she said. "It made the most sense."

Scott opened the gym bag and went to the back of the car. It only took him a few minutes to exchange the Massachusetts license plates for the set from Rhode Island he'd taken off a car the night before. A small socket wrench and pliers were also in the bag. He placed the car's actual plates in the duffel and handed it to Hope. "Don't forget," he said. "Got to change back before you return that vehicle."

Hope nodded. She already looked pale.

"Look, call me if you have any hassle. I'll be close enough, and—"

"You think if there's a problem, I'll have time to make a phone call?"

"No. Of course not. All right, I'll just guide myself . . ." His voice trailed off. Too much to say. No words to say it with.

Scott stepped back. "Sally should be on her way down the turnpike by now."

"Then I'll go," Hope said. She placed the gym bag on the seat beside her.

"Keep to the speed limit. I'll see you in a bit."

He thought he should say *Good luck* or *Be careful* or something bland and encouraging. But he did not. Instead, he watched as Hope quickly exited the parking area, and he glanced at his watch, trying to imagine where Sally would be. She was taking a parallel route east. It seemed like a small touch, changing license plates for the day, but he understood that when Sally had talked to both of them about paying attention to small, seemingly insignificant details, there was much truth in what she'd said. For the first time he'd come to understand that everything he'd learned in life up to that point had little relevance to what he was about to do.

On the precipice of sudden cowardice, Scott returned to his truck and readied himself to head east into uncertainty.

Hope drove toward the intersection where the interstate highway branched off to the northeast. She followed Sally's directions as carefully as possible, keeping her speed within the limits so as not to attract any attention, heading to the spot that Sally had designated, where they would meet up later that day. She decided that it was best if she tried to compartmentalize everything. She thought of what she was about to do as mere items on a checklist, and that she was moving steadily from one to the next.

She tried to think analytically and coldly about the last three entries on her list.

Commit the crime.
Get away. Meet Sally.
Leave no trace of yourself behind.

She wished that she were a mathematician who could see everything she was doing as nothing more than a series of numbers building into theories and probabilities, and who could imagine lives and futures with nothing more passionate than the statistics of an actuary.

This was impossible. So, instead, she tried to work herself into some sort of righteous anger, fixating on Michael O'-Connell and his family, insisting to herself that the course they were taking was the only one that he had left open to them, and the only one that he would not have anticipated. If she could make herself angry enough, perhaps rage alone would carry her forward far enough to do what she had volunteered to do.

Someone has to die, she told herself. Before he kills Ashley. She repeated this, like some perverse mantra, over and over for several miles of highway.

Hope remembered games when everything hung in the balance during the last minutes before the referee's whistle.

Reaching deep into that athlete's dark reservoir for some bit of magic would free her for just the half second needed to decide the contest. As a coach, she had always urged her players to visualize that moment when success or defeat hung in the balance, so that when it inevitably arrived, they were psychologically prepared to do what was necessary, and to act without hesitation.

She imagined that this experience would be the same.

And so, biting down on her lip, she started to picture events as they were imagined by Sally, with the assistance of Scott's description of the location. She imagined the run-down, decrepit house, the rusted-out car in the front yard, the garage filled with engine parts and debris. She thought she knew what would be inside: the clutter of newspaper, beer bottles, and take-out food, a stale aroma of uselessness. And he would be there. The man who'd created the man who'd created the threat to all of them. She knew that when she faced him, she had to picture Michael O'Connell.

She saw herself waiting.

She saw herself entering.

She saw herself facing the man they had designated for death.

Hope drove east, her mind cluttered, wishing that she could act as if this particular trip were nothing in the least bit out of the ordinary.

By midafternoon, Sally had driven to Boston and parked on the street opposite Michael O'Connell's apartment building, with a clear view of the entrance. In her hand, she clutched the key that Hope had given her.

She was scrunched down behind the wheel of her car, try-ing to appear as inconspicuous as possible, while all the time believing that everyone on the block had already seen her, memorized her face, and taken down her license plate num-ber. She knew these fears were groundless, but they were there, right on the edge of her imagination, right at the point where fear threatens to start taking over emotions and actions, and it was all Sally could do to keep things in check.

She wished she had O'Connell's easy familiarity with darkness. It would help her—and Scott and Hope, as well—with what they were trying to do.

Again, she shook her head. Her sole act of rebellion, of stepping outside the routine strictures of society, was her relationship with Hope. She wanted to laugh at herself. A middle-aged, middle-class woman, unsure about her relationship with her partner, didn't really amount to much of an outlaw.

And certainly didn't amount to much of a killer.

She picked up her sheet of yellow notepaper and tried to picture where all the others were. Hope would be waiting for her. Scott would be in position. Ashley would be at home with Catherine. And Michael O'Connell would be inside—she hoped.

What made you think you could plan this and pull it off? she suddenly demanded of herself.

It.

She felt her throat go dry. *It* wasn't a fair contraction. Call *it* what *it* is. A murder. Premeditated. First-degree murder. The sort of scheme that in some states would send you to the electric chair or gas chamber. Even with the extenuating circumstances, *it* would still buy twenty-five years to life.

Not for Ashley, she thought. Ashley would remain safe.

And then, just as abruptly, she realized what she was thinking. Everyone's life would be ruined. Except O'Connell's. His would remain on the same path as before, and there would be little in the way of his pursuit of Ashley, or, if he so chose, some other Ashley.

There would be no one left to defend her.

Make it work.

She looked up, saw shadows start to creep over the building rooftops, and, she told herself, It begins now.

*   *   *

He clutched the cell phone in his hand and felt a thrill of excitement, but kept himself calm until he heard the familiar voice on the other end.

"Michael? Is that you?"

He inhaled sharply. "Hello, Ashley."

"Hello, Michael."

They were both quiet for a second. Ashley took a moment to stare down at the papers her mother had prepared for her. A script, with key sentences underlined three times. But the pages seemed blurry, indistinct. In the silence of Ashley's hesitation, Michael O'Connell rocked forward in his seat. The phone call was wonderful and terrible at the same time. It told him he was winning. He could barely contain the grin that creased his face. His right leg started to twitch, like a drummer using his foot to control the thunder of the bass drum.

"It's wonderful to hear your voice," he said. "It seems as if so many people are trying to keep us apart. You know that will never happen. I won't let it." He smiled, laughed a little, and added, "It does no good for them to try to hide you. You've seen that, haven't you? There's nowhere that I can't find you."

Ashley closed her eyes for a moment. His words were like splinters in her skin.

"Michael, I've asked you over and over to leave me alone. I've tried everything I could to help you understand that we are not going to be together. I don't want you in my life. Not at all." Everything she said, she knew she'd said before. To no effect. She didn't expect anything different this time. The world she lived in was mad, and no amount of reason or rationale was going to change it.

"I know you don't mean that," he said, an instant chill in his voice. "I know that you've been put up to say that. All these people who want you to be someone that you aren't. I know that it's other people who are dictating everything you say. That's why I'm not paying any attention to it."

Ashley almost panicked at the word *dictating* as she

glanced down at her script. What if he'd somehow seen everything, somehow managed to learn everything?

"No, Michael. No. A million times, no. You've got it wrong. You've gotten it wrong from the very start. We are not going to be together."

"It's destiny, Ashley. It was meant to be."

"No. How can you think that?"

"You don't understand love. True love. Complete love. Love never ends," he continued coldly, letting every word echo across the line. "Love never stops. Love never leaves. It is always right inside. You should know that. You imagine yourself to be an artist, but you cannot understand the simplest thing. What's wrong with you, Ashley?"

"There's nothing wrong with me," she said sharply.

"Yes, there is." O'Connell rocked in his seat. "Sometimes I think you're really sick, Ashley. Diseased. There's got to be something wrong with someone who can't understand the truth. Who refuses to listen to their heart. But you shouldn't be worried, Ashley, because I can fix you. I'm going to be there for you. No matter what happens, no matter what bad things take place, you need to know, I will always be there for you."

Ashley could feel tears welling up in her eyes. She felt utterly helpless.

"Please, Michael."

"You don't need to be afraid of anything." His voice was filled with dark anger that lay right below the words he spoke. "I will protect you."

Everything he said, she thought, was the exact opposite. *Protect* meant *hurt*. *Don't be afraid* meant *Be scared of everything.*

The hopelessness of her situation nearly overcame her. She felt a wave of nausea, and a flood of heat on her forehead. She closed her eyes and leaned against the wall, as if she could stop the room from spinning around her. It will never end.

Ashley opened her eyes and looked wildly at Catherine. Catherine could only hear one-half of the conversation, but she knew it was going poorly. She thrust her index finger down hard on the script, jabbing at the words as hard as she could. "Say it! Say it, Ashley!" she whispered frantically.

Ashley lifted her hand and wiped away the tears. She inhaled deeply. She did not know what she was setting in motion, but she knew it was something terrible.

"Michael," she said slowly, "I've really, really tried. I've tried to say no to you in every way I could. I don't know why you can't understand it. Really, I don't. There's something inside of you I will never understand. So I'm going right now to speak with the only person I could think of who ever managed to get you to do what they tell you to. Someone who might be able to tell me what I need to say to you to make you understand. Someone who will know how I can get you out of my life. Someone I'm absolutely one hundred percent certain will help me get rid of you. Someone I can trust to help me."

Everything she said, she knew, was designed to provoke every ounce of rage he held.

O'Connell didn't reply, and Ashley thought perhaps for the first time that he might be listening to her.

"There's only one person in the world I think you're really scared of. So I'm going to see him tonight."

"What are you saying?" O'Connell asked abruptly. "Who are you talking about? Someone who can help you? No one can help you, Ashley. No one except me."

"You're wrong about that. There is one man."

"Who?" O'Connell's shout leaped across the line.

"Do you know where I am, Michael?"

"No."

"I'm a short ways from your home, Michael. Not the apartment where you live, but the home where you grew up. I'm on my way right now to see your father," Ashley lied as coldly as she could, pausing slightly between each word. "He can help me." And then she hung up. And when the phone started to ring within seconds, she ignored it.

*   *   *

Sally looked up from behind the wheel and felt a current of electricity surge through her entire body. Michael O'Connell, moving furiously quickly, had exited the apartment building. He was jamming his arms into his overcoat as he took the steps in a single leap, then hurried down the block, almost sprinting. Sally reached down and grasped a cheap stopwatch from the passenger-side car seat. She punched the ON button when she saw O'Connell lurch into his car and rapidly pull out, tires complaining loudly.

She picked up the cell phone and hit the speed dial.

When she heard Scott's voice on the other end, she replied, "On his way right now," before hanging up.

Scott would start his own stopwatch.

She could not hesitate. There was so little time. Sally grabbed a backpack that contained several critical items and immediately exited her car, rapidly crossing the street toward O'Connell's apartment. She kept her head lowered and pulled a ski cap down as low as she could. She was dressed in Salvation Army clothes: jeans, worn sneakers, and a man's peacoat. She wore leather gloves over a skintight set of latex surgical gloves.

She told herself, The gun will be there.

There was no backup plan if it wasn't. Only an agreement that they would abort the entire scheme, go back to western Massachusetts, and try to invent something new. She thought it possible that O'Connell might take the gun with him to visit his father. His sudden rage was one variable that she hadn't been able to anticipate. In a way, she hoped he would take the gun with him. Perhaps he would use it in the way they had hoped to; that he would make the mistake that would solve all their problems.

Or, he might take the gun and use it on them.

Or, he might take the gun and use it on Ashley.

There was no plan except flight and panic if this one blew up.

Sally followed the same route that Hope had traveled a few days earlier. Within seconds, she found herself standing outside the apartment. She was alone, key in hand.

No neighbors. The only eyes that watched her belonged to the clutch of cats mewling in the hallway. Did he kill one of your number today? she wondered. She slipped the key into the lock and let herself in as quietly as she could.

Sally told herself not to look around. Not to examine the world where Michael O'Connell lived, because she knew it would only fuel her own terrors. And speed was critical to everything that she'd mapped out. Get the gun, she repeated to herself. Get it now.

She found the closet. She found the corner. She found the boot, with the dirty sock stuffed in the top.

Be there, she whispered to herself.

She lifted the sock, taking note as to how it was placed. Then she leaned in and reached inside the boot.

When her gloved fingers touched the steel of the barrel, she gasped out loud.

Gingerly she pulled the weapon free.

For a second, she hesitated. This is it, she thought. Go forward or go back.

She could see no option other than fear. Taking the gun terrified her. Leaving the gun terrified her.

Feeling as if someone else were guiding her hand, she carefully slipped the gun into a large plastic bag inside her backpack. She left the sock on the floor.

One more thing to do. She walked quickly into the small living room and stared at the battered desk where Michael O'Connell kept his laptop computer plugged in. He'd created a great deal of trouble for all of them while he was seated at that desk, she thought. And now it was time for her to do the same for him. As scared as she was, this next step gave her a nasty sense of satisfaction. She removed the similar-model computer from her backpack, then quickly replaced his computer with the one she had prepared for him. She didn't know whether he would immediately see the difference, but he would, sooner or later. She was pleased with this. She had spent some hours in the past day downloading a variety of pornographic materials, and from extreme right-wing antigovernment websites, filling the computer's memory with as much rage-filled, satanic-inspired, heavy-metal rock music as she could find. When she was persuaded that the computer was laden with enough incriminating items, she had used one of the word files to start writing an angry letter, one that started, *Dear Dad, you son of a bitch,* claiming that O'Connell now knew that he should never have lied on his father's behalf years ago, and that he was now prepared to rectify that one big mistake in his life. He was the only person on this earth capable of dealing out the appropriate kind of justice to pay back his mother's murder. Scott's research of the O'Connell family history had helped her immensely.

Sally had done two other things to the computer. She had unscrewed the back panel, giving her access to the innards of the machine, and had carefully loosened the connection where the main power cord entered the machine, so that it wouldn't start up. Then she had replaced the back entry with one additional detail: she had taken two drops of Super Glue and made sure that one of the screws that held it all together was completely locked in place. O'Connell might know how to fix the machine, she thought, but he wouldn't be able to get into it. A police forensic technician would.

She quickly double-checked its position. It seemed to be just the way he'd left it.

Sally stuffed O'Connell's computer into the backpack, next to the gun.

She looked down at her stopwatch. She was at eleven minutes.

Too slow, too slow, she told herself as she threw the backpack over her shoulder. She could feel the weight of the gun bouncing against her back. She took a deep breath. She would be back, before too long.

The cell phone on the car seat rang urgently. Scott had not been certain that he would get this call, but thought it highly possible, so he was fully prepared when he heard the voice on the other end.

"Hey, this Mr. Jones?"

O'Connell's father sounded rushed, a little unsteady, but excited.

"Smith, here," Scott replied.

"Yeah, right. Mr. Smith. Right. Hey, this is—"

"I know who it is, Mr. O'Connell."

"Well, damned if you weren't right. I just got a call from my kid, like you said I would. He's on his way over here now."

"Now?"

"Yeah. It's about a ninety-minute drive from Boston, except he's gonna be moving fast, so maybe a little less."

"I will make arrangements. Thank you."

"The kid was yelling something about some girl. Sounded real upset. Crazy almost. This got something to do with a girl, Mr. Jones?"

"No. It's about money. And a debt he owes."

"Well, that isn't what *he* thinks."

"What he thinks is irrelevant to our business, Mr. O'Connell, isn't it?"

"Yeah. I suppose so. So what should I do?"

Scott didn't hesitate. He'd expected this question. "Just wait there for him. Hear him out. No matter what he says."

"What're you gonna do?"

"We will be taking some steps, Mr. O'Connell. And you will be earning your true reward."

"What do I do when he decides to leave?"

Scott felt his throat go dry. He could feel a spasm in his chest.

"Step aside and let him go."

Hope sipped a cup of coffee while she waited for Sally. The bitter taste burned her tongue.

She was parked in a strip-mall lot, perhaps a hundred yards from the entrance to a large grocery store. There was plenty of traffic, but she was a little farther away from the entrance than she needed to be, having left perhaps two dozen parking spaces between her and the next car.

When she spotted Sally in her own nondescript rental, moving slowly through the aisles of the mall lot, she stiffened. She placed the coffee in a cup holder and quickly rolled down the window, giving Sally a small wave to get her attention. She waited for Sally to park two aisles away, then walk in her direction. She could see that Sally was looking around nervously, and she seemed pale.

Sally was already shaking her head. "I can't let you do this. It should be my job—"

"We've been over that," Hope said. "And things are in motion now. Making a change might throw it all off."

"I just can't."

Hope inhaled. This was her chance, she thought. She could back out. Refuse. Step back and ask, What the hell are we thinking?

"You can. And you will," Hope replied. "Any chance Ashley has rests with us. Probably any chance we have lies in each of us doing what it is we're capable of. It's as simple as that."

"Are you scared?"

"No," Hope lied.

"We should stop, right now. I think we're out of our minds."

Yes, we probably are, Hope thought.

"If we do not go through with this, and then the worst happens to Ashley, we will never, not for one instant of one day for however many years any of us has left, forgive ourselves for letting it happen. I think I can forgive myself for what I'm about to do. But for standing aside and letting something terrible happen to Ashley, that would be something we would carry to our graves."

Hope took a deep breath. "If we fail to act, and *he* does, we will never rest again."

"I know," Sally said, shaking her head.

"Now the weapon. It's in the backpack?"

"Yes."

"There's not much time, is there?"

Sally looked down at her stopwatch. "I think you're about fifteen minutes behind him. Scott should be moving into position now, as well."

Hope smiled, but shook her head. "You know, when I was growing up, I played so many games against a clock. Time is always a crucial factor. This isn't any different. I have to go. Now. You know it. If we're going to play this game, then failing because we weren't quick enough would be a terrible thing. Just leave, Sally. Do what you're supposed to do. And I will do the same, and maybe, at the end of the day, everything will be okay."

Sally had many things she could say, right at that moment, but she chose none of them. She reached out and squeezed Hope's hand hard and tried to fight back tears. Hope smiled and said, "Get going. There's no time. Not anymore. No more talk. Time to act."

Sally nodded, left the backpack on the floor of the car, stood a few feet back while Hope started up the car, and gave a small wave as she exited the parking lot. It was only a quarter mile to the interstate highway entrance, and Hope knew that she needed to move rapidly, to close the difference in time between her and Michael O'Connell. She made a point of not looking in the rearview mirror until she was well away from the rendezvous location, because she did not want to see Sally standing forlornly behind.

Scott pulled the battered truck into the student parking lot at a large community college some six or seven miles away from the house where Michael O'Connell had grown up. The truck was instantly absorbed into the general mix of vehicles.

After looking around carefully to make sure no one was nearby, he slid out of his clothes and rapidly pulled on an old pair of jeans, a sweatshirt, beaten blue parka, and running shoes. He jammed a navy watch cap over his head and ears, and although the sun was setting, he slid on sunglasses. He grabbed a backpack, made sure his cell phone was in his jacket pocket, and stepped from the truck.

His stopwatch told him that Michael O'Connell had been traveling just shy of seventy minutes. He would be speeding, Scott reminded himself, and wouldn't stop for any reason whatsoever, unless he was pulled over by a policeman, which would only help the situation.

Scott hunched up his shoulders and headed across the parking area. He knew that a bus route was near the entrance to the school. It would take him to within a mile or so of O'Connell's house. He had memorized the schedule, and he had the necessary change for a one-way trip in his right pocket, and the return trip in his left.

A half-dozen students of various ages were waiting underneath the canopy of the bus stop. He fit in; at a community college, you could be a student at nineteen or fifty-nine. He made sure that he didn't make eye contact with any of the waiting people. He told himself to think anonymous thoughts, and perhaps that would make him seem invisible.

When the bus came, he found a seat near the back, alone. He turned and peered out the window at the brown, beaten landscape of the countryside as the bus wheezed along.

Scott was the only person to get off at his stop.

For a second he remained still, alone on the side of the road, as he watched the bus disappear into the evening gloom. Then he set off along the side of the road, walking quickly, wondering precisely what he was hurrying toward, but knowing that time was of the essence.

•

Crime-scene photographs have an otherworldly quality to them. It's a little like trying to watch a movie frame by frame, instead of in continuous action. Eight-by-ten, glossy, full color, they are pieces of a large puzzle.

I tried to absorb each shot, staring at them as I might the pages of a book.

The detective sat across from me, watching my face.

"I'm trying to visualize the scene," I said, "so I can better understand what happened."

"Think of the pictures like lines on a map," he said. "All crime scenes make sense eventually. Although, I got to admit, this one wasn't a picnic."

He reached down and pawed through some of the photographs.

"Look here." He pointed at furniture in disarray, blackened and charred. "Sometimes, it's just a matter of experience. You learn to look beyond the mess, and it tells you something."

I stared down, trying to see with his eyes.

"Exactly what?" I asked.

"There was a hell of a fight. Just one hell of a fight."

43

The Open Door

Scott's survey of the neighborhood several days earlier had told him where to wait.

He knew he had to be inconspicuous; if anyone saw him and made the connection between the figure dressed in dark clothes watching the O'Connell house from the shadows, and the man in the suit and tie who had been asking so many questions, it would create a significant problem. But he needed to be able to see the front of the house, in particular the dirt driveway. He needed to do this without raising the interest of any neighborhood dogs or residents. The spot where he chose to wait was perhaps a little distant, but it accommodated his needs. The battered onetime barn with half its roof caved in was now nothing more than an eyesore. From the corner, where he crouched, he could just see the entranceway to the O'Connell home. He was counting on Michael O'Connell to be driving fast, maybe even squealing

the tires as he came around the last corner, spitting gravel
and dirt when he turned into the place that was once his
home. Make noise, Scott whispered to himself, as if he
could encourage O'Connell's recklessness. Make sure
someone sees your arrival.

Lights were on in the adjacent houses. Scott breathed in
the cold air. He could see an occasional form flit by a window and the ubiquitous glow of television screens.

He lifted his hand and held it in front of his face, to see if
it quivered. Maybe a little, he imagined. But not enough to
make a difference.

Lots of answers this night, he told himself. Any lingering
questions he might have had about who he was, or who Sally
was, or even who Hope was, were destined for responses.

He thought about Hope for an instant. He felt a surge of
near panic.

I don't know her, he thought. I have only the barest grasp
of who she is.

But everything in his life suddenly pivoted on her capabilities.

Scott breathed in hard, tried to imagine what made him
think even for the barest of moments that the three of them
could pull off something that was so alien to their lives. In
that brief second of doubt, he heard the sound of a car rapidly approaching.

By this time, Sally had returned to the Boston area. She
headed to a particularly fancy shopping area in the Brook-
line area. Her first stop was at an ATM machine right outside the collection of stores, where she used her card to
obtain $100 in cash. She made certain, right after the ma-
chine spat out her money, to lift her head so that the security
camera clearly recorded her face. She made a point of placing her time-stamped receipt in her pocket.

Then she walked into the mall and made her way to a
fancy lingerie store.

For a second, she hesitated amid the racks of silk and lace, until she spotted one of the younger saleswomen. The girl was probably no older than Ashley.

Sally approached her. "I wonder if you might help me with something."

"Of course," said the young woman. "What are you looking for?"

"Well, I wanted to get something for my daughter, she's about your height and size. Something special, because she's had a rocky time the last couple of weeks. Broke up with a boyfriend, you know how it is, and I wanted to get her something that would make her feel sexy and beautiful, when some jerk boy has made her feel just the opposite. Do you know what I mean?"

"Yeah. Do I ever," the salesgirl said, nodding. "You're being thoughtful."

"Well, what's a mother to do? And, you know, I'd like to get something nice as a gift for a special friend, as well. Someone I haven't been, well, very nice to lately. Maybe some silk pajamas?"

"I can help with that, too. Do you know the size?"

"Oh, yes. These would be for a very special friend. We share a lot together, out in western Massachusetts, where we live. And things have been very up and down of late, and I'd like to try to make up for that. Flowers are always nice, but when you have a special relationship, sometimes it's better to come up with something that will last longer, don't you think?"

The salesgirl smiled. "Absolutely."

Sally thought the mention of western Massachusetts—with its reputation across the state for accommodating women with partners—would underscore what she needed to get through to the young woman. She followed her toward the racks of expensive undergarments, thinking that she had already said enough so that the young lady would remember her. Sally reminded herself to use a credit card as well, because that would also put her in the location. She thought she might also make a point of speaking to the store manager before she left, just to compliment her on her choice of employees. That was the sort of conversation that was always recalled, if necessary, at a later point.

Sally thought she was on a stage, reciting lines invented by necessity.

"These are some of our nicest things," the salesgirl said.

Sally smiled, as if what she was doing were the most natural thing in the world. "Oh, yes. Indeed."

At more or less the same moment, Catherine and Ashley were in a Whole Foods supermarket less than a mile from Hope and Sally's home, wheeling a cart that they filled with a variety of fancy, organic foodstuffs. The two of them had been silent throughout the shopping expedition.

When they turned down an aisle near the front of the store, Ashley spotted a large display of fresh pumpkins built into a tower, decorated with dried cornstalks. It was a Thanksgiving-oriented theme, with a row of walnuts and cranberries and a paper turkey in the center. She nudged Catherine and gestured toward the display.

Catherine nodded.

The two of them pushed the cart close to the display. Just as they swung next to the edge of the table that served as the foundation, Catherine loudly said, "Oh, damn, we forgot the bean dip."

As she said this, they swung the cart so that the front wheel caught the table leg. The entire display teetered for an instant, and Ashley let out a small yelp and bent forward, as if she were trying to keep it from tumbling, when, in actuality, she grabbed at one of the largest foundation pumpkins.

Within seconds, the entirety had tumbled in a loud crash, dried gourds, Indian corn, scooting across the floor, while yellow pumpkins and squash started rolling about haphazardly.

Catherine gasped. "Oh my goodness!" she shouted loudly.

Within a few seconds, several stock boys and the store manager had descended upon the mess. The stock boys set to repairing the display, while Catherine and Ashley profusely apologized and insisted upon paying for any damage. They were turned down by the manager, but Catherine reached into her pocketbook and withdrew $50, which she thrust toward the manager. "Well, then at least make sure that these nice young men who have cleaned up the mess Ashley and I have made are properly rewarded for their assistance."

"No, no," the manager said. "Really, ma'am, that's not necessary."

"I insist."

"Me, too," said Ashley.

The manager, shaking his head, took the money, to the great relief of the stock boys.

Then Ashley pushed their cart into the checkout line, while Catherine pulled out a bank card to pay for the items. Both women made sure that they, too, turned directly toward the store's security cameras. There was little doubt in their minds that they would be remembered that particular night. That had been Sally's final message to the two of them: *Make certain that you do something public that establishes your presence at home.*

This they had accomplished. They did not know what was happening in some other part of New England at the same time, but they imagined it was something truly dangerous.

Michael O'Connell's car headlights cut across the dim front of his onetime home. The lights reflected off the polished side of his father's truck. A car door slammed loudly and Scott saw O'Connell striding toward the entrance to the kitchen. The urgency in Michael O'Connell's pace seemed to light through the darkness.

O'Connell's anger was critical, Scott thought. Angry people don't notice the small things that could later be important.

He watched as O'Connell grabbed at the side door and disappeared inside. He hadn't been in Scott's sight line for more than a few seconds. But every motion that Scott had seen told him that whatever Ashley had said to him, it had driven him single-mindedly right to the house.

Taking a deep breath, Scott hunched over and ran across the roadway, trying to keep to the shadows. He sprinted as quickly as he could up the drive to where O'Connell had left his car. He ducked down and reached inside the backpack, first removing a pair of surgical gloves, which he slipped on. Then he pulled out a hard-rubber-headed mallet and a box of galvanized roofing nails. He took a single glance toward the back of the house, breathed in sharply, then drove one of the nails into the sidewall of Michael O'Connell's rear tire. He bent down and heard a slow hiss of escaping air.

He then took another couple of the nails and tossed them haphazardly around the driveway.

Moving as stealthily as he could, Scott made his way to the back of the elder O'Connell's truck. He left the rest of the box of nails open in the back. He also left the mallet nearby, just another one of the many tools that cluttered the back of the truck and the carport.

His first task completed, Scott turned and walked steadily back to his hiding spot. As he crossed the street, he heard the first raised voice, electric with anger, coming from inside the house. He wanted to wait, to make out the precise words, but understood he could not.

When he reached the decrepit barn, he pulled out his cell phone and hit the speed dial.

It rang twice before Hope picked it up.

"Are you close?" he asked.

"Less than ten minutes."

"It's happening now. Call me when you stop."

Hope disconnected without a reply. She pushed down on the gas, picking up her pace. They had figured on at least a twenty-minute lag time between Michael O'Connell's arrival and her own. They were pretty close to schedule, she thought. This did not necessarily reassure her.

Inside the house, Michael O'Connell and his father stood a few feet apart, in the bedraggled living room.

"Where is she?" the son shouted, his fists clenched. "Where is she?"

"Where is who?" his father replied.

"Ashley, God damn it! Ashley!" He looked around wildly.

The father laughed mockingly. "Well, this is a hell of a thing. A hell of a thing."

Michael O'Connell pivoted back in the older man's direction. "Is she hiding? Where did you put her?"

The older O'Connell shook his head. "I still don't know what the hell you're talking about. And who the hell is Ashley? Some girl you knew back in high school?"

"No. You know who I'm talking about. She called you. She was supposed to be here. She said she was on her way. Stop screwing with me, or so help me God, I'll . . ."

Michael O'Connell raised his fist in his father's direction.

"Or you'll do what?" the father asked, a sneer filling his voice.

The older man remained calm. He took his time sipping at a bottle of beer, staring across the room at his son, eyes narrowed. Then he deliberately walked over to his lounge chair, slumped into it, took another long pull on the beer bottle, and shrugged. "I just don't know what you're getting at, kid. I don't know anything about this Ashley. You suddenly call me up after being out of touch for years, start screaming about some piece of tail like you're some punk in junior high school, and asking all sorts of questions I got absolutely no idea what the hell it is you're talking about, then you all of a sudden show up like the whole world's on fire, demanding this and that, and I still don't have no clue what's going on. Why don't you pop a beer and calm down and stop acting like a baby."

As he spoke, he gestured toward the kitchen and the refrigerator.

"I don't want a drink. I don't want anything from you. I never have. I just want to know where Ashley is."

The father shrugged again and held his arms wide. "I have absolutely no goddamn idea what and who you're talking about. You ain't making any sense."

Michael O'Connell, steaming, pointed at his father. "You just sit there, old man. Just sit there and don't move. I need to look around."

"I ain't going nowhere. You want to take a look around? Go ahead. Ain't changed much since you moved out."

The son shook his head. "Yeah, it has," he said bitterly as he pushed across the small living room, kicking some newspapers out of the way. "You've gotten a whole lot older and probably drunker, too, and this place is more of a mess."

The father eyed his son as Michael O'Connell swept past him. He didn't move from his seat as the younger man entered the back rooms.

He went first into the room that had been his. His old twin bed was still jammed into a corner, and some of his old AC/DC and Slayer posters were still where he'd tacked them up. A couple of cheap sports trophies, an old football jersey nailed to the wall, some books from high school, and a bright red painting of a Chevrolet Corvette filled the remaining space. He paced across the room and flung the closet door open, half-expecting to see Ashley hiding in the back. But it was empty, except for an old jacket or two that smelled of dust and mildew, and some boxes of out-of-date video games. He kicked at the box, strewing its contents across the floor.

Everything in the room reminded him of something he hated: what he was, and where he came from. He saw that his father had simply thrust many of his mother's old things onto the bed—dresses, pantsuits, overcoats, boots, several painted boxes filled with cheap jewelry, and a photo triptych of the three of them on one of their rare vacations at a camping ground up in Maine. The picture stirred up nothing but terrible memories: too much drinking and arguing and a silent ride home. It was a little as if his father had simply dumped everything that reminded him of his dead wife and his estranged son into the room, kicking it away, where it collected dust and the smells of age.

"Ashley!" he cried out. "Where the hell are you?"

From his seat in the living room, his father shouted, "You

ain't going to find nothing and nobody. But you keep on looking, if that's gonna make you feel better." Then he laughed, a false, phony laugh, provoking even more rage.

Michael O'Connell gritted his teeth and threw open the bathroom door. He pulled aside a shower curtain that was grimy with mildew and mold. A vial of pills perched on the sink corner suddenly tumbled to the floor, spreading tablets across the tile. He bent down and picked up the plastic bottle, saw that it was heart medication, and laughed.

"So, the old ticker giving you some troubles, huh?" he said loudly.

"You leave my things alone," the father shouted in reply.

"Screw you," Michael O'Connell whispered to himself. "I hope whatever is wrong hurts like hell before it kills you."

He tossed the vial back down on the floor, crushed it and all the scattered pills beneath his foot, and left the bathroom. He walked into the other bedroom.

The queen-size bed was unmade, its sheets filthy. The room smelled of cigarettes, beer, and soiled clothing. A plastic laundry basket in one corner was overflowing with sweatshirts and underwear. The bedside table was cluttered with more pill canisters, half-filled liquor bottles, and a broken alarm clock. He emptied all the pills into his hand and stuffed them into his pocket, tossing the canisters back on the bed. That will be a surprise when you need them, he thought.

Michael O'Connell walked to the closet and jerked open the double doors. Half the closet—the half that had once held his mother's things—was empty. The rest was occupied by his father's clothing—all the slacks and dress shirts and sports coats and ties that he never wore.

He left the doors open and went to the sliding glass door that led out to the backyard. He pulled on it, but it was locked. He pressed his face up against the glass, peering into the darkness. He unlocked the door and stepped outside, ignoring the cry from his father behind him: "What the hell you doing now?"

Michael O'Connell peered right and left. No place back there to hide, he thought.

He turned and went back inside. "I'm going to look in the basement," he shouted. "You want to save me some trouble, tell me where she is, old man? Or maybe I'm going to have to ask you the hard way."

"Go ahead. Check the basement. And you know what? You don't scare me much now. You never did."

We'll see about that, Michael O'Connell said to himself.

He went over to the single hallway door that led to the basement. It was a dark, closed-in place, filled with spiderwebs and dust. Once, when he was nine, his father had forced him down there and locked the door. His mother had been out and he'd done something to anger the old man. After whacking him on the side of the head, he'd thrust the child down the stairs and left him in the dark for an hour. Michael O'Connell stood at the top of the stairs and thought that what he'd hated the most about his father and his mother was that no matter how many times they had shouted and screamed and traded punches, it only seemed to link them more tightly. Everything that should have driven them apart had actually cemented their relationship.

"Ashley!" he shouted. "You down there?"

A single overhead bulb threw a little light in the corners. He peered through each shadow, searching for her.

The room was empty.

He could feel anger building in his chest, like heat racing down his arms into clenched fists. He turned and went back to the small living room, where his father waited for him.

"She was here, wasn't she?" Michael O'Connell asked. "Earlier. To talk to you. I just didn't get here in time, and then she told you to lie to me, right?"

The older man shrugged. "You still not making any sense."

"Tell me the truth."

"I am telling you the truth. I don't have any idea what you're talking about."

"If you don't tell me what happened, what she told you

when she got here, where she went, I will hurt you, old man. I am not joking about this. I can do it and I will do it, and trust me, I will deliver a world of pain, and I won't give a damn about you any more than I ever have. So, tell me, when she called on you, what did you tell her?"

"You're either crazier than I remember or stupider. Right now, I can't tell which." The old man lifted his bottle to his lips and leaned back in his seat.

Michael O'Connell stepped forward and in a single violent swipe knocked the beer bottle from his father's hand. It slammed against the wall, breaking into pieces. The father barely reacted, although his eyes lingered on the broken bottle, before he turned back and stared at his son.

"It was always a question, wasn't it? Which one of us was gonna grow up meaner?"

"Screw you, old man. Tell me what I want to know."

"Get me another beer first."

Michael O'Connell reached down and grasped his father by the shirt, half-pulling him out of his seat. In the same moment, the father's right hand shot out and seized the son around the collar, twisting his sweater so that it choked him. Their faces were only inches apart, their eyes locked together. Then O'Connell thrust his father back, and the old man released his son.

Michael O'Connell walked over to the television set. He stared at it for an instant.

"This how you spend your nights? Getting drunk and watching the tube?"

The father didn't answer.

"Too much of the old idiot box is bad for you. Didn't you know that?"

Michael O'Connell waited for a second, so that the mocking words would settle in, then he drew back his foot and delivered a karate-style kick to the television, sending it crashing down, the screen shattering.

"Bastard. You're gonna pay for that."

"Am I? What else do I have to break to get you to tell me what happened when she called you? How long was she here? What did she promise you? What did you tell her you would do?"

Before his father could reply, he walked over to a book-case and swept a shelf of knickknacks and photographs to the floor.

"That was just some of your mother's leftovers. Don't mean nothing to me."

"You want me to look around until I find something that does? What did she tell you?"

"Kid," the old man said through tightly pursed lips, "whatever it is this bit of tail is to you, I don't know. And what she's got you into, I don't know either. You in some kind of trouble? Money trouble?"

Michael O'Connell looked at his father. "What are you talking about?"

"Who's looking for you, kid? Because I think they're gonna find you just about any minute, and when they do, they aren't gonna be nice about it. But maybe you know that already."

"All right," Michael O'Connell said slowly. "Last chance before I come over there and start to pay you back for all the times you beat me when I was a kid. Did a girl named Ashley call you today? Did she say she wanted your help in breaking up with me? Did she say she was on her way to talk to you?"

The older man continued to eye his son through narrow, rage-filled eyes. But through the sheet of fury that seemed to be just a second or two away from breaking free, he managed to clench his lips and spit out, "No. No, God damn it. No Ashley. No girl. No nothing like what you just said. And that's the goddamn truth, whether you want to believe it or not."

"You're lying. You old bastard, you're lying."

The old man shook his head and laughed, which infuri-ated Michael O'Connell even more. He felt as if he were on a ledge, trying to keep his balance. What he wanted, more than anything else, was to feel his fists smashing against the old man's face. But he took a deep breath and told himself that he still needed to know what was happening, because there was some reason he'd been called here. He just couldn't see what it was.

"She said . . ."

"I don't know what she said. But Miss whoever-the-hell-she-is hasn't called here or shown up at the side door."

Michael O'Connell took a step back. "I don't . . ." His mind was rapidly churning. He could not see why Ashley would send him on a trip to his home unless she had something in mind. What she expected to gain seemed just beyond his reach.

"Who you in trouble with?" the old man asked again.

"Nobody. What do you mean?" Michael spat back, angry at having the train of his thoughts interrupted.

"What is it? Drugs? You pull some kind of low-rent robbery with some guys and then stiff them on the cut? What are you doing that would have guys with money looking for you? You steal something from them?"

"I've got no idea what you're talking about." He was confused by the smug look on his father's face. He realized, in that second, that the old man should be a lot angrier about the shattered television set. The reason he's not angry is because he knows a new one is heading his way, Michael O'Connell thought.

"Who've you been fucking around with, kid? Because there's someone real pissed with you."

"Who told you that?"

The older man shrugged. "I ain't saying. I just know."

Michael O'Connell straightened up. Nothing makes sense, he thought. Or maybe it does.

"Old man, I will hurt you. You should understand that. You are old and weak and I will cause you great pain. Now tell me what you're talking about!" he shouted across the room. He took two quick strides, so that he was again looming over his father, who remained in his chair, grinning, wondering whether he'd managed to keep his son in the house long enough for the mysterious Mr. Smith to make the correct arrangements, whatever they might be.

*   *   *

Less than a half mile away from the O'Connell house, on an adjacent street, Hope spotted several beaten old cars and pickup trucks sporting Harley-Davidson wings on stickers, all pulled to the side of the roadway, parked haphazardly. She could see some lights coming from a worn and battered ranch-style home set back from the street and could hear loud voices and hard-rock music. She realized someone was having some sort of get-together. Beer and pizza, she guessed, with a methamphetamine dessert. She stopped her rental car a few feet behind one of the parked cars, so she appeared to be just another visitor.

As quickly as she could, she pulled on the black coveralls that Sally had purchased. She jammed a navy blue balaclava-style face mask and hat into her pocket. Then she slipped on surgical gloves, and a pair of leather gloves over those. She wrapped several strands of black electrician's tape around her wrists and her ankles, so that no flesh was exposed between the coveralls and her gloves and shoes.

She threw the backpack with the gun over her shoulder and started to jog in the direction of the O'Connell house, her outfit helping her to blend into the night. She had the cell phone in her hand, and she dialed Scott.

"Okay. I'm here. A couple of hundred yards away. What am I looking for?"

"The boy drives a five-year-old red Toyota, with Massachusetts plates," Scott said. "The father has a black pickup truck, which is parked halfway beneath a carport. The only exterior light is by the side door. That is your entry point."

"Are they still—"

"Yes. I could hear some things breaking inside."

"Anyone else?"

"Not that I can see."

"Where should I—"

"By the carport. On the right side. It's cluttered with all sorts of tools and engine parts. You will be able to see them, but not be seen."

"Okay," Hope said. "Keep an eye out. I'll talk to you afterwards."

Scott hung up. He leaned against the side of the old, ramshackle barn and watched. There was very little light, he thought. No streetlamps in this rural section of the world. As long as Hope clung to the shadows, she would be fine.

Then he stopped, because the notion that *she would be fine* made absolutely no sense whatsoever. None of them were going to be fine, he realized. Except maybe Ashley, and she was the whole reason they were doing what they were doing.

Scott wondered, if he was so crippled and scared by the night that was unfolding, how did Hope, who was the actual performer on the stage the three of them had created, manage to control her doubts?

Running crouched over at the waist, more like some feral animal than the athlete she had once been, Hope cut across the side yard and slid herself up against the back wall of the carport. She pivoted about, lowered herself to the ground, and took a moment to get her bearings. The closest houses were all at least thirty or forty yards away, across the street.

She rolled her head back against the wall of the carport and shut her eyes.

Hope tried to do some sort of odd inventory of her emotions, as if she might be able to find the one that would power her through the next few minutes. She pictured Nameless lying dead in her arms and then, in her mind's eye, substituted Ashley for her dog.

This toughened her.

She managed to find a little more iron in the thought that O'Connell would come after Catherine, as well. She knew her mother would fight hard, but that wasn't a fight she thought the older woman could win.

She added up all the threats to their lives and did the equation. She tried to subtract doubt and uncertainty from the sum. Everything that had seemed so clear-cut and obvious when the three of them were sitting in their comfortable living room now seemed perverse, wrong, and wildly impossible. She was sweating hard, and she knew her hands were shaking.

Who am I? she suddenly asked herself.

There was a moment, she remembered, shortly after her father had died, that she had truly been scared. It wasn't so much the fear of being left behind; it was instead a fear of not being able to live up to what he'd wanted her to be. She tried to imagine that her dead father would have wanted her to be precisely in the position she was, with her head up against a wall, the night surrounding her, the damp ground seeping through her coveralls. He would understand taking a chance to protect others. He always wanted her to take charge, whether it was for good or for bad. *You're the captain,* she could hear his voice in the darkness.

Hope thought that in that moment she was truly on the verge of madness.

Clear your mind, she told herself.

She pulled the balaclava down over her head, so that her face was obscured.

She reached inside the backpack and removed the gun from its plastic bag.

She slid her finger around the trigger. It was the first time in her entire life that she'd actually held a handgun. She wished she had more experience with weapons, but was surprised to feel a certain electricity flowing from the steel handle into her hand, an unfamiliar, almost intoxicating power.

Hope scrambled to the edge of the carport and listened to angry voices coming from inside the home as she waited for the right moment to arrive.

"I need to know what's going on," Michael O'Connell burst out. Every word he spoke was laden with years of hatred for the man smugly rocking in his lounge chair across from him, and with all the weight of his love for Ashley. He could feel his heart racing; it nearly made him dizzy with rage.

"What's going on? You're here, shouting about some girl, when you ought to be a whole lot more worried about who-ever it is that you've made into an enemy," his father said, waving his hand in the air.

"I don't know what you're talking about. I haven't burnt anyone."

The old man shrugged infuriatingly. Michael O'Connell took a step forward, fists clenched, and the older man finally pushed himself out of the chair, squaring his shoulders to his son. "You think you've gotten old enough and strong enough to take me on?"

"I don't think you want to ask that question, old man. You're looking a little paunchy and out of shape. That fake back injury of yours might start acting up for real. What you were good at was beating up on women and kids, and that was a real long time ago. I'm not a kid anymore. You might think hard about that."

The chill in his voice caused the older man to stop. He puffed out his chest and shook his head.

"I never had any trouble handling you back then. You may think you're all grown up, but I'm still a whole lot more trouble than you want to try to take on. I can still crush you."

"You were a weakling then, you're a weakling now. Mom used to hold her own against you. In fact, if she wasn't drunk, you couldn't even have beaten her. That's how it re-ally happened, isn't it? The night she died? She was too drunk to fight back, and you saw your opportunity and that's when you killed her."

The older man snarled.

"I should never have lied for you. I should have told the cops the truth all along," Michael O'Connell said bitterly.

"Don't be pushing things," the father replied coldly. "Don't be going places where you got no right to go."

As their words dropped in volume and increased in hatred, the two men had closed to within a few feet of each other, like dogs in that instant before growls turn into a fight.

"You think you could kill me and get away with it, like you did her? I don't think so, old man."

The father suddenly jerked forward and slapped his son hard across the face. The sound of the blow echoed in the small room.

Michael O'Connell grinned savagely. He shot out his right arm and seized his father by the throat. Closing his hand around the old man's windpipe was instantly satisfying. As he could feel muscles contract, and tendons start to crush beneath his grip, he felt a passion that almost overwhelmed him. Panicked, the older man grabbed at his son's wrist, digging his fingernails into the flesh, trying to pull free, while he felt the breath quickly choke out of him. As his father's face turned a deeper red, Michael O'Connell suddenly pushed him back, releasing him. The older man slammed against a coffee table, spilling its contents. He grabbed at the arm of the lounge chair as he fell to the ground, pulling it over, and lay back, gasping on the floor, his eyes wide with surprise. His son laughed and spat at the older man.

"Stay there, old man. Stay there forever. But hear me on this: if you ever get a call from Ashley, or anyone connected to Ashley, and you promise them you will help them in any way, I will come back here and kill you. First I will hurt you, so that you will be begging for me to stop. And then I will kill you. Do you understand that? I'd like to kill everything in my past. It would make me feel a whole lot better. And the place I'd like the most to start with is you."

The father remained on the floor, frozen. The son saw fear spread throughout the old man's eyes and, for the first time that night, thought that the drive north had been worthwhile.

"You need to hope that you never see me again, you pathetic old man. Because the next time, you will end up in a box in a hole in the ground, which is where you belong. Where you've belonged for years."

Michael O'Connell turned and, without a single glance back, went out the side door.

The cool night air hit him like another bad memory, but all

he could think of was what game Ashley had invented, and why she had thought that his father could help her. Someone had been lying.

He slid behind the wheel of his car, fired up the engine, and decided he needed the answer to those questions immediately.

Hope had listened to the argument, then the clatter of a short fight. She gripped the automatic in her hand tightly, holding her breath when she saw Michael O'Connell lurch through the door and stride to his car only a few feet away from where she was hidden. She waited for him to back down out of the driveway, then accelerate rapidly into the night.

The next moment, she knew, was critical.

Sally had told her, *Do not delay. Not for one second. As soon as he exits, you must enter.*

She rose up.

Hope could hear Sally's voice in her ear.

Do not hesitate. Do not wait. Go straight inside. Don't say a word. Just pull the trigger. Don't look back. Leave.

Hope took a single deep breath and emerged from behind the carport. She rapidly crossed through the small arc of light to the side door. She looked down and saw her left hand close on the door handle and thrust herself into the house.

Hope was in the kitchen, but she could see through the entryway into the living room, just as Scott had described. She stood there, nearly frozen, and watched Michael O'Connell's father begin to pick himself up off the floor.

He turned toward her. He did not look surprised.

"Mr. Jones send you?" he asked as he straightened himself up, dusting himself off. "You missed the punk by less than a minute. That was his car peeling out of here."

Hope lifted the weapon and assumed a firing stance.

The older O'Connell looked confused.

"Hey," he said sharply. "It's the goddamn kid you want, not me."

Everything in the world was suddenly exaggerated. Every color was brighter, every sound louder, every smell more pungent. Hope's breathing seemed to echo in her ears, a cascade of rushing noise. She tried not to think about what she was doing.

Aiming directly at the old man's chest, she pulled the trigger.

And nothing happened.

·

The detective carried a large box with a broken red-tape seal over to his desk. He dropped it in the middle with a thudding sound, then leaned forward with a small grin and asked me, "You know how kids are on Christmas morning? When they stare at all those packages wrapped up underneath a tree?"

"Sure. But what . . ."

"Collecting evidence is a little like all those presents. The kids always think that the biggest present will be the best, but often it isn't. It's the less-significant, less-flashy box that really holds the most valuable gift. In a sense, that's what happens with us. It might be the smallest thing that becomes the biggest, when you finally get to trial. So, when you arrive at a crime scene and pick up this or that, or when you execute a search warrant, you need to consider all the pieces."

"And in this case?"

The detective grinned. He pulled out a handgun, encased in a plastic bag, with another red evidence seal closing it. He handed me the weapon, and I peered at it through the transparent shield. I could see the residue of fingerprint dust on the handle and the barrel.

"Be careful," he said. "I don't think that sucker's loaded, but the clip is in the handle, so I can't be sure." He smiled. "You'd be surprised how many near-fatal accidents occur in property rooms when people start waving around guns that are supposed to be unloaded."

I held the weapon cautiously. "Doesn't look like much."

The detective nodded. "Piece-of-shit weapon," he said with

a small shake of his head. "About as cheap as you can find. Manufactured by some company in Ohio that machine-stamps out each part of the weapon and then screws it together, sticks it in a box, and ships it off to some disreputable dealer. A good gun shop would never carry crap like this. And no real professional would ever use it."

"Still, it works."

"Sort of. Twenty-five automatic. Small caliber. Lightweight. Professional killers—and we don't get a whole lot of those around here as you might imagine—like twenty-two- and twenty-five-caliber weapons, because they're easy to fit a homemade silencer to and, when loaded with a magnum bullet, do the job clean and nice. But they'd never use a throwaway gun like this. Too unreliable. It's not easy to handle, the safety and the action both jam, and unless it's fired at extremely close range, it's not very accurate. And it doesn't pack much punch, either. Wouldn't stop a moderately sized pit bull or rapist, unless you managed to get 'em in the ticker or some other fatal spot with the first shot."

He smiled again as I turned the weapon over in my hands.

"Or you fired it real, and I mean real, close. Like lover close."

Again he grinned.

"And, generally speaking, it isn't wise to get that near the person you're trying to kill."

I nodded, and the detective plumped back down in his seat.

"See, learn something new every day."

I held the weapon up again, holding it to the light, as if it could tell me something.

"Of course," the detective said, "now that I've told you how damn bad that weapon is, on the other hand, it seemed to do the trick. Sort of."

44

Making Choices

Hope realized instantly that she had made a mistake.

Her mind racing with the wildest of possibilities, she placed her thumb against the safety switch and pushed it down, making certain it was in the firing position. She lifted her gloved left hand and fumbled with the action to push a round into the firing chamber—all of which she should have had the sense to do before she'd entered the house. The top snatched back, cocking the weapon. She had a terrible thought that neither she nor Sally had even bothered to check if the gun was properly loaded.

In that second, she did not know whether to flee or continue.

O'Connell's father, his hands starting to rise in a gesture of surrender, suddenly let loose an immense bellow and threw himself across the room toward Hope.

As she raised the gun into a firing position for the second time, he closed the distance between them. As she pulled the trigger, he slammed into her.

She could feel the gun buck in her hand, heard a snapping sound and a thud, and then she spun backward, slamming into the kitchen table, upending it with a crash, sending empty liquor bottles flying across the room, shattering against walls and cabinets. Hope was knocked to the floor, the breath almost smashed out of her. O'Connell's father, growling visceral, terrifying noises, fell on top of her. He was clawing at her face mask, trying to get his fingers around her throat, punching her wildly.

If her first shot had hit him, she could not tell. She tried desperately to lift the weapon, to fire again, but O'Connell's hand suddenly clasped down viselike on her own, and he tried to force the weapon up into the air.

Hope kicked out, jabbing her knee into his groin, and she felt him gasp in pain, but not so much that his assault diminished. He was stronger than her, she could sense this immediately, and he was trying to bend the weapon back, so that its barrel would rest against her chest, not his. At the same time, he continued to pound her with his free hand, flailing away. Most of the blows missed, but enough landed so that sheets of red pain appeared behind her eyes.

Again she kicked, and this time the force of her leg slammed both of them back, sending more debris flying around the room. A wastebasket tumbled, spreading pungent used coffee grounds and empty egg shells across the floor. She could hear more glass breaking.

O'Connell's father was a veteran of bar fights and knew that most battles are won in the first few blows. He was wounded and could feel pain shooting through his body, but he was able to ignore it, fighting hard. Far more than Hope, he sensed deep within him that this fight against the hooded, anonymous foe was the most important of his life. If he did not win, he would die. He pushed on the weapon, trying to force it down against his assailant's body. It was not lost on him that he'd done almost exactly the same thing once many years earlier, when he'd battled with his drunken wife.

Hope was well beyond panic. Never in her life had she felt the sort of muscle that was pushing at her. Adrenaline screamed in her ears, and she grasped at air, trying to find the strength to win. With an immense thrust, she slammed O'Connell's father sideways, and the two of them half-rolled against a counter. Dishes and silverware cascaded around them. The movement seemed to achieve something; O'Connell's father bellowed with pain, and Hope caught a glimpse of red blood streaking against the white paint of the cabinet. Her first shot had caught him in the muscle and bone of his shoulder, and despite shredded tissues and cracked bone, he was fighting through the pain.

He grasped at the weapon with both hands, and Hope suddenly slammed him with her free arm, smashing his head against the cabinet. She could see his teeth bared, his face a mask of anger and terror. She raised her knee again, and again it found his groin. She pushed back and smashed at his jaw with her free hand. He was reeling, staggered by the blow, but still she remained pinned beneath him.

She pounded away with her left arm, keeping a fierce grip on the gun, demanding with every muscle she had to make certain that it did not turn and point at her.

And in that second, she suddenly felt the pressure on her gun hand diminish. She imagined that perhaps she was winning, and then, she gasped as an immense shock of pain creased through her entire body. Her eyes rolled back, and she nearly passed out. The blackness that threatened to overtake her spun her about dizzily.

O'Connell's father had grasped a kitchen knife out of the debris that had tumbled about them. Holding her hand with the gun away with one arm, he had plunged the knife into Hope's side, searching for her heart. He bent all his weight to this task.

Hope could feel the tip of the blade slicing into her. Her only thought was *This is it. Live or die.*

She reached across with her left hand and grabbed at the gun, jerking it toward O'Connell's father's face as it contorted with its own combination of pain and rage. She jabbed it up under his chin, just as the knife blade seemed to carve into her soul, and yanked on the trigger.

Scott wanted to glance down at the luminescent face of his watch, but didn't dare take his eyes off the carport and the side door to the O'Connell house. Under his breath, he was counting the seconds since he'd seen Hope's dark figure disappear inside.

It was taking far too long.

He took a step away from his hiding place, then shrank back, uncertain what to do. He could feel his heart pounding away. A part of him was screaming that everything had gone wrong, everything was messed up, that he needed to get away, right at that moment, right then, before he was sucked any further into some disastrous whirlpool of events. Fear, like a riptide, threatened to drown him.

His throat was dry. His lips were parched. The night seemed to be choking him, and he grabbed at his sweatshirt collar.

He told himself to leave right then, to get away, that whatever had happened, he needed to flee.

But he did not. Instead, he remained frozen. His eyes penetrated the dark. His ears were sharpened to sound. He glanced right, then left, and saw no one.

There are moments in life when one knows one must do *something,* but each option seems more dangerous than the next, and every choice seems to herald despair. Whatever was happening, Scott knew that somehow, in some oblique way, Ashley's life might depend upon what he did in the next few seconds.

Maybe all their lives.

And, while desperate to give in to the panic growing within him, Scott took a deep breath and, trying hard to clear his head of all thoughts, considerations, possibilities, and chances, started to run fast toward the house.

Hope wanted to scream, opened her mouth in terror, but did not. No high-pitched fear emerged, just a raspy, weakened noise of harsh breath.

Her second shot had caught O'Connell's father directly beneath the chin, crashing upward through his mouth, shattering teeth and shredding tongue and gums, and finally lodging deep in his brain, killing him almost instantly. The momentum of the shot had pitched him back, almost lifting him off her, then he had crashed down on top of her, so that she was almost pinned beneath his body, suffocating under the weight of his chest.

His hand still gripped the knife blade, but the force driving it into her body had evaporated. She almost blacked out with a sudden surge of pain. It sent streaks of fire through her side, into her lungs and heart, and sheets of black agony to her head. She was abruptly exhausted, and a part of her urged her to close her eyes, to go to sleep, right there, at that moment. But a force of will kicked in, and she gathered herself to push the dead man's body off her. She tried once, but she didn't have the strength. She pushed a second time, and he seemed to tumble a few inches. She pushed a third time. It was like trying to move a boulder, embedded in the earth.

She heard the door open, but could not see who it was.

Again she fought off unconsciousness, gasping for air.

"Jesus Christ!"

The voice seemed familiar. She groaned.

Suddenly, magically, the weight of O'Connell's father holding her down, as if she were underneath an ocean wave, disappeared, and she surfaced. The shape that had once been O'Connell's father slumped to the linoleum floor next to her.

"Hope! Jesus!" she could hear her name being whispered, and she gathered herself to turn toward the sound.

"Hello, Scott." She managed a little smile through the pain. "I had some trouble."

"No shit. We've got to get you out of here."

She nodded and struggled to sit up. The knife still protruded from her side. Scott started to reach for it, but she shook her head. "Don't touch it," she insisted.

He nodded. "Okay."

He half-lifted her up, and Hope pushed herself to her feet. The movement increased her dizziness, but she overcame the sensation. Gritting her teeth and leaning on Scott, she stepped over O'Connell's father's body. "I need help." She draped an arm around his shoulder, and he started to steer her to the door. "The gun," she whispered. "The gun, we can't leave it."

Scott looked around and saw the weapon on the floor. He picked it up and removed Hope's backpack. He dropped the gun back into the plastic bag, sealed it, then threw the backpack over his free shoulder. "Let's get outside," he said.

They stumbled through the door, and Scott helped Hope to the dark side of the carport. He propped her up against the wall. "I've got to think."

She nodded, drinking in the cold air. It helped to clear her head, and just exiting the close confines of death strengthened her. She pushed herself up a bit. "I can move."

Scott was someplace between horror, panic, and determination. He understood he had to think clearly and efficiently. He lifted Hope's face mask and could see why Sally had fallen in love with her. It was as if the pain of what she had done had etched itself on her face in the bravest of strokes. In that second, he realized that what she had done had been as much for him as it had been for Sally and Ashley.

"I must have bled, on the floor. If the police . . ."

Scott nodded. He thought hard, then knew what he had to do.

"Wait here. Can you manage?"

"I'm okay," Hope said, although she clearly was not. "I'm hurt. Not injured," she said, using an old athletic cliché. If you are merely hurt, you can still play. If you are injured, you cannot.

"I'll be right back."

Scott ducked around the corner of the carport and crouched down, hiding as best he could as he surveyed the mess of machine parts, stray tools, empty paint cans, and stacks of roofing shingles. He knew that somewhere within a few feet was what he needed, but was unsure whether he would be able to spot it among the weak shadows.

Be lucky, he whispered to himself.

Then he saw what he needed. It was a red plastic container.

Please, he spoke to himself. Don't be empty.

He picked up the container, shook it, and could feel about a third of the container sloshing liquid back and forth. He unscrewed the top and immediately smelled the unmistakable odor of old gasoline.

Scott bent over and, as quickly as he could, slipped from the carport, into the light and through the door.

For an instant, he wanted to be sick, and he fought off a

sudden surge of nausea. The first time he'd entered the house that night, he had been completely focused on Hope, and extricating her from the scene of her fight. This time he was alone with O'Connell's father's body, and for the first time he looked down and saw the gore, the man's gargoyle-like, ravaged face. He gasped and told himself to remain calm, which was useless. He could feel his heart pounding, and everything around him seemed somehow illuminated. The mess from the fight and the blood seemed to glow as if painted with vibrant colors. He thought that violent death made everything brighter, not darker.

Scott was stealing every breath he could, moving unsteadily.

He looked over to the spot where he'd found her pinned beneath O'Connell's father, where there was likely to be blood, and he saw red droplets marring the floor. He sloshed some of the gasoline in that spot. Then he poured the remainder on the father's shirt and slacks. He looked around, saw a dish towel, and dipped it into the mixture of blood and gas on the man's chest. He stuck this in his pocket.

Again a wave of nausea threatened him, and he reached out to steady himself, then stopped. Every second he was inside the murder place, he thought, the likelihood of leaving some telltale clue increased. He stood up, dropped the container into the pools of gasoline, and stepped to the stove. There were matches on the counter next to the gas burners.

He stepped close to the door, lit the entire box, and tossed it onto O'Connell's father's chest.

The gasoline exploded into flame. For a second, Scott remained frozen, watching the fire start to spread, then he spun about and ducked back into the night.

He found Hope leaning against the carport. She had her gloved hand wrapped around the knife handle, still protruding from her side. "You've got to be able to move," he said.

"I can walk." Her words seemed raspy.

The two of them clung to the shadows until they reached the street. Scott slid his arm under Hope, so that she could lean against him, and they stepped slowly through the darkness. She was steering him toward her car. Neither looked back at the O'Connell house. Scott prayed that the fire he'd set would take some time to get going, that it would be several minutes before anyone in any of the adjacent homes spotted the flames.

"Are you okay?" he whispered.

"I can make it," Hope replied, leaning against him. The night air had helped to clear her thoughts, and she was controlling the hurt, although every step she took sent a spike of electric pain through her. She ricocheted between confidence and strength and despair and weakness. She knew that no matter how Sally had plotted the remainder of the night, it wasn't going to happen as planned. The blood she could sense pulsing through the wound told her that.

"Keep going," Scott urged.

"Just a couple out for a brisk night stroll," Hope said, joking through the pain. "Left at the corner, and the car should be just ahead, halfway down the street."

Each step seemed slower than the last. Scott didn't know what he would do if a car came along, or if someone came outside and eyed them. In the distance he could hear dogs barking. As they staggered around the corner, looking like a couple that had belted down too much at dinner, he saw her car. The party going on in the house nearby had gotten a bit louder.

Hope managed to stiffen herself. She felt as if she were using every muscle in her body, taking every ounce of strength she had.

"Get me behind the wheel." She tried to speak with the authority that would leave nothing to debate.

"You can't drive. You need a doctor and a hospital."

"Yeah. But not here. Not anywhere close to here."

Hope was calculating, trying to remain clearheaded, although the pain made it difficult. "The goddamn license plates," she said. "The ones that were such a big deal to change. Change 'em back."

Scott was confused. He didn't see why this was a priority

when stanching the wound in her side and getting her to an emergency room seemed far more critical. "Look—" he started.

"Just do it!"

He steered her into the driver's seat as she'd requested. He grabbed at the bag with the plates and, with a frown and deep breath, a single glance at the house where the party was, ducked to the front and back of the car as rapidly as he could, putting the proper Massachusetts plates on the rental car. He took the others and threw them into the backpack along with the gun, and he stuffed the dish towel marred with gasoline and blood into the plastic bag alongside the weapon.

He went back to the driver's side. Hope had put the key into the ignition, and he could see her face contort with pain as she stripped the tape from her ankles and pulled the tape and the two sets of gloves from her hands. She handed these and her balaclava to Scott. He stood by helplessly as she pulled the knife blade out of her body.

"Jesus!" she gasped. Her head lolled back, and she nearly passed out. But as quickly as this wave came, another arrived. The pain kept her alert. She breathed in sharply.

"I've got to get you to a hospital."

"I'll get there myself. You've got too much to do." She gestured at the knife. "I'll keep that." She dropped it to the floor of the car and pushed it out of sight.

"I could get rid of it," Scott said.

It was hard for Hope to think completely straight, but she shook her head. "Get rid of that stuff, and the plates, somewhere where they won't be connected to this car." She was trying hard to remember everything, trying hard to be organized, but the pain prevented true calm, reasoned thinking. She wished Sally were here. Sally would see most of the angles, all of the details. It was what she was good at, Hope thought. Instead she turned to Scott and tried to look at him as if he were somehow a part of Sally, which, she imagined, he once was.

"Okay," she said. "We're back following the plan. I'm

okay to drive. You do what you're supposed to." She gestured toward the backpack with the gun.

"I can't leave you. Sally would never forgive me."

"She won't have a chance to forgive you if you don't. We're way behind schedule. What you have to do now is crucial."

"Are you sure?"

"Yes," Hope said, although she knew this was a lie. She wasn't sure about anything. "Go. Go now."

"What should I tell Sally?"

Hope paused. A dozen thoughts went through her head, but she said only, "Just tell her I'll be okay. I'll speak to her later."

"Are you sure?" He glanced down to where the knife handle had protruded from her side. He could see where the black mechanic's jumpsuit was stained with blood.

"It's not nearly as bad as it looks," Hope lied again. "Just go, before we lose our opportunity."

The idea that, after everything she'd done, they might fail almost crushed her. She waved her hand toward Scott.

"Go."

"Okay," he replied, standing up, stepping back.

"Oh, Scott."

"Yes?"

"Thanks for coming to help."

He nodded. "You did all the hard work." He closed the driver's-side door and watched as Hope bent to the wheel and started the car. He stepped back, and she pulled away steadily. He continued to watch as she drove down the road, standing alone in the darkness until the red rear lights disappeared in the ink that enveloped him. Then he flung the backpack over his back and started to jog toward the bus route. He was late, he knew, and it might be disastrous, but he still had to play out the hand as Sally had dealt it. He was unsure what Hope was going to accomplish the remainder of that night, but most of their luck needed to ride with her. Then he realized that that might be wrong. Much luck was still needed in other locations that night.

*   *   *

Sally was parked on the edge of a strip-mall lot, waiting for Scott. She glanced down at her watch, then checked the stopwatch, picked up the cell phone, and thought hard about calling, but decided against it. She was perhaps forty-five minutes out of Boston, close to the interstate, a place selected for the same reasons she had selected the spot where she had met with Hope to transfer the gun, but different, in that it would provide Scott easy access to the route back to western Massachusetts.

She leaned her head back against the seat headrest and closed her eyes. She would not allow herself the fear of going through all the possible disasters that might have taken place that night. They were amateurs at the art of killing, she thought. They might each have had some expertise that made the planning, organization, and conceptualizing of death seem manageable and feasible, but when it came down to the actual execution of the plan, they were the rankest of novices. In a way, when she had designed the machinations of that night, she had thought that their inexperience would be their strongest suit. Experts would not have done what they did. The plan was too erratic, too haphazard, and far too dependent on each person managing certain tasks efficiently. That was the strength of the whole idea, she thought.

Educated people would not be doing what they were doing. Drug addicts or violent people might work their way up the ladder of criminality to murder. That was logical.

She squeezed her eyes shut.

Perhaps the idea that they could function in a landscape of murder was a fantasy all along. She immediately envisioned Scott and Hope in handcuffs, surrounded by policemen. O'-Connell's father would be giving a statement, and she would be next, as soon as either Scott or Hope broke down under questioning.

And Ashley, even with Catherine at her side, would be facing a future of Michael O'Connell alone.

She opened her eyes and surveyed the green-tinged light of the parking lot.

No sign of Scott.

Hope should be on her way home.

Michael O'Connell should be on the side of the road either trying to repair his flat or waiting for a tow truck. He should be angry and cursing and wondering what the hell was going on. The one thing he wouldn't be expecting was that he was caught up in a performance in which he was a critical player. Sally smiled. She thought that the part that was most likely to have been performed without dropping a line, or taking a misstep, had been his, and he did not even know it. He was being choked and he wasn't even aware that he was being neutralized, removed from Ashley's life right at that moment.

She clenched her fist and imagined, *We've got you, you bastard.*

She breathed out slowly. Maybe.

Scott should be pulling in. Any second.

She pounded on her steering wheel in frustration and despair.

"Where the hell are you?" she whispered fervently, sweeping the area with her eyes again. "Come on, Scott. Get here!"

She reached for the cell phone again, then put it down. Waiting, she understood, was the second-hardest thing. The hardest thing was trusting someone she had once told herself she loved, had left behind, cheated on, and then divorced. In truth, the only thing that maintained any kind of civility between her and her ex-husband was Ashley. That, she guessed, would be enough to get them through the night.

Then her thoughts turned to Hope. She shook her head and felt tears in her eyes. She knew she could trust her completely, though she had done precious little over the past months to deserve that trust. She felt as if she were floating in the air of uncertainty.

"Come on!" she whispered again, as if words alone could make things happen.

*   *   *

A large green Dumpster was located in a far corner of the parking lot where Scott had left his truck. To his immense relief, it was nearly full, not only with plastic bags jammed with debris, but also stray bottles and cans, and uncollected trash. He seized one of the bags that seemed only partway filled, undid the fastener at the top, and thrust the stolen plates and the rest of the leftovers of tape and gloves deep inside. Then he carefully retied the top so that it wouldn't break free and replaced the bag in the midst of the pile of waste. He guessed that the container would be emptied soon, probably the next day.

He walked back to his truck rapidly and waited until no other cars were leaving before starting the engine.

After placing the backpack on the floor, Scott changed back into a suit and tie. He knew he had to hurry, but more important, he knew he had to avoid attention. He wished that he could speed, but dutifully stayed within the posted limits. Even up on the interstate, he diligently remained in the center lane as he headed to his meeting with Sally.

He did not know what he would say when he saw her.

Trying to formulate words, to fill her in on what had taken place that night, seemed impossible. If he told her nothing, she would hate him. If he told her everything, she would be terrified and hate him. She would want to go to Hope's side immediately and not do what was next in line on the plan.

It could all fall apart.

He drove through the night knowing that he was going to lie. Perhaps not much, but enough. It made him angry and it made him sad, but mostly it made him feel incompetent and deeply dishonest.

When he pulled into the parking lot from the highway ramp, he spotted Sally. It did not take him long to accelerate into the space next to her. Scott grabbed the backpack with the gun and the dish towel covered with gas and blood and stepped from the car.

Sally remained behind the seat, but she turned on the engine.

"You're late," she said. "I don't know if I have enough time left. Did it go as planned?"

"Not exactly," Scott said. "It wasn't as simple as we thought."

"What do you mean?" Sally asked in her brisk lawyer's tones.

"There was a bit of a struggle. Hope succeeded, she did what she volunteered to do." He hesitated. "But she might have gotten hurt a little bit in the confrontation. She's in the car now, heading home. And I was worried there might be something left behind that indicated she had been there, so I set a small fire."

"Jesus!" Sally exclaimed. "That wasn't in the plan!"

"I just was worried about the scene, you know. I thought that would be the best way to compromise what some cop might think had taken place. Isn't that exactly the sort of thing you told us about?"

Sally nodded. "Yes, yes. Okay. I don't think it's a problem."

"There's a towel in with the item in the backpack. It will transfer some of the gas to the gun barrel. Get rid of it afterwards."

Sally nodded again. "That was smart. But Hope, what were you saying about Hope?"

Scott wondered whether he wore the lie on his face. "She's on schedule now. Do what you have to do and speak with her later."

"What exactly happened to Hope?" Sally demanded sharply.

"You have to leave. You have to get back to Boston. Time is critical. There's no way to tell what O'Connell will do."

"What happened to Hope?" Sally repeated, bitter anger in her voice.

"I told you, she was in a fight. She got cut with a knife. When I left her, she said to tell you she was okay. Got it? That's exactly what she said. *Tell Sally I'm okay.* You need to finish the job tonight. We all do. Hope did her part. I did mine. Now do yours. It's the last thing, and . . ." He didn't finish.

Sally hesitated. "Cut with a knife? What do you mean *cut with a knife*? Tell me the truth."

"I am telling you the truth," Scott answered her stiffly. "She was cut. That's it. Now go."

Sally imagined a hundred different responses to her ex-husband right at that second, but stopped. As angry as she was, she knew that once, years earlier, she had lied to him, and that right then he was lying to her, and that there was absolutely nothing she could do about any of it. She nodded, not trusting her voice anymore, took the backpack, and drove off into the night. Once again, Scott was left behind, staring at car lights disappearing in the darkness.

•

"And so," the detective said as he pointed to the crime-scene photographs, "the fire really messed everything up. And, even more than the fire, it's the damn water that gets poured over everything by the fire department. Of course, you can't really ask them not to do that," he said with a wry laugh. "We were just really lucky the whole house didn't go up in flames. The blaze was pretty much contained to the kitchen area. See the back wall there, all scorched? The arson guy said whoever it was that set the damn thing didn't know what they were doing, so that instead of spreading across the room, the fire went up the wall and into the ceiling, which was how it got spotted by the neighbor across the way. So all in all, we were fortunate to be able to piece things together."

"Have you worked many homicides before?" I asked.

"Here? We're not like Boston or New York. We're a pretty modest-size department. But the state bureau of forensics is pretty good, and the medical examiner's office isn't filled with slouches, so when a killing does come along, we generally get a pretty good handle on it. Most of the homicides we see are like domestic disputes that got out of hand, or else drug deals that turned sour. Most of the time the bad guy is standing there, or at least his buddy is, so someone tells us who we're looking for."

"That wasn't the case this time, was it?"

"Nah. There were some questions made us scratch our heads at first. And there was a whole lot of folks who weren't going to shed a tear over O'Connell buying the farm. He was a nasty husband, a nasty father, a nasty neighbor, and as dishonest a son of a bitch as the day is long. Hell, if he'd owned a dog, he probably would have starved the beast and kicked it twice a day just on principle, you follow? Anyway, there was just enough left in the house and in the crime scene for us to go on."

I nodded my head. "But what put you in the right direction?"

"Two things, really. I mean, you have a fire and a dead body that was partially burnt, and truly dumb guys that we are, we initially just figured that the older O'Connell got drunk and somehow managed to set the place on fire along with himself. You know, passes out with a cigarette and a bottle of Scotch in his hand. Of course, that more than likely would have been in the living room in a chair, or in the bedroom, on the bed, instead of the kitchen floor. But when the medical examiner gets the body back on a table, peels away some charred flesh, sees the gunshot wound, and finds a twenty-five-caliber round in his brain, and another in his shoulder, well, that made things a whole lot different. So we were back at that soaking mess, looking for something to get us going, you know. But the doc also finds scrapings under the guy's fingernails, as well, so we've got some pretty interesting DNA, and then all of a sudden, the mess in the house looks like a fight that went poorly for the old bastard. And then when we canvas the place, one of the neighbors recalls seeing a car with Massachusetts plates squealing out of there not too long before the smoke started. That and the DNA results got us a search warrant. And then what do you suppose we find?"

He was smiling, and he snorted a small laugh. A policeman's satisfaction in once again learning that the world occasionally works the way it is supposed to.

I was less sure I would have reached that same conclusion.

45

A One-sided Phone Call

Hope drove north, through the tollbooths at the border to Maine, heading toward a spot near the shoreline she remembered from a summer vacation, many years earlier, shortly after she and Sally had first fallen in love. They had taken the young Ashley there on their first trip together. It was a wild spot, where an overgrown park of dark trees and tangled underbrush went straight to the water's edge, and the rocky shoreline caught the breakers that rolled in from the Atlantic, sending sprays of salt water into the air. In the summer it was magical, seals playing against the rocks, a dozen different species of seabirds crying against the onshore breezes. Now, she thought, it would be a lonely and abandoned spot, and it was the only place that she could think of that would be quiet enough for her to figure out what exactly she was to do.

She tucked her elbow down, keeping pressure on the wound in her side. This helped stymie the flow of blood, and the injury itself had slid into a constant throbbing pain. On more than one moment, she thought she was going to pass out, but then, as the miles slid beneath the wheels of the car, she had gathered some strength and, keeping her teeth clenched against the hurt, believed she could tough out the entire trip.

She tried to imagine what had taken place within her. She pictured different organs—stomach, spleen, liver, intestines—and like playing a child's game guessed which ones had been sliced and creased by the knife blade.

The countryside seemed darker even than the night that enveloped her. Great stands of black pines, like witnesses by the side of the road, seemed to be watching her progress.

When she exited the turnpike, she gasped with a sudden pain as she gently turned the wheel, steering the car down the ramp, then twisting through back roads that reminded her of her childhood home. She tried to measure her breathing, telling herself to take cautious pulls of the night air.

She let herself imagine that she was really on the road to the house where she had grown up. She could picture her mother years earlier, hair up, in the garden, wrangling with the flowers, while her father was in the back on the field he'd built for her, trying to juggle a soccer ball in the air. She could hear his voice calling for her to put on her cleats and come out and play. He sounded strong, not at all as he was later, in the hospital being stalked by disease.

I'll be right there, she thought.

Small brown signs every few miles pointed her in the direction of the park, and now she could smell a little salt in the air. She remembered a hidden parking lot, which she knew would be empty on a cold November night. A single, yardwide pathway thickly padded with pine needles led through the stands of trees and brush, past a picnic area, then another three-quarters of a mile to the ocean. She lifted her eyes and saw the full moon. She knew that she might need its meager light. Hunter's moon, she thought. It was rimmed with yellow, and she imagined that the first snows and ice weren't far off. She doubted anyone else would come along; she did not know what she would say if someone did. She did not have the energy left to lie even to the most mildly inquisitive policeman or park ranger.

Hope saw another sign, a blue background with a large white *H* in the middle.

This was an unfair temptation, she thought. She had not remembered that the park was only a couple of miles from a hospital.

For a moment, she envisioned turning in that direction. There would be a large swath of bright light, and a sign in neon red spelling out EMERGENCY ENTRANCE. Probably an ambulance or two parked nearby, on a circular entry. Right inside there would be a nurse, behind a desk, doing triage.

She imagined the nurse: a sturdy, middle-aged woman, unfazed by blood or danger. She would take one glance at the wound in Hope's side, and the next thing Hope would be aware of would be the fluorescent lights of the exam room, and the murmured voices of a physician and nurses as they bent over her trying to save her life.

Who did this to you? someone would ask. They would have a notepad handy to record her words.

I did it to myself.

No, really, who did it? The police are on their way, and they will want to know. Tell us now.

I can't say.

We have questions. We need answers. Why are you here? Why are you so far from your home? What have you been doing this night?

I won't say.

That's not the same as you can't say. We are suspicious. We have doubts. If you live through this night, we will have many more questions.

I won't answer.

Yes, you will. Sooner or later, you will. And tell us, why is there someone else's blood on your coveralls? How did that get there?

Hope gritted her teeth and kept driving.

Sally pulled her car into almost the same spot opposite Michael O'Connell's apartment that she had occupied earlier that evening. The street was empty, save for the cars parked up and down the block. It was urban dark, where the night blackness tried to creep into corners, join shadows together, fight against all the ambient light that crept out from more vibrant parts of the city.

She looked down first at her wristwatch, then at the stopwatch, which was keeping a running time for the entire day. She breathed in slowly. Time was moving far too slowly.

Sally stared up at the façade of Michael O'Connell's building. His apartment windows remained dark.

Gazing up and down the street, Sally could feel heat building within her. How close was he? Two minutes? Twenty minutes? Was he even heading this direction at all?

She shook her head. Proper planning, she told herself, would have designated someone to follow him out of his father's home, so that every step he took that day was monitored. She bit down on her lip. But doing that would have endangered them all, for it would have put one of them in closer proximity to O'Connell than she wanted. That was why she had created the gap—between his exit and his return. But Scott had been dangerously slow at returning the weapon, and now she had no real grasp on where O'Connell might be. Did the air seep from his tire as Scott had promised it would? Had he been sufficiently delayed? Maybes screamed at her like a dissonant symphony of out-of-tune instruments.

Glancing sideways, toward the backpack that contained the gun, she fought off the urge to simply stick it into a trash container behind the building. There would be a more than good chance the cops would still find it. But it lacked the certainty of what she needed, and in a night filled with doubt, this part had to be conclusive.

For a moment, she grasped at the cell phone. Her mind spun wildly to Hope.

Where are you? she asked herself.

Are you okay?

Her hands were shaking. She did not know whether it was out of fear that O'Connell would catch her and destroy everything by doing so, or whether she was afraid for Hope. She pictured her partner, tried to imagine just exactly what had happened to her, tried to read between the lines of what Scott had told her, but every step she took along this path of imagination only frightened her more.

O'Connell was closing in on her, getting nearer with every passing minute; she could sense it. She knew she had to act without delay. And yet, crippled by uncertainty, she hesitated.

Hope was out there, in pain; she could sense that as well. And she could do nothing about it.

She let out a low, slow moan.

And then, with an overwhelming force of will, Sally seized the backpack and launched herself out of the car. She prayed that the night would conceal her as she ducked her head down and rapidly crossed the street. She knew that if anyone saw her and connected her and the backpack to O'Connell and his apartment, everything might unravel. She knew enough not to run, but to measure her pace. Eye contact with anyone would be fatal. Conversation with anyone would be fatal. Anything that made the next few moments noticeable in any manner or form would be fatal. To all of them.

She knew that this was the moment she had to rise to. It was the second where everything that had happened that night hung in some balance. A failure on her part would doom all of them, and possibly Ashley as well. She had the murder weapon in her possession. It was a minute of complete vulnerability.

Sally whispered to herself, Keep going.

As she moved through the vestibule of the apartment, she could hear voices on the elevator, so she ducked into the stairwell and ran up the stairs, taking them two at a time.

She paused by the solid fire door, trying to listen through, then, realizing that that was impossible, she stepped through and walked steadily down the corridor to O'Connell's apartment. She held Mrs. Abramowicz's key in her hand, just as she had earlier that day. For a terrible second, she imagined him inside, lying on the bed, the lights out. She should make a plan. What if he was inside? What if he showed up before she finished her task? What if he spotted her in the hallway? What if he saw her on the elevator? Or exiting the building, on the street? What was she going to say? Would she fight him? Would she try to hide? Would he even recognize her?

Her hand shook with questions as she opened the door.

She stepped inside rapidly, closing it behind her.

She listened for breathing, for footsteps, for a toilet flushing, for the tap of computer keys—anything that might tell her she wasn't alone—but she could hear nothing beyond the tortured noise of her breathing, which seemed to grow in sound and intensity with each passing second. *Do it now! Do it now! There's no time!*

She ducked across the entryway, afraid to turn on any light, cursing herself as she bumped against a wall. A little streetlight slipped through the bedroom windows, giving her just enough illumination to see. She caught a glimpse of herself in a mirror. It almost made her scream.

She dashed toward the closet and frantically unzipped the backpack, removing the gun. She could smell the pungent odor of gasoline, just as Scott had warned her. She slipped the gun back into the shoe and rammed the stray sock down over the top to stifle the smell. After pushing it back into position, hoping everything was placed exactly as she had memorized earlier, she rose.

Sally told herself to move calmly, efficiently, to think every step of the way, but she could not. She took the now empty backpack, glanced around rapidly, thought it all looked as it had earlier that day, and turned to head out.

Once again riveted by darkness, she stumbled.

She tried to control her racing fears, told herself not to run. She did not want to crash into anything, maybe knock something over. There had to be no sign at all that someone had been inside the apartment twice that day. Nothing, she told herself, as she waited for her heart to slow, could be more important.

Delaying her exit was almost painful.

When Sally finally reached the door, she almost panicked. *He's there,* she thought. She imagined that she could hear his own key in the lock. She thought she heard voices, footsteps.

Sally told herself to ignore the tricks fear was playing on her, and she pushed her way out of the apartment. She swept her eyes right, then left, and saw that she was alone. Still, her hand twitched, and she thought she could hear telltale sounds approaching from every direction. She steeled herself, told herself to hold it all together.

Just as she had done earlier, she locked the door and made

her way down the hallway. Again, she chose the stairs. Again, she made her way through the vestibule and out into the night. Suddenly she was flooded with a glow of success. She crossed the street, embracing anonymity.

In the street just in front of her car was a storm drain. She dropped Mrs. Abramowicz's key between the grate spaces, hearing it plop into muddy water at the bottom.

Not until she got into her car, closed the door, and pushed her head back did she feel tears welling up within her. For a second, she believed it would all work, and she told herself, She's safe. We've done it, Ashley is safe.

And then she remembered Hope and a new panic set in. One that seemed to rise up out of some black space deep within her, rushing forward inexorably, threatening to sweep her up in some new, shapeless fear. Sally gasped out loud, catching her breath. She reached for the cell phone and punched the number for Hope's phone.

Scott felt relief as he pulled into his driveway. He tucked the truck back behind the house, to its usual spot, where it was hard to see from the roadway, or by any of the neighbors. He grabbed all his clothing from that night, got into the Porsche, and pulled back out into the street. He revved the engine, making sure that he made enough noise to be noticed by anyone still up and watching television or reading.

In the center of town was a pizza restaurant favored by students. This late—it was closing in on midnight—the presence of a professor was likely to be noted. It wasn't that unusual—teachers correcting papers were known to seek out the occasional late-night burst of energy. It was as good a place as any to be seen.

He parked directly in front, and the sports car caught the attention of some of the young men seated at a counter by the window. The car always got noticed.

He bought a slice of grilled-chicken-and-pineapple pizza and deliberately used his ATM debit card to pay for it.

If asked, he would not be able to account for his presence earlier that night. *Home, grading papers,* he would say. *And, no, I don't answer the phone when I'm going over student work.* But it would not have been possible for him to drive from O'Connell's father's home, all the way to Boston, and then back to western Massachusetts in the relevant time. *Kill someone and then buy a slice of pizza? Detective, that's absurd.* It was not the best of alibis, but it was at least something. It was dependent, in more than a small way, upon Sally doing what she had promised she would with the weapon. So much hinged on that gun being discovered in the same spot that Scott almost coughed out loud as he choked with tension.

He took his slice over to an empty spot at the counter and ate slowly. He tried not to think of that day, tried not to replay every scene in his head. But a picture of the murdered man slid into his consciousness as he stared at his pizza. When he thought he smelled the unmistakable odor of gasoline, and then the equally sickening scent of burning flesh, he almost gagged. He told himself, You were at war again. He breathed in, continued to eat, and concentrated on what remained for him to accomplish. He had to drop off every item of clothing that he'd worn inside O'Connell's father's house at the local Salvation Army clothing dump, where it would disappear into the maw of charity. He reminded himself not to forget the shoes. They might have blood on their soles. He recognized the double entendre that had inadvertently scoured his mind: we all might have blood on our souls.

He looked down at the slice and saw that his hand trembled as he lifted the food to his mouth.

What have I done?

He refused to answer his own question. Instead, he found himself thinking about Hope. The more he envisioned her situation, the wound in her side, the more he understood there was a long way to go before he could breathe easily again.

Scott looked around the restaurant wildly, staring at the other late-night diners, almost all of whom kept to themselves, their eyes dutifully fixed ahead, looking beyond the window or gazing at the wall. For a moment, he thought they would all be able to see the truth about him that night, that somehow he wore guilt like a vibrant streak of crimson paint.

He felt his leg twitch spastically.

It will all fall apart, he thought. We are all going to prison.

Except Ashley. He tried to keep a vision of her firmly in his head as a way out of the overwhelming despair that threatened to overcome him.

The pizza suddenly tasted like chalk. His throat was dry. He desperately wanted to be alone, yet did not, both at the same time.

He pushed the paper plate away.

For the first time, Scott realized that everything that they had done, designed to return certainty to Ashley's life, had thrown all of them into a black hole of doubt.

Scott slowly walked out of the restaurant, returned to his car, and wondered whether he would ever be able to sleep peacefully again. He did not think so.

Hope was still seated in her rental car, but the engine was off, the lights were extinguished, and she was resting with her head against the wheel. She had pulled into the deepest part of the small parking lot at the entrance to the seaside park, farthest away from the main road, as hidden as she could manage.

She felt light-headed, but exhausted, and she wondered whether she would have the strength to complete the night. Her breathing was shallow and labored.

On the seat next to her, she had the knife that had done so much damage, a cheap ballpoint pen, and a sheet of paper. She ransacked her mind, trying to think if there was anything else that might compromise her. She saw the cell phone, told herself that she had to get rid of it, and as she reached out, it rang.

Hope knew it would be Sally.

She picked it up, lifted the phone to her ear, and shut her eyes.

"Hope?" Sally's voice came across the line, scratchy with anxiety. "Hope?"

She did not reply.

"Are you there?"

Again, she did not answer.

"Where are you? Are you all right?"

Hope thought of many things she could say, but none would form on her tongue, pass through her lips. She breathed in heavily.

"Please, Hope, tell me where you are."

Hope shook her head, but did not say anything.

"Are you hurt? Is it bad?"

Yes.

"Please, Hope, answer me," Sally pleaded. "I have to know you're all right. Are you heading home? Are you going to a hospital? Where are you? I'll come there. I'll help you, just tell me what to do."

There's nothing you can do, Hope thought. *No, just keep talking. It's wonderful to hear your voice. Do you remember when we first met? Our fingertips touched when we shook hands, and I thought we were going to catch on fire, right there, in the gallery, in front of everyone.*

"Are you unable to talk? Is there someone else around?"

No. I'm alone. Except I'm not. You're here with me now. Ashley is with me. Catherine and my father, too. I can hear Nameless barking because he wants to go to the soccer fields. My memories are surrounding me.

Sally wanted more than anything else to panic, to give in to all the fear that blew around her with hurricane force, but she managed to grip tight to something within her, containing all the winds of tension.

"Hope, I know you're listening to me. I know it. I'll talk. If you can say something, please do. Just tell me where to go, and I will be there. Please."

I'm at a place you will remember. It will make you smile and cry when you understand.

"Hope, it's done. We're finished. We did it. It's all past us. She's going to be safe, I know it. Everything will go back to being how it was. She will have her life and you and I will have our lives together, and Scott will have his teaching, and it will all be as it was when we were happy. I've been so wrong, I know I've been awful, I know it has been hard on you, but please, together, we will go forward from this point on, you and I. Please don't leave me. Not now. Not when we have a chance."

This is our only chance.

"Please, Hope, please. Talk to me."

If I talk to you, I won't be able to do what I have to do. You will talk me out of it. I know you, Sally. You will be persuasive and seductive and funny, all at once, the way you used to be; it's what I loved about you from the beginning. And if I allow myself to talk to you, I won't be able to argue with all the reasons you will use to dissuade me.

Sally listened to the silence, racking her brain for what it was she could say. She could not put what was happening into words; it was far too black and nightmarish. She knew only that there had to be some phrase, some concoction of language, that she could utter that might change what she was afraid was happening.

"Look, Hope, love, please let me help."

You are helping. Keep talking. It makes me stronger.

"No matter what has happened, I can get us out of it. I know I can. Trust me. It's what I'm trained to do. It's what I have my expertise in. There is no problem too big that we can't extricate ourselves from, working together. Didn't we learn that tonight?"

Hope reached over and brought the piece of paper and pen in front of her. She crooked the phone between her shoulder and her ear, so that she could continue to listen.

"Hope, we can manage. We can win. I know it. Just tell me you know it, too."

Not this. Too many questions. We will all be in jeopardy. I need to do this. It's the only way I can be sure we're all safe.

Sally was quiet, and Hope wrote on the page, **There is too much sadness in my life.**

She shook her head. The first lie of many, she thought. She continued writing.

I have been unfairly accused at the school I love.

Sally whispered, "Hope, please, I know you're there. Tell me what is wrong. Tell me what to do. I'm begging you."

And the woman I love no longer loves me.

Hope shook her head slightly as she wrote these words. She bit down on her lower lip. She needed to find some way to indicate that this was all a bunch of lies, find a way to say this so that only Sally would know the truth, not the park ranger who would find the note, nor the detective who would read it.

So I have come to this place that we once loved, so that I could remember what it once was like, and what I know the future would be, if only I were stronger.

Sally, tears flowing down her face, gave in to something that went way beyond terror. It was the sensation of inevitability. *She wants to protect us.*

"Hope, love, please," she coughed out the words between gasps of complete despair. "Let me come be with you. Always, since the first, we relied upon each other. We made each other right. Let me do that again, please."

But, Sally, you are.

I tried to stab myself with a knife but that only made me bleed all over the place, and I'm sorry. I wanted to stab myself in the heart, but I missed. So, I've chosen another route.

There it is, Hope thought.

The only route still open to me. I love you all, and trust you will all remember me the same way.

She was exhausted.

Sally's voice had diminished to a whisper. "Look, Hope, my love, please, no matter how badly you are hurt, we can just say that I did it to you. Scott said you were cut. Well, we'll just tell the cops I did it. They'll believe us, I know it.

You don't have to leave me. We can talk our way out of this, together."

Hope smiled again. It was a most attractive offer, she thought to herself. Lie our ways out of all the questions. And maybe it would work. But probably not. *This is the only way to be sure.*

She wanted to say good-bye, wanted to say all the things that lovers and partners would whisper to each other in the dark, wanted to say something about her mother and Ashley and everything that had happened that night, but she did not. Instead, she merely touched the END button on her cell phone to disconnect the line.

In her car, still parked on the street outside Michael O'Connell's apartment building, Sally gave in to all the emotions cascading within her and sobbed uncontrollably. She felt as if she were shrinking, that she had abruptly grown smaller, weaker, and was only a shadow of the person she had been at the start of the day. Whatever they had done, she wasn't sure that it was worth the cost that had been paid. She bent over, kicked her feet, and pounded on the wheel, flailing her arms about wildly. Then she stopped and moaned as if she'd been punched in the stomach. She closed her eyes and rocked back and forth, slinking down in her seat, in total agony, and completely oblivious that Michael O'Connell, cursing loudly, openly enraged, glowing with red anger and black bitterness, and blinded to the world around him, had passed by only a few feet away as he stomped his way toward his own front entranceway.

Epilogue

"So, Do You Want to Hear a Story?"

"I see," she said a little cautiously, "you managed to meet with the detective who investigated the case?"

"Yes," I replied. "It was most enlightening."

"But you have returned because you have a few more questions, correct?"

"Yes. I still think there are other people I need to speak with."

She nodded, but did not reply at first. I could see that she was calculating carefully, trying to measure details against memories.

"This would be the same request, would it not? To speak with Sally or Scott?"

"Yes."

She shook her head. "I do not think they would speak with you. But regardless, what would you expect them to say?"

"I want to know how it worked out."

This time she laughed, but without humor. "Worked out? What a truly inadequate phrase to describe what they went through and what they did, and how it might have impacted their lives in the days that followed."

"Well, you know what I mean. An assessment."

"And you think they would tell you the truth? Don't you imagine that when you knocked on their door and said, 'But I need to ask you some questions about the man you killed,' that they would simply look at you as if you were completely crazy and then slam the door in your face? And even if they were to invite you in, and you were to ask, 'So, how *have* your lives been since you got away with murder?' what incentive would they have for unburdening themselves of the truth? Can't you see how ridiculous that would be?"

"But you know the answers to those questions?"

"Of course," she said carefully.

It was early in the evening, just past the end of the summer afternoon, that undecided time between day and night when the world takes on a faded look. She had opened the windows in her home, letting in the stray sounds that I had grown accustomed to from many visits: children's voices, the occasional car. The drawing down of another benign day in the suburbs. I went over to the window and took in a breath of air.

"You will never think of this as home, will you?" I asked.

"No. Of course not. It is a deadly place. Sad because it is so normal."

"You moved, right? After all these events took place."

She nodded her head. "Perceptive of you."

"Why?"

"I no longer felt I could safely rely on the solitude that I had surrounded myself with for so many years. Too many ghosts. Too many memories. I thought I might go crazy." Again she smiled. "So, what did the policeman tell you?"

"That what Sally predicted did indeed take place. Actually, he didn't say that; it's what I extrapolated. When the detectives went to Michael O'Connell's apartment, they found the murder weapon concealed in the boot. It was his DNA beneath his murdered father's fingers. At first, he admitted being there, fighting with the old man, but denied killing him. Of course, a person who sadistically crushes another man's heart medication beneath the sole of his shoe lacks some credibility on that score, and so they didn't believe him. Not for a second. No, they had him, even without a full confession, and when they recovered the computer, which he'd dropped off at a repair shop, and found the angry letter to his old man . . . well, motive, means, opportunity. The holy trinity of police work. Isn't that what Sally called it, when she first designed the plan?"

"Yes. Exactly," she said. "This is what I suspected they would tell you. But they must have told you more?"

"He tried to blame it on Ashley, on Scott and Sally and Hope, but . . ."

"A conspiracy that would require so many unlikely things, correct? One, stealing the murder weapon, giving it to another, having it pass through three sets of hands before returning it to O'Connell's apartment, a fire . . . Really, it hardly made sense, correct?"

"That's right. It didn't make sense. Especially when coupled with Hope's suicide and the distraught note she left behind. The detective told me that to believe O'Connell, one would have to imagine that a woman bent on killing herself stopped off mid-drive to murder some man she'd never seen before, in a location she'd never been to, drove all the way back to Boston, replaced the gun in O'Connell's apartment, and then drove all the way back to Maine and threw herself into the ocean after leaving behind a note which neglected to mention any of this. Or maybe you would think that Sally was the killer, but she was in Boston buying frilly lingerie right about the time of the killings. And Scott, well, maybe it was him, but he didn't have the time to perform the act, then get to Boston and then back to western Massachusetts to his slice of late-night pizza. Again, not within the realm of probability."

As I talked, I could see tears welling up in her eyes. She seemed to be seated ever more straight and upright in her chair, as if each word managed to tighten the nut and screw of some memory within her.

"And so?" she asked, but this time her words seemed choked.

"And so, what Sally had envisioned eventually took place. Michael O'Connell copped a plea to second-degree murder. Apparently he wanted to fight in trial, continued to claim his innocence right up to the last minute. But when the cops told him that the caliber gun used in the murder of his father was the same as the one used to kill the private eye, Murphy, and that maybe they'd look at him for that crime, too, he took the easier way out. Of course, that was just a bluff on their part. The shots that killed Murphy produced bullet fragments far too deformed for forensic comparison. The police told me that. But it was a useful threat. Twenty to life. Eligible for his first parole hearing after eighteen years."

"Yes, yes," she said. "This we know."

"So, they got what they wanted."

"Do you think?"

"They got away with it."

"Really?"

"Well, if I'm to believe what you've told me, they did."

She stood up, walked around the room, went to a sideboard, and poured herself a small drink. "Not too early, I guess," she said. I could see that tears were forming at the corners of her eyes.

I remained quiet, watching her.

" 'Got away with it' you say? Do you really think that's the case?"

"They aren't going to be prosecuted in a court of law," I said.

"But don't you imagine that there are other courts within us, where guilt and innocence are always in the balance? Does anybody—especially people like Scott and Sally—ever get away with anything?"

I didn't reply. I guessed that she was right.

"Do you imagine that Sally doesn't lie alone in the darkness at night, sobbing the hours away, feeling a coldness in the bed where once Hope lay? What did she get away with? And the weight that Scott carries now, don't you wonder how the events of those days batter him every waking second? Does he smell that odor of burnt flesh and death on every stray breeze? Can he face all those eager young faces in his school knowing what lie rests within him?"

She paused, then said, "Do you want me to go on?"

I shook my head.

Then she added, "Think hard about it. They will continue to pay a price for what they did for the rest of their days."

"I should speak to them," I repeated.

She sighed deeply.

"No, really," I insisted. "I should interview Sally and Scott. Even if they won't speak with me, I should try."

"Don't you think they should be left alone with their own nightmares?"

"They should be free."

"Free of one—maybe. But are they really?"

I didn't know what to say.

She took a long pull on her drink. "So, now we're near the end, are we not? I've told you a story. What did I say, at the start of all this? A murder story? A story about a killing?"

"Yes. That's what you said."

She smiled behind her tears. "But I was wrong. Or, to be more accurate, I wasn't telling you the truth when I said that. No. Not at all. It's a love story."

I must have looked surprised, but she ignored this and walked over to a sideboard and opened a drawer.

"That's what it was. A love story. It's always been a love story. Would any of it have happened if someone had really loved Michael O'Connell when he was growing up, so that he knew the difference between real love and obsession? And did not Sally and Scott love their daughter enough so that they would do anything—anything at all—to protect her from harm, no matter what price they would have to pay? And Hope, did she not love Ashley, too, with something far more special than any-one ever realized? And she loved Sally, as well, more deeply than even Sally knew, so that the gift she gave them all was a kind of freedom, wasn't it? And really, when you look at any of the actions, any of the events, anything that happened along all those days and nights when Michael O'Connell came into their lives, wasn't it about love, really? Too much love. Not enough love. But, when all is said and done, love."

I remained silent.

As she was speaking, I saw her pull a pad of paper out from a drawer and write down several lines.

"You have," she suddenly said, "a couple more things to do, here, to really understand all this. It seems to me that there is indeed an interview of some importance that you need to conduct. Some critical information you need to acquire and, well, *distribute*. I will be counting on you."

"What's this?" I asked as she handed me the slip of paper.

"After you have done what is necessary, go to this location at this hour and you will understand."

I took the paper, glanced at it, and put it into my pocket.

"I have a few photographs," she said. "I keep them in drawers mainly, now. When I pull them out, I just cry and cry uncontrollably and that's not a good thing, now, is it? Still you probably ought to see one or two."

She turned again to the sideboard, opened a drawer, shuffled through some frames, and finally removed one. She looked down at it, smiling through glistening eyes.

"Here," she said, her voice cracking a little. "This one is as good as any. It was taken after the state championship game and she was just a few weeks shy of her eighteenth birthday."

Two people were in the picture. A muddy, joyous teenage girl, hoisting a golden trophy above her head, while being lifted into the air by a balding, hulking older man, who was clearly her father. Both their faces glowed with the unmistakable joy of victory after sacrifice. I stared at it. The picture seemed to be alive, and for a moment I could almost imagine the cheering and the excited voices and the tears of happiness that must have surrounded that moment.

"I took the picture," she said. "But really, I wished I had been in it, as well."

Again she took a deep breath.

"They never found her body, you know," she said. "It was several days before someone spotted her car and found the note left on the dashboard. And there was a big storm the day after, one of those classic late-fall nor'easters, and they couldn't put divers into the water to search for her. The outgoing tides were very strong along the shoreline that November and must have swept her miles out to sea. At first, I could hardly bear this, but as time went on, I understood perhaps it was better that way. It allowed me to remember her at so many better times. You asked me why I told you this story?"

"Yes."

"Two reasons. The first is because she was braver than anyone had any right to expect, and someone ought to know that."

Catherine smiled behind her tears and then pointed at my pocket, where I'd put the piece of paper.

"The second reason?" I asked.

"That should become apparent to you soon enough."

We were both quiet, then she smiled.

"A love story," she repeated. "A love story about death."

The setting differs, depending upon the age of the prison, and how much money the state is willing to invest in modern penal technology. But strip away the lights, motion detectors, sensors, electronic eyes, and video monitors, and prison is still just one thing: locks.

I was frisked in an anteroom, first with an electronic wand, and then the old-fashioned way. I was asked to sign a paper stating that if for some reason I was taken hostage, I would not expect the state to go to any extraordinary measures to rescue me. My briefcase was inspected. Every pen I carried was unscrewed and examined. The sheets of paper in my notebook were ruffled, to make sure I wasn't trying to smuggle something between the pages. Then I was led down a long corridor, through an electronic sally port, where the bars behind me snapped shut. The escort brought me to a small room, just off the prison library, he told me. Usually, it was for meetings between prisoners and lawyers, but a writer looking for a story seemed to meet the same qualifications.

There were bright overhead lights, and a single window on one wall that looked out on a glistening razor-wire fence and an expanse of empty blue sky. A sturdy metal table and cheap folding chairs were the only furniture in the room. The escort motioned me to sit, then pointed at a side door.

"He'll be here in a minute. Remember, you can give him a pack of cigarettes, if you brought them, but that's it. Nothing else. Okay? You can go ahead and shake hands, but that would be the extent of any physical contact. According to rules established by the state Supreme Court, we're not allowed to listen to your conversation, but the camera up there in the corner"—he gestured up into the far edge of the room—"well, that records the entire meeting. Including me giving you this warning. You got it?"

"Sure," I said.

"Could be worse. We're a whole lot nicer than some states. Don't want to be in stir down in Georgia, Texas, or Alabama."

I nodded, and the guard added, "You know, the monitor, it's for your protection, too. We got some guys in here likely to slice your throat if you said the wrong thing. So we keep a close eye on all meetings like this."

"I'll keep that in mind."

"But you don't have to worry none. O'Connell is what passes for a gentleman in this place. All he wants to do is tell people how he's innocent and all."

"That's what he says?"

The guard smiled as the side door opened, and Michael O'Connell, in handcuffs, wearing a blue denim work shirt and dark jeans, was escorted into the room. "That's what they all say," the guard said as he went over to unsnap the cuffs.

We shook hands, then sat across from each other at the table. He had grown a scraggly beard and cropped his dark hair into a crew cut. There were some lines around his eyes that I guessed hadn't been there a few years earlier. I arranged a notepad in front of me and toyed with a pencil while he lit a cigarette.

"Bad habit," he said. "I took it up in here."

"It can kill you."

He shrugged. "In this place, it seems like the least of my worries. A lot of things can kill you. Hell, look at some dude cross-eyed and he'll kill you. So, tell me why you're here."

"I've been looking into the crime that landed you here," I said cautiously.

His eyebrows lifted slightly. "Really? Who sent you?"

"No one sent me. I'm just interested."

"How did you get interested?"

I wasn't sure how to respond. I had known that this question was coming, but hadn't really formulated an answer beforehand. I leaned back a little, and said, "I overheard something at a cocktail party, of all places, that sparked my curiosity. I did a little looking around, and thought I'd come and speak with you."

"I didn't do it, you know. I'm innocent."

I nodded, didn't reply, hoping he would simply continue. He watched for my reaction, taking a long drag on the cigarette, then blew a little smoke in my direction.

"Did they send you?"

"Who do you mean?"

"Scott. Sally. But mainly Ashley. Did they send you, just to make sure I was still here, behind bars?"

"No. No one sent me. I sent myself. I've never spoken with any of those people."

"Sure." He snorted a laugh. "Sure you haven't. How much are they paying you?"

"No one is paying me."

"Right. You're doing this for free. The fucking bastards. You'd think they'd leave me alone now."

"You can believe what you want."

He seemed to think hard for an instant, then leaned forward.

"Tell me," he said slowly, "when you met with them, what did Ashley say?"

"I haven't met with anyone." This wasn't true, and I knew he knew it.

"Describe her for me." Again he was crouched forward, as if driven halfway across the table by the force of his questions, a sudden, profound eagerness in each word. "What was she wearing? Has she cut her hair? Tell me about her hands. She has long, delicate fingers. And her legs? Still as long and sexy? But I'd really like to hear about her hair. She hasn't cut it, has she? Or colored it? I hope not."

His breathing had increased, and for a moment I thought he might be aroused.

"I can't tell you," I said. "I've never seen her. I don't know who you're talking about."

He breathed out, a long, slow exhale of breath. "Why do you waste my time with lies?" Then he ignored his own question and said, "Well, when you do meet her, you will see exactly what I'm talking about. Exactly."

"See what?"

"Why I won't ever forget her."

"Even in here. For years?"

He smiled. "Even in here. For years. I can still picture her from when we were together. It's like she's always with me. I can even feel her touch."

I nodded. "And the other names you mentioned?"

Again he smiled, but this was a far different sort of smile. A hunter's grin.

"I won't be forgetting them, either." A corner of his lip suddenly lifted in a half snarl. "They did it, you know. I'm not sure how, but they did it. They put me in here. You can count on it. Every day, I think about them. Every hour. Every minute. I will never forget what they managed to do."

"But you pleaded guilty. In a court. You got up in front of a judge, swore an oath to tell the truth, and said you committed the crime."

"That was a matter of convenience. I didn't really have a chance. If convicted, in a trial, I would have gotten a mandatory twenty-five to life. By pleading, I shaved maybe seven years or more off the back end of prison and bought myself a parole board hearing. I can do the time. And then I'll get out and put things right."

He smiled again. "Not what you expected to hear?"

"I had no real expectations."

"We are meant to be together. Ashley and I. Nothing has changed. Just because I'm in here for years, nothing is different. It's just time that has to pass before the inevitable happens. Call it destiny, call it fate, but that's the way it is. I can be patient. And then I'll find her."

I nodded. This I believed. He leaned back in his seat and looked up at the surveillance camera, stubbed out the butt of his cigarette, picked out a crumpled pack from his shirt pocket, and lit up another. "It's an addiction," he said, letting smoke dribble out between his lips. "Almost impossible to quit, or so they say. Worse than heroin or even crack co-caine." He laughed. "I guess I'm something of a junkie."

Then he stared across the table at me. "You ever been ad-dicted to something? Or someone?"

I didn't reply, letting silence be my answer.

"You want to know if I killed my father? Nah. I didn't do it," he said stiffly with a smirk on his lips. "They got the wrong man."

Some information I needed to distribute.

That was what she had told me, I was sure of it. It didn't take me long to figure out what she had meant.

I pulled my car into the driveway and stepped outside. The daytime heat had risen. I imagined that pushing the wheels of a wheelchair on a hot afternoon like this would be partic-ularly hard.

I knocked on the door to Will Goodwin's house, then stepped back and waited. The flower garden that I'd first seen weeks earlier had bloomed into colorful, orderly rows, like a military unit on parade. I heard the noise of the chair scraping against the wooden floor, then the door swung open.

"Mr. Goodwin? I don't know if you remember, but I was here a few weeks back."

He smiled. "Sure. The writer. Didn't think I'd ever see you again. Got some more questions?"

Goodwin was grinning. I noticed there were some changes since I'd seen him earlier. His hair was shaggier, and the in-dentation in his forehead, where he'd been smashed by the pipe, seemed to have filled out slightly and was better ob-scured by the tangle of locks. He'd started a beard, as well, which framed his face so that his jaw had a sense of determi-nation to it.

"How are you?" I asked.

He gave a small wave with his hand, toward the chair. "Ac-tually, Mr. Writer, I've made some strides. More of my mem-ory returns every day, thank you for asking. Not of the attack, of course. That's lost, and I doubt it will ever return. But school, studies, books read, courses taken, you know, some of that creeps back every day. So, I'm at least modestly upbeat, if that's possible. May be able to see something of a future one of these days."

"That's good. That's real good."

He smiled, spun back on the chair a bit, balancing himself, then leaned forward toward me. "But that's not the reason you're here, is it?"

"No."

"You've learned something? About my mugging?"

I nodded. His jocular, outgoing manner changed immediately, and he pushed himself forward toward me, instantly insistent.

"What? Tell me! What have you found out?"

I hesitated. I knew what I *might* be doing. I wondered if this was what went through the judge's mind when he heard the verdict from the jury box. Guilty. Time to pronounce sentence.

"I know who hurt you." I watched his face for a reaction. It wasn't long in coming. It was as if a shadow fell across his eyes, deepening in the space between us. Black darkness and stiff hatred. His hand quivered, and I saw his lips set tightly.

"You know who did this to me?"

"Yes. The problem is, what I found out isn't something you could take to a detective, isn't the sort of information that someone can make a case out of, and sure wouldn't get you any closer to a courtroom."

"But"—he was speaking with a high-pitched intensity—"you still know? You know and you're sure?"

"Yes. I am absolutely, completely certain. Beyond a reasonable doubt. But, understand, not the sort of information that a cop would be able to use, like I said."

"Tell me." He was nearly whispering, but the demand in his voice was ancient, and awful. "Who did this to me?"

I reached into my briefcase and removed a copy of the mug shot photographs of Michael O'Connell and handed it to him. *Two reasons,* Catherine had said to me. And this was the second.

"This is him?"

"Yes."

"Where is he?"

I handed him another piece of paper. "He's in prison. That's his address, his prison identification number, a few of the particulars of the sentence he's serving, and the tentative date of his first parole hearing. It's many years away, but there it is, along with a phone number that one can call to get further information, if one decides they want it."

"And you're sure?" he asked again.

"Yes. One hundred percent."

"Why are you telling me this?"

"I thought you had a right to know."

"How do you know?"

"Please, don't ask me that."

He paused, then nodded. "Okay. I guess. Fair enough."

Will Goodwin looked first at the picture, then at the sheet of paper. "This is a tough place, this prison, isn't it?"

"Yes. Hard time."

"Almost anything could happen to someone in there."

"That's correct. You could get killed for a pack of smokes. He told me that himself."

He nodded. "Yes. I imagine that's true."

He looked past me for a second, then added, "That's something to think about."

I stepped back, ready to leave, but then hesitated. For a moment I felt dizzy, and the temperature seemed to spike. I wondered what it was that I had just done.

I saw that Will Goodwin was rigid, and that the muscles on his arms were taut with tension. "Thank you," he said slowly, his words moving slowly, but each carrying the weight of the cruelty that had been done to him. "Thank you for remembering me. Thank you for giving me this."

"I'll be leaving then." But what I was leaving behind would never depart.

"Hey, one more question," he said suddenly.

"Sure. What is it?"

"Do you know why he did this to me?"

I took a deep breath. "Yes."

Again his face clouded, and his lower lip twitched.

"Well, why?" He could barely spit out the question.

"Because you kissed the wrong girl."

He paused, breathing out hard, as if his wind had been ripped right from his lungs. I could see him absorbing what I had said. "Because I kissed . . ."

"Yes. Just once. A single kiss."

He seemed to teeter, as if there were suddenly dozens of other questions he wanted to ask. But he did not. Instead, he merely shook his head slightly. But I saw that his hand on the wheel of the chair had tightened, his knuckles whitened, and that deep within him the coldest rage I'd ever imagined had taken root.

The piece of paper Catherine had given me directed me to a street outside a large art museum in a city that wasn't Boston or New York. It was shortly after five in the afternoon, traffic filled the streets, and the sidewalks were jammed with people heading home. The sun was just beginning to descend beyond the rows of office buildings, and the opening bars of the evening symphony of urban life were just starting up. I could hear car horns, wheezing bus engines, and the hurrying hum of voices. I stood at the bottom of a wide set of stairs, and the flow of people carved around me, as if I were a rock in a stream, with water rushing past on either side. I kept my eyes locked ahead, staring up the expanse of stairs, not really believing that I would recognize her. When I saw her, I had no doubt. I'm not sure why. Many other young women were leaving the museum at that hour, and they all had that casual end-of-the-day look, with backpack or satchel slung over their shoulder. They were all striking, all compelling, magical. But Ashley seemed more of everything. She was surrounded by several other young people, all stepping out, their heads bent together, talking eagerly, all on the verge of some adventure that surely couldn't be more than a day, maybe two, away. I watched her as she descended toward me. It seemed as if the fading light and the mild breeze caught her hair and lifted her laughter. As she floated past me, I wanted to whisper her name and ask her if what she saw ahead was worth what had gone past, but then, I knew that was the least fair question of all, because the answer was somewhere in the future.

So I said nothing and watched her pass. I don't think she noticed me.

I tried to detect something in her voice, in her step, that might tell me what I needed to know. I thought that I might have seen it, but couldn't be certain. And as I watched, Ashley was swallowed up by the press of the evening crowds, disappearing into her own life.

If it really was Ashley. It could have been Megan or Sue or Katie or Molly or Sarah. I wasn't sure it made a difference.